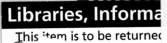

## LUCY KING
## KIMBERLY LANG
## ANNE OLIVER

Harlequin (UK) Limited's policy is to use papers that are natural, renewable
and recyclable products and made from wood grown in sustainable forests.
The logging and manufacturing processes conform to the legal environmental
regulations of the country of origin.

Printed and bound in Spain
by CPI, Barcelona

MILLS &
BOON

Published in Great Britain 2015
by Mills & Boon, an imprint of Harlequin (UK) Limited,
Eton House, 18-24 Paradise Road, Richmond, Surrey, TW9 1SR

SCANDAL IN THE SPOTLIGHT © 2015 Harlequin Books S. A.

*The Couple Behind The Headlines, Redemption Of A Hollywood Starlet* and *The Price of Fame* were first published in Great Britain by Harlequin (UK) Limited.

*The Couple Behind The Headlines* © 2012 Lucy King
*Redemption Of A Hollywood Starlet* © 2012 Kimberly Kerr
*The Price of Fame* © 2012 Anne Oliver

ISBN: 978-0-263-25240-8

05-1215

Harlequin
and recycl
The loggi
regulation

Printed ar
by CPI, B

# THE COUPLE BEHIND THE HEADLINES

BY
LUCY KING

**Lucy King** spent her formative years lost in the world of Mills & Boon romance when she really ought to have been paying attention to her teachers. Up against sparkling heroines, gorgeous heroes and the magic of falling in love, trigonometry and absolute ablatives didn't stand a chance.

But as she couldn't live in a dream world for ever she eventually acquired a degree in languages and an eclectic collection of jobs. A stroll to the River Thames one Saturday morning led her to her very own hero. The minute she laid eyes on the hunky rower getting out of a boat, clad only in Lycra and carrying a three-metre oar as if it was a toothpick, she knew she'd met the man she was going to marry. Luckily the rower thought the same.

She will always be grateful to whatever it was that made her stop dithering and actually sit down to type Chapter One, because dreaming up her own sparkling heroines and gorgeous heroes is pretty much her idea of the perfect job.

Originally a Londoner, Lucy now lives in Spain, where she spends much of the time reading, failing to finish cryptic crosswords, and trying to convince herself that lying on the beach really *is* the best way to work.

Visit her at www.lucykingbooks.com.

For William.

# CHAPTER ONE

Two hundred and fifty thousand pounds?

*Two hundred and fifty thousand pounds?*

Imogen gaped at the catalogue, her jaw practically hitting the floor. It had to be a mistake. A typo or something. Because surely no one could be expected to fork out a quarter of a million pounds for that…that *thing*.

Bracing herself, she turned back, stared at the canvas hanging on the wall, and winced. 'The Sting in Society' was so eye-poppingly ugly it made every cell in her body shrivel in protest. So primitive it looked as if it had been executed by her five-year-old nephew in one of his tantrums. So absolutely hideous that not even the copious amounts of vintage champagne on offer could dent its impact.

And it was enormous. The artist, who'd splashed a blaze of clashing colours onto the canvas in a seemingly random fashion, clearly felt his creativity was too great to contain, which while undoubtedly satisfying some sort of artistic bent for himself, was excruciating for everyone else.

It would be one thing if 'The Sting in Society' were a one-off. That she could just about deal with while fulfilling her aim to take every advantage of the free-flowing champagne. But it wasn't. The plain white walls of the gallery were littered with the things. Beneath unforgivably bright lights hung two dozen canvases, all splattered with the same great swathes of colours, all equally dreadful, and all going for the same mind-blowing sums of money.

Imogen grimaced. She was the first to admit that she was no expert on modern art, but in her opinion whatever its worth, the whole lot should be consigned to the Thames.

Not that anyone else appeared to think so, she thought, glancing around at the trendily dressed throng. Everywhere she looked, people milled about, tilting their heads and tapping index fingers against their mouths while spouting esoteric nonsense about allegory and metaphysics.

Swinging her gaze back to the piece she was standing in front of, Imogen stifled a shudder. It was madness, she mused, narrowing her eyes as she tried to work out its appeal and failed. Complete insanity.

Who in their right mind would pay that amount of money for such a horrendous thing anyway?

She mentally ran through a list of all the things a quarter of a million pounds could achieve. Only yesterday her department had had to allocate exactly that sum to one of the projects run by the Christie Trust, and the options were still fresh in her memory. Spending it on an eye-watering splatter of colours had not, strangely enough, been one of them.

But then what did *she* know about anything?

Imogen took a step back, bit her lip and frowned. Recent events had proved that her judgement sucked. Big time. So who was she to decide whether or not this stuff was any good? As bizarre as she might think it, little red dots were popping up next to the paintings like chicken pox, so the evidence appeared to be speaking for itself.

Which only hammered home the painful realisation that her judgement was indeed still in bits.

Not that *that* was any surprise.

Only two months had passed since Connie, her once-upon-a-time partner-in-crime and best-friend-since-school had run off with Max, Imogen's then boyfriend, and, although the pain had ebbed to a dull ache instead of the agony it had once been, it still hurt.

More so this evening, thought Imogen morosely, her already battered spirits taking a nosedive. The last time she'd been to a private view, Connie had been with her. They'd laughed and talked loudly and pompously about light and depth and perspective, ransacked the canapés and then hit the latest club.

Tonight, however, she was alone, and Connie, the sneaky snake-in-the-grass, was in all likelihood at home, snuggling up to Max on the sofa and hatching wedding plans.

Imogen's heart twanged. She'd told herself to get over it a million times and she reckoned she was making good progress, but from time to time—usually when she was least expecting it—the whole sorry affair swooped down and smacked her around the head.

Like this afternoon.

Like now.

The backs of her eyes prickled but she blinked the sting away and yanked her shoulders back. What did she care what Connie was up to? So what if the friendship they'd had, the one that had started at kindergarten and had continued for the past twenty-five years, had disintegrated in the ten seconds it had taken to read Max's note? And so what if her ex-boyfriend and her ex-best friend were getting married?

She didn't give a toss, did she?

No. She'd had plenty of time to reflect on the betrayal, and with hindsight she'd come to realise that actually they'd done her a favour. Because who needed friends who could do something like that to you?

And as for Max, well, yes, he was undeniably gorgeous—all dark floppy hair, twinkling eyes and oodles of charm—but he was a complete waste of space and she was well shot of him.

If the press had levelled the same waste-of-space accusation at her—which they had, frequently and not entirely un-fairly—that was fine because she had plans to reverse that and to prove to herself and her critics that she *did* have something to offer the world.

Max, on the other hand, seemed happy to spend the rest of his life perfecting his air of insouciant ennui. So if Connie wanted to spend the rest of *her* life massaging that ego, she was welcome to it.

Imogen shook her head at her own naïve foolishness. Far from being the perfect couple she'd always assumed she and Max had been, they were, she now knew, chalk and cheese. The really astounding thing about their relationship was not how it had ended, but how it had limped along for so long in the first place.

Truly, the mind boggled, she thought, casting another glance at the monstrosity calling itself 'The Sting in Society'. And she was through with it all. Bored, rich playboys, fickle best friends and staggeringly pretentious so-called art.

She'd got what she'd come for. Two glasses of ice-cold bone-dry champagne had done an excellent job of obliterating the shock and torment of learning of the engagement. Her body was buzzing and her mind was numb, and she had better things to do than waste any more time in front of this kind of rubbish.

Determinedly banishing the blues and reminding herself that she was far luckier than most, that she had no business wallowing in misery and that she ought to focus on what she *did* have rather than what she didn't, Imogen gritted her teeth and spun on her heel.

And crashed into something hard and unyielding.

Something that let out a soft 'oof' and flung its arms around her for balance.

For a second it felt as if the world had stopped. She stood there, stunned, crushed up against whoever it was she'd cannoned into, the breath whooshing from her lungs and her head spinning with shock.

Then the shock receded and her surroundings settled and other things filtered into her brain. Like the fact that he was male. Tall. Broad. Solid. Warm. And strong. His arms were like bands of steel around her back and she could feel the restrained power in the hardness that was wrapped around her. Plus he smelled amazing.

Imogen couldn't remember the last time she'd found herself in such close proximity to a man like that—if ever—and to her horror her body automatically began to respond. Her stomach quivered. Her heart lurched and her temperature rocketed. For one crazy split second she wanted to press herself closer. Wanted to snuggle up to him and feel those arms wrap themselves tighter around her. Enveloping her. Protecting her.

Which was nuts. Completely nuts.

Imogen blinked as sanity put in an appearance and nudged aside the fancifulness. She could stop that right now. She'd been through the emotional wringer recently and the last thing she needed was to fall head first into the arms of another man. Metaphorically speaking, of course.

And what on earth made her think she needed protecting anyway? She was perfectly capable of doing that herself. Heaven knew she'd had enough practice.

Summoning up every ounce of self-control she possessed, Imogen gulped in a breath and forced herself not to react to the intoxicating waft of soap and sandalwood that shot up her nose.

'Oh, sorry,' she muttered, jerking back and looking up to see who it was that was having such an odd effect on her.

And nearly swooned all over again.

All thoughts of Connie and Max and self-protection vanished as she found herself staring up into the most gorgeous eyes she'd ever seen.

To begin with he had the kind of thick, dark eyelashes she'd give her designer wardrobe for. Then there were the fine lines that fanned out from their corners and suggested he laughed a lot.

Swallowing back the lump in her throat at the reminder of how little *she* laughed at the moment, Imogen focused on the colour of his irises instead. That kind of blue was unusual. It made her think of the sky in summer and the shallows of the Mediterranean Sea. Which would have had her envisaging long, languid summer afternoons and the long languid ways in which one might spend them with a man like this had she not ruthlessly shut down that strand of her imagination for ever.

And as if all that weren't potentially sense-scrambling enough, there was the glint. The glint lurked in the depths of his eyes and suggested danger and excitement and naughtiness. The glint promised fun. A lot of fun. For a woman who was into that sort of thing, which, being too emotionally scarred, she wasn't. But if she *had* been, the heat sweeping through her would have been down to instant chemistry, and not what must surely be a fault with the air-conditioning.

Whatever it was that was causing her to overheat, Imogen hauled herself back under control as she dragged her gaze over the rest of his face, which would have more than lived up to her expectations if she'd had any. His dark hair looked as if it were made for rumpling and his mouth looked as if it would deliver the most devastating of kisses.

All in all, the combination of that face and that body was lethal, she thought, suppressing a shiver. If you were interested in that sort of thing. Which, dammit, she wasn't. She really wasn't.

'My fault,' he said with a smile that had her stomach somersaulting before she could stop it.

He unwound his arms from around her and she took a hasty step backwards.

'And not a drop spilt,' she said, glancing at the glasses of champagne that had only moments ago been flung around her. 'Impressive.'

'I've had plenty of practice.'

Of having random women barrel into him? She could just imagine. 'How fortunate.'

The smile deepened and Imogen felt something inside her melt. Her pathetically weak resistance probably. 'For you it is.'

She raised her eyebrows. 'For me?'

He held out a glass to her. 'One of these. You looked like you could do with it.'

Had he been watching her? Checking her out?

At the thought of those eyes roaming over her, Imogen's heart began to race and she swallowed hard to combat the sudden dryness of her mouth. 'I was just leaving,' she said a lot more breathily than she'd have liked.

His mesmerising gaze slid to the painting behind her and then back to hers. The glint twinkled. 'Not because of the scorpion, I hope?' he said.

'Is that what it is?'

He nodded. 'It is.'

'I'd never have guessed.'

'It's obscure.'

'Very.'

'It represents man's fight against the injustice of capitalism.'

Imogen tilted her head and frowned as she finally managed to locate her brain. 'It seems a bit hypocritical to charge a quarter of a million pounds for a piece of canvas and a few brush strokes that apparently represent the injustice of capitalism, don't you think?'

'To be honest I hadn't given it much thought,' he said dryly.

Vaguely wondering what was happening to her intention to leave, Imogen took the glass he was holding out and lifted it to her lips.

'Thank you,' she murmured and took a sip.

'You're welcome,' he said, watching her as she parted her lips and let a mouthful of champagne slide down her throat. 'So what do you think of it?'

She thought she heard a trace of hoarseness in his voice and it sent a shiver down her spine. 'The painting?'

He nodded. Then cleared his throat a little.

'Honestly?'

'Oh, I'm all for honesty,' he said.

Hmm. If he was, and frankly she doubted it because he was, after all, a man, then it was more than Max had been, the lying, cheating scumbag. 'Then honestly,' she said a touch more tartly than she'd intended, 'it makes my eyes bleed.'

Without warning he threw his head back and let out a roar of laughter and her stomach tightened at the sound. 'And there was me thinking it had great light, searing depth and imaginative perspective,' he said, shoving a hand through his hair and grinning.

Imogen went still for a second, her eyes colliding with his, and her heart stuttered. The warm amusement in his voice that suggested he thought the exact opposite reminded her of the gaping hole in her life left by the treacherous Connie, and her eyes stung again.

And then an appalled thought crossed her mind and she snapped herself away from the memories. 'Oh, no, you're not the artist, are you?'

His eyebrows shot up. 'Do I look like the artist?'

Imogen let her gaze run over him from head to toe, felt her blood begin to simmer and managed to convince herself it was a perfectly normal reaction to an extremely handsome man and there was no need to get her knickers in a twist over it.

He certainly didn't look like any artist she'd ever met, she reflected, vaguely distracted by the thought of her knickers getting, not just in a twist, but totally removed, slowly and seductively, by the man smouldering down at her. He looked dark and dangerous and wicked. The sort of man that could make a woman lose her head if she wasn't careful. 'Come to think of it,' she said as coolly as she could manage, which wasn't coolly at all, 'no.'

'Thank heavens for that.'

Ignoring the odd fizzing of her veins, Imogen pulled herself together. If he'd gone to the trouble to bring her a glass of champagne, the least she could do was engage in a minute or two of conversation before leaving. After all, his smile might be lethal and the glint was downright criminal, but conversation had never killed anyone, had it? 'So how do you know so much about this particular—ah—piece?'

'I own it.'

'God, why?' she asked aghast, rapidly revising her opinion of him. He might be gorgeous but his taste in art left a *lot* to be desired.

His eyes gleamed. 'I won it at a charity auction.'

Her eyebrows shot up. 'Someone else was bidding for it?' That at least two people had wanted the thing was astounding.

He nodded and grinned. 'A friend of mine.'

'Some friend.'

'One of the best. It was quite a tussle.'

'But he eventually bowed out?'

'He did.'

'Sensible man.'

He shrugged. 'He didn't have much of a choice. I like to win.'

Hmm. She cast him a sceptical glance and noticed the determined set to his jaw as well as the now decidedly ruthless glint in his eye. Oh, yes, he liked to win. And, she deduced, at any cost.

'Well, it seems to me that on this occasion you lost,' she said, stifling a shudder at the dangerously enticing thought of being pursued and conquered by someone like him.

He gazed at her for so long and so intently that her mouth

went dry and her body began to buzz. 'You know, you could be right,' he murmured.

She tried to blot out the buzzing by telling herself that the man was an idiot who had more money than sense, but it didn't appear to be working. 'So really you acquired it by accident?'

He tilted his head and grinned. 'It would seem so. Although not an unhappy one, given the increase in its value over the years.'

She lifted her eyebrows. 'And that's important?'

'Profit is always important.'

Imogen frowned. 'Well, I suppose in this case the simple appreciation of something beautiful doesn't really come into the equation.'

At that his eyes gleamed and her heart unaccountably skipped a beat. His gaze suddenly dropped and then slowly roamed over her. 'Oh, I don't know,' he murmured, and to her alarm she felt her cheeks going bright red. Heat shot through her and she began to tingle in places she'd thought she'd never tingle in again.

Didn't intend to ever tingle in again, she reminded herself, straightening her spine and lifting her chin. 'Nevertheless you have my commiserations.'

He smiled that smile of his and to her irritation she could feel her blush deepening. 'But not an offer to buy it?'

Right now, what with being on the verge of becoming putty in his hands, Imogen thought she could well end up offering him anything he asked for.

And didn't that bring her up short?

Forcing herself to imagine the painting on her wall, having to stare at the hideous thing day in day out, and concentrating on not turning into that putty, she shuddered. 'You must be joking,' she said, adopting a look of horror for good measure. 'This isn't my kind of thing at all.'

'Pity,' he said, then sighed and rubbed a brown hand along his jaw. 'I have a depressing feeling it's never going to sell.'

'Are you surprised?'

'Not particularly. But if it doesn't, Luke, that friend of mine who bowed out of the bidding, will never let me forget it. He needles me about it enough as it is.'

He looked so cross that Imogen couldn't help smiling. 'Well, that's what comes of indulging in silly displays of competitive pride,' she said solemnly, tutting and shaking her head in mock admonishment.

'You're probably right.'

'And can you blame him?'

He arched an eyebrow as he gazed at her, his mouth eventually curving into a rueful smile. 'Not really. If the roles had been reversed I'd do the same.'

'Of course you would.'

'So,' he said, draining his glass and handing it to a waiter who was weaving past, 'I know why I'm here, but, if this isn't your kind of thing, why are *you* here?'

Imogen went still, her smile fading and her temperature plummeting as her fingers tightened around the stem of her glass.

Oh, heavens. What could she say? No way could she tell him the truth. That only half an hour ago she'd learned about Max and Connie's engagement, on Facebook of all places. That she'd been so stunned, so thrown off balance and tossed upside down, and so hurt by the fact that they hadn't bothered to call her up and tell her personally that she'd fled the office in search of the nearest source of alcohol, which happened to be the gallery next door to the office where she worked. No way. That kind of revelation she'd be keeping to herself.

So, aware that he was waiting for an answer and not liking that probing gaze one little bit, Imogen shrugged and fixed a bland smile to her face. 'I've decided lately that my horizons need broadening,' she said, thinking it was, after all, at least the partial truth.

'I see.' He gave her a sexy kind of half smile and his eyes glittered. 'Need any help?'

She stared at him as shivers raced up and down her spine. Help? Oh, goodness. From the way the glint was glinting she could guess exactly the sort of help he was offering. The sort she wasn't interested in, she reminded herself. Not. Interested. In.

'Thank you, but no,' she said, sounding a lot firmer than she felt.

'Are you sure? Because I'm good at broadening horizons.'

'I've no doubt you are.'

He smiled into her eyes, and even though he hadn't moved it felt as if he'd somehow got closer. 'Have dinner with me and I'll show you how good.'

# CHAPTER TWO

IMOGEN blinked, faintly stunned, although why the invitation should be quite such a surprise was beyond her. It wasn't as if she'd never been asked out to dinner before.

Maybe it was the fact that the intensity of his attention was so all-encompassing it had robbed her of reason. Or maybe it was simply the fact that, as he'd apparently stolen all the air around her, her brain was being starved of oxygen. 'Dinner?' she murmured.

He nodded. 'That's right. Dinner. Comes after lunch and before breakfast. Around this time.'

'Ah, *that* dinner.'

'That's the one. So?'

Imogen was almost certain her answer ought to be no. More than almost certain, actually, because hadn't she just been telling herself that she'd had enough of men for the fore-seeable future, the whole lousy lot of them? Wasn't she just the tiniest bit unhinged at the moment? And didn't she need to concentrate on repairing her poor battered emotions in-stead of letting herself be dragged under the spell of such a dangerously magnetic man?

But it was so tempting, she thought, her common sense beginning to unravel beneath his unwavering gaze. After two months of miserable soul-searching, her self-esteem could really do with the attention, and after nearly three glasses of champagne her stomach could really do with the food.

Besides she hadn't sworn off all men, had she? She blotted out the little voice in her head jumping up and down, waving its arms in alarm and demanding to know what on earth she thought she was doing, and concentrated on justifying the decision she was pretty sure she was going to make. She might have had her fingers burnt recently but she wasn't *that* jaded. And dinner didn't have to go anywhere, did it? How could a couple of hours in the company of a gorgeous attentive man hurt?

Feeling her spirits creeping up, Imogen laughed for what seemed like the first time in weeks and felt lighter than she had in months. 'I don't even know your name.'

'Jack Taylor.' He held out his hand.

'Imogen Christie,' she said, taking it.

For a moment she was so startled by the feel of his hand wrapped around hers and the energy that suddenly spun through her that the name didn't register. She was too busy marvelling at the way every nerve ending she possessed tingled. The way her whole body was suddenly coming alive, and thinking about how much fun dinner was going to be.

But when it did, seconds later, her smile froze and her stomach disappeared. Her heart sank and the heat pounding through her turned to ice.

Oh, hell.

Jack Taylor? Not *the* Jack Taylor? Not the one she'd read about. Heard about. Been warned about...

How typical was that? She reluctantly pulled her hand out of his as disappointment washed through her.

Random snippets of information started whipping round her head. Facts she must have subconsciously gleaned over the years that now spun and whirled and settled into one long list.

According to the financial press, the man was some kind of investment superstar. He made millions on a daily basis, backing ventures most people wouldn't touch with a barge-pole and taking risks considered to be either insane or genius depending on one's point of view. His funds were huge and his successes were global.

As, apparently, were his extra-curricular activities.

According to her friends and the kind of press that fa-voured gossip over finance, Jack Taylor was legendary. He was gorgeous and charming. Smooth and charismatic, yet ice cool and elusive. He was, by all accounts, a true heartbreaker.

As poor wretched Amanda Hobbs had eventually found out, she recalled. The story of Amanda, who she didn't per-sonally know but was the friend of a friend of a friend, had recently taken the grapevine by storm, causing hands to be clapped to mouths and gasps of shock and pity. Poor, tragic Amanda, who'd been going out with him until he'd callously ditched her, and had had to flee to Italy to recover.

With all the details of the whole saga zooming to the fore-front of her mind Imogen bridled, and the disappointment turned into something colder, harder and stonier because, apart from the work aspect, Jack Taylor was exactly the sort of man Max was. Exactly the sort of man she'd vowed to steer well clear of.

Rumour had it that a few years ago he'd even engaged in an Internet bidding war over some woman. From what she could remember he'd opted for *greatsexguaranteed* as a user name and didn't *that* tell her everything she needed to know? And not just that he was a fan of online auctions.

As she stared up at him standing there oozing self-confident charm, his eyes gleaming with that wicked glint, she wondered how on earth she could have missed it. It was there for anyone with half a brain to see. The laid-back insou-ciance. The unmistakeable air of wealth. Of innate arrogance. The dazzling smile of a man who knew he had the ability to make women fall into his bed like dominoes.

Well, not this woman, thought Imogen grimly, gathering

her scattered wits and pulling herself together. In targeting her he'd chosen badly. Really badly.

The little part of her that was deeply flattered at being hit on by the infamous Jack Taylor, that wondered if he really could guarantee great sex, could forget it. So could the gleam of expectation in his eye, because she wasn't falling into his bed or anywhere else. She was immune. And dinner was most definitely off.

'I know a great little place just round the corner,' Jack was saying, and Imogen dragged herself back to the conversation.

Oh, she just bet he did, she thought, going numb. She bet he knew great little places round every corner of London.

'Actually,' she said smoothly, drawing her shoulders back and giving him a tight smile, 'I don't think dinner is such a good idea after all.'

There was a pause. A flicker of surprise in his eyes as he tensed a little. 'No?'

He sounded distinctly put out and satisfaction surged inside her. Hah. He probably hadn't been turned down in his life. Well, the experience would do him good. 'No,' she said, lifting her chin a little higher and injecting a hint of steel into her voice.

He tilted his head and regarded her with that disconcertingly probing gaze. 'Why not?'

'I'm busy.'

'Then how about another night?'

'Thank you, but no.'

'Sure?'

God, he was unbelievable. Why had no one ever mentioned his persistence along with everything else? 'Tell me, Jack,' she said, delighted to hear that she was sounding as withering as she'd intended, 'has anyone ever said no to you?'

He grinned, her arch tone clearly rolling off him like water off a duck's back. 'Not recently.'

Typical. 'Well, there's a first time for everything,' she said deliberately waspishly.

And that ought to have been that. By now he should have got the message that she wasn't interested and should be shrugging, turning away and going off in search of easier prey.

But much to her irritation, his smile barely faltered. If anything, it turned more seductive, and for some reason her mouth went dry. Something about the way his eyes were glittering, the way he'd shifted his weight sent warning bells tinkling around her head.

Which started clanging violently when without warning he reached out, put a hand on the side of her neck and leaned forwards.

Imogen couldn't move. At the feel of his hand, singeing her skin where it lay, the thudding of her heart turned to a hammering and her breathing shallowed, and to her horror there wasn't a thing she could do about it. Not when her feet seemed to be rooted to the floor and her body had turned to stone.

Every one of her senses, pretty much the only part of her that hadn't been stunned into immobility, leapt to attention and zoomed in on Jack and what he was doing.

And what exactly was that? she wondered dazedly as she gazed up at him. The ghost of a smile played at his lips, lips that parted a fraction and dragged her attention down, robbing her of what little of her breath remained and flipping her stomach.

Oh, God, he wasn't going to kiss her, was he? Not now. Not right here among all these people.

Not that an audience was her greatest concern. No, her greatest concern was what she'd do if he did.

But just as she was trying to work out what that was and panicking at the idea that she even had to think about it, just as her heart was about to stop and she thought she might be about to pass out, he angled his head and murmured right into her ear, 'OK, if you're tight for time, how about skipping dinner and moving straight on to dessert?'

For a moment there was a kind of vibrating silence while his words made their way to her brain. Long heavy seconds during which everything but the two of them and the electric field that they generated disappeared. Imogen was so wrapped up in not responding to his nearness, in not shivering as the warmth of his breath caressed her cheek, and so preoccupied with not closing the minute distance between them and winding her arms around his neck to kiss him that his proposition took quite a while to arrive.

Then it did, and she thought she must have misheard. Misunderstood or something, because surely he couldn't be suggesting what she thought he was suggesting.

But when he drew back and she saw the glimmer of intent and desire in the depths of his eyes she realised she hadn't misheard. Or misunderstood. And he was suggesting exactly what she'd thought he'd been suggesting.

'That's outrageous,' she breathed, although whether this was directed at his audacity or at the sharp thrill that was spinning through her she wasn't sure.

He took a step back and ran his gaze over her face, slowly and thoroughly as if committing every square millimetre to memory before letting it linger on her lips. Which, to her horror, automatically parted to emit a tiny dreamy gasp.

'Is it?' he murmured.

Barely able to breathe, she watched his smile become knowing and the gleam in his eyes turn to something that looked suspiciously like triumph and quite suddenly Imogen had had enough.

Of everything.

All the pain and frustration of the past few months wound together in one great knot in the pit of her stomach and began to pummel her from the inside out. So hard, so relentlessly that she nearly doubled up with the force of it.

Memories and thoughts and feelings cascaded into her head, each one tumbling over the other, fast and furious and unstoppable.

Of her own battered heart carelessly ripped from her chest and then stamped all over by two people she'd cared so much about.

Of poor Amanda weeping and wailing her way across Italy.

Of the cool arrogance of the man standing before her. Of the God-given right he thought he had to seduce people—women—into falling in with his plans. The idea that anyone, he of all people, had the nerve to guarantee great sex.

As the whole gamut of emotions swept through her with the force of a tidal wave, the urge to strike a blow for every woman worldwide who'd had her heart broken by a lothario like Jack surged up inside her.

It was overwhelming, overpowering. It overrode any sense of civility, of politeness, of reason, and obliterated the lingering heat and any trace of desire.

Dimly aware that she was out of control but unable to do anything about it, Imogen lifted her chin and said coldly, 'If you're hungry, I suggest you find some other poor victim to devour.'

And with that, she spun on her heel and marched off.

When it came to ways of occupying himself on a Tuesday night, Jack had options. Lots of options.

Last Tuesday he'd accompanied a sleek blonde to a classical concert in aid of medical research. The Tuesday before that he'd wined and dined a rumpled brunette at a newly opened restaurant so sought-after it already had a six-month waiting list. And the Tuesday before *that* he'd been discussing investment strategy with clients over cocktails in Geneva.

*This* Tuesday night, however, was apparently payback for all that fun.

It hadn't started well. For one thing he loathed modern art.

Absolutely loathed it. The pretension of the paintings and the people who waffled on about them invariably made him want to hit something hard. This allegedly exclusive one-night-only art exhibition in the West End of London was one of the worst he'd ever encountered and the only reason he'd come was to see his own unforgivably awful contribution sell.

And even *that* hadn't been going his way. While a number of the other exhibits had attracted buyers, his hadn't, and it had started to occur to him that he might be forced to take the bloody thing back home with him.

With the evening plumbing depths he could never have anticipated, Jack had decided to write the whole episode off as a complete disaster and had been on the point of leaving when he'd spotted Imogen.

She'd been standing with her back to him in front of his six-foot-by-four-foot painting, gazing up at it, utterly still, her head tilted to one side. Something about her had caught his eye and held it. Made his muscles contract a little and his heart beat a fraction faster. And not just because she was the only person to display any interest in his painting.

Out of habit, he'd checked her out. He'd run his gaze over her, taking his time as he registered long, wavy, gold-streaked hair fanning out from beneath her black beret, generous curves moulded by a figure-hugging black knee-length coat, and the best pair of calves he'd ever seen encased in sheer silk and tapering down to sexy black high heels.

He'd felt a fierce stirring of attraction, his body tightening with awareness and his mouth going dry. His pulse had picked up and the blood rushing through his veins had heated.

And then, just as he'd been wondering why he was responding so strongly to a woman whose face he hadn't even seen, just as he'd managed to dredge up some kind of self-control and get his heart rate and breathing back to normal, she'd turned to hold the catalogue up to the light, and he'd lost his breath all over again.

She was quite simply stunning. Light from the spotlight overhead had spilled over her face, illuminating high cheekbones, a straight nose and creamy skin. Her mouth was wide, her lips full and pink and extremely kissable.

It had struck him then that, despite her considerable assets, his response to her had been startlingly unusual in its intensity. He'd never lacked for female company—quite the opposite in fact—but the immediacy and the strength of it had been new. And actually not just new. He'd found it intriguing. Tantalising. Deliciously unsettling.

Which was why, thinking optimistically that despite its inauspicious start the evening had started to look up, he'd levered himself off the pillar he'd been leaning against and had gone in search of a couple of glasses of champagne.

Well, that had been a spectacular waste of time, Jack thought darkly, rooted to the spot as he stared at Imogen's retreating figure, shock reverberating through him as he tried to work out what had happened.

Victim?

*Victim?*

Where the hell had *that* come from?

All he'd suggested was dinner and what on earth was wrong with that? Where had all that vitriol sprung from? Anyone would think he'd suggested slinging her over his shoulder and carting her off somewhere dark and private so he could have his wicked way with her. Which he hadn't, quite.

He dragged in a breath, shoved a hand through his hair and scowled after her as the latter part of their conversation rattled around his brain.

Up until the point Imogen had gone all psycho on him, he'd thought things had been progressing marvellously. Even their initial collision, though unplanned, had worked to his advantage. His head might have gone momentarily blank at the feel of her body plastered up against his and at the scent of her winding through him, but he'd heard her breath catch.

He'd seen the flash of interest in her eyes. And felt the hammering of her heart against his chest.

And it had been all the encouragement he'd needed. He'd done what came as naturally as breathing, and flirted with her. And she'd flirted right back. She'd shot him sexy little smiles, let out breathy little sighs and he'd instinctively had the feeling that she was as attracted to him as he was to her. Inviting her to dinner to see how the attraction—and the evening—might develop had seemed an entirely logical step forwards.

Jack rubbed his hand along his jaw and frowned as he remembered the moment his radar had picked up her unexpected switch in mood. He'd been holding her hand, recovering from the jolt of electricity that had shot through him the moment their palms had met and wondering whether he should be feeling disconcerted or delighted by the obvious chemistry.

He'd been vaguely asking himself whether the floor really was tilting and whether he ought to be concerned by the way the words '*this* one' were flashing in his head in great neon letters when he'd felt her tense. She'd whipped her hand out of his as if his touch had suddenly scorched her, and he'd realised that something had changed. Dramatically.

To say he'd been wrong-footed was the understatement of the century. He'd always believed he had an uncanny ability to read women, but never in a million years would he have seen the chilly, supercilious air that she had adopted coming.

His jaw tightened as the disdainful expression on her face and the scorn in her voice when she refused his offer of dinner slammed into his head. He couldn't remember the last time he'd been rejected. People—women in particular—generally didn't, and, ever since his mother had pretty much abandoned him at birth, rejection was something he'd taken great care to avoid. Which was why he only ever issued dinner invitations to women he was convinced would say yes.

Until now.

But what the hell had gone wrong?

OK, so he probably shouldn't have made that comment about dessert, but he'd been so disconcerted by her change in attitude, and, if he was being honest, disappointed, that winding her up as much as she'd wound him up had proved irresistible.

Which meant that when she'd accused him of being outrageous, she might have had a point. But he'd never anticipated that she'd react in quite such a melodramatic way. Why should he? He'd seen the flicker of desire in her eyes and he'd heard her shallow breathing. For a split second he'd thought that perhaps he'd got away with it after all. That mutual attraction might have come to outweigh her indignation.

And that made her rejection, her parting shot, all the more devastatingly brutal.

Jack glowered after her. So much for thinking the evening had been looking up. He'd just crashed and burned spectacularly and he didn't like it. Any of it.

Ignoring the smattering of interested glances being cast in his direction, he let the anger and frustration that had been simmering inside him surge through his veins.

How dared she assume he had victims? How dared she assume he devoured anyone? How dared she make him feel he'd been harassing her?

And what exactly was so off-putting about him anyway? He'd never had any complaints before. He'd never had anything but sighs of appreciation and requests for repeat performances.

So what was her problem? And frankly why was he bothering to try and work it out? Imogen clearly had it in for him and he wasn't a masochist. The best thing he could do would be to forget the last half an hour and get the hell out of here.

The rational part of his brain told him to chalk this evening up to experience, that, apart from everything else he'd had to endure, no woman was worth the hassle. Especially not one as shallow as Imogen Christie.

He knew who she was. The minute he'd heard her name he'd recognised it. It would have been hard not to, given the number of times it had appeared in the press. Imogen Christie was nothing more than a vacuous socialite. The kind of pointless woman who did nothing but flit from party to party and hit the headlines with her antics. The kind of pointless woman his mother was.

So what if during their brief conversation she'd made him laugh? So what if she'd made his body respond so intensely that all he could think about was how much he wanted to wrap her round him and keep her there for hours? She was the sort of woman he despised, the sort he'd spent most of his adult life avoiding, and if he ever bothered to look back on this evening he'd be grateful he'd had such a lucky escape.

That was what the sane, logical part of his brain was telling him.

However, another louder, more insistent part of his brain, the part that housed a deeply ingrained, deeply hidden craving for approval, and the part that would, if he let it, wonder what was wrong with him, demanded to know why she'd said what she had and why she'd changed her mind.

Not because he wanted to change it back. No. Now he was finally listening to that warning voice inside his head, he had no intention of pursuing her. He just wanted to know what she thought gave her the right to be so rude, and what exactly it was that she had against him.

There was no way he was allowing someone like Imogen Christie to just waltz off with the last word and no explanation, he thought grimly, watching her push through the door and disappear into the night. No way.

So forget the gold-streaked hair that made him want to tangle his hands in its silky softness. Forget the eyes of such deep brown that looking into them was like falling into a of molten chocolate. Forget the curves that his hands itched to caress. He really didn't need the distraction.

What he needed were answers, and he'd get them, whether she liked it or not.

# CHAPTER THREE

WHAT an idiot, Imogen told herself for the hundredth time as she stood on the street and shivered in the chilly February breeze.

What on earth had possessed her to say *that*? Why, oh, why hadn't she just smiled serenely, told Jack she had a boyfriend or something and left it there?

Whatever had happened to her decision to stay cool and collected at all times? To do absolutely nothing that might attract the attention of the press? It was a good thing she hadn't given in to temptation and flung that glass of champagne all over him. That really would have been the pits.

Maybe the whole Connie/Max engagement thing had affected her more than she'd thought, because the way everything inside her had merged into one hot seething tangle of emotion and then swooped up, seizing control of her brain and her senses, had been weird.

How could she have been so *rude*? she asked herself yet again, stamping her feet in an effort to inject a degree of heat into her body and scouring the shadowy, empty street for a taxi. Jack might be everything she detested in a man—well, aside from his considerable physical attributes, of course—but that was no excuse. She was never rude.

Imogen winced with shame as her words flew back into her head. What had she been *thinking*? OK, so she'd bare been thinking at all, let alone rationally, but that was no excuse, either.

Not that there was anything she could do about it now. She couldn't rewind time and she could hardly go back and apologise, could she? An apology—even assuming he'd be willing to listen—would lead to conversation and undoubtedly a request for an explanation, and she really didn't want to go into the reason for her temporary mental meltdown.

No. All she could do was hope that Jack had written her off as bonkers, slope off home, open a bottle of wine and forget all about the entire excruciating afternoon.

If her brother and his family had been around she'd have invited herself over for supper and let herself be plied with wine and sympathy, clambered all over by her niece and nephew, and maybe let herself not feel quite so lonely and messed up for a while. But unfortunately they were skiing in the Alps.

And yes, there were a couple of parties that she'd been invited to, but having to dodge the inevitable loaded questions about the newly betrothed couple didn't appeal in the slightest.

The worst thing was that with the defection of Connie she no longer had the sort of girlfriend she could call up and drown her sorrows with. Not for the first time, Imogen asked herself how it was possible to feel so alone in a vast city like London, where she knew loads of people and there was always something going on.

Pushing that thought aside before she became even more maudlin, she hauled her spirits up. Home—a cosy mews house in Chelsea—wasn't *such* a bad option, she thought dryly, spying the yellow light of a cruising taxi and throwing her arm up to hail it. It had always been something of a haven, a place to shut herself away from the occasional unpleasantness of life. A scathing newspaper report, a deliberately awful paparazzi photo, a lousy boyfriend... She'd licked her wounds there many times, and would probably do so many times in the future.

Tonight she'd run a bath, pour herself a glass of wine, light a few candles and relax. She might even allow herself to contemplate the press-free and purposeful life she'd have in the States if her application to study there was accepted.

She watched the taxi execute a U-turn and pull up at the pavement where she was standing, and chewed on her lip as a flicker of optimism flared into life inside her.

Yes, that was what she'd do, she thought, leaning forwards to give the taxi driver her address and then reaching for the door handle. She'd package everything that had happened this afternoon and stuff it in the cupboard called Denial, and wallow in that blissful daydream. And then she'd—

'Just a minute.'

At the sound of the deep, dry voice behind her and the sudden scorching heat of the hand covering hers, Imogen jumped, and then, as her back brushed against him, froze. Her heart leapt into her throat. Pure terror shot through her and as her head went fuzzy she automatically jerked her elbow back. Up and hard.

She heard a growl of surprise, of pain, and with adrenalin whipping through her veins she snapped round. Instinctively, braced herself.

And crashed back to reality as she clapped eyes on the man who'd sneaked up on her.

Oh, dear.

As all the adrenalin and energy drained away, Imogen bit her lip and grimaced. Jack was almost doubled up, one hand planted on the window of the taxi, the other clutching his stomach as he gasped for breath.

'What on earth did you do that for?' he said when he was finally able to speak.

'It was an automatic reaction. You startled me. Sorry.'

'Remind me never to do *that* again,' he muttered and, w

a wince, straightened. Which brought him almost as close as he'd been when he'd crept up on her in the first place.

A shiver that this time had nothing to do with the cold or fear or adrenalin scuttled down Imogen's spine, and she sighed. So much for hoping that Jack might decide to write her off and forget what she said. It was stupid of her to think he would. To think that anyone would. 'Did you want something?' she said, blinking with what she hoped looked like innocence.

'You walked off in the middle of our conversation,' said Jack, rubbing his ribs and glowering at her. 'That wasn't very polite.'

'As far as I was concerned,' she said, lifting her chin and giving him a cool smile, while determinedly ignoring the stab of guilt that she might have hurt him, 'it was over.'

'I'm sure you think so,' he said, clearly disagreeing.

Actually, maybe it was no bad thing he'd followed her, because now would be an excellent time to apologise. She could clean the slate, clear her conscience and draw a line under their brief but surprisingly turbulent acquaintance. And then she could nip into the taxi and disappear into the night and put an end to what had been a day she hoped never to repeat.

'OK, look,' she said, making herself keep eye contact, while groping behind her for the door handle. 'I apologise for the whole victim-devouring-comment thing. It was uncalled for. I'm sorry.'

He frowned. 'What prompted it?'

Imogen swallowed. No way was she going to go into the frightening cocktail of emotion that had surged through her and obliterated every shred of common sense. Instead, she recalled the 'skipping straight to dessert' remark, and raised her eyebrows. 'You have to ask?'

'I wouldn't if I didn't.'

'I don't do dessert.'

'Ever?'

'For the time being.'

His mouth curved into a faint smile. 'Don't tell me you're sweet enough.'

Imogen rolled her eyes. 'Oh, please.'

'I thought not.' He paused. Then frowned as the smile faded. 'Nevertheless, that was quite an overreaction.'

Very probably. 'For which I apologise. Again.' She stopped, tilted her head as she waited for some kind of response. Which appeared to be a long time coming. 'You could do the gentlemanly thing and accept it,' she said archly.

'What makes you think I'm a gentleman?'

Imogen shrugged and ignored the way her body hummed with anticipation at the idea of Jack being very ungentlemanly indeed. 'Suit yourself,' she said with as much indifference as she could muster, which wasn't a lot. 'As delightful as it's been to have this little chat, I have somewhere to be. So if there's nothing else, I'll say goodnight.'

'Nothing else?' he murmured, fixing her with a hypnotising glance as the frown disappeared and his lips curved into that lethal smile. 'Imogen, darling, we've barely begun.'

Imogen swallowed as she stared up at him, her heart suddenly thumping with something other than anticipation and her mouth going dry. 'Well, I guess it's possible we'll bump into each other again.' Although given that they hadn't to date it didn't seem likely. Which was something of a relief because she had the feeling that too much of Jack would be so dangerous to her health he ought to come with a government warning. 'But for now, goodnight.'

Suddenly desperate to get away, she flashed him a quick smile, yanked on the handle and pulled the door open. She clambered in and turned to close the door behind her, but to her dismay saw that Jack had planted one hand on the edge and the other on the taxi, and was showing no signs of getting out of the way.

'What?' she muttered, catching the determined look in his eye, her pulse fluttering with nerves.

'Would you mind if I joined you?'

Imogen started. He wanted to join her? In the close confines of the taxi? For how long? Oh, no. No way. That would be nuts. With the skittish way she was feeling, it would be inviting trouble, and she'd had more than enough of that already. 'I doubt we're going in the same direction.'

'We will be,' he countered, and she had the feeling he wasn't talking about their respective geographical destinations.

'I'm sure another taxi will come in a minute.'

'It's starting to rain and I don't have an umbrella.'

At his woeful expression, cracks appeared in her resistance. Jack didn't look like the sort of man to be bothered by a few drops of water, but deliberately leaving him standing there in the rain would be plain cruel and while she might have many failings cruelty wasn't one of them. Besides, if she protested any longer it would look as if she had a problem with him. Which of course she did, but she didn't want him to know that.

And as if those weren't reasons enough, the glint in his eye was turning ruthless and his comment about winning at all costs crossed her mind. Jack clearly wanted an explanation for her behaviour earlier and he probably deserved one.

So how could she refuse? With a fresh wave of the shame that was never far away washing over her, she couldn't. It would be churlish and immature and she hoped she was neither.

With a sigh she gave in. 'I'm heading west.'

'Great. So am I.'

'Then jump in,' she said, scooting across the leather to the far side of the taxi.

As Jack climbed in, slammed the door shut behind him and threw himself onto the seat beside her, Imogen felt faintly foolish. What was there to worry about? It was a taxi ride and a short one at that. There were at least a couple of feet between them and absolutely no need to breach the distance. It would be fine.

And it was until the taxi pulled away with a sharp swerve. Caught unawares, Imogen let out a gasp of shock as she was flung sideways and thrown against him. Her head banged against his shoulder and her hand landed on his upper thigh, perilously close to his groin. She felt him jolt. Heard him inhale sharply. And felt herself go beetroot as she peeled herself off him, muttered an apology and twisted back and away.

'That's the second time that's happened this evening,' said Jack, slanting her a glance, a grin playing at his lips as he shifted and started undoing the buttons of his coat. 'If it wasn't for that parting shot of yours earlier, I might be tempted to think you're finding it hard to resist me.'

Seriously, could today get any worse? Imogen inwardly wailed as mortification joined all the other emotions crashing around inside her. 'You're the one who followed me and wanted to share my taxi,' she muttered, and then because she was in such mental disarray added, 'and, you know, that could be construed as stalking.'

At that, Jack tensed. The hands busy at the buttons of his coat stilled. With her heart beating a fraction faster, she met his suddenly chilly gaze and noticed an almost imperceptible tightening of his jaw.

'Stalking…devouring…' he said in a dangerously low voice. 'You want to watch where you throw those accusations, Imogen.' Drawing the lapels of his coat apart, he tugged at the knot of his tie. He pulled it off, rolled it up and put it in his pocket, then undid the top button of his shirt.

Ignoring the fact that he might have a point, Imogen bristled and told herself that staring at the wedge of flesh now exposed at the base of his neck wasn't going to achieve anything. 'And you ought to know that I don't use the term lightly.

I had a stalker a few years ago and *he* ended up in jail.' The memory of the man who for six long months had followed her, sent her horrible emails and repeatedly ignored the restraining order imposed on him flashed into her head and she shuddered.

He shot her a quick glance and the odd look in his eye made her pulse leap. 'A stalker?'

'A stalker.'

'I guess that would explain your elbow in my stomach.'

'Would it?' she replied sweetly. Whatever that look had been it had better not have been pity. 'Maybe I just don't like you.'

He smiled. 'Yes, you do. You might not want to, but you do.' And then his expression turned serious. 'I'm sorry if I scared you.'

She frowned and decided that getting into a no-I-don't-yes-you-do kind of tussle about whether she liked him or not, which she didn't of course, wasn't going to get her anywhere. 'You didn't. You startled me. There's a difference.'

'If you say so.'

'I do.'

'As a matter of interest, where *are* you going?'

'That's none of your business.'

'Now, now, darling,' he said with a grin. 'You're not being very friendly.'

'You've practically hijacked my taxi. I'm not feeling very friendly.'

Although to be honest she wasn't quite sure what she was feeling. Edgy, definitely. Skin-pricklingly aware of every inch of him as he sat back and ran his hands through his hair. All weirdly quivery, too.

Those 'darlings' had her wondering what it would be like to have him say them and mean them. They had her imagining him saying them in a whole load of other scenarios, all of which involved her naked and in his arms.

How on earth did he do it? she wondered dazedly. Yes, he was extraordinarily good-looking and his body was something else, but she'd met loads of handsome well-packaged men over the years and none of them had made her go fluttery and molten and teenagery like this.

All she wanted to do was clamber onto his lap, yank up his shirt and get her hands on him. While planting her mouth on his and kissing him as if her life depended on it. In fact it was taking every ounce of self-control she possessed not to slide across the leather and do precisely that.

Even more confusing was how she could react to him like this when she knew who he was and what he was really like. It was perverse.

But perhaps that was what chemistry was, she reflected, surreptitiously letting her eyes drift over him and almost scientifically noting her body's inevitable response. A searing attraction that had no regard for logic or reason or circumstance.

Well, that was fine, she told herself, sliding her gaze down over the powerful muscles of his thighs, remembering the feel of those muscles tensing beneath her hand and wishing she could just switch herself off. She might be as attracted to him as an iron filing to a magnet, but she was simply going to have to defy the laws of physics and resist. It was a question of control. That was all.

'If you're not feeling very friendly, why are you eyeing me up?'

Jack's voice jerked her out of her musings and Imogen felt her face blush a bright red. Thank goodness it was dark inside the taxi, she thought, and leaned forwards to lower the window a little. 'No particular reason,' she said and hoped she wouldn't be struck down for the whopping lie. 'I'm simply trying to work out what I'm—' She stopped. Hmm. On reflection, 'up against', which was what she'd been about to say, didn't seem all that prudent. 'I'm simply trying to assess an adversary,' she said instead.

Jack's eyebrows rose. 'You see this as a battle?'

Only an internal one, she thought darkly, pulling herself together and crossing her arms as if that might provide some kind of defence against his impact. And one she had to take control of. Now. Before the conversation headed down an avenue that led who knew where? 'What do you want, Jack?'

'What do you think I want?'

'I have no idea,' she said, lying for the second time in minutes.

'I'd like an explanation.'

'Oh? What for?' As if she didn't know.

'All I did was ask you out for dinner.'

'Really?' she said, arching an eyebrow as she mentally revisited their conversation at the gallery. 'It seemed to me like you were asking for a whole lot more than just dinner.'

'Yes, well, it seemed to me that a whole lot more than just dinner was on offer.'

Imogen let out a gasp and her jaw nearly hit the floor. For a second she just gaped at him, her mind reeling. 'My God,' she breathed, 'you really are incredible.'

'Now why doesn't that sound like a compliment?'

'Because it isn't,' she all but snapped, feeling her temper beginning to stir as much at her own hopelessness as his outrageousness, and banking it down.

Jack shook his head in mock exasperation. 'Imogen, Imogen, Imogen, what *is* your problem?'

She wished he wouldn't say her name like that. She'd never thought of it as a particularly sexy name, but on his lips it sounded like every wicked thought she'd ever had. '*I* don't have a problem.' Although actually, she did. Because the way she was actually enjoying this whole conversation was just plain odd. 'Is it really so hard to believe that I just don't want to have dinner—or anything else—with you?'

He stared at her for a while, his expression utterly unfathomable, and then to her consternation a smile curved his mouth and his eyes took on a dangerous gleam. Achingly slowly, he began to run his gaze over her. Lingering on her face, then moving down, drifting over her breasts, her waist, her hips and her legs, right down to her toes.

Her body tingled, fizzed beneath the smouldering gaze, and the beat of something hot and achy thudded deep inside her. Helpless to do anything to stop him, Imogen watched him look, her heart pounding. As his gaze roamed back up her in the same languid way, flames of desire licked at her stomach and her bones melted. If it hadn't been for the wool of her dress rubbing over her sensitised skin, she'd have thought he'd just stripped her naked and then set her on fire.

'Frankly, yes,' he murmured, and she bristled because the realisation that not even several layers of winter clothing could disguise the reaction of her body was frustrating in the extreme.

'Well, believe it,' she said sharply.

He gave her a knowing smile. 'You might not want dinner, but you definitely want me.'

Imogen blinked as his words hit her brain and she yanked herself out of the rapidly unravelling sensual web he'd woven around her.

There it was again, she thought, giving herself a mental slap. The rock-solid conviction of a man who thought he knew everything about everything. Including her. And, quite suddenly, instead of wanting to scoot across the leather and snuggle up to him, she wanted to smack him across the head.

'In your dreams,' she said, jutting her chin up to add strength to her words. But all that did was jerk his gaze down to her mouth, which instantly tingled.

'You know I could prove you wrong, don't you?' he murmured.

'You could try,' she said, arching a challenging eyebrow. She did *not* want to know what his mouth would feel like on hers. Definitely not. She'd focus on the button beneath that wedge of chest instead. 'But I wouldn't fancy your chances of success.'

'I would.'

Barely able to believe his cheek, Imogen snapped her eyes to his face, all thoughts of focusing on his shirt button vanishing. It was the smile playing at his lips that did it. A knowing, confident smile that acted like a match tossed onto the smouldering embers of her indignation.

Forget that he was probably right. This wasn't about rightness. This was about him and those like him. Anger suddenly raced along her veins and her head went fuzzy with the intensity of everything she'd thought she'd packaged away but evidently hadn't.

But then, just as she was about to lean over, jab him in the chest as she told him exactly what she thought of him, something made her pause. Made her ask herself what losing her temper would get her. She'd already exhibited more emotional volatility in the last six hours than she had in her entire life, and a further display would simply reinforce the impression, on both herself and Jack, that she was seriously unstable. And recent events aside, she wasn't. Much.

Losing her temper now, getting all hot and fiery while he sat there as cool as an ice sculpture, would merely give Jack more ground. She'd be far better off staying calm and collected and in some sort of control.

Closing her eyes, Imogen inhaled deeply and went to her happy place where the sun warmed her skin and Martinis flowed.

How hard could it be?

# CHAPTER FOUR

Now what was she doing?

Jack frowned as he stared at Imogen, who was sitting with her head bent, pinching the bridge of her nose and muttering to herself.

She really was peculiar. Intriguingly peculiar, but peculiar nonetheless. He didn't think he'd ever met anyone so mercurial, who smouldered and sizzled one minute and bristled and bridled the next. No wonder he found himself caving in to the compulsion to needle her; her mood swings were enough to drive a man to drink.

Was she meditating? Or mentally preparing herself for battle?

Whatever it was, maybe he ought to cut his losses and leave her to it, because intentions were all very well, but forgetting about the frantic urge to run his hands over her curves when she was sitting a couple of feet away was proving harder than he'd anticipated. Especially now that, thanks to the taxi driver's desire to get going, he knew what she felt like.

But when she eventually opened her eyes and gave him a serene smile his senses tumbled into such chaos that any idea he'd had of cutting and leaving completely vanished.

'You really want to know what my problem is?' she said silkily.

'I do,' he said, vaguely wondering why he was so keen to

know when every instinct was telling him it wasn't going to be good.

'Well, *this* is exactly it.'

'Exactly what?'

She gave him another beguiling smile and his stomach clenched. 'There's so much I barely know where to start.'

'You could always try the beginning.'

'You're right. I could.' She nodded and he had the unsettling feeling he'd just handed her a knife with which to eviscerate him. 'OK, well, for a start you have a seriously over-inflated ego.'

An over-inflated ego? Jack felt his eyebrows shoot up. Of all the accusations she could have hurled at him that was the most inapplicable. 'What makes you think I have an over-inflated ego?'

'Outside the realm of this evening's conversation, you mean?'

Now why did that sound as if she knew something he didn't? Jack tilted his head as he regarded her, and racked his brains. 'Have we met before?'

'No.'

'I thought not.' If they had, he'd definitely have remembered. And come to think of it— 'Why not?'

'Oh, just lucky I guess.'

'Ouch,' he said, muttering and rubbing his chest. 'Tell me, what precisely do you have against me? Or do you have it in for men in general?'

'No, no,' she said with a dazzling smile. 'At the moment, just you.'

'I'm flattered.' He tilted his head and narrowed his eyes. 'So?'

Imogen arched an eyebrow. *'Greatsexguaranteed?'*

'What?' His jaw dropped and his pulse spiked. 'Are you offering?'

Her eyes flashed for a second and relief spun through him

because all that cool detachment had been faintly disconcerting. 'No, of course I'm not offering,' she said witheringly. 'I'm referring to the eBay incident.'

Ah, that. Four years ago he'd prodded Luke into getting over the death of his first wife by entering into a bidding war over the woman who eventually became his second. Interesting how, of all the things Imogen could have started with, she'd chosen to focus on the user name he'd chosen in a moment of flippancy. Almost Freudian. 'Oh, yes, I remember.'

She sniffed. 'An over-stated claim if ever I heard one.'

Jack grinned, fascinated despite himself. 'What makes you so sure?'

He'd never received any criticism of his performance in bed and Imogen was just too easy to wind up. Steam was whooshing out of her ears and she was rolling her eyes.

But that didn't stop the blush creeping into her cheeks. Nor did it stop his gaze dipping to her mouth, where the tip of her tongue darted out to sweep along her lower lip.

His body contracted with a sudden powerful wave of desire. The air inside the taxi thickened and vibrated with an almost tangible tension and a series of X-rated images slammed into his head. Of Imogen panting and writhing as he moved on top of her, with her, buried deep inside her. Having sex. Great sex.

His head went fuzzy, his mouth went dry and his pulse thundered. The urge to haul her into his arms and set about making the fantasy a reality took him completely by surprise and he had to curl his hands into fists to stop himself from reaching for her.

'Which only goes to prove my next point.'

As the cool tone of her voice filtered into his head, Jack blinked and willed his pulse to slow down.

Point? What point? He could barely remember his own name, let alone think about any point. He was rock hard and aching. He'd never felt such an overwhelming need to possess, such a primitive urge to claim. And it scared the living daylights out of him.

Telling himself not to be absurd, that physical attraction—even when it involved someone who had it in for him—was nothing to worry about, he cleared his throat. He ran his hands through his hair. Went to adjust the knot of his tie before remembering that he'd already removed it.

'Which is?' he said, eventually folding his arms across his chest and hoping he sounded calmer than he felt.

'I've heard that you're arrogant and presumptuous.'

*What?*

Jack frowned as Imogen paused and raised her eyebrows, evidently waiting for some kind of response. What was she expecting him to do? Apologise? Deny it? Or confirm she was right?

'Oh, please don't hold back on my account,' he said dryly, having no intention of doing any of that and deciding to see what else she threw at him before responding.

She smiled a smile that didn't reach her eyes. 'I wasn't going to.'

'Then do continue.'

'I've also heard that you're callous, cold and emotionally bankrupt.'

Jack kept a neutral expression fixed to his face but behind it he was reeling. Forget knife in the singular. Imogen was attacking him with an entire kitchen drawer full of the things, and to his surprise her accusations stung.

Being called *arrogant* and *presumptuous* he could just about deal with. There might even have been a smidgeon of truth in the charges, although he'd have preferred 'confident' and 'spotting an opportunity and taking it'.

But callous, cold and emotionally bankrupt? That was going too far. He wasn't either callous or cold. And so what if he kept his emotions to himself? Not everyone liked flaunting them left, right and centre.

'I didn't realise dinner called for much emotional depth,' he said, his voice not betraying a hint of what he was thinking.

'I doubt anything you do calls for much emotional depth,' she said with faint amusement that did nothing to soften what sounded rather like an insult.

And where had she got this stuff from anyway? 'You don't even know me.'

'I know men like you.'

'Men like me?' The idea he was a type was oddly distasteful. And wrong.

'OK,' she conceded. 'Men with your reputation.'

Jack went still. 'That's what you're basing your accusations on?' he said deceptively mildly. 'Gossip, rumour and hearsay?'

She shrugged. 'It's as good a place to start as any.'

No, it wasn't. He wasn't nearly as notorious as his reputation liked to make out. Not that he'd ever done anything to contradict it. Most of the time it suited him to have people—women especially—think the worst of him. Then unattainable expectations were less likely to arise. On either side.

Now, however, having people—Imogen—think the worst of him didn't seem appealing at all.

'You seem to have judged me exceptionally quickly,' he said, unaccountably irritated by the notion because it had never bothered him before.

Imogen bit her lip and frowned. 'Possibly. But I do have grounds.'

Oh, this he'd love to hear. 'Which are?'

'Amanda Hobbs, for one thing.'

Amanda Hobbs? He frowned as he racked his memory. Oh, yes. 'What about her?'

'You broke her heart.'

'Did I?' he said, knowing perfectly well he hadn't because he never let things ever get to the stage where hearts became involved.

Her jaw dropped and she stared at him. 'You mean you don't *know*?'

'I mean I really don't know.'

Imogen spluttered in outrage, her grip on her control clearly unravelling. 'I can't *believe* you could be so callous as to not even acknowledge what you did.'

As far as he was aware he had nothing to acknowledge, but Imogen's outrage and the way it made her eyes flash was utterly absorbing, and besides he was intrigued by what fresh rumours the mill had been grinding. 'So enlighten me.'

'Are there really so many women you can't remember them?' she said scathingly.

Not nearly as many as rumour would have it. But she didn't need to know that right now, so Jack merely shrugged and smiled in a 'what can I say?' kind of way, which made her eyes flash even more.

'OK, fine,' she said, nodding and pushing herself upright. 'You went out together. For three months.' *Three months?* Jack's eyebrows shot up. 'You were about to move in together but then you ditched her. By text. Of all the rotten, lousy things to do.' She glared at him, her chin up and her body quivering with emotion.

'Anything else?' he said.

'Isn't that enough?'

'I'm sure you have more.'

'Did you even *care* that the poor girl was heartbroken? That she was a complete wreck and had to flee to Italy to recover?'

Well, no, he didn't. Why would he? And what was it to her anyway? Why was she so offended? Were they friends? They certainly shared the same melodramatic tendencies.

'So you're some sort of avenging angel? Getting your own back for all the crimes I've supposedly committed?' he said. Was that really why she'd flung the 'victim devouring' comment at him? 'Because let me assure you, sweetheart, there's absolutely no need.'

'Really,' she said witheringly, obviously not believing him for a second.

Right. That was enough, Jack decided, twisting round and giving in to the increasingly pressing desire to set her straight. 'Look, here are the facts. The facts,' he repeated, fixing her with a stare, 'not some twisted third-hand gossip.'

She opened her mouth to say something, but he was fed up with the accusations and the scorn so he uncrossed his arms and clamped a hand over it. 'Quiet.'

Ignoring the feel of her soft skin and her mouth beneath his palm and the way her eyes were widening with shock and something else, Jack made himself focus on the facts.

'Amanda and I went out two or three times,' he said. 'Four at the most.' And even that was several times too many. Although beautiful, Amanda had been a drama queen with a penchant for flouncing, which was one of the reasons he'd stopped seeing her. 'We didn't have a relationship and we certainly never discussed moving in together.'

Which he knew was true because relationships and co-habitation didn't feature in his game plan. Never had done and never would, even if he wanted them to. Which he didn't.

Jack watched Imogen blink as her brain processed the information, and he felt her mouth move. Without taking his eyes off hers for a second he leaned a fraction closer. 'That's right,' he said silkily. 'Whatever Amanda is doing in Italy, it isn't getting over me. OK?'

She tilted her head a little, stared at him for what felt like ages, then nodded.

'And while we're at it,' he murmured, thinking he might as well set her straight on a few other things, too, seeing as he had her here, 'my reputation, unlike my ego, *is* over-inflated.'

That was evidently one fact too many to digest, Jack

thought, watching as Imogen's eyes widened. 'You don't be-lieve me?' he said, tutting in mock disappointment.

She narrowed her eyes then shook her head.

'I see,' Jack said, nodding and frowning as if in deep thought. 'I've heard that you're shallow and vacuous. Nothing more than a party girl who leads an utterly pointless life.' She tensed and narrowed her eyes even further. 'I guess that's all true, too.'

At the fiery dagger-shooting glare she gave him, he added with feigned ignorance, 'You mean it isn't?'

She shook her head again.

'I see. So why would things be different for me?'

He waited while she thought it over. And when she shrugged, he leaned forwards a fraction and murmured, 'Perhaps I'm not as bad as you'd like me to be.'

He felt a shudder run through her. Saw her eyes darken, thought he felt her mouth open, and lust burst through him.

Visions of what might happen if they were both as bad as could be bombarded his head, and again he wanted to slide his hand down her neck round to her nape and pull her head towards him. He wanted to slam his mouth down on hers and wrap her in his arms and assuage this desire that itched inside him.

Which would be the worst idea on the planet.

Quite why, Jack couldn't fathom. If his reputation was largely fabricated, there was every chance hers was too. Despite what he'd heard, Imogen certainly didn't come across as shallow and vacuous. She came across as spiky, fearless and utterly intriguing.

So if her reputation *was* as fabricated as his, there wasn't anything stopping him from suggesting dinner again. Nothing to stop him persuading her to acknowledge the attraction that sizzled between them and nothing to stop them pursuing it.

Nothing, that was, apart from the weird warning flag that was waving frantically in his brain. The one that had taken up residence the minute the words '*this* one' had popped into his head when he'd first shaken her hand and was now insisting on being noticed. The one that had his blood chilling and his stomach clutching with something that felt suspiciously like panic.

Not that he ever suffered from panic, of course. No. On reflection, that odd sensation was undoubtedly hunger. But still…

Jack cleared his throat and drew back a little. It would probably be an idea to bring this whole evening to a close. He'd found out what Imogen's problem was, and had rectified it. He'd done what he'd set out to do and there was no need to stick around. In fact, he should get out. Now. While the taxi was stationary at the lights.

'OK,' he said with a firmness designed to convince himself as much as her. 'Is that it? Are we done with the accusations?'

She nodded.

'Sure?'

She nodded again.

'Then I'll say goodnight.'

And before he could change his mind, he whipped his hand from her mouth, opened the door and leapt out.

# CHAPTER FIVE

THAT Jack had got out of the taxi when he had was a good thing, Imogen told herself, pummelling her pillow into shape a few hours later, then flinging herself back and staring up at the ceiling. Definitely a good thing.

Because if he hadn't...

As the scene in the taxi slammed into her head all over again, she shivered beneath the thick duvet and threw her arms over her head in frustration. What might have happened if he hadn't was precisely what she'd been trying *not* to think about all evening. And failing miserably.

Not that that was any surprise. She could still feel the imprint of his hand clamped over her mouth. Her lips still tingled. Her skin still burned. She could still remember how dizzy with desire she'd been at the intoxicating nearness of him. Desire that had been whipping through her long before he'd leaned forwards and touched her, and still was.

The moment she'd got home, she'd decided she might as well try to get on with the things she'd planned. She'd poured herself a glass of wine and run herself a bath, but neither had had the intended effect. The wine had tasted like acid in her mouth and the bath had merely heightened the buzzing in her body to such a degree that not even the bubbles could disguise the effects of the lingering traces of desire.

And as for daydreaming about life in the States, well, that

had been utterly pointless. Every time she told herself to concentrate on what might happen if she was really lucky and they accepted her, she'd found herself fantasising about Jack instead.

It hadn't helped that her brain kept rehashing the latter part of their encounter, starting with the minute she'd brought up the whole *greatsexguaranteed* thing. Of all the places she could have begun… Imogen let out a soft wail and threw one arm across her eyes. Who knew what he must have made of *that*?

Naturally, once she'd mentioned it, it was all she'd been able to think about. Great sex. With Jack. Guaranteed. Even when she'd been calling him arrogant and cold and callous she'd been going so hot and tingly that she'd wanted nothing more than to hurl herself onto his lap and ravish him.

Once he'd covered her mouth she'd tried to concentrate on all those questions, all those very valid points of his, but his voice had been so soft and so low that she'd felt hypnotised and she rather thought she couldn't have said a word even if his hand hadn't been in the way.

In fact, the only things that had stopped her tearing his fingers away and launching herself at him right there and then had been the presence of the taxi driver and her distaste of exhibitionism.

Imogen sighed again and gave up, because there was little point in denying it. She wanted him and had done from the moment they'd met. He'd certainly been right about *that*.

Not that it mattered one way or the other any more, she thought, scowling up at the ceiling. There she'd been, going all soft and swoony, coming to the realisation that struggling to control the desire racing through her body was like trying to paddle against the current, and wondering if giving in would really be so bad, and he'd been planning his escape.

Which with hindsight was completely understandable. Her behaviour, rattled by the effect he had on her and the events of the afternoon, had been unbelievably deranged and if she'd been in his position she'd have done exactly the same.

Imogen screwed her eyes tight shut and pulled the duvet over her head as if that might somehow obliterate the memories and the images because all in all the whole evening had been mortifying and she'd give anything to be able to forget every ghastly second.

The only reason she wasn't going to give in to the temptation to barricade herself in her bedroom for the next ten years was the knowledge that she had no need to lay eyes on him ever again.

Something was wrong, thought Jack the next day, running a finger around the inside of his collar, and shifting on his chair as he tried to concentrate on the menu.

Very wrong.

Maybe he was coming down with something. A cold. The flu. Pneumonia perhaps. Whatever. *Something* had to account for the achiness and the restlessness that had invaded his body some time during the night.

Usually he had no problem sleeping. Usually he crashed out the minute his head hit the pillow and fell into a deep dreamless sleep. But last night he'd slept terribly. He'd tossed and turned, then prowled and paced around his bedroom until he'd finally given up and gone to the office.

However, given that he'd been in since six, he'd achieved remarkably little. All morning he'd been feeling on edge. He'd growled at his secretary, when he never normally growled, barked unfairly at one of his traders, and had made some stupidly rash investment decisions.

Eventually, unable to stand the four walls of his office and the tension any longer, and realising he could do some serious damage to his funds—and his team—if he stuck around when he was in this perplexing mood, he'd called Luke and dragged him out for lunch.

'So what's up?'

At the sound of Luke's voice, Jack jerked himself out of his dark thoughts and glanced up to find his friend staring at him with avid curiosity.

'Nothing's up,' he said. 'What makes you think anything's up?'

'Well, the fact that you haven't been listening to a word I've been saying for the past five minutes is a bit of a clue.'

God, had it been that long? 'Sorry,' Jack muttered and frowned.

What was going on? He never felt like this. Never lost track of conversations. On the contrary, his ability to stay focused at all times was legendary. It was what had made him millions. And he never normally had such trouble ordering off a menu, either.

Hmm. Maybe he ought to grovel to his secretary and ask her very kindly to make an appointment with the doctor, because he couldn't go on like this. He'd drive himself demented and his business into the ground. 'I was miles away.'

'Clearly,' Luke said. 'Visiting anywhere interesting?'

Feeling distinctly uneasy at the glint in Luke's eyes, Jack pulled himself together. He had no intention of discussing his symptoms. He'd sound nuts. Besides, it was probably nothing. Everyone had a bad night once in a while, didn't they? He was just suffering from lack of sleep and overwork. That was all. And he'd have the steak.

'Nowhere at all,' he said, snapping the menu shut and fixing the easy life's-a-breeze smile that he'd mastered from an early age to his face. 'So what were you saying?'

'Just checking you're still on for Saturday.'

Ah. At the thought of Saturday and Daisy, Jack's smile turned genuine. In a moment of recklessness he'd offered to babysit his god-daughter while Luke and Emily went to a wedding in Cornwall.

What he thought he'd been doing he had no idea. He had

zero experience of looking after three-year-old girls and had no desire to do so on any kind of a regular basis. But Luke's parents were out of the country, and Emily's sister was busy, and when, with a slightly desperate note to her voice, Emily had told him that she didn't trust anyone else but him, he hadn't been able to resist.

Personally, Jack thought her trust in him was highly misplaced, but, although he'd never admit it, he'd do pretty much anything for Luke and Emily, and sacrificing a Saturday night for his gorgeous god-daughter wasn't exactly a hardship. 'Of course I'm still on for Saturday.'

'Because if you had other plans,' said Luke conversationally, 'I'm sure we could work something out.'

'I don't.'

'Are you sure?'

'I'm sure.'

'OK.' Luke grinned and turned his attention to his own menu. 'But if you change your mind all you have to do is let us know.'

'Thanks, but I won't.'

'Just offering you a get-out clause if you need one.'

Jack fought the urge to grind his teeth. What the hell was this? He didn't need a get-out clause. He might have his faults, but backing out of an arrangement—especially one that concerned the only two people in the world whose loyalty and friendship he could count on—wasn't one of them.

And Luke knew that, which meant that this conversation had some sort of agenda.

'If there's a point you're trying to make, Luke,' said Jack, sitting back and bracing himself, 'why don't you come out and make it?'

'Fine.' Luke grinned and looked up. 'I was just thinking that if you wanted to take a certain Imogen Christie out on Saturday night instead of babysitting Daisy, all you have to do is say. I'm sure we can make other arrangements.'

Jack went still, any semblance of relaxed ease evaporating. 'What makes you think I'd want to take Imogen Christie out on Saturday night?'

'Only that this morning Emily had a call from a friend of hers who spotted the two of you at an art exhibition last night. Chatting and then getting into a taxi and looking extremely cosy.'

Cosy? *Cosy? Cosy* was the last thing it had been. This friend had clearly missed the 'victim devouring' comment. 'I see.'

'Apparently she was after all the gory details.'

'There aren't any.'

Luke arched an eyebrow and grinned. 'That I find hard to believe.'

Jack shrugged. As far as he was concerned, Luke could believe what he liked. 'Why are you so interested?'

'You're my oldest and best friend. Why wouldn't I be interested?'

Ah, thought Jack wryly. How could he have forgotten? Of course Luke would be interested. Ever since he'd married three years ago, he'd been dropping not very subtle hints that Jack should think about following his example and settle down himself.

Hah. As if. As much as Luke and Emily might wish otherwise, the last thing he wanted was what they had. They had each other, and Daisy, and another baby on the way. Which was great for Luke, but that kind of family set-up wasn't for him. Never had been, never would be.

'So Emily put you up to this?' he said, stifling a shudder at the thought of settling down.

'She asked me to get the low-down,' said Luke, completely without shame.

'Well, you can tell her to tell her friend that there's nothing to report. Imogen and I met at the gallery and had a conversation, which continued in a taxi. Then I got out and she carried on to wherever she was going. That was it. End of story.'

'OK, great.' Luke grinned and sat back, his mission clearly accomplished. 'Because if you weren't up for babysitting, I'm not sure what we'd have done.'

Which only went to prove how subtly Jack had been finessed. Not that he cared about that at this particular moment. The sudden contraction of his muscles had nothing to do with being skilfully finessed. Nor did the pounding of his head and the rocketing of his heart rate.

No. The cause of all that was the thought now ricocheting around his brain to the annihilation of everything else: what if it *wasn't* the end of the story?

Jack went hot, then cold, and felt a bead of sweat trickle down his spine as the idea stopped racing round his head and began to take root.

Wow, he thought, his stomach churning. If it wasn't and he did in fact consider Imogen unfinished business, then that would certainly explain his unease and his restlessness over the past twelve hours. Was it a coincidence that he'd started feeling like this the minute he'd left her? He didn't think so.

As realisation dawned all the thoughts his subconscious had been keeping at bay broke though the fragile barrier it had erected and rained down on him.

If he'd done the right thing by getting out of that damn taxi last night, why had it felt the exact opposite? Why had he marched down that street towards his flat feeling as if he had hundred-tonne weights attached to his ankles? Why had the broken dreams he'd had during the moments of sleep he *had* managed to snatch been filled with such erotic images? Why did his blood heat and desire race though him at the mere thought of her? And why couldn't he get the memory of her sprawled against him as the taxi had pulled away, her mouth inches from his and her hand clamped to his thigh, out of his head?

Oh, yes, he thought grimly, that definitely sounded like unfinished business.

'But I can't help wondering why.'

'Why what?' said Jack, dazed by the intensity with which he ached to finish what he'd started with Imogen.

'Why you aren't seeing her again. I've heard she's very pretty.'

Imogen was more than pretty. She was beautiful, contrary, fascinating and as sexy as hell, and there was no point in denying it. A wave of heat rocked through him and he shifted on the chair to ease the pressure building in his lower body. 'She is.'

'Then what's wrong with her?'

Jack inwardly winced. 'She's just not my type,' he muttered, thinking that Luke might be his best friend but there was no way he was about to confess how badly he'd crashed and burned.

'Not your type? She has a pulse, doesn't she?'

'Ha-ha.' Jack frowned and tried to ignore the sting of the seriously lame joke.

'Sorry. I couldn't resist.'

'Well, try.'

Luke's eyebrows shot up at the sharp tone of Jack's voice, as well they might. Luke, who was one of the few people who knew Jack wasn't as dissolute as he'd have everyone believe, often took the mickey. Usually it never bothered him, so why did it now?

Telling himself to get a grip, Jack shot his friend an apologetic smile. 'Sorry,' he said. 'Just knackered.'

'No problem,' said Luke with a quick smile of his own. 'I shouldn't have brought her up in the first place.'

Jack sighed and pushed his hands through his hair. 'If you must know, I did ask her out. She turned me down.'

'God, why?'

'She disapproved of my reputation.'

'I see.' Luke nodded. Tilted his head and frowned. 'Didn't you set her straight?'

'Of course.'

'Then I don't get it. What happened?'

Jack resisted the urge to grind his teeth. That was a billion-dollar question, and the one he'd been avoiding ever since he'd made the decision to get out of that taxi, if he was being brutally honest.

The truth of it was that he'd got spooked. He'd known that Imogen was as attracted to him as he was to her. He'd seen and heard the evidence. Hell, he'd even told her she wanted him.

But had he taken advantage of it? No. Instead, he'd opted for the easy way out, dogged by the weird sensation that Imogen was somehow dangerous. That she could very easily pose some kind of threat to his peace of mind if he got involved with her.

Which was absurd, he thought, conjuring up the image of her sitting there eyes wide and darkening with heat as he leaned in close to set her straight. The woman was as much of a threat as a marshmallow, and his overreaction had been melodramatic to say the least.

But then why wouldn't it have been? Over the course of a matter of hours he'd had to endure agony-inducing art, been struck by the severest case of lust he'd had in a long time, had had an invitation to dinner hurled back in his face, suffered a jab to the ribs and then been accused of being arrogant and cold.

With such a battering assault on his senses was it any wonder his equilibrium had been somewhat off?

But now, however, he could see that Imogen was just one in a long line of women who'd caught his eye. She was business he badly wanted to finish, that was all.

'I was an idiot,' said Jack, feeling the restlessness and tension ease from his body at the burgeoning notion of pursuing and capturing Imogen.

'So what are you going to do?'

'Track her down.'

And when he did he'd make her acknowledge the attraction that flared between them if it was the last thing he did. He'd employ every tactic he knew—and he knew plenty—and by the time he was through with her, she'd be begging him to take her in his arms and assuage the ache he'd stir up in her.

'How?'

'I have absolutely no idea,' Jack said, telling himself that with the energy and focus suddenly spreading through him it wouldn't present too much of a problem.

'Need any help?'

Jack caught the trace of yearning in Luke's voice and grinned. Years ago the two of them had been a lethal double act in their pursuit of women, but now he operated alone. 'Thanks,' he said and glanced over at the approaching waiter, 'but I should be able to manage.'

# CHAPTER SIX

TONIGHT was going to be grim, thought Imogen for the billionth time that Friday. Utterly grim, and if she hadn't been the only person available to represent her family at tonight's Valentine's Day Ball, she'd have stayed at home, curled up with a good book and a glass of wine.

For one thing she was exhausted. Not because she'd been putting in sixteen-hour days at work or anything. Her lowly nine-to-five job in the funding department at the Christie Trust—which she'd only been given because of who she was—wasn't, unfortunately, hugely demanding.

And not because she'd been out until the early hours, either, as in an effort to avoid Max and Connie she'd largely shunned the social scene ever since they'd got together.

No. The cause of her restless nights was Jack.

To her intense, teeth-grinding frustration, she hadn't been able to get him out of her head. The minute she closed her eyes at night, there he was, frazzling her brain with his voice, his eyes, his scent and the feel of his hand on her mouth.

As if disturbing her dreams wasn't bad enough, he had an annoying tendency to invade her thoughts during the day, too. Often at the most inconvenient times. Like yesterday when she'd been in the supermarket contemplating what to buy for supper. She'd been lurking in the frozen food aisle and eyeing up the pizzas when, completely apropos of nothing, the image of him in the back of the taxi had flown into her head.

However, in her now hyperactive imagination, Jack hadn't got out. In her mind's eye the driver had magically disappeared and Jack had stayed put. With a smouldering smile, he'd pulled her towards him and kissed her until her stomach disappeared and she forgot her name. And then he'd done all manner of indescribably delicious things to her with his hands that had had her temperature rocketing and her knees turning to jelly right there by the frozen peas.

If it hadn't been for the shop assistant asking if she was all right and bringing her crashing back down to earth, she'd have found herself hopping into the freezer to cool off.

It really had to stop because she'd come to the unwelcome and disturbing conclusion that she was developing a seriously unhealthy obsession with Jack.

Why else would she have got hold of Amanda Hobbs' details in Italy the morning after the art exhibition and called her to wheedle out the truth?

Why else had she spent hours fantasising about him when she'd managed to convince herself that she'd never be seeing him again?

Why else had she had to unplug her laptop and stuff it in a cupboard at home if not to stop herself from doing a Google search on him relentlessly?

And why else had she endlessly tortured herself with the acknowledgement that her wanting him wasn't the only thing he'd been right about?

Imogen sighed and nibbled on her lip as once again her thoughts helplessly barrelled off in that direction. Jack had been right about everything else he'd pointed out too. She *had* misjudged him. Even in her frazzled state she'd managed to work that out. Her reputation was hugely exaggerated—if not completely inaccurate—so why wouldn't his be, too? Frankly some of the stuff she'd heard had been so outlandish she'd thought at the time that it had to be fabricated.

Not that that made him a saint, of course, but if Jack really was a louche layabout he wouldn't be heading up one of the most successful investment companies in the country, would he? And yes, he might have had more than his fair share of women, but a man who looked like that, had a voice like that and such charismatic magnetism would.

And that meant that perhaps she'd made a mistake in rejecting his offer of dinner quite so out of hand.

The taxi she'd called to take her to the five-star hotel overlooking Hyde Park hurtled round a corner as if on two wheels and Imogen, too lost in thought to grab onto the handle in time, crashed into the side. Which didn't hurt, but did bring her careering back to her senses.

God, she was doing it again, she thought, rubbing her shoulder and then checking her hair. Obsessing over Jack when there was absolutely no point. Even if she *had* reached the realisation that he was nothing like Max and might quite like the idea of joining his bevy of conquests, it was far too late.

Besides, Jack Taylor was way out of her league in every respect, and she hadn't exactly put herself across in the best of lights that evening.

Imogen closed her eyes and pressed her fingers to her temples as she fought a rising blush and tried to calm down. Not that there was much hope of that when her stomach was churning, her head was pounding and her nerves were wound so tight she thought they might be about to snap.

Because her sense of impending doom about this evening wasn't entirely down to exhaustion. Or her frustration at her inability to wipe Jack from her brain.

As if either of those factors weren't enough to tempt her to tell the taxi driver to take her back home and dive under her duvet, she also had to deal with the fact that tonight it was almost inevitable she'd come face to face with Max and Connie. She'd seen their names on the guest list, and in a crowd of a hundred there'd be little place to hide. And she wouldn't be able to avoid the whispers and sidelong glances that were bound to be cast her way, either.

Sensing the taxi coming to a halt, Imogen opened her eyes and took a deep breath. Never mind, she told herself, getting out and stiffening her spine. All she had to do was keep her cool and remain poised, and everything would be fine.

Adjusting her stole and rubbing her teeth to remove any errant lipstick, she opened the door and, with a grace that years of practice had bestowed on her, got out. She flashed a blinding smile at a loitering photographer and then made her way up the wide stone steps and through the huge glass doors.

This was an important night for the trust, she reminded herself, holding her head high as she shrugged off the stole and handed it to the waiting attendant. Stashing the ticket she received in return in her clutch bag and giving the attendant a beaming smile of thanks, she walked across the black-and-white-chequered marble floor towards the handful of people who'd already arrived. The annual Valentine's Day Ball raised thousands, if not millions, for good causes, and she wouldn't do anything to jeopardise that.

She'd given herself a string of hearty pep talks and gone over how she'd behave and what she'd say a thousand times. Should she happen to bump into either Max or Connie, or heaven forbid the two of them together, she'd resist the urge to claw their eyes out and instead would be charming, witty and chatty. The life and soul of the party, in fact. She'd show everyone that she couldn't care less about what they'd done, or how much they'd hurt her, because she was over it.

'Imogen?'

At the sound of the familiar female voice behind her, Imogen froze. Her heart thumped and her blood roared in her ears before shooting to her feet. As if in slow motion, she turned.

And there they were. Max and Connie. Standing right in front of her, arms linked, clinging to each other like limpets and grinning like maniacs. Connie's hand was wrapped around Max's arm and the whopping diamond on the third finger of her left hand sparkled as if on fire.

Feeling as if someone had walloped her in the solar plexus and then sucked all the air from around her, Imogen looked from Connie to Max and back again. And to her horror, her vision blurred, her throat closed over and her head went completely and utterly blank.

Aha, thought Jack with a surge of satisfaction as he scanned the lobby of the hotel and spotted Imogen. There she was. Over there by the fireplace. Standing next to a tall, dark-haired man and a short blonde woman.

Excellent.

It seemed that his mother, for once in her shallow, flaky life, had actually come up with the goods.

Calling her to make discreet enquiries about when and where he might find Imogen had been something of a last resort. However, despite assuring Luke he'd manage perfectly well alone, tracking Imogen down had proved trickier than he'd thought.

After lunch he'd gone back to the office, his mind trawling through the options and discarding each one almost as soon as it entered his head. Chasing around London on the off chance of bumping into her he'd deemed inefficient and unlikely to result in success. Obtaining her contact details and sending her an email or giving her a call would give her the chance to ignore him. And if he'd pitched up on her doorstep, her stalking accusation might actually have held some merit.

Which had left him with no alternative but to try his mother. He'd figured that no one knew the London social scene better—with her penchant for partying 'til dawn with men younger than *he* was, she'd had enough practice—and if anyone knew where Imogen was going to be it was her.

Not that he'd needed to be subtle when making his enquiries, he thought, adjusting his bow tie as he weaved his way towards Imogen. His mother was so self-absorbed she'd never spare the time to wonder why her son would be asking about the whereabouts of a girl.

Of course, there wasn't anything particularly newsworthy about the fact that he had. His wanting to track Imogen down wasn't a big deal. So what if he'd never cared in the past about who knew who he was dating? And so what if he'd previously sought a girl's contact details from friends and acquaintances without a care for the gossip doing so might generate?

With the possibility of Imogen's resistance being a large obstacle in his intention to make a conquest of her, this operation required delicacy. Subtlety. A different approach.

And one that required his full focus, he reminded himself, keeping her in his line of sight. Focus that mustn't be derailed at any cost. Especially not by the spectacular way she looked.

As he got closer he could see that she was wearing a strapless black full-length dress that clung everywhere and had a split up to the top of her thigh. Her hair was swept up and looked like spun gold. Diamonds glittered at her throat and ear lobes.

A weaker man would have been dazzled. A weaker man would have cast aside any tactics he might have had, fallen to his knees at her feet and begged her for a smile. Luckily for him and his life-long adherence to strategy, Jack had self-control and strength in spades and didn't possess one iota of weakness.

Although actually, he thought, narrowing his eyes as something about the tense set of her shoulders snagged his attention, Imogen wasn't looking quite as radiant as she should be. In fact, she was looking rather pale. Somewhat stunned. And increasingly as if she was going to pass out.

He quickened his pace, concern rushing through him at the realisation that something was badly wrong.

'Imogen?' he said, coming to a halt a foot from her and steeling himself against the effect she'd have on him if he let her. 'Are you all right?'

For a moment she simply stared at him, her eyes huge and troubled, and he had the strangest feeling that she was looking straight through him. But then, just when he was beginning to get really worried by her pallor, she blinked. Pulled her shoulders back, gave herself a quick shake and then shot him a stunning smile.

'Jack, darling,' she purred, and to his astonishment reached up, wrapped a hand around his neck and planted a kiss at the corner of his mouth. 'You made it.'

At the brush of her lips so soft and full and so tantalisingly close to his own and at the touch of her hand on his neck, Jack felt as if he'd been electrocuted. Her breast was squashed up against his arm, her body was warm and soft against his, and her scent was intoxicating. She shot every one of his senses to pieces and blew his strategy to smithereens, and he wanted nothing more than to haul her into the shadows and tug that mouth to his properly. So he could explore it with his, thoroughly and at length.

She drew back, her eyes dark and now sparkling, and Jack ruthlessly stamped out the urge. Strength and self-control, he reminded himself. Strength and self-control. Because right now he wasn't here to show her how pointless denying the chemistry they shared was. He was here to help.

Catching the flicker of pleading in her eyes, he ignored the voice inside his head demanding to know what made him think he could help when he didn't have a chivalrous bone in his body. Whatever was going on, Imogen clearly needed him to be attentive, so attentive he'd be.

After all, he reflected, belatedly gathering his scattered wits and switching to Besotted Lover mode, he'd planned on being extremely attentive to Imogen this evening and he'd envisaged having to put in a lot more groundwork. If circumstances expedited matters he'd be a fool not to take advantage of them.

Wrapping an arm around her waist and pulling her tight against him, he smiled down into her eyes and murmured, 'Did you really think I wouldn't?'

He felt her relax. Saw the clouds drift from her eyes, the trouble gradually fade, and as heat and desire crept in to take its place all he could think about was how much fun getting Imogen to unravel in his arms was going to be.

'I wasn't sure.'

'Such little faith.'

'Forgive me?'

Right now, with her voice all soft and breathy and her body moulded to his, he thought he'd probably forgive her anything. Faintly disconcerted by the thought, Jack released his grip on her slightly and dragged his gaze from hers to cast a quick glance at the couple she was with. 'Aren't you going to introduce me to your friends, darling?'

Imogen blinked. 'What? Oh. Yes. Of course. Jack, this is Max Llewellyn.' Her smile faltered and it made Jack wonder if *friends* was quite the word. 'And Connie Nicholson.'

'Jack Taylor,' he said, nodding briefly and shaking their hands in turn.

Something about Max made his hackles shoot up. Made him take an instant dislike to the man even though he couldn't for the life of him work out why. Maybe it was the fact that he was altogether too smooth. His teeth were too white, his hair too perfectly coiffured, his nails too manicured.

'Max and Connie are engaged,' Imogen said with a tightness that confirmed his earlier suspicion that whatever the three of them were they weren't friends.

'Congratulations,' said Jack.

'Thanks,' said Connie, her wide smile fading as she shot a quick glance at Imogen, whose own smile was now so brittle it looked as if it might be about to shatter.

An awkward kind of lull fell, during which no one apart from Jack looked at anyone else. As long seconds passed, the strained silence worsened and he sensed Imogen's anxiety grow.

Deciding that, as fascinating as the dynamics of this group were, someone needed to do something to ease the situation, Jack was just about to lob in a polite but inane comment about the weather when Imogen pulled herself together and did the job for him.

'Well, isn't this nice?' she said brightly.

'Delightful,' Jack murmured, thinking *nice* was *not* the word.

'I must say,' said Connie enthusiastically, clearly overcompensating for the palpable tension vibrating around their little group, 'your events department has done an excellent job.'

He followed her gaze as it skipped around the tastefully lavish Valentine's Day decorations that adorned both the lobby and, from what he could see through the giant half-open doors, the ballroom.

'And so it should have with tickets costing four figures each.' Imogen let out a laugh that sounded high and false, and, to his ears, verged on hysterical. 'You see the rose petals?' she said, waving a hand in the direction of the petal-strewn floor. 'Damask. Flown in from Morocco, would you believe? All two hundred thousand of them. And the candles? Bought from the same people that supply Westminster Abbey. And let's not forget the casino. I understand the croupiers have been specially brought in from Monte Carlo. You must try it later. There's roulette, not of the Russian kind, luckily, ha-ha-ha.'

'Are you a gambling man?' Jack said, cutting into Imogen's rapidly spiralling-out-of-control rambling, not because he was the slightest bit interested in Max's gambling habits, but because he thought she might thank him later.

'No.' Max laughed and Jack inwardly winced. The man sounded like a horse neighing. 'Far too risky. Modern art's more my thing.'

Idiot. 'Really?'

'Yes. In fact, I recently picked something new up.' He waited, evidently expecting to be asked all about it, and when no one did, went on, 'Well, when I say *I*, I mean I instructed my man to buy it on my behalf, of course, haw-haw-haw. Very exclusive. Very exciting.'

'I'm sure,' Jack muttered, fervently hoping that whatever Imogen's relationship was with this pompous prat, it wasn't close.

'Cost me a bomb, naturally, but I always think you can never put a price on truly great art, don't you?'

'Oh, I couldn't agree more,' he said.

'Yes,' said Connie, loyally picking up the conversational thread. 'Apparently, it's supposed to represent man's fight against the injustice of capitalism, but personally I can't see it. I just like the colours.'

Jack stilled as a horrible thought darted across his mind. No. It couldn't be…

But with the way Imogen was tensing at his side, apparently it just possibly could. He glanced down at her to find out if she'd come to the same conclusion he had and at the same time she turned her head to look up at him.

Their eyes met. And locked. He saw a flash of amused horror sparkle in the brown depths. Felt a corresponding smile tug at his lips, and for one heady moment everything receded. The brightly coloured mass of people gathered around them… The low hum of conversation… The crackling and spitting of the fire… The gentle clink of glasses and the fizz of champagne… It all faded away until the only two things he was aware of were Imogen's warm, soft and pliant body clamped to his side and the growing sense of need clawing at his gut.

'Well, that's always important,' Jack murmured, his voice sounding strangely hoarse as desire began to hammer through him.

'And I'm sure it'll make a great investment,' said Imogen, nodding gravely, her eyes still glued to his.

'So they tell me,' brayed Max from somewhere that sounded miles away.

And quite suddenly Jack had had quite enough of Max and Connie and this excruciating conversation. And quite enough of sharing Imogen with them. With anyone, for that matter.

His pulse was racing and his mouth was dry. He'd come here with one purpose in mind, and his hard, aching body was telling him to get on with it. He'd come to her aid. Now it was time she repaid the favour.

'Darling,' he murmured, heat whipping through him so fiercely his body pounded with the force of it, 'I think we should circulate, don't you?'

His hand tightened around her waist, bringing her in closer contact with his hard, aroused lower body and she blinked, her eyes darkening and her breath catching.

'What?' she breathed. 'Oh, yes. You're right. Absolutely right. Circulate. Good idea.' She flashed Max and Connie a bright smile and raised her hand in a jaunty wave. 'Well, we must be off. So lovely to see you both. Toodle pip.'

# CHAPTER SEVEN

Toodle pip? *Toodle pip?*

Oh, good Lord.

Still clamped to Jack's side as he whisked her out of the lobby, around the corner and along a corridor, Imogen stifled a wince and wished she could go back and redo that conversation with the cool, collected poise she'd intended.

How could she have crumbled quite so hideously? How could she have forgotten every word of those pep talks? And how could she have behaved so recklessly?

As she sneaked a glance at Jack and the stern set of his face, her body buzzed with a mind-altering combination of adrenalin, desire and wariness. What must he be *thinking*?

When he'd first materialised, she'd thought she must have conjured him up. Because having exchanged a series of stilted 'how are you?'s and 'what have you been up to lately?'s with her bêtes noires, she'd been racking her brain for some way out of the desperately awkward situation she'd found herself in and had come up with nothing that would allow her to extricate herself with any kind of dignity.

And then there he'd been, all dark and gorgeous and gazing down at her with that mesmerising look of concern on his face, and with barely a thought for the consequences, and because it had struck her that Jack outclassed Max in every way, she'd decided to use him. Quite shamelessly.

Not that he'd seemed to mind. After what must have been considerable initial surprise Jack had thrown himself into the role of besotted lover with admirable aplomb, and if she hadn't known better she'd have been totally convinced.

Of course, unlike herself, he'd merely been putting on a performance, and it was little wonder he'd borne her off. After the way she'd been gabbling on about the decorations like an interior designer on acid, on top of everything she'd done on Tuesday night, he must think her completely nuts. In fact, he was probably removing her for her own safety.

But where *were* they going? she wondered as alarm began to trickle through the adrenalin, the desire and the wariness. Wanting to give her time to collect herself in private was one thing, but he'd better not be planning to stash her in a cupboard or something. She had a speech to give.

Just as she was toying with the idea of wrenching herself from the tight embrace of his arm and legging it, Jack drew to a halt at the far end of the corridor. He set her against the wall and, shoving his hands in his pockets, took a step back. His deep blue gaze fixed on hers, pinned her there and in the silence that ensued all she could hear was the rapid thump of her heart.

Dimly aware that the guests were far away and that the corridor was dusky and completely deserted, she realised that they were completely alone and Jack wasn't nearly as relaxed as she'd imagined. And her heart beat even faster.

'So, *darling*,' he said, leaning in a fraction and apparently stealing all her oxygen, 'what exactly was that all about?'

At the low seductive tone of his voice and the glitter in his eyes, her mouth went dry. Resisting the urge to run her tongue along her lips, Imogen swallowed. 'Would you believe me if I said I behaved like that with every man I'm pleased to see?'

'No.'

'I didn't think so.' She sighed and bit her lip as shame,

which had been an embarrassingly long time coming, struck her square in the chest. 'I'm sorry.'

Despite the tension in him one corner of his mouth hitched up. 'Don't be. I actually found the whole thing hugely entertaining.'

Imogen blinked in surprise and not a little pique. Entertaining? That was not what she'd been expecting. 'I'm delighted you enjoyed the show,' she said tartly.

Jack raised an eyebrow and grinned, then twisted round to lean one shoulder against the wall, far too close for her peace of mind. 'You don't really behave like that with every man you're pleased to see, do you?'

'Of course not.'

'Good.'

'I was just a little—ah—jumpy.'

'I'd never have guessed.'

She ignored that and sought refuge in manners. 'Anyway, thank you for coming to my rescue.'

'It was my pleasure. I'm glad I was able to help out. Why the jumpiness?'

Imogen tried come up with a suitable explanation but it was tough when she only had a variety of unsuitable ones to choose from.

She could attribute her nerves to the awkwardness that had hit her when she'd first laid eyes on Max and Connie. But that had disappeared the minute she'd seen Jack. From then on her jumpiness had been firstly down to the feel of his body against hers and the corresponding desire that had swept through her and wiped out every scrap of self-possession she had, and then the sense of connection she'd had when their eyes had met over the realisation that Max could well have bought Jack's painting.

But as she had no intention of giving him the pleasure of knowing how jumpy he made her, she was going to have to explain about Max and Connie. Which wouldn't exactly put her in a good light, but then given the nature of their acquaintance to date she doubted she could sink any lower in his estimation.

'If you must know,' she said, straightening her spine against the wall and ignoring the twinge she felt at the notion of sinking lower in his estimation, 'I used to go out with Max.'

She turned her head in time to see Jack's eyebrows shoot up and a flicker of something flare in the depths of his eyes. 'I see.'

Hmm. Intriguing. What had that been? Disappointment? Anger? Jealousy? Imogen's heart fluttered for a second and then she told herself not to be so absurd, because why would he be any of those things?

When he didn't say anything else, she shifted round to face him and folded her arms across her chest. 'What?' she asked, jutting her chin up partly in response to the frown creasing his forehead and partly because she was annoyed with herself for actually wanting him to be jealous.

'I must say I'm surprised.'

'Why?'

'Well, for one thing, he has abysmal taste in art.'

At the memory of how dazed she'd felt when her gaze had locked with his and they'd just stared at each other while coming to the same conclusion her heart gave a little lurch. 'Did he really buy your painting, do you think?' she said.

Jack shrugged the shoulder that wasn't propped against the wall. 'I had a phone call from the gallery the morning after the show, and apparently *someone* bought it, so it isn't beyond the realms of possibility.'

A tiny smile tugged at her lips. 'Oh, dear, poor Max.'

From the way Jack grunted, she guessed he didn't share the sentiment.

'So what's the other thing?' she asked.

He arched one dark eyebrow. 'What other thing?'

'You said "for one thing", which would imply there's another.'

'He's a jerk.'

Imogen frowned, faintly put out that Jack had deduced in five minutes what it had taken her the last two months to figure out. 'Well, yes, but he was *my* jerk. Now he's Connie's jerk and that hurts.'

'Why? I'd have thought you'd be glad to be rid of him.'

'Oh, I am. *Now*.' She bit her lip. 'But I wasn't for a long time.'

'What happened?'

Imogen sighed and decided that she had nothing to lose by telling him. 'We went out together for about a year. I thought everything was going fabulously, until one weekend a couple of months ago when I got home from staying with my parents and found a note, telling me he was leaving me to shack up with Connie.'

His jaw tightened. 'Like I said, he's a jerk. And she's not much better.'

'She was my best friend. *My best friend*. How could she?' Imogen frowned and shook her head at her own naiveté. 'I thought I knew her inside out. We grew up together. Started at the same school on the same day. Hung out all the time in the holidays. That sort of thing. It's the ultimate betrayal.'

'It sounds like you're more upset at the loss of a friend than a boyfriend.'

Imogen snapped her gaze up to find him looking at her thoughtfully. Maybe he had a point. Connie's betrayal *had* cut far deeper than Max's. 'I'm upset full stop,' she muttered, slightly thrown by the realisation.

Although actually she wasn't all that upset, was she? At least not about the disgustingly happy couple. Not any more.

Now that she thought about it, over the last couple of days she'd been so caught up with thoughts of Jack and the way he made her feel that Max and Connie and their forthcoming nuptials had barely crossed her mind.

She cast her memory back to the traumatic afternoon she'd discovered they'd got engaged, and to her bewilderment she felt nothing. Not a pang, not a twinge, not an ache. Which was as unnerving as it was a relief.

'Or at least I *was*,' she added, thinking that since Jack had come to her rescue so splendidly and as it no longer appeared to hurt perhaps she owed him the rest as well. 'The afternoon we met at the gallery when I was a little, ah…' She paused as she searched for any word that wouldn't make her sound demented.

'Unhinged?'

'Vulnerable,' she corrected, flashing a glare at him, 'I'd just found out they'd got engaged.'

'I see.'

'And it kind of threw me.'

'Well, that explains a lot,' he said with a satisfied nod.

'Don't look so pleased with yourself,' she said archly. 'You didn't exactly help.'

'Oh?'

'You reminded me of Max.'

Jack's eyebrows shot up and then he scowled. 'I'm nothing like Max.'

He looked so affronted she couldn't hold back a smile. 'Well, I realise that now, but I didn't know that at the time, did I? All I could see then was that you were both good-looking, charming with a fine line in banter, and heartbreaking players.'

Jack flinched. 'You jumped to an awful lot of conclusions.'

'And you didn't?' she countered as she thought of the character flaws he'd flung at her.

He frowned. Tilted his head as he stared at her with such an intense expression on his face her stomach squeezed. 'You're right. I did. I'm sorry.'

Mollified, Imogen gazed up at him until something that had been niggling away at her ever since he'd pitched up at her side struck her again. 'What are you doing here anyway?' she said. 'I don't remember seeing your name on the original guest list.'

'It wasn't. My ticket was a last-minute thing.'

'Why?'

'I wanted to see you.'

His eyes darkened and the glint appeared. As the air seemed to thicken around them Imogen gulped, her heart rate rocketing.

'What for?' she said a little huskily. 'You must think I'm insane.'

He pushed himself off the wall and turned so that he was standing so close she could feel the heat radiating off him. 'I don't think you're anything of the sort.'

'Really?'

'Really.' He tilted his head and gave her a smile that frazzled her senses. 'Would you like to know what I *do* think?'

She'd *love* to. 'I'd be fascinated,' she said evenly, trying not to sound too desperate.

'I think you must have had a rough time recently.'

'Oh, I have.' That he appeared to understand was doing strange things to her brain.

'And I think you're beautiful.'

Every bone in her body melted. 'You do?'

'I do.' His gaze dropped to her mouth and his eyes darkened to navy. 'I also think that you and I have unfinished business.'

Oh, heavens. Perhaps she hadn't sunk quite as low in his estimation as she'd imagined. 'Do we?'

'I think so.'

'In what way?'

'We started something on Tuesday night. Something that got held up by misunderstandings and assumptions.' He reached out to tuck a stray lock of hair behind her ear and she jumped. 'But now,' he added, lowering his hand to her wrist and slowly stroking it up to her shoulder, 'it seems to me that there isn't anything standing in the way of the basic facts any longer.'

'What basic facts?' she breathed because, although she was getting a pretty good idea, she was finding it hard to concentrate with his hand gliding over her skin.

'That I want you and you want me.'

Relief flooded through her. 'Ah, those facts.'

His fingers were now spreading over her skin where her neck met her shoulder and his thumb was on the pulse that hammered there. 'I hope you're not going to try and dispute them again.'

Imogen swallowed. 'I wouldn't dream of it.'

What would be the point? He was right. She did want him. More than she'd ever wanted anyone ever before. Had done for ages. And right now she wanted every smidgeon of danger, excitement and fun that that glint had to offer, because the realisation that he wanted it, too, was destroying what little was left of her self-control.

'Jack—' she said hoarsely.

But as his thumb circled relentlessly over her skin her head swam and she couldn't remember what she'd been intending to say. Still only touching her along her collarbone, he reached behind her and opened the door and backed her into whatever lay behind it.

'What are you doing?' she breathed as she stepped into darkness.

'Finishing that business we started. Do you have any objections?'

Somewhere through the fog swirling around her head, she was pretty sure she did. Not least because of where she was and what she was supposed to be doing. Reason made one pathetic last-ditch attempt to do the right thing. 'Dinner's about to begin.'

His gaze dropped to her mouth. 'You're so right.'

She shivered at that. 'I'm the guest of honour. I can't hide out in a—' she glanced round, her eyes adjusting to the dimness '—in a broom cupboard.'

'Five minutes,' he murmured, holding her transfixed with a look of pure need.

Oh, God, she thought, her heart beginning to thud crazily. Her nerve endings were sizzling so manically that the idea that she might be able to resist him was laughable. 'Two.'

'We'll see.'

And then he lowered his head to hers and all Imogen could see was him. Enveloping her and intoxicating her.

Her breath caught, her heart stopped and just when she thought she might pass out with the sheer weight of anticipation, his lips brushed hers. Lightly. Fleetingly. She trembled and let out a breathy little sigh. So he did it again. And again. The third time her moan was one of frustration because surely after all the build-up he wasn't planning to spend the whole two minutes doing that, was he?

But just in case that *was* his plan, just in case he *was* intending to give her only a tantalising hint of what he had to offer and truly drive her insane, Imogen reached up and wound her arms around his neck. She threaded her fingers through his hair, then tilted her hips and wiggled.

Which seemed to do the trick.

The hand that was on her shoulder whipped round to the nape of her neck while his other arm snapped around her and then to her delight and relief she was being hauled against him. Stunned by the speed and suddenness with which he moved, Imogen let out a startled gasp, which he took advantage of immediately by slamming his mouth down on hers.

The minute his lips met hers, properly this time, the remaining fragments of her brain disintegrated. As their tongues tangled and devoured, heat shot through her from head to toe. Her heart crashed against her ribs while her stomach swooped.

Barely able to control her movements, she pressed herself closer and he deepened the kiss. She heard him groan, felt the hot, hard evidence of his arousal against her and every inch of her body throb with need. He was all hard, powerful muscle and strength and the idea that right now every drop of it was hers was making her head swim. It was a good thing he had such a tight hold of her. If she hadn't been clasped so tightly in the strong, warm circle of his arms she'd have crumpled to the floor in a quivering, molten heap.

'You pack quite a punch,' Jack muttered, dragging his mouth from hers to explore the skin of her neck and upper chest.

'So do you,' she said raggedly as a series of uncontrollable shudders ripped through her. 'You know, never have I been so glad to be wearing a strapless dress.'

She was even more so when he slid his hand up her side to cup her breast. At the jolt of desire, Imogen let out a whimper of pleasure.

'Shh,' Jack murmured.

'Make me,' she said, desperate for his mouth to find hers again.

Which, to her fevered relief, it did. While he continued his devastating assault on her mouth, he pushed the top of her dress and her bra down and, taking the weight of one breast in his palm, he rubbed his thumb over her nipple.

Beneath his touch her nipple hardened and ached and Imogen groaned and arched her back. And then his mouth moved down to her other breast, closing over that nipple, and she screwed her eyes tight shut and dug her teeth into her lower lip, because, wow, she'd never felt pleasure like it.

Sparks showered through her, straight down to the hot,

aching centre of her, and she shuddered against him, trembling with the desire to have him thrusting up hard inside her.

But just when she thought she was about to collapse with need, Jack lifted his head and stared down at her, breathing heavily, his eyes blazing and dark and his face tight with restraint. Swallowing hard, he dragged in a ragged breath and took a step back.

'No,' Imogen muttered in protest.

'We have to stop,' he said roughly, drawing her dress and bra back into place with shaking fingers.

'Why?'

His eyes dropped to her mouth and for a moment she thought he would declare he was joking and drag her back into his arms.

But he didn't. Instead, he backed away even more and set his jaw. 'Because we've already been more than five minutes,' he said grimly, 'and if we carry on like this I might very well end up getting us a proper room.'

'A proper room?' she echoed dazedly.

'Well, this *is* a hotel, and beds are in dangerously close proximity.'

Imogen went dizzy at the thought of her and Jack hot and sweaty and naked in bed. 'That would be fine by me.' In fact, the sooner, the better.

'What happened to you being the star of the show and all that concern about being missed?'

Oh. Damn.

She blinked as reality crashed back into her head and obliterated the heat. Yes. Of course. The Ball. Dinner. Her speech. She blanched. Her speech! In a matter of minutes, she had to get up in front of a hundred people and speak. Agh. 'You're right.'

'You'd better go. Now. Before I change my mind and book that room.'

'What about you?' she said, wishing she didn't have to leave.

'I'll follow in a few minutes.'

'Will I see you after dinner?'

Jack hauled her into his arms and gave her a swift, hard kiss that made her head reel, and then shot her a look full of hot, dark promise before nudging her through the door and pointing her in the right direction. 'You can count on it.'

# CHAPTER EIGHT

Count on it?

Hah. She couldn't count on anything, thought Imogen, stalking into the conservatory after dinner with as much speed and force as her dress would allow, which infuriatingly wasn't a lot. Ideally, she'd have liked to pace and stomp but all she could do was totter over to an armchair and throw herself into it.

At least the glowering she could manage, she thought, staring gloomily out into the softly lit gardens.

Where had the evening gone so wrong?

After leaving Jack, she'd sailed into the dining room as if she were floating across the floor, aware that the electricity still flowing through her must be evident to anyone with eyes in their head, but unable to summon up the energy to do anything to hide it.

She'd taken her seat and smiled a hello to the other people at her table. She'd murmured her appreciation of the food and dipped in and out of the conversation. And all the while her thoughts had kept drifting back to that broom cupboard.

How she'd managed to get through the short speech she'd had to give thanking the sponsors and the guests she'd never know. Even as she'd been elaborating on the causes the trust had recently supported she'd felt a self-destructive urge to rip up her prompt cards and ask the audience, in a choose-your-own-adventure kind of way, what they thought might have happened next if Jack hadn't stopped when he had.

Which would really *not* have impressed the illustrious gathering. Nor the trust's board. And had it made its way into the press, it certainly wouldn't have gone down well with the submissions committee at the university she'd applied to in the States.

Imogen let out a sigh and frowned. Oh, who was she kidding? She knew exactly when the evening had started to go downhill. It had taken a turn for the worse the moment she'd stepped down from that podium and spotted the woman Jack was sitting next to.

She'd been a blonde of indeterminate age. Beautiful in a ravaged kind of way. The sort of woman who commanded the centre of attention and revelled in it. And, judging by the way her hands had been all over him, one who'd clearly set her sights on Jack.

Not that he'd seemed to object, she thought sourly. Throughout dinner her gaze had kept sliding to him and every time she'd looked, he'd just been sitting there, letting himself be pawed to pieces.

Probably still was, because where was he anyway? Dinner had been over for ages and she'd hung around but there'd been no sign of him. So much for his promise to come and find her after supper.

Logic and common sense told her that there were a dozen different reasons he might have been delayed, but neither stood a chance against the overwhelming suspicion that he could well be checking out the broom cupboard with the blonde.

And how had he known about that anyway? Imogen frowned and swung her feet up to rest on the window sill. The way he'd steered her out of the lobby and down that corridor, as if he knew exactly where he was going...

She nibbled on her lip, vaguely aware that her mind was

careering off in a dangerously extravagant direction, but too wound up to stop it. Why was she even bothering to wonder? For all she knew Jack was acquainted with the whereabouts of all the broom cupboards in every top London hotel.

That little voice hammering away inside her head and insisting she was wrong, that he wasn't like that, was all very well but, despite what he'd told her that night in the taxi, and despite what she'd told herself over the past few days, she couldn't get what she knew of his reputation entirely out of her mind.

Irrational, undoubtedly, but there it was. What with the betrayal she'd suffered recently and the knowledge that Max and Connie's affair must have been going on right under her nose was it any wonder she was predisposed to mistrust?

Imogen glanced at her watch and sighed. Five more minutes to compose herself and then she'd be saying her goodbyes and getting out of here, because the night had turned out to be just as grim as she'd thought—although for entirely different reasons—and she'd had enough.

Jack scoured the ground floor of the hotel for Imogen. The things he had to suffer in the pursuit of a date!

As if having to bring ferocious desire and the memories of those scorching kisses under control hadn't been trial enough, Jessica had been on particularly demanding form this evening.

From her behaviour at dinner one would never guess she'd ignored him most of her life, but it had taken Jack less than two minutes to figure out that his mother's brief foray into lavish maternal affection was nothing more than an effort to impress her latest conquest, who happened to work in the same field as he did.

Which couldn't have bothered him less. Jessica, who'd had him when she was a teenager and had promptly handed him over to her parents to raise him so that she could carry on partying, didn't have a maternal bone in her body, and he'd never deluded himself into thinking otherwise.

So the stabbing at his gut was nothing more than indigestion, although if someone had asked him what had been on the menu he couldn't have said. All he'd been able to think about for course after course was what had gone on in that broom cupboard and what might have happened if he hadn't heard the echo of the gong announcing dinner.

Jack strode through the lobby, his temper beginning to simmer. He didn't think he'd ever had such an uncomfortable couple of hours and Imogen's disappearing act wasn't helping.

Where was she? Did she think playing hard to get would somehow reel him in even more? Well, he thought, setting his jaw grimly, she needn't have bothered. He was reeled in quite comprehensively already.

Or at least he would be if only he could find her.

Right. This was it. The last room. If she wasn't here, he was going home. Yes, he very much wanted to continue where they'd left off but there was only so much volatile behaviour he was prepared to take and hers was hitting his limit.

Jack pushed open the door to the conservatory and scanned the space. Tall, lush palms brushed the walls, the subtle lighting casting long, dark shadows over the cane furniture, the pillars and the marble floor. But other than the fixtures and fittings, that was it. There was no sign of her here, either.

Disappointment walloped him in the stomach, roiling and churning and making him go all light-headed.

He shoved his hands through his hair and pulled himself together. So that was that, then. He'd be off. He'd forget all about Imogen and the insane notion that he somehow wouldn't survive if he didn't finish the business they'd started, and get back to being in control of his life.

It had been an absurd idea anyway. When had he ever chased a woman he was interested in quite so determinedly?

When had he ever had to? And as for not surviving, well, that was ridiculous. Of course he'd survive. He always did.

Calling himself all kinds of fool, Jack turned on his heel and was about to march out, when something caught his eye and made him freeze.

It was a pair of feet. Clad in black high-heeled shoes and propped up on the window sill.

They could be anyone's, of course, but what the hell, it was worth checking out. He strode over to the huge armchair that faced away from him and stopped in front of it.

And there she was, calmly sitting there, her elbows resting on the arms of the chair, her hands clasped, her fingers entwined and tapping against her mouth. Her legs stretched out, one exposed where her dress had fallen open, and as his gaze travelled the length of it from hip to ankle and back again all thoughts about leaving and forgetting about her vanished beneath a tidal wave of relief. 'So this is where you got to.'

She glanced up at him and it was then he noticed the frown and the lack of warmth in her eyes. 'Top marks for observation.'

The relief ebbed and he inwardly flinched. That didn't sound like the voice of a woman keen to continue where they'd left off in the broom cupboard. In fact, it sounded like the voice of a woman who was grumpy and fed up. Very possibly—although he had no idea why—with him.

'Are you all right?'

'Fine,' she said, clearly anything but.

'So what are you doing here all by yourself?'

'Well, I was hoping to have a few moments of peace...'

Jack rubbed a hand along his jaw and frowned. If that was a not-so-subtle hint that he should leave, then she was going to be disappointed because he wasn't going anywhere. Instead, he pulled up a chair and sat down facing her. 'I did say I'd come and find you after dinner.'

'You took your time.'

Jack's eyebrows lifted in surprise. Was that what was annoying her? The fact that he hadn't come looking for her the minute coffee had been served? Was she really that high maintenance? 'I got waylaid by someone wanting to invest in one of my funds.'

'Oh.' Her gaze jerked to his and he saw something flash in her eyes. Something that looked a little like relief and Jack inexplicably felt like grinning. Imogen might be hard work at times, but he had no doubt she'd be worth it.

'And you didn't exactly make it easy by hiding out here.'

'I wasn't hiding.' She sniffed. 'I was merely taking a little time out to think.'

'About what?'

'Things.'

'Where I was being one of them?'

She flushed. 'Possibly.'

'And what conclusion did you draw?' he asked, intrigued because whatever it was she'd been thinking about it was highly likely to be the cause of her frostiness.

'It occurred to me you might have been…how shall I put it…otherwise engaged.'

'What?'

'Oh, nothing,' she said with an airy wave of her hand. 'It's irrelevant now anyway. Have you had a pleasant evening?'

His smile tightened a little at the thought of the ordeal he'd had to endure so far this evening and still was. *Pleasant* was not the word he'd have used. 'Not particularly.'

'Oh?' She raised her eyebrows and regarded him coolly. 'From where I was sitting it looked like you were having a whale of a time.'

'Believe me, I wasn't.'

'The blonde virtually sitting in your lap certainly looked as if she was enjoying herself.'

Jack frowned. What on earth was she talking about? What blonde? There hadn't been a blonde.

Unless she meant Jessica.

Jack went still as the memory of his mother's overblown behaviour at dinner flew into his head. She *did* mean Jessica.

As realisation dawned he felt like laughing because if he wasn't mistaken Imogen was jealous. It wasn't an emotion he'd ever experienced himself, of course—that weird tightening of his body when she'd told him she'd once gone out with Max had been nothing but surprise—but he could recognise it in others.

'Ah, the blonde,' he said, feeling the tension ease from his shoulders as he leaned forwards and, unable to resist any longer, wrapped his hand around her ankle and slid it up her bare calf.

With a sharp gasp Imogen snatched her legs away and clutched the edges of the lower half of her dress together.

'Don't think you're going to get out of this by virtually sitting in *my* lap,' she said tartly, although, with her breath catching the way it was, it didn't come out as tartly as he imagined she'd have liked.

'I'm not trying to get out of anything,' he said, grinning. 'But I can see how it must have looked.'

'Really? I'm surprised you could see anything at all what with that cleavage constantly being shoved in your line of sight.'

'Jessica can be a little over-demonstrative at times.'

'A little over-demonstrative?' said Imogen. 'Hah. I've never seen anyone so tactile. Honestly, it was appalling. All that pawing and leaning over you. I'm surprised she didn't have a wardrobe malfunction.'

Jack's grin widened as he watched her eyes flash and colour rise in her cheeks. 'Yes, well, I don't think it was quite as bad as that, but she's always been on the tactile side. It's part of her whole "dahhhling" persona. It drives me insane but, seeing as she's the one who wangled me the space at her table, it seemed rude to cause a scene.'

Imogen scowled. 'Do the two of you have history?'

'You could say that.'

She harrumphed. 'And a future?'

'Unfortunately, that, too.'

'Well, then, don't let me keep you.'

'You aren't,' he said, sitting back, stretching his legs out and crossing them at the ankles as he looked at her. 'My mother's currently strutting her stuff on the dance-floor with her latest boyfriend and I doubt she could care less what I'm up to.'

For a moment Imogen thought she must have misheard. That, despite being so cross with him she'd been so caught up in white-hot jealousy, so thrown off balance by the searing jolt of electricity that had shot up her leg when his hand had caressed it, that she'd completely lost the plot.

Either that or he was joking.

But Jack didn't look as if he was joking. Far from it. His expression was one of faint distaste and the blue of his eyes looked strangely flat.

In the long seconds of silence that stretched between them, all she could do was stare at him in astonishment while he looked unwaveringly back. The strains of music coming from the ballroom and the distant buzz of conversation barely registered as the realisation that he was one hundred per cent serious dawned.

'Your mother?' she said once she'd regained the power of speech.

Jack grimaced, his eyes dark and unfathomable. 'I'm afraid so.'

'That was your *mother*?'

'So she claims.'

'But she can't be.' She thought of her own mother, who was in her fifties and favoured tweed. Her mother, who was happiest on her knees in a flowerbed, trowel in hand, and wouldn't be seen dead with a neckline that plunged to her navel or a hemline that skirted her buttocks, let alone shaking her groove on the dance floor.

Jack let out a deep sigh. 'That's what I've wished for many times over the years, but she is, and unfortunately there isn't a thing I can do about it.'

So many questions raced around her head that she didn't know where to start. 'But how…?'

'Oh, the usual way, I should imagine.'

'I mean she looks about twenty-one.'

'I'll tell her you said so. She'll be delighted.'

'How old was she when she had you?'

'Sixteen.'

'Crikey.' She paused. 'And how old are you?'

'Thirty-three.'

Imogen did the calculation, then blew out a breath. Jack's mother might not be twenty-one, but she was spectacularly, and no doubt expensively, well preserved. 'Goodness.'

His eyes glittered. 'Quite.'

She blinked. 'Well, I must say, I'm speechless.' And more relieved than she could possibly have imagined.

'Good, because I don't particularly want to talk about my mother.'

That was a pity because she did. She really ought to have given in and searched him on the Internet, because she'd bet her entire shoe collection that it would all be there. 'No?'

'No.'

'But—' There was so much more she wanted to know. Who was his father? Who'd brought him up? What had his childhood been like? How did he feel about having a mother who behaved like that?

'I said no.'

And presumably just in case she was thinking of pressing the point, which she was, Jack sprang to his feet and, taking hold of her elbows, pulled her out of the chair and up into his arms. Barely before she could work out what was happening he was winding her arms around his neck, then hauling her tight against him and lowering his head to capture her mouth with his.

The minute their lips melded and tongues met, Imogen was lost. As ways of shutting her up went, she thought a second before her brain addled, this one was pretty effective. No doubt exactly as he'd intended, all traces of her idiotic jealousy and every drop of curiosity about his mother vanished in a wave of lust.

'That dinner was agony,' she mumbled when Jack broke for breath.

'I'm sorry you got the wrong impression about Jessica,' he muttered, trailing a series of hot kisses along her jaw.

Imogen shivered. 'It wasn't just that.'

He lifted his head to shoot her a quizzical glance before turning his attention to her ear lobe. 'What else was it?' he muttered.

'I kept thinking about that broom cupboard.'

She felt his mouth curve into a slight smile against her skin. 'You, too?'

Biting her lip to stop herself from whimpering, Imogen whispered, 'How did you know about it?'

'What?'

'How did you know it was there?'

'Sign on the door.'

'Oh,' she said on a shuddery sigh, her head falling back to allow him better access to her neck. 'How did you know it would be unlocked?'

'I didn't. Just got lucky.' He paused. Lifted his head and stared down at her, his brows drawing together in a faint frown. '*That's* what you were thinking about? The extent of my knowledge of the whereabouts of hotel broom cupboards?'

'A bit,' Imogen said, bringing her head back up and fervently hoping he wasn't going to ask her why, because having to explain would certainly kill the moment. So she gave him what she hoped was a mind-boggling smile and deliberately seductively said, 'What about you?'

Which, judging by the glint that appeared in his eyes, worked beautifully. 'Nothing so complicated,' he murmured. 'I simply kept wondering what might have happened if I hadn't stopped.'

Imogen's heart tripped at the heady realisation that they were as muh at the mercy of this as they were of each other and that just maybe he wasn't completely out of her league. 'Oh.'

'Want to know what I came up with?'

Watching his eyes darken, she nodded, and then he was leaning forwards, pressing her into the back of the chair and murmuring into her ear.

As what he told her filtered into her brain, Imogen's temperature shot so high she went dizzy. All she could think about was dragging him off and demanding he fulfil every one of the exotic scenarios he suggested.

'So what do you think?'

Think? She could barely breathe. 'Is some of that even anatomically possible?' she managed shakily.

'I have no idea. But we could have a hell of a lot of fun finding out.'

'Well, as you know,' she said gravely, 'I'm all for fun.'

'I was hoping you might say that.' He stared down at her and the desire and need she saw in his eyes nearly brought her to her knees. 'Are you done here?'

Definitely, yes. She nodded. 'All done.'

'Then let's go.'

# CHAPTER NINE

GOING anywhere, however, when her bones had melted and her body had turned to one great quivering mass of need, was easier said than done, and by the time they reached the huge glass-and-steel building that housed Jack's flat, Imogen was a mess.

After discarding the idea of booking a room at the hotel as way too risky and her house as way too far, they'd walked the five hundred metres or so to his. And even that had been agony.

She was so hot and itchy with desire, so dazed by the knowledge her fantasies were about to become reality that she didn't think she could stand it, and if it hadn't been for the threat of a lurking photographer she'd have given in to temptation, dragged Jack into a shadowy doorway and begged him to take her right then and there.

Jack, however, didn't seem to be having nearly such a problem with self-control. He might have kissed her as if his life depended on it back in that conservatory, and he might want her equally badly, but he clearly wasn't reduced to watery knees and dissolving bones by the experience.

While she'd been tottering around, swooning and losing her breath all over the place, there'd been nothing trembly or quivery about the way he'd marched her here. Nothing clumsy about his steps as he strode across the marble floor towards the lift. And nothing shaky about his fingers as they punched a series of numbers into the keypad.

Jack was eerily calm, as if he was used to doing this kind of thing all the time. Which he might well be, Imogen realised with a pang of envy that she quickly squashed. But so what if he was? It wasn't as if she wanted him for ever. She just wanted one night of guaranteed great sex. Maybe two. Starting, with any luck, right now, because, as he'd pointed out earlier, their business needed finishing and what with the desire zooming around inside her she was more than ready to help.

The doors to the lift swished open and Imogen brushed past him, stepped in and leaned against one mirrored side. She gripped the rail in order to prevent herself from slithering to the floor and shivered as he stepped in after her and instantly took up more than his fair share of air.

The minute the doors closed behind him, the air that was left turned electric, heavy and hot. Jack leaned against the opposite side of the lift and stared at her, his eyes dark and intense, his face tight with desire, and Imogen trembled. A muscle pounded in his jaw, and as he curled his fingers around the rail she saw that his knuckles were white and she couldn't help thinking that perhaps he wasn't as cool as she'd thought.

'Come here,' he said hoarsely.

Hmm. Definitely not cool. She gripped harder on the rail, her heart hammering so wildly she thought it might be about to break free. 'What if someone else wants to get in?'

'Private lift. It stops at my floor only.'

'Convenient.'

'For getting to the penthouse, extremely.'

'And for seducing unsuspecting innocents?'

His jaw clenched with tightly controlled effort. 'Are you the unsuspecting innocent in this scenario?'

'Could be,' she said, although in reality she was neither unsuspecting nor innocent.

'And I'm the seducer?'

'So I've heard.' She paused, then added with a slow smile, 'So I'm hoping.'

'Then why do I suddenly get the feeling that the roles are reversed?' he said, tilting his head and staring at her as if he wanted to look into her soul.

At the suddenly serious expression on his face, Imogen's heart skipped a beat and her mouth went dry. He had to be joking. Had to be. Because he couldn't possibly think he was in any danger from *her*, could he? That was ridiculous. This was the legendary Jack Taylor. The man who left a trail of broken hearts wherever he went while his own remained completely untouched.

Of course he was joking, she told herself, because while she didn't mind the idea of being the seducer at all, there was no way he was an unsuspecting innocent. Which was a good thing because the last thing she wanted was for either of them to be unsuspecting or innocent about this. This was simply about sex. Hot passionate sex.

And speaking of which...

'I can't imagine,' she said, her pulse racing and her blood roaring in her ears as she let desire take over and gave him her most smouldering smile. 'But if you feel like that,' she added, sliding the zip at the side of her dress down and feeling the silk slither over her skin to fall in a black shimmering pool on the floor, 'then you come here.'

How on earth had he ever thought Imogen was nothing more than a vacuous frothy socialite? Jack wondered, utterly stunned by the sight of her. She was gorgeous. Intriguing. Wholly unpredictable. And total dynamite.

And how had he ever thought that not seeing her again was a good idea? He must have been out of his tiny little mind. Because right now, with the four mirrored walls of the lift giving him every view of her he could possibly want, Jack thought he'd never seen anything so magnificent.

She was standing there wearing nothing but the strapless bra that barely contained her breasts, the tiniest excuse for knickers he'd ever come across, those black sky-high heels and a seductive smile, and he was about to collapse with need.

So much for fooling himself he was in some sort of control over this, that he was somehow in charge. For a while he'd actually thought he had it nailed. After all, it might have taken a Herculean effort, but he'd done a pretty good job of holding it together on the way here.

Now, however, with all that soft creamy skin encased in black lacy underwear on display and with Imogen smouldering at him, he was so riddled with desire and so wary of what might happen when his control snapped he didn't dare move.

With an impatient little sigh, she arched an eyebrow and cocked a hip, and his vision blurred. 'Well?' she said softly.

What the hell? Who cared who was in charge anyway? This had been going on way too long and he'd had enough.

'In agony, actually,' he muttered, prising his fingers off the rail, lunging forwards to close the distance between them and slamming his mouth down on hers.

Oh, thank God for that, thought Imogen, closing her eyes and winding her arms round his neck as she kissed him back as hungrily as he was kissing her. For a moment she thought he'd been about to pass out and she'd had the stomach-curdling feeling that he'd been horrified by what she'd done and, even worse, by what he'd seen.

But to her relief and delight that didn't seem to be the case. Not judging by the hot insistence of his mouth and the rock-hard length of his erection pressing against her pelvis.

His hands spanned her waist, holding her tight against him as his tongue and lips ravaged hers. Her ears popped and she wasn't sure if it was from the lift zooming them up to the penthouse or the effect of his kiss. Either way her mind was being well and truly blown.

As Jack slid his hands round to her back, down over her bottom and pulled her hips even tighter to his Imogen writhed against him, rubbing herself up and down his hardness in a desperate attempt to assuage the ache that was throbbing between her legs.

The sound of the lift door swishing open dimly penetrated the fog of desire in her head and she felt his hands slip lower, curving round her upper thighs. He pressed her back against the wall of the lift for support and, pulling her legs up, wrapped them around his waist. Breaking off the kiss and breathing heavily, he took her weight and turned.

Imogen could feel the thundering of his heart against her chest and it made every muscle quiver, every nerve ending sizzle. As he carried her out of the lift she caught a glimpse of the image of the two of them so intimately entwined, Jack fully clothed, herself practically naked, reflected a thousand times over, and it turned her on even more.

And then he was striding with her across the hardwood floor of the apartment, making a beeline for what she sincerely hoped was the bedroom. Clinging on for dear life, Imogen tightened her legs around his waist and buried her head in his neck. She could feel the tension gripping his powerful frame as he stopped to kick off his shoes and then remove hers, she could feel his pulse hammering beneath her cheek and she couldn't resist. As Jack strode through a doorway she nipped the skin covering his pulse with her teeth then soothed it with her tongue, relishing the salty taste of him and the growl that rumbled low in his throat.

He stopped, and she slowly disentangled herself, taking care to brush him with every part of her body before standing on the jelly that seemed to have replaced her legs.

Jack let out a harsh breath and she didn't think it was from the exertion of carrying her from the lift to the bedroom.

She took a tiny step back and the backs of her knees hit the edge of the bed. His eyes roamed over her and she watched him swallow hard then shove his hands through his hair as if to stop himself from reaching for her, as if reaching for her might lead to things getting out of control way too fast.

'I appear to be at something of a material disadvantage,' she said, achingly aware of how little she had on.

'If you felt like balancing things up a little,' he said, his voice hoarse, 'I'd have no objection.'

'Now there's an idea,' Imogen murmured, smiling a little and letting her gaze wander all over him as she wondered where to start.

Jack's jaw clenched and his hands curled into fists at his sides. 'You carry on looking at me like that and there won't be a whole lot of foreplay.'

'Fine by me. The way I see it we've indulged in more than enough foreplay already.' So much so that the minute he touched any one of her erogenous zones she'd probably splinter right then and there. And, besides, they had all night, didn't they?

Jack's eyes blazed. 'You forget I have a reputation to live up to.'

'I haven't forgotten,' she said with a shiver. 'But if it would help, I could try not looking at you.'

'It would.'

So Imogen closed her eyes and, as every one of her remaining senses switched to high alert, lifted her hands to his chest. She felt him tense, heard his breath catch. Her fingers brushing over the thick cotton of his dress shirt, she undid the studs, taking her time, dropping them one by one into the pocket of his trousers and revelling in every sound and every movement he made.

As she slipped her hands beneath his shirt, and finally, *finally* laid them on his skin, he shook violently. Groaned.

'This isn't helping.'

His voice grated across her senses and she shivered. 'So stop me,' she murmured.

'I can't.'

Feeling a surge of power, she moved her hands up and outwards, her fingers brushing over the smattering of hair that covered his chest, over his nipples and up over his shoulders. His muscles contracted beneath her touch and when she shrugged off his shirt and jacket and let them drop to the floor she felt a shudder rip through him.

She let her hands drift down, over the defined, taut muscles of his abdomen, and had a sudden desperate urge to find out what he tasted like. While her fingers worked at the button of his trousers and slid down the zip, she leaned forwards, pressed her open mouth against the skin of his chest and touched her tongue to him.

And then it was as if her body had a will of its own and she couldn't have controlled it even if she'd wanted to. As she dropped a series of tiny wet kisses across his chest, she pushed his trousers and shorts down. Her fingers curled around his hard length and caressed, and she heard him exhale a long shuddery breath.

'Enough,' he muttered hoarsely, wrapping a hand around her wrist and putting a halt to her strokes. 'Open your eyes.'

Imogen wasn't sure she had the strength. She'd gone all weak and languid, as if desire had melted every cell in her body. Every drop of her focus had headed south, zooming in on the feel of him in her hand. All she could think of was being flat on her back with Jack looming over her and the weight of his body pinning her to the bed. Of that hard, silken length pushing up inside her, filling her, driving her mindless with pleasure, and the anticipation was almost too great to bear.

Where she found the effort she had no idea, but when she did finally manage to open her eyes the sight that met them made her breath stick in her throat and her head go dizzy.

Her gaze drifted over him hungrily. Tanned, lean and powerful, his body was mouth-watering, and she wanted to touch
everywhere.

'Better?' she breathed.

'Infinitely worse.'

And then he caught her by the waist and twisted round and
back, falling onto the bed and taking her with him so that she
lay sprawled all over him.

Imogen didn't have time to worry about how undigni-
fied that nifty move must have made her look, because one
of Jack's arms whipped round her bottom, the other planted
itself on the back of her neck, bringing her head down. His
mouth met hers and her mind went blank.

As their tongues tangled the hand on her bottom slid slowly
up her spine and then back down, creating shivering ripples
of delight over every inch of skin it moved.

He unclipped her bra and, when she eased herself off him
a little, pulled it from her and threw it to join his clothes. Her
nipples brushed against his chest and it was electric. Hearing
Jack's sharp intake of breath at the contact, she did it again
and again until she couldn't stand it any more and crushed
her chest to his.

Feeling as though a bonfire had sprung into flame in the
pit of her stomach, Imogen shifted on top of him so that his
erection pressed against her hot, aching centre. And then
couldn't stop herself grinding against him and moaning with
frustration at the thin lace of her knickers that was the only
thing separating them.

As the heat coiled deep within her suddenly burst apart
and powered through her it all became too much. No more
barriers, she thought frantically as she jerked herself up and
tried to twist round.

'Where do you think you're going?' muttered Jack, tightening his arm around her.

'I need…' she panted, her voice broken and croaky, and

then swallowed hard with the effort of containing her craving to get him inside her. 'I have to get these off,' she breathed. 'Now. Help me, Jack.'

His eyes turned to midnight and blazed up at her. 'How could I possibly refuse?'

With one smooth move he flipped her on her back and then her breathing went haywire as he hooked his fingers over the sides of her knickers and pulled them down her legs.

He tossed her knickers away and slid his hands back up, taking his time as he explored every inch of skin, every dip, every muscle slowly and thoroughly, until she was quivering and whimpering, her skin tingling wherever his fingers brushed.

And then he was rolling onto his side, propping himself up on one elbow, his leg nudging her knees apart, his other hand inching up her thigh round her hip and sliding through the soft curls at the top of her thighs.

Imogen watched his eyes darken with passion, heard his breathing hitch as his lips came down on hers, and her heart raced with anticipation. As his tongue pushed into her mouth he slipped a finger inside her, and she groaned.

He stroked her relentlessly, sliding another finger into her, his thumb finding her swollen clitoris and rubbing, and something hot and powerful began to unfurl deep within her.

She dragged her mouth from his to gulp in a ragged breath and nearly jumped out of her skin when his lips began roaming over her neck, her collarbone and then down the slope of her breast before closing over her nipple. Sensation cascaded through her and wiped out every thought in her head.

She felt a wave of ecstasy rolling towards her from way off, gathering strength and speed, unstoppable and relentless, coming closer and closer until it slammed into her and she shattered into a million tiny pieces. Convulsing and drowning with pleasure, Imogen clutched at Jack's shoulders, flung her head back and cried out his name.

Jack felt her clenching around his fingers, felt the shudders racking her body beneath him, and as he lifted his head from her breast and stared at her flushed face he didn't think he'd ever seen anything so wild, so wanton or so beautiful.

His body throbbed with a need stronger than anything he'd ever experienced before and his head was pounding so hard with the effort of not twisting to come down on top of her and driving into her that he was on the point of exploding.

Withdrawing his fingers from her as gently as he could, he focused on her breathing to try and calm himself down. And he was doing fine, listening to her breaths gradually shallow and lengthen, until she stretched languidly and gave him a slow, satisfied smile.

'Well, I think we can say your reputation definitely remains intact,' she said huskily.

Jack brushed a lock of hair off her forehead. 'I'm not sure you've experienced enough to base that assumption on.'

'No? You think you can do better?'

'Aren't you expecting guaranteed great sex?' He leaned over, opened the drawer in his bedside table and reached for a condom.

'Promises, promises.' Imogen smiled and lifted herself onto her elbows as he ripped open the packet and rolled the condom on, gritting his teeth against the almost unbearable surge of desire.

His heart thudded and he stared down at her. 'I make no promises other than this.'

'I know,' she said softly. 'And this is all I want. Truly. You have no idea how much.'

However much she wanted him it couldn't be a patch on how much he wanted her. Way beyond the point of trying to work out whether she meant what she said, or what the intensity of his need might mean, Jack shifted his weight on top of her, crushed his mouth to hers and, letting out a rough muffled groan, pushed inside her.

He'd meant to go slowly, to give Imogen time to adjust to him. But going slowly was impossible when she was moaning and clutching at his shoulders and tilting her hips, and he couldn't stop himself thrusting forwards and up and burying himself as deep inside her as he could.

'Oh, wow,' she breathed, and the desperation in her voice did something strange to his chest.

Every inch of him wanted to pound into her, possess her and make her his. It was primitive and urgent and he had to grind his teeth to stop himself from giving in. With agonising care, he began to move, sliding in and out of her, slowly and rhythmically as if to prove to himself that he knew how to keep himself under control.

But that was a joke, wasn't it? Because as he thrust in and out of her slippery heat he heard the quickening of her breathing through the mind-blowing desire rocketing through him, and he felt his control unravelling. As pure need took over, his movements became harder, faster, wilder, her moans, her writhing and her panting destroying the remnants of his control and urging him on.

And then, just when he thought he couldn't take any more tension, couldn't stand any more agonising ecstasy, she exploded in his arms, shaking and quivering and gasping his name, and as she rippled around him it was more than he could bear. With a harsh cry he drove into her one last time and hurtled into white-hot oblivion.

# CHAPTER TEN

For several long minutes there wasn't a sound in the room except the harsh, then softening, pants of ragged breathing.

Reeling from the intensity of his climax, Jack focused on the slowing of his thundering heart until it was back to normal, then shifted and took his weight on his elbows. He felt Imogen shudder and clamp around him as a series of tiny aftershocks rippled through her.

'Well, you certainly deliver,' she said, gazing up at him with a quivery kind of smile. She lifted her head to plant a sizzling kiss on his mouth before sighing with languid satisfaction and flopping back against the pillows.

So did she, he thought, gazing down into her eyes, a glazed soft dark brown, and for a moment losing himself in their depths. Aftershocks of a different kind were racing around his head, because that had quite simply been astonishing. *She'd* been astonishing, and if there was one thing he'd realised it was that they weren't finished. Not by a long shot.

'I aim to please,' he murmured, rolling off her and sitting on the edge of the bed to deal with the condom.

'Oh, you do. And I'm *definitely* going to have to rethink my stance on dessert,' said Imogen. She manoeuvred herself to her knees, pressed herself against his back and ran her hands over the muscles of his shoulders.

'Dessert?' he echoed, so distracted by the soft warmth o

her wrapped around him that he didn't have a clue what she was talking about.

'Remember when you first suggested dinner?'

Jack winced. 'How could I ever forget?'

'You also suggested skipping it and heading straight to dessert.'

'So I did.' He twisted around and pressed her back and down. 'As I recall you weren't particularly impressed.'

'I was very much impressed.' She lay there, her hair tumbling over his pillows as she clutched the sheet to her chest and grinned up at him. 'But I was trying desperately hard not to be.'

He shook his head. 'What a lot of time we've wasted.'

'It's only been three days.'

So it had. Hard to believe when their bodies moved together as if they'd known each other for years.

'Still too long,' he murmured, attributing that disconcerting thought to extraordinary sexual compatibility, and then burying it. 'Just think,' he added, running a hand over her shoulder and slipping it beneath the sheet, 'we could have been doing this since Tuesday.'

She batted her eyelashes up at him, a seductive smile curving her mouth and her eyes turning so dark they were almost black. 'Then why are we talking when we should be making up for lost time?'

As his body hardened Jack lowered his head. 'Beats me,' he muttered, and set about making up for lost time the best way he knew.

Well, that had been quite a night, thought Imogen, blinking lazily at the weak early sunshine that spilled in through the gaps in the blind and hearing the soft swoosh of the lift doors closing.

And actually quite a morning…

She shivered and sighed and stretched, knowing full well

that her smile was wide and sated but not caring one jot. Because, frankly, why would she?

She'd never had so many mind-blowingly intense orgasms in her life and she'd never expected her sexual horizons to have been broadened to quite such an extent. But to her delight, over the course of the night—and the morning—she'd learned that many of the outrageous things Jack had murmured into her ear in the inky darkness of the hotel's conservatory *had* been anatomically possible, and their extensive research into the matter had led to pleasure so great it had almost hurt.

Imogen's eyes drifted shut as her imagination replayed scene after scene after scene. Jack was amazing. His stamina was incredible, his desire for her dauntless, and as for what happened when he lost his grip on his control… Well, that was just staggering.

And she badly wanted some more of it, she realised, feeling her body stirring once again. The minute he got back from picking up the wrap she'd abandoned at the hotel she'd suggest it. So far they hadn't made it out of bed, and while she had nothing against beds—when they came with Jack in situ she was positively in favour of them—a change of venue might be nice.

Maybe she'd go and get in the shower so that when he came back he'd find her all hot and naked and wet and wouldn't be able to resist joining her.

Or maybe she'd wander into the kitchen so that he'd find her dishevelled and slumberous, wearing nothing but a bedsheet while she made coffee.

Or maybe—

At the shrill ring of the phone, Imogen jerked out of her imaginative bubble with a pop and realised she was hot, blushing and tingling. Goodness, what had happened to her? Twelve hours of some seriously great sex and she was addicted.

She heard Jack's voice echoing through the flat asking the
caller to leave a message, and yanked a pillow over her head
to blot it out. For one thing, listening to that voice, even on a
machine, was not conducive to her attempts to calm down,
and for another she didn't feel entirely comfortable about
eavesdropping.

However, as the beep sounded and dulcet female tones
began to replace his seductively deep ones any scruples she
might have had about not wanting to eavesdrop vanished.
Tossing the pillow to one side, Imogen lay there, her ears
pricked and her antennae quivering, but rigidly still, as if the
woman on the other end of the line would be able to tell she
was listening if she moved.

'Jack?' came the soft voice that made all the tiny hairs on
the back of her neck bristle and jump to attention. 'It's Emily.
I'm just ringing to confirm we're seeing you later. I hope you
haven't forgotten or anything. Daisy's *so* looking forward to
it… Hang on… What?' There was a pause. The sound of a
phone being muffled and the mumble of another female voice
in the background. And then she was back. 'Oh, and Anna
says don't forget to bring something to sleep in.'

Huh? What? Imogen jerked upright, the curiosity racing
through her so powerful it could have killed a dozen cats.

'OK, then, we'll see you later. Bye, darling.'

Darling? *Darling?* Who on earth was Emily? Who was
Daisy? And who the hell was the Anna who knew so much
about what Jack wore or rather didn't wear in bed? Were they
all friends? Ex-girlfriends? Current girlfriends? Or—

Imogen bit her lip and slammed the brakes on her spinning imagination before she had Jack getting up to all kinds
of dissolute and debauched antics. Her stomach could stop
that churning and those little arrows of jealousy could get
lost because she wasn't bothered one little bit by what he got
up to. She was only after his body, and even that on a highly
temporary basis.

Nevertheless, it did hammer home how little she knew about him. For all she knew he might be into threesomes. Foursomes. Orgies. He might have fetishes, visit clubs and who knew what else?

With her body and brain on the point of overheating, Imogen let out a groan of frustration at her inability to control her wayward imagination. What with all this extra work it was having to cope with, it was a surprise it hadn't short-circuited.

She threw back the sheet and swung her legs to the floor. It really was none of her business. Jack could get up to whatever he wanted to with whoever he wanted to. And as he clearly had plans for later, that might or might not involve three women and very little clothing, she ought to head off and leave him to it.

Besides, she reminded herself as she padded into the bathroom and flicked on the shower, she'd already jumped to a dozen erroneous conclusions where he was concerned and she was *not* going to jump to any more.

Of course, she'd never dream of asking, but there was bound to be some logical *innocent* explanation for why Jack had a woman ringing him up requesting he remembered his pyjamas when he came round later that night. Absolutely bound to be.

Jack strode through his flat, draped Imogen's wrap on the back of the sofa and dumped the bag of *pains au chocolat* he'd picked up on the way back on the kitchen counter. It really was extraordinary, he thought. After the night—and morning—they'd had, he ought to be exhausted. At the very least be done with her for a while. But was he? It would appear not. He'd only been out for ten minutes but the image of her lying sprawled and sated in his bed had accompanied him all the way to the hotel and back, and every second he was away from her had felt like an hour. So no, it seemed he wasn't done with her at all.

But that was hardly a surprise. Never had a woman responded so swiftly, so instinctively or so wildly to his touch. Never had anyone thrown caution so splendidly to the wind nor been quite such an enthusiastic research assistant.

Jack grinned at the memory of the sexual gymnastics they'd practised, and headed to the bedroom. The whole night had switched between being intense, dark and explosive then light, teasing and fun. And he wanted more. A lot more.

He paused mid-stride and frowned, his heart skipping a beat as alarm bells rang. More? Oka-a-ay. So that was new. It wasn't that he chose to have one-night stands exactly. It was simply that that was how things generally turned out, which was fortunate as he liked variety.

But there was no need to panic. Just because sex with Imogen had surpassed all his expectations—and he'd had a few—and just because it put pretty much every other sexual experience he'd ever had in the shade, it didn't mean anything. It was the roller coaster of the build-up that had made it so explosive. That was all.

Given that they'd put it off for so long wanting more was only natural, and, if he kept things strictly to sex, what was the problem with seeing her again? As far as he could work out there wasn't one because he never did anything else. He certainly never combined sex with anything as messy as emotion. Quite apart from the fact that he didn't do emotion, he never made—nor would make—the mistake of thinking that sex ever meant anything other than the mutual satisfaction of completely natural needs.

So it—he—would be fine.

Satisfied that he'd got things clear in his head, Jack switched his attention to the sound of running water coming from his bathroom.

At the thought of Imogen in the shower hot and wet and

covered with bubbles his body instantly hardened. He stripped off his jumper and jeans, then plucked a condom off the bedside table, tore open the packet and, gritting his teeth against the exquisite agony, sheathed himself.

As desire whipped around inside him, he walked into the bathroom. Steam billowed around the marble surfaces and curled off the limestone-tiled walls, and a fine film of sweat coated his skin.

The outline of Imogen's body was just about visible through the foggy glass. She had her back to him and her arms were raised, her hands in her hair, and the intensity of what he wanted to do to her slammed into his head and made his heart thunder.

Oh, he wanted more. Much more.

Opening the door, Jack stepped in and flinched as needles of hot water pounded his skin. Blinking the water out of his eyes, and mindful of what had happened the last time he'd startled her—and how much more damage she could inflict this time—he lifted his hands and wrapped them round her wrists.

Imogen froze then jumped. She let out a gasp and made a move to turn but he held her where she was and pulled her back against him. He felt her shiver. Heard her murmur, 'I thought I warned you not to startle me.'

'Why do you think I have my hands on your wrists?'

'Restraint, Jack?'

'Not my kind of thing.'

'Then let me go.' She squirmed against him, but not in an effort to get free, and it sent need shooting through him.

'In a minute,' he said. 'I think I could be changing my mind.'

He inched her forwards and pressed her hands up against the cool limestone tiles that lined the wall of the shower.

'I thought that was supposed to be my prerogative,' she

said, her voice laced with such hoarse desperation that it did dangerous things to his self-control.

'You can stop me any time you like,' he muttered, thinking that nobility was all very well, but if she did stop him he might expire.

So just in case she *was* tempted to think along those lines, he slowly slid his hands down her arms, then round to cup her breasts. Her head dropped back against his shoulder, and when his mouth came down on the pulse throbbing at the base of her neck, he felt her shudder.

'Now why would I want to do a thing like that?' she mumbled and arched her back to push her breasts harder into his hands.

He brushed his thumbs over her nipples and closed his eyes against the warm water sluicing relentlessly over them, then trailed one hand lower, slowly stroking over her ribcage, the slight curve of her abdomen, down to the centre of her.

She moaned low in her throat when he slid his fingers into her, and she ground her bottom into his pelvis. He heard her breathing shallow. Felt her shake. And unable to take the burning pressure growing inside him any longer, he backed up a little, bent her forwards, and, gripping her hips, drove into her.

'So, any excitements while I was gone?' asked Jack, quite a while later.

Imogen watched him move around the kitchen, switching on the kettle and rummaging around in a cupboard for the coffee grounds with impressive efficiency, and frowned as she contemplated his question.

Any excitements other than the fact that at some point during the ten minutes he'd been out she'd clearly lost her mind? Because that surely was the only explanation for her complete inability to resist him.

There she'd been, in that shower, determinedly not think-

ing about what Jack might be up to later and telling herself
she'd be calling a taxi the instant he returned with her stole,
when he'd materialised behind her.

Seconds later she'd been lost. With the feel of his hard
body enveloping her, his voice reaching right down inside
her and winding round her nerves, and the erection hot and
hard and pressing into her bottom, she'd folded like a pyra-
mid of cards in a breath of wind.

And now look where she was. Perched on a bar stool in
his kitchen and leaning against the counter, wearing nothing
but one of his shirts and her knickers, her stomach rumbling
at the prospect of breakfast.

Which so hadn't been the plan.

Wishing her resistance were stronger, Imogen stifled a
sigh. 'You had a phone call.'

Jack glanced up from the cafetiere into which he was
spooning coffee. 'Who from?'

'How should I know?' she said, shrugging deliberately
carelessly, then dragging her gaze from his and taking an avid
interest in the granite surface of the breakfast bar. 'They left
a message, but I didn't listen.'

'How very admirable of you.'

The amusement in his voice told her he didn't believe her
for a second, but that was fine because that was her stand and
she was sticking to it. 'It didn't seem polite.'

'Of course it didn't,' he murmured, brushing past her to
press the red button flashing on the base of the telephone that
sat in the corner of the kitchen.

As Emily's voice rang through the flat again, and all the
scenarios she'd tried not to envisage came rushing back,
Imogen forgot herself and winced. It sounded even worse the
second time round, she thought, frowning and biting her lip.

'Didn't hear it, huh?'

She jerked her gaze to Jack's, and to her mortification the

blush that she'd been battling back broke free and flooded into her face. 'Absolutely not.'

'Well, that's good,' he said, coming back and pouring boiling water into the cafetiere, 'because if I'd heard that message, I'd have jumped to some pretty spectacular conclusions.'

Imogen swallowed and felt her cheeks burn even more fiercely. 'I'm sure you would, what with your imagination.'

Jack glanced at her and grinned. 'I guess I'd be thinking threesomes. Foursomes even. Possibly an orgy or two.'

'That would be that dirty mind of yours,' she said primly, silently cursing her transparency. 'My pure and innocent one would never have come up with anything so...' She trailed off as she racked her brains for a word that wouldn't inflame her already burning body any further.

'Carnal?'

'Complicated.'

His hand stilled mid-plunge, and his eyes gleamed and darkened in a way that made her think he was remembering last night. 'As I think we've established,' he said softly, 'there's nothing pure and innocent about you.'

'You've corrupted me.'

'No more than you've corrupted me.' He reached for a couple of cups and then took a jug from the fridge. 'Milk?'

'Yes, please.'

'Anyway,' he said, pouring coffee into the cups and adding milk to one, 'I'm sure you're not interested in the slightest but those conclusions—the ones you didn't come to—would be wrong.'

'Would they?'

'Uh-huh.'

'Why?'

Jack pushed the cup across the counter towards her and grinned. 'I've never been good at sharing. I'm far too selfish.'

Imogen's eyes widened. Selfish? Jack? No doubt he had

flaws—who didn't?—but after the attention he'd lavished on her last night, she didn't think selfishness was one of them.

'Something to do with being an only child I should think,' he was saying, 'but whatever the reason, more than one woman at a time has never appealed.' He flashed her a lethally sexy smile. 'And if there were two like you I doubt I'd survive.'

'Then what *are* you doing tonight?'

Oh, no, thought Imogen, immediately clamping her lips together although it was far too late. That had just blown her protestations of innocence to smithereens, hadn't it? And what the hell had happened to her supposed lack of interest in what he got up to?

Jack grinned triumphantly and pounced as she'd known he would the second the words had left her mouth. 'Aha! I knew it.'

Inwardly fuming at the piteous nature of her will power, Imogen scowled. 'Has anyone ever told you you can be unbelievably smug at times?'

Jack's eyebrows rose. 'Smug?' he said. 'Well, let me see...' He frowned and tapped his fingers against his mouth as he pretended to consider. 'I've been called arrogant, presumptuous, cold, callous and emotionally bankrupt, but smug?' He paused and glanced up at the ceiling as if racking his brains, then gave his head a quick shake. 'Nope, that's one I haven't heard before.'

As the memory of the insults she'd thrown at him flew into her head Imogen felt her blush turn to one of shame. How had she ever thought him all that? He was turning out to be so different from what she'd initially imagined. So much more. Yes, he was gorgeous and sexy, but he was also funny, thoughtful and surprisingly gallant.

She blinked and put a stop to her analysis of his considerable attributes because thinking of Jack as anything other than the guarantor of great sex was pointless on a dozen different levels.

'So?' she asked, sitting up and resolutely hauling herself back on the conversation.

'I'm babysitting.'

Babysitting?

Imogen's jaw dropped as she stared at him and she nearly fell off the stool. It was a good thing she'd just put her cup down otherwise there'd be shards of porcelain and coffee all over the floor. 'Babysitting?' she echoed.

'That's right.'

'You?'

'Me.'

'Are you serious?'

'Totally.' He paused, then tilted his head as he gauged her reaction. 'You know,' he added mildly, 'your astonishment isn't exactly flattering.'

Imogen pulled herself together and flashed him a quick smile. 'Sorry, but I'm finding it a little difficult to get my head round the idea.' Then she frowned as a disturbing thought crossed her mind. 'Whose baby is it?'

'Not mine, if that's what you're thinking.'

'It wasn't,' she said with a speed that she suspected rather weakened that denial.

'Yes, it was,' he said, switching the oven on. 'But don't worry. I'm not that irresponsible. The baby belongs to that friend of mine, Luke, and Emily, his wife. Daisy's my god-daughter and Anna is Emily's sister.'

'Who happens to know you sleep without anything on?'

Jack grinned. 'Her notion of a joke, I imagine.'

'She sounds hilarious.'

'She has her moments.'

'So how old is she?' Imogen asked, still trying to come to terms with the fact that Jack had a god-daughter who he was babysitting tonight.

'No idea. Late thirties, early forties, maybe.'

'Ha-ha. Very funny. I meant Daisy.'

'She's three.'

'Do you have much experience of babysitting three-year-old girls?'

'None at all. This is my first time.'

Oh, dear. If the trauma she'd suffered as a result of running through all those possible explanations for Emily's phone call hadn't been so fresh in her mind, she'd have given him her sympathies. But it was, so instead she settled for what she hoped was an enigmatic smile. 'Then in that case, good luck.'

'Will I need it?'

All of a sudden he looked worried and Imogen grinned and resisted the temptation to reach out and pat his hand. 'I'm sure it'll be a walk in the park.'

Jack nodded. 'That's what I thought. I mean, she's three. How hard can it be?'

If Daisy was anything like her niece, Jack was in for one hell of a weekend. The poor guy really had no idea what was about to hit him. And on top of such little sleep...

Nevertheless, at the thought of a man like Jack giving up his weekend, his Saturday night, to spend time with a little girl, something in the region of her chest melted and she let out a gentle sigh.

'What?' he asked, frowning at her.

'Who'd have thought?' she said dreamily.

'Who'd have thought what?'

'You're a softie.'

Jack tensed and scowled. 'No, I'm not. This is a one-off favour for friends who were desperate. That's it. So don't tell anyone, because just think what it would do to my reputation if it got out.'

She could imagine; he'd have even more women flocking to him than he did at the moment. Ignoring the jealousy that darted through her at the idea, Imogen took a sip of coffee and regarded him over the rim of the cup. 'Doesn't it bother you?'

'What? My reputation?'

She nodded.

'Not in the slightest,' he said, evidently happier to be on different ground if the way his scowl cleared and his mouth curved into a grin was anything to go by. 'Why would it when I've gone to such great lengths to cultivate it?'

Imogen's eyebrows shot up. 'You actively encourage it?'

Why on earth would he want to do that? Was he nuts? From what she'd heard his reputation wasn't one to be particularly proud of, so why, when he had so much more going for him, would he want people to think otherwise?

The only answer she could come up with was that maybe he used it as some kind of shield, a defence mechanism of sorts. But that would imply he needed protection and what would he need protecting against? It didn't make any sense.

However, there was little point in asking because it didn't look as if she was going to get an answer. Not now, with the way his smile was vanishing and a frown was furrowing his brow. In fact, she had the feeling he hadn't meant to let that slip, which only made it all the more intriguing.

'You know,' said Jack, moving round the breakfast bar to stand in front of her, his eyes glittering with such intent that Imogen's heart began to hammer and all the questions that she'd wanted to ask evaporated, 'I don't have to leave for another couple of hours.'

'A couple of hours?' she breathed as he nudged her knees apart, then lifted her onto the counter.

'At least.' He eased her back and slipped his hands beneath her shirt. 'So maybe you'd like to help me find a way to fill the time.'

# CHAPTER ELEVEN

By the time the following evening came around Imogen, having spent the weekend drifting around in something of a deliciously achy daze, had come to a number of conclusions.

First, as she'd relived Friday night, it had occurred to her how short-changed she'd been by boyfriends over the years. She hadn't exactly had loads of sex, but she'd had enough to realise that with hindsight she should have been a lot more assertive in the bedroom. And a lot pickier in her choice of the men who'd occasionally occupied it.

Secondly, she'd decided that now she'd experienced the mind-blowing variety with Jack she wanted more of it. Not the 'for ever' kind of more, of course, but certainly the 'take it one day at a time' kind of more, because as a way of banishing the loneliness that had been swamping her for so long it was unbeatable.

Unable to resist any longer, and becoming increasingly frustrated that she couldn't seem to stop mooning over Friday night, she'd hauled her laptop out of the cupboard, fired it up and had settled down to find out as much about Jack as possible.

As she'd suspected there was a lot to go through, but after hours of poring over the links she'd discovered, among many other things, that, thirdly, their short-term goals might actually be compatible.

From what she'd gleaned Jack wasn't big on relationships, and, given that she would hopefully be on her way to the States in the autumn, neither was she. But she would definitely be up for a string of dates or a brief fling or anything else he might be able to offer. It would be thrilling and exciting, and exactly what she needed before she embarked on the next stage of her life.

The only fly in the ointment was the fourth conclusion she'd come to. That wanting a fling with Jack was all very well, but as he'd shown no signs of intending to see her again, things didn't look hugely promising on that front.

After they'd filled the couple of hours he had free yesterday most satisfactorily, Jack had dropped her home. He'd given her a searing kiss, rather perfunctorily muttered he'd be in touch, and then sped off.

Which did leave her in a bit of a quandary, because how could she engage in a fling with him if he didn't in fact ever call?

Still pondering the problem that had been occupying her mind all day, Imogen climbed out of the bath, dried herself off, then pulled on her favourite leggings and top. She'd figure something out, she thought firmly, padding into the sitting room. She had a medley of eighties' music blaring out of her iPod and a roaring fire in the grate. She had a chicken roasting in the oven and a glass of wine waiting for her on the coffee table, and a whole relaxing Sunday evening in which to come up with a way to firstly get in touch with him and secondly persuade him to agree to a fling.

With all that for inspiration, how could she fail?

What he was doing here, thought Jack, frowning up at the bank of windows that ran along the length of Imogen's first floor and shoving his hands through his hair, he had no idea.

He hadn't planned on dropping by. Quite apart from the fact that he'd decided it would be a good idea to leave it for a while before seeing her again and to give himself time to re-establish his equilibrium and fortify his self-control before she could destroy it totally, after the weekend he'd had he'd intended to drive straight home and crash into bed.

So why had he made the detour to see if Imogen was home? Why was he so pleased to see her lights on? And why when he'd pulled over and parked outside had his pulse started racing like a teenager's on a first date?

Jack gave his head a quick shake, then rubbed a hand over his face and stifled a yawn. Did it really matter? He opened the door and levered himself out of the car. Was there really any need to make a big deal over it? Of course there wasn't. After thirty-six hours in the company of a three-year-old girl he simply felt like a while in the company of a twenty-eight-year-old one and there was nothing odd about that.

Nor was there anything odd about the unsteadiness of his hand as he jabbed a finger at the doorbell. That was simply down to chronic sleep deprivation and an unexpectedly tough weekend.

He shoved his hands in the pockets of his jeans and listened to the echo of the bell ringing upstairs. A couple of minutes later he heard the sound of footsteps heading to the door and his pulse sped up.

There was a pause while Imogen presumably checked him out through the spyhole, then the click of the lock and the sliding of the chain. The door swung open, and when he looked down at her, standing there with tousled hair, glowing cheeks, sparkling eyes and a wide, dazzling smile, Jack knew exactly why he'd come.

'Hi,' she said with a breathlessness he hoped came from pleasure at seeing him and not from skipping down the stairs.

'Hi,' he said a little hoarsely.

'What are you doing here?'

Jack cleared his throat. 'I was passing. On my way home.'

'Thank God for that.'

Her grin widened beguilingly and for a second his mind went blank. 'What?'

She waved a hand vaguely. 'Oh, nothing. I was hoping for a distraction, that's all.'

'From what?'

'Ah, just a little problem I was grappling with. Most unsuccessfully. But it doesn't matter any more. Come in.'

'Thanks.'

She held the door wide open and stood back. 'Go straight up and turn right.'

Jack brushed past her, followed her instructions and found himself in the sitting room, which was so warm and calm and relaxing that his exhaustion seeped right away.

Soft light from the lamps dotted around the room spilled over a pair of squishy-looking sofas and a battered leather armchair, all positioned round a low glass coffee table that was piled high with magazines, books and trinkets. A fire blazed in the fireplace, either side of which were floor-to-ceiling bookshelves filled with books, files and photos.

As a strange sense of contentment settled over him, Jack took off his coat and dropped it on one of the sofas, then turned. Imogen stood in the doorway, watching him with an expression that flickered between pleasure and longing, and wariness and uncertainty.

'You look wiped out,' she said.

'You look gorgeous.'

An eyebrow arched in disbelief as she glanced down at what she was wearing. 'In this?'

'In that.' Whatever it was—and it could hardly be called glamorous—it hugged every beautiful curve of her body. 'You look very strokeable.'

She smiled and his hands began to itch with the need to reach out and show her exactly what he meant. 'Would you like a glass of wine?' she asked.

'I'd better not. I'm driving.'

'I see.' Her smile faded and she seemed to deflate right in front of him. But suddenly she lifted her chin up and pulled her shoulders back. 'You could stay,' she said quickly, her cheeks going bright red. 'For supper, I mean. And whatever…'

Supper and whatever sounded like heaven. 'Thank you.'

'Great.' She gave him a wonky kind of half smile but she didn't look away. Didn't turn away, either. 'I'll just go and get that wine, then, and—ah—check on the chicken.'

Which was, presumably, her cue to leave. But to his fascination and to her obvious consternation she didn't appear to be going anywhere. Her eyes didn't leave his. And as she continued to hold his gaze Jack heard her breathing shallow and felt a reciprocal quickening of his pulse.

Wondering if it would be entirely inappropriate to stride over, haul her into his arms and drag her to the floor, he saw her blink. Then sweep the tip of her tongue over her lips before letting out a tinkling little laugh. 'It's not fancy or anything,' she said, her words tripping over each other so fast it occurred to him that she was nervous. 'Just a roast. I often do them on the Sundays I'm around. Chicken, this time, obviously, otherwise why would I have said I'd better check on the chicken? And some vegetables. Carrots and leeks, from what I can remember. Oh, and potatoes, of—'

Taking a couple of quick long steps towards her, Jack wrapped one arm around her waist, buried the other in her hair and put a stop to the torrent of words with his mouth.

As he kissed her, hot and hard, he felt her melt against him, heard her moan, and the sound of it sent desire rocketing through him. She sighed against his lips, tilted her hips and pressed herself closer, and Jack thought he'd better stop before he lost all control.

Reluctantly lifting his head, he drew back and stared down at her. Her cheeks were pink, her eyes glazed and her lips red and swollen and she looked so desirable he told himself that, whatever the initial reason for it, his decision to detour via here was the best move he'd ever made.

'Thank you,' she breathed.

'What for?'

'Shutting me up.'

'It was a pleasure.'

'It was indeed. As you may have noticed, I tend to talk too much when I'm nervous.'

He had, and he thought it rather adorable. 'Are you nervous now?' he muttered, faintly perplexed because he rarely found anything adorable.

She leaned back in his arms and smiled up at him. 'Not any more.'

'Good,' he said firmly because he didn't need to be thinking of Imogen as adorable.

'I'll just be a minute. Make yourself at home.' Extricating herself from his arms, she backed away. Straight into the wall. She jumped and winced, then shrugged and flashed him a self-deprecating 'ignore me, I'm an idiot' kind of grin before disappearing through the door.

The chicken was fine. Imogen, who was taking a wine glass from a cupboard and shaking her head in frustrated bewilderment, however, was not.

She was twenty-eight, for heaven's sake. She wasn't naïve. Or inexperienced. So why did she have to be so gauche? Why did she have to rattle away like that in his vicinity? She'd always thought she'd got over that particular habit years ago, but she clearly hadn't.

And what exactly was it about Jack that reduced her to such a tangled bundle of nerves anyway? It wasn't as if she didn't know him, was it? And it wasn't as if she had to worry about whether he was going to stay for more than just supper. The hungry way he'd been looking at her and the hot fierceness with which he'd kissed her moments ago gave her the impression that she only had to give him the nod and she'd be on the floor on her back and naked within seconds.

Obviously his unexpected appearance at her door had thrown her more than she'd thought. When she'd first spotted him through her spyhole she'd been overwhelmed by a wave of delight, then relief at the realisation that she'd been presented with a solution to the problem she'd been mulling over without any success whatsoever.

But when she'd seen him prowling round her sitting room, her haven, his large body taking up such a great chunk of space and his presence wiping out all the air, her brain had kind of short-circuited. And then gone into complete meltdown when he'd told her he thought she looked gorgeous.

Imogen felt a reluctant grin tug at her mouth as she ran her wrists under the cold tap and took a series of deep, steadying breaths. He must be completely shattered if he thought that, because without a scrap of make-up on and her oldest clothes she was not looking her best.

She poured Jack a glass of wine, pleased to note her hands were no longer trembling, then pulled her shoulders back and headed into the sitting room. He was holding one of the many photos that sat on her shelves and staring down at it, the expression on his face so unfathomable that she instantly longed to know the reason for it.

Her hours browsing the Internet, which hadn't revealed as many in-depth personal details as she'd expected, had whetted her appetite and she wanted to know more. She shouldn't, yet she did, so there'd be no giving of any nod and no tumbling to the floor and getting naked just yet.

'How did the babysitting go?' Imogen asked lightly, as if the mortifying previous ten minutes had never happened.

Jack turned and looked up, then took the glass she held out. 'Thank you. It was knackering,' he said, regarding her thoughtfully. 'But then you knew all along it would be, didn't you?'

Imogen hid a smile. 'I did have an inkling.'

'Because of these two?'

She glanced down at the photo he was holding and nodded. 'My nephew and niece. They're five and three respectively. Gorgeous but tyrannical.'

'You could have warned me,' he murmured, putting the photo back.

'And spoiled all your fun?'

She sat at the end of one sofa while Jack settled himself into the armchair and grimaced. 'It wasn't fun. It was hell.'

'Really?' She frowned. He couldn't mean that.

'No, not really.' He sighed, the grimace slowly morphing into a smile. 'It was fine, but you are still a wicked wicked woman.'

'Thank you,' she said demurely. 'I do my best.'

'You have a close family,' he said, flicking a glance at the dozens of photos on the shelves.

Imogen nodded. 'Yes. It's not that big, but we are close.'

She thought she saw something flicker in the depths of his eyes, something that in anyone else she'd have suspected was envy, but couldn't possibly be that in Jack. He seemed to value his solitariness highly—thrived on it even—so there was no way he'd ever want a noisy, messy family, the kind hers was.

Or would he?

Imogen blinked as the thought ricocheted round her head, and immediately warned herself not to go there. She was *not* going to try and inveigle her way into his psyche. She wouldn't be welcome and she didn't need to know his feelings about marriage or family or anything, in fact, other than whether he'd be up for a fling.

'So what did you and Daisy get up to?'

Jack rubbed a hand over his face and smiled, the shadows thankfully disappearing. 'What didn't we get up to? I thought I had a fairly short attention span but it's not a patch on Daisy's. We went to Regent's Park, then the zoo and had an ice cream. And that was just the first hour.' He shuddered. 'I don't think I'll ever be the same again.'

Imogen laughed. 'She ran rings round you.'

'She did.'

And he didn't sound entirely happy about the fact. 'So I take it you're not tempted to join the ranks of fatherhood just yet?'

Jack's hand froze mid rub, his gaze jerked to hers and he tensed. 'No way.'

At the vehemence in his voice curiosity spun through her hard and fast and made a complete mockery of her determination to stay away from his psyche.

'What, never?'

'Not planning to,' he muttered, relaxing his shoulders, she thought, with rather more effort than was natural.

Now she really was intrigued. 'Why not?'

'Why would I?' he said, taking a sip of wine, then sitting back, to all appearances the epitome of indifference. 'You've seen my mother.'

'Well, yes, but she's not exactly typical, is she?'

'Perhaps not, but she didn't make for an idyllic childhood. Certainly not one I'd want to inflict on anyone else.'

'Do you think you would?'

Jack shrugged, and she had the feeling that this wasn't the first time he'd had this conversation. 'I work hard. I travel a lot. It could happen.'

'But presumably there'd be another party involved.' The hypothetical child's mother, for instance, not that she particularly wanted to think about anyone else enjoying Jack's considerable charms.

'They could be worse, and I'm not prepared to take the risk.'

No, well, she could see how having a mother like his might make a man wary of parenthood. At the memory of Jessica's flamboyant behaviour on Friday evening, Imogen inwardly winced. While Jessica looked like fun, she couldn't honestly admit she'd like her as a mother. And imagine having a *grand-mother* like that.

'I must say your mother didn't look particularly maternal,' Imogen murmured.

'She doesn't have a maternal bone in her body,' Jack said, and she wondered if he was aware of the bitterness that laced his voice. 'The minute I was born she handed me over to her parents and carried on partying. She's barely stopped since.'

'So you were brought up by your grandparents?' She'd read something about that on the Internet, but the details had been sketchy.

He nodded, but his jaw was tight. 'And a string of au pairs.'

'What was that like?'

Jack shrugged and she could see shutters slamming down over his eyes, instantly masking anything of importance. 'My grandparents did their best.'

'And the au pairs?'

'Marginally better.'

Imogen frowned. 'What about your father?'

'What about him?'

'Do you know who he was?'

His mouth twisted into a humourless smile. 'Oh, yes. He was a fellow pupil at my mother's very expensive but surprisingly lax boarding school. He was shipped off to the States the minute the pregnancy became apparent, and stayed there.'

'Do you see anything of him?'

'No.'

That seemed a shame. Her father and brother got on brilliantly and, she knew, deeply valued their relationship. 'Why not?'

'Why would I? I'm the product of an accident. A reckless mistake.' He shrugged as if it was all neither here nor there. 'Anyway, he married years ago and has his own family now.'

And that was quite enough of that, thought Jack, not liking the note of resentment that tinged his voice one little bit.

He might not have a crystal-clear idea of why he'd dropped by this evening, but it definitely hadn't been for a discussion about his childhood. Never mind that it was remarkably easy to talk to Imogen. Careless talk could cost him an emotional fortune and he had the deeply uneasy feeling that all she'd have to do was probe a bit further and he'd end up horizontal on the sofa spilling it all out while she made sympathetic noises and took notes on an imaginary clipboard.

Which meant it was time to change the subject, he thought, stifling a shudder at the image, because he had no intention of spilling anything out. There was no way in hell he was going to elaborate on the trauma of the years of maternal neglect that had been inflicted on him when he'd been young. The aching loneliness. The constant awareness that he didn't matter. That his mother was more interested in the social scene than her son and that somehow the blame for her indifference must lie with him. That he simply hadn't been good enough.

No, he had no desire to dwell on the past. No desire to go into the strict and critical attitude of his grandparents, who'd been terrified that, if they weren't, genes would out and that he'd grow up to be as flighty and irresponsible as his parents.

And he certainly had no desire to let in all the old feelings of inadequacy and hurt and confusion that had coloured his childhood and were now banging at the door of his conscience.

So he did the only thing he could under the circumstances and went in search of distraction.

He let his gaze run over Imogen, and as his body tightened with need, Jack leaned forwards and set his glass down on a pile of magazines on the coffee table. 'I didn't come here to talk about families,' he murmured, shooting her a smouldering smile and not taking his eyes off her for one second.

Imogen swallowed and her breath caught. 'No?' she said

with a huskiness that scraped across his nerve endings. 'Then why did you come?'

In one fluid move, Jack was on his feet and came down on the sofa right next to her. Her mouth dropped open with a little O of surprise and the banked flames in her eyes flared to life.

'I came for this,' he muttered, pulling her into his arms and reaching for the zip of her top as his mouth captured hers.

As his hands slid over her body, his heat and strength wrapped around her and his mouth devoured hers, Imogen closed her eyes. Part of her thought she ought to be outraged at the admission that he'd only popped by on the off chance of a booty call. Another, far greater part, was so pleased he'd decided to put a stop to her interrogation that she didn't care.

Because her heart had started twisting and aching for the lonely confused boy he must have been and she didn't want it to. She didn't want to want to seek out his mother and shake her by the shoulders until she acknowledged what a wonderful man her son was. She didn't want to envy her brother or think about marriage and family or Jack in that context. All she wanted was more of this. More of the incredible way he made her feel and spectacular sex.

So she shut it all off and gave herself up to sensation. To the hands roaming over her skin and deftly removing her clothing. To the weight of his body pressing her back into the sofa and the feel of his muscles beneath her hands. To the heat of his mouth on her throat, her breasts and then blissfully lower. To the sound of his harsh breathing and the thundering of her heart. And then to the glorious feel of him sliding into her and casting her into a fierce whirlpool of pleasure.

The following morning, as dawn filtered through the curtains, Imogen watched Jack pull on his clothes and considered her dilemma. After the long, hot night they'd just had, she was convinced more than ever that a fling was what she wanted. The problem she had was that time was fast running out and she didn't have a clue how to go about asking if he was up for one.

'Well, that was fun,' she said lightly, wondering how on earth to broach the subject.

'It was.' Jack snapped on his watch and prowled around her bedroom in search of his belt.

'I think it's on the floor by the sofa.'

'Thanks,' he muttered and disappeared into the sitting room.

From where he could well yell a goodbye and go.

Letting out a deep sigh, she flopped back, nibbled on her lip and wished she had the guts to just come out and say it. Because frankly, why shouldn't she? The worst he could do was say no, and what did she have to lose? A potential fling, and what was such a big deal about that anyway?

Oh, sod it, she thought, sitting up suddenly and leaping to her feet. Since when was she such a wimp? She'd go in there, tell him what she wanted and do her damnedest to ensure that he couldn't say no.

Wrapping the duvet around her and holding her head high, Imogen wandered into the sitting room to see Jack rummaging around for his shoes.

'I'd better make a move,' he muttered.

'Of course,' she said, letting the duvet slip a little as he glanced up at her. 'The markets won't wait for you.'

Jack's gaze dropped to her cleavage and he stopped what he was doing, the glint in his eye suddenly gleaming fiercely. 'Which is unfortunate,' he murmured, walking over to her, grasping the top of the duvet and pulling her towards him.

The searing kiss gave her the encouragement and lack of inhibition she needed. 'So what would you say to doing this again some time?' she murmured giddily when he finally lifted his head.

Jack grinned. 'I'd say I'm free on Wednesday if you are.'

# CHAPTER TWELVE

AND that was how it had been ever since.

Jack grated lime zest into a bowl and wondered if he ought to be worried. Not about the fact that he and Imogen arranged their dates from one to the next—that was the way he liked it, the way he'd always liked it. No. It was the fact that there had been so many of them that was so unsettling. Six weeks of them to be exact, which was five weeks more than usual, and he couldn't see an end in sight. Strangely, he didn't seem to want to.

As if all that wasn't disconcerting enough, he thought, squeezing the lime juice and adding it to the bowl, here he was at home. In his kitchen, cooking. For her. And not for the first time.

He spooned a dollop of fromage frais into the lime, sprinkled a teaspoon of sugar on top and gave it a stir. In the six weeks of random dates, which, as they happened two or three times a week, hadn't been quite as random as he'd have liked, he and Imogen had stayed in as much as they'd gone out. Sometimes she cooked for him, on other occasions he for her. They'd joked that her kitchen had never been so well used, and that his fridge, used to housing nothing but beer and milk, had never been so well stocked.

But actually it wasn't much of a joking matter, was it? he reflected, filling a pan with water and sticking it on the hob.

Because if he'd been on the outside looking in, he'd have described the whole thing as domesticated. Cosy. Something that looked suspiciously like the beginnings of an affair. Or even a relationship.

And that definitely *was* worrying.

As much as he might tell himself he didn't do relationships, he had the unsettling feeling that he was getting used to Imogen. Getting used to having her around.

Jack poured himself a glass of wine, then walked into his study, sat in his chair and stared out at the darkening London skyline, his brow furrowed. What was it about her that he found so appealing? OK, so she was undeniably gorgeous and incredible in bed, but that combination—while rare—he'd come across before. So it had to be more than that.

Was it her wickedly dry wit? The way her eyes sparkled with passion and admiration when she talked about the work the trust did? Or the honesty with which she regarded her place within it?

Was it her ability to laugh at herself? The biting, self-deprecating humour she used to deflect the barbs of others? Or was it the warmth and affection with which she spoke of her family?

Jack frowned and pressed the rim of the glass to his chin. Whatever it was, it held him weirdly enthralled.

So far they'd lived entirely for the present. They never discussed the past or the future. They didn't talk about hopes and dreams or anything remotely personal. As if by some kind of unspoken agreement they kept things light, their conversation sticking to how their days had been, when they were going to meet up next and what they were going to do when they did. Besides, they spent so much of their time together in bed, there hadn't exactly been a lot of time for chatting.

Which had suited him perfectly initially.

But now…

Now he found himself wanting to know more. He wanted

to know about her past. Her plans for the future. What her hopes and dreams were and what she wanted out of life. He wanted to find out what had happened with that stalker and then personally go and hunt him down and string him up. Swiftly followed by everyone who'd criticised and mocked her over the years.

Basically, he thought, he just wanted more of everything.

He stilled, and his fingers tightening around the bowl of the glass, his blood chilling because wanting more of everything hadn't been in the plan. It had *never* been in the plan. It simply wasn't an option, and to ensure it never happened Jack had taken the precaution of building up defences so high, so impenetrable that he'd been sure they were unbreachable.

But somehow Imogen, with her warm smile and disconcertingly penetrating gazes, had sneaked straight past them, he realised with a start. And as a result, after a lifetime of denial, she'd got him hoping for things he'd never dreamed he'd be able to have.

On the increasingly frequent occasions he thought of Luke and Emily and their little family unit, he now found himself responding, not with heartfelt relief that it would never happen to him, but with an extremely unfamiliar and deeply unsettling pang of envy.

He kept thinking about that exhausting but entertaining weekend with Daisy and wondering 'what if?'. Which invariably led him to go over the conversation he and Imogen had had about his upbringing.

What if she'd had a point when she'd queried his assertion that history would undoubtedly repeat itself? What if he'd been denying himself something deep down he'd always wanted just because of some ancient misplaced feelings of inadequacy?

As those defences he'd spent years fortifying cracked and wobbled, Jack's heart pounded and his head swam. If Imogen was right about that, what else might she be right about and he be wrong about?

Maybe it wouldn't hurt if he opened up and let her in a bit to see what she had to say about things. And then if that turned out to be relatively painless, maybe he could open up and let her in a bit more.

Noticing the hand that was holding the wine glass was trembling, he set the glass down and rubbed his chest to ease the tightness that was suddenly gripping it.

He'd never thought he'd get the chance to have a relationship, but it seemed that whether he'd planned it or not that was exactly what had been going on with Imogen.

So maybe now was the time to give it a proper shot, he thought, his mouth going dry as his pulse raced. Put things on a firmer footing. See where things went. She might have told him that first time that she wanted nothing more than sex, but as far as he could make out she was as into this as he was.

Would it really be such a terrible idea to suggest they give it a go? Yes, he'd be putting more on the line than he had for years but maybe this time, *this time*, it would be OK. Maybe more than OK even...

At the sound of the buzzer, Jack jumped. Adrenalin raced along his veins and a thousand different emotions suddenly thundered through his body as he leapt to his feet and strode to the intercom in the hall to buzz Imogen in.

He'd suggest it the minute she arrived, before either his nerve failed him or one of his many hang-ups kicked in and demanded to know what the hell he thought he was doing.

Assuming she didn't have something else in mind, of course. Unzipping her dress in the lift after the Valentine's Day Ball seemed to have sparked her imagination, and he never knew quite what vision he'd be presented with when the lift doors drew back. If she was wearing as little as the last time she'd come over, his proposition might be delayed a while.

Jack waited and counted the seconds with fidgety anticipation. He tried leaning casually against a wall, but as he stood there rigid and tense, he realised that doing anything casually when he'd come to such an earth-shattering decision was hopeless. So he marched over to the console table to rearrange the pile of post he'd tossed there earlier.

And stopped. What the hell was he doing? Since when did he fidget like this? And what was this jittery feeling? Surely it couldn't be nerves. He'd never experienced a moment of nervousness in his entire life. It was impatience, he told himself. That was all. Now he'd made his mind up he wanted to get on with it.

He really had to calm down, he thought, shoving his hands through his hair and ignoring the bead of sweat trickling down his spine. Now, before she came in and asked if there was anything wrong.

He heard the lift arrive and managed to pull himself together seconds before the doors opened and Imogen burst into his apartment, wearing all her clothes and a beaming smile. For a moment he didn't know whether to be disappointed or relieved, but then it was all immaterial anyway because she was dropping her bag, shrugging off her coat and sidling up to him and he was busy being bamboozled by a surge of heat and longing.

His heart banged against his ribs as she wrapped her arms around his neck and gave him a hot, hard kiss that blew his mind. He was on the verge of tumbling her to the floor when she pulled back and grinned up at him.

'You look happy,' he said, smiling down at her.

'I am.'

'Me too.' And possibly for the first time in his life he genuinely was. 'I have news.'

'Oh? So do I.'

Whatever hers was, his definitely needed the buffer of alcohol. 'Would you like a drink?' he asked.

'I brought champagne.' She twisted back, bent down and dug around in her bag.

Jack arched an eyebrow at the very expensive bottle she held aloft. 'Are we celebrating?'

'We are.'

'Excellent,' he said, heading for the kitchen and unable to stop himself wondering if by any possible chance she'd come to the same conclusion he had.

Imogen leaned against the counter while Jack took a couple of glasses from a cupboard. He popped the cork, then deftly filled each glass and handed one to her.

'So what are we celebrating?' he asked, his pulse racing as he geared himself up to tell her about the momentous conclusion he'd come to.

Her eyes sparkled and shone and his chest ached. 'My news.'

'Which is?'

'I got in,' she said, grinning and punching the air with a little 'Yay'.

Jack tilted his head and smiled, her enthusiasm infectious even though he had no idea what she was talking about. 'Got in where?'

'University.'

He went still, for a moment stunned into speechlessness, all thoughts of sharing *his* news spectacularly derailed. What? University? She was going to university? 'I didn't know you'd applied,' he said, the realisation she hadn't told him stinging so badly that he was totally taken aback.

'No, well, I didn't tell anyone.'

'No one?'

'Not a soul.'

Oh. Well, that wasn't so bad, then. But still… 'Why not?'

She gave him a look that suggested she was surprised he even had to ask. 'You know what the press is like. They'd have mocked me, ripped me to shreds, given me hell. And imagine what they'd have said if I hadn't got in.'

Jack thought of all the stories he'd read and heard about her and decided that she was undeniably right. Again. 'So who knows you've been accepted?'

Imogen blinked. 'No one yet. Well, apart from you now.'

Something warm unfurled in the pit of his stomach at that. 'What are you going to study?'

'Behavioural Economics.'

'How long's the course?'

'Three years. And when I finish I'm going to wave my bit of paper at the board of the trust and make them give me a job where I can really make a difference.'

'It sounds like you've got it all mapped out.'

She nodded. 'For once.'

Jack grinned. He was delighted for her. And weirdly proud. She might not have said as much in so many words, but he'd got the impression lately that she rather regretted her misspent, frivolous youth. 'Congratulations.' He held up his glass and she clinked hers against it.

'Thank you.'

'So where are you heading?' If she wasn't staying in London, then, wherever it was, they should be able to make it work somehow. They'd both be busy during the weeks, but there were always weekends... And long, long holidays...

Her eyes shone and he could feel the excitement vibrating through her. 'America. New York, to be precise.'

And just like that, Jack felt as if someone had socked him in the solar plexus. His head went fuzzy and his heart rate slowed right down. All the blood that had been surging through his veins shot to his feet and for a moment he thought his legs were about to give way.

'Well, that is worth celebrating,' he said, his voice sounding as if it came from far far away.

'Isn't it?' She beamed and took a mouthful of champagne,

completely unaware her words were smashing all those achingly fragile fledgling hopes of his to smithereens. Because
while London would have been perfect, the UK doable, the
States was impossible.

'When do you leave?'

'August. To give me time to settle in and things.'

As something in his chest tightened Jack turned his back
on her before his expression of careful neutrality cracked, and
dropped a handful of linguine into the pan of boiling water.

'I see,' he muttered.

And he did, because it was blindingly clear. There he'd
been, tentatively thinking he might like something more with
her, and all along Imogen had been making plans to leave.

Wishing he could kick himself, Jack felt a strange kind
of numbness seep through him. How the hell could he have
been such a fool? How could he have ignored the one rule
he'd sworn to live by, and made the disastrous mistake of
confusing sex and emotion?

And what on earth made him think he was entitled to even
a sliver of happiness anyway? Had he learned *nothing* from
the past? He'd been nuts to even allow himself to go there.

Well, whatever, he thought grimly, throwing the bowl of
marinated prawns into the frying pan and focusing on the
sizzle instead of the thousands of tiny sharp arrows stabbing
at his chest. At least he hadn't made a complete idiot of himself and spilled out his news first.

Feeling his blood freeze at the thought of how close he'd
come to doing just that, he buried all the blossoming thoughts
he'd foolishly and recklessly let poke their way through his
defences. He wouldn't be letting them out again. Ever.

And just in case they dared try when he wasn't paying attention, he'd do what he'd done when as a child he'd begged
his mother to spend time with him and she'd told him to go
and bother someone else. He'd do what he'd done every time
his grandparents had shot him one of their disapproving looks,

every time one of the au pairs he'd come to adore had left and never come back.

He'd shut himself down.

'So what was it you wanted to say?' said Imogen, leaning over, peering into the pan and sighing appreciatively, her breast brushing against his arm.

Blocking out everything apart from his body's physical reaction to her proximity, Jack shrugged, shook his head and gave her the kind of smouldering smile he'd spent years perfecting. 'It doesn't matter,' he said coolly, as if nothing had changed even though it irrevocably had. 'It can wait.'

Until hell froze over.

# CHAPTER THIRTEEN

'GOOD afternoon, can I help you?'

Now there was a question.

Imogen stood in front of the reception desk at Jack's Mayfair office and looked down at the receptionist who was regarding her with a pleasant but neutral expression.

She definitely needed help of some sort, because lately she'd been at a complete loss as to what was going on between her and Jack, and if the situation continued she'd go nuts.

The only thing she knew for certain was that over the past few months things between them had changed. She couldn't put her finger on what exactly, but ever since she'd told him she was off to the States he'd become sort of cold. Distant and withdrawn. It was as if he'd closed off the fun, warm part of him, and nothing she did—and she'd tried everything—seemed to be able to open it up again.

They'd carried on seeing each other, but a lot less frequently than in the beginning. In fact, they'd gone from meeting up two or three times a week to once, if she was lucky. In the past month they'd got together four times, and every one of those had been at her suggestion.

To her increasing distress and confusion there'd been no romantic dinners, no laughter and no warm teasing. Just sex. It was still explosively intense sex, but it had been becoming increasingly soulless—at least to her mind—and she couldn't work out why.

It had briefly occurred to her that given the timing it might have had something to do with her leaving, but the minute the thought had popped into her head she'd deemed it ridiculous and had discarded it. Jack had told her that he could promise her nothing but sex, and she saw no reason why he'd have changed his mind. So she'd assumed it must be something else. Something to do with his work, maybe. A friend. Or even his mother.

But whatever the cause for it, Jack was freezing her out and she didn't like it one little bit. She missed the warmth and the laughter. She missed their conversations. The more he retreated, the more she missed him, and, although she knew it shouldn't, it hurt.

The last straw had been his reply to the email she'd sent him earlier asking if he wanted to meet up this evening. 'Fine' had been his one-word answer, and she'd suddenly had enough of being on the receiving end of such icy indifference without knowing the reason for it. Which was why the minute she'd finished work she'd walked out into the warm sunshine and headed straight here. Whatever was going on she had an all-consuming need to know. Right now.

'Is Jack Taylor available?' she asked.

The professional smile and cool expression remained in place. 'Do you have an appointment, Miss—?'

'Christie. Imogen Christie.'

'Oh, yes,' said the receptionist, her smile brightening as the cool facade vanished. 'We've spoken on the phone. It's nice to meet you in person.'

'Likewise. Hannah, isn't it?'

'That's right. Jack's out at the moment, but he shouldn't be long,' she said, glancing at the clock on the wall behind her. 'You're welcome to wait in his office if you'd like.'

Imogen nodded and smiled. She most definitely would like. 'Thank you.'

\* \* \*

Jack was in a filthy mood. He was tense, on edge and the lousy meeting he'd just screwed up hadn't helped.

There was no point whatsoever wondering what the matter was. This time he didn't bother asking himself if he was coming down with a cold. Or the flu. Or even pneumonia. He knew perfectly well what was wrong with him. As much as he'd struggled against it, as much as he might wish for anything but, he'd come down with a bad case of Imogen.

Climbing out of the taxi and striding up the steps to his office, he shoved his hands through his hair and scowled.

Why the hell was it so hard to cut her out of his life? God knew he'd tried. The morning after she'd revealed her plans he'd ruthlessly wiped all her contact details from his phone and his computer. He'd removed every trace of her from his flat and told himself he couldn't care less what she did or where she went. That in fact he'd had a narrow and extremely lucky escape.

For a day or two it had worked beautifully, helped by some unexpected news coming out of Asia that sent the markets into a spin and demanded every ounce of his concentration.

As Imogen hadn't crossed his mind once, he'd assumed he'd got over her and had congratulated himself on a job well done. But then she'd called him. She'd asked if he wanted to meet up, and with the way his pulse had leapt and his resistance had caved in he might as well not have bothered going to all those lengths to forget her.

None of the precautions he'd taken had made a scrap of difference on any of the other occasions she contacted him, either, because the minute he heard her voice, images of her, conversations they'd had and the laughter they'd shared slammed into his head and he couldn't help wanting to see her again.

He'd told himself that as long as he kept things strictly to sex he'd retain control and he'd be fine. But he wasn't fine, because keeping things strictly to sex, seeing the permanent bewilderment on her face at his deliberately cold demeanour, was just about killing him.

He hated it, he realised, pushing through the revolving glass door, his head pounding. All of it. He hated the fallibility of the will power and inner strength he'd always taken for granted. He hated the loss of control and the volatility of the stuff churning around inside him and the fact that he couldn't seem to stay away from her. Most of all he hated the indisputable truth that she was leaving and there wasn't a bloody thing he could do about it.

'Ah, Jack...?'

He stopped, halfway across the lobby, and glared at Hannah. 'Yes?' he snapped.

Her eyebrows shot up at his tone and a pang of remorse thumped him in the gut. Whatever was going on inside him it wasn't his receptionist's fault. 'Sorry,' he muttered. 'What is it?'

'Imogen's here.'

Jack froze as the blood roared in his ears. Imogen was here? Why? She'd never visited before. And how the hell was he supposed to cut her out of his life if she took to invading his space like this? *Hell*. 'Where is she?'

'I told her she could wait in your office.'

'Thanks. Make sure we're not disturbed.' He gave Hannah a dazzling smile to make up for the way he'd growled at her and swivelled on his heel.

As he strode down the corridor, his heart thumping with who knew what, Jack realised that for the first time in his life he had absolutely no idea what to do. He was all at sea, most likely on a collision course with disaster, and it was terrifying.

He stopped stock still in the middle of the passageway, his pulse racing. Terrifying? *Terrifying?* Since when had he ever been terrified—or even remotely scared—of anything? He frowned and with great effort pulled himself together. This was getting ridiculous.

Shoving his hands through his hair, he told himself to calm down, because the notion that he was all at sea was absurd. He was blowing what was really nothing more than a niggling little problem completely out of proportion. All he needed to do was find out what Imogen wanted and then send her on her way. Simple.

Reminding himself that this was *his* turf and that *he* was in control, he sprang forwards, continued down the corridor and opened the door to his office. As he shut it behind him and closed the blinds to give them privacy he was aware of Imogen jumping up from the sofa and spinning round.

Deliberately not looking at her, Jack strode across the wide expanse of carpet and perched on the edge of his desk. And only when he was sure he was fully prepared, only when he'd braced himself against the mind-boggling effect she always seemed to have on him, did he do so.

He folded his arms across his chest and regarded her with a steely coolness because the last thing his mind needed right now was boggling. 'So to what do I owe this honour?' he drawled.

He watched her throat move as she clearly swallowed back a bunch of nerves and told himself he didn't care how nervous she was, nor why. Then her eyes, filled with the bewilderment and uncertainty he'd seen a lot over the past few weeks, locked onto his and he set his jaw, because he didn't care about that, either.

'You said you were up for meeting,' she said.

'I assumed you meant later.'

'Do you have a moment now?'

The rest of his afternoon was free, but nevertheless Jack glanced at his watch. 'I can give you ten minutes.'

Imogen frowned and gave a little nod, then she pulled her shoulders back and lifted her chin. 'I'd like to know what's going on,' she said coolly.

Jack arched an eyebrow. 'What do you mean?'

'Well, with us.'

'I'm afraid I'm going to need a bit more to go on than that.'

She tilted her head and stared at him as if trying to work out whether he was being deliberately obtuse or genuinely didn't know. 'Haven't you noticed things are different?'

Jack wasn't sure he could work it out, either, so he shrugged as if he genuinely didn't have a clue. 'Different how?'

'I don't know,' she muttered. 'Just strange.' She frowned, bit her lip and then fixed him with a fierce look. 'I don't get it. What happened? What changed? Did I do something wrong?'

Jack felt his jaw tighten but he was pretty sure that was his only reaction to her string of questions. He knew his expression was unreadable and his eyes were flat because it was a look he'd become adept at adopting over the years. 'Does it matter?'

'It shouldn't, but strangely it does.'

'Why?' he drawled, stamping down hard on the hope that surged through him at that. 'You're leaving. What do you care?'

She took a quick, deep breath. 'Look, if you want to finish things, Jack, then all you have to do is say. I'm a big girl. I can take it.'

'I don't.' The words were out before he could stop them, and as he watched the tension in her body ease a little, it struck him that if he wanted to remain in control of this conversation he was going to have to be very careful.

'So you want to carry on?' she asked.

'Do you?'

'I still have a while before I have to leave, so, yes, of course I do. But not like this.'

'Like what?'

Imogen let out a sigh. 'Well, the sex…' she began and then tailed off, her cheeks reddening.

Jack went cold. Of course. That was what this boiled down to. Sex. It always had and he'd been an idiot to think that she might have come here for anything else. To think she might actually be missing him or something. 'What's wrong with it?' he said flatly.

'Well,' she began again, and then her courage clearly failed her because she gave him a shaky kind of smile and made a lame stab at humour. 'Nothing apart from there being not enough…'

'I see,' said Jack, nodding slowly and letting his gaze drift over her. Her hair was down and tumbled over her shoulders. The jacket she was wearing fitted her as if she'd been stitched into it and her skirt was tight and short. Her endless legs were bare and he could see her red-varnished toes peeping out of her very high, very sexy shoes. As the memory of how those legs felt wrapped around him flew into his head, desire surged though him, and he pushed himself off the desk. 'Then I suppose I'd better see what I can do to remedy the situation.'

Reaching out, he caught her by the waist. Imogen jerked her gaze to his and gasped, but he merely pulled her tight against him and twisted her round to press her against the edge of the desk. And before she got it into her head to demand to know what the hell he thought he was doing, before she could protest about the dozens of people on the other side of the door, and certainly before his common sense could wake up and object, he slammed his mouth down on hers, hot and hard and furious.

To his grim relief, Imogen put up no resistance. As their tongues met and tangled she moaned and melted against him. Her hands whipped up to bury themselves in his hair and his shot down to the hem of her skirt. Pushing it up, Jack gripped her thighs and lifted her onto the desk.

She let out a soft whimper and he reminded himself that this was what she'd come here for. This was what she wanted from him. All she'd ever wanted from him, would ever want from him and it would be the last time.

Imogen tore her mouth from his. 'You know, I really didn't come here for sex, Jack,' she panted.

'Are you sure about that?' he muttered, slipping his fingers beneath her knickers, stroking her between her legs before thrusting them inside her.

'One hundred per cent,' she gasped, and as he felt her muscles instantly clench around his fingers another great wave of desire slammed into him.

'Do you want me to stop?' he said, his voice rough and unsteady with every volatile thing churning around inside him.

She pressed herself closer. 'Don't you dare.'

As he rubbed and stroked her hands shot to the buckle of his belt and wrenched it open. She yanked his zip down and then shoved his trousers and shorts down and wrapped her hand around the hot, hard length of him.

Jack inhaled sharply, lurched to one side to grab his wallet, which lay on the desk, and pulled out a condom.

And then he was tugging her knickers to one side, holding her hips in place and driving into her. He crushed his mouth to hers to swallow her hoarse groan.

As he pounded into her she clung to his shoulders and wrapped herself around him and his mind blew. It was frantic and raw, her desperation matching his own, and he couldn't hold himself back. His thrusts became increasingly harder and faster, and then she was whimpering and moaning and letting out a harsh muffled cry and he was coming with a scorching rush of pleasure while she shattered and convulsed around him.

In the aftermath, with his head buried in the crook of her neck, her body shuddering against his and their ragged breathing the only sounds in the room, Jack shook and something inside him cracked open and fell apart. The vestiges of his crumbling defences vanished, and, with his pulse thundering and drowning out the voice in his head telling him he was insane, he heard himself mutter, 'Stay.'

Imogen stilled in Jack's embrace, her heart slowing right down and the heat and pleasure dissipating like a warm breath in cold air. Something told her he wasn't talking about right now, and that something made her shiver, despite the heat of the body still plastered against her.

And come to think of it how the hell had that happened anyway? One minute he'd been all steely calm and icy control while she'd waffled and dithered and generally floundered in bewilderment at his attitude, and the next he'd been grabbing her and ravishing her right here on his desk. While she assisted.

But whatever the reason for it the intensity of his kisses and the frantic desperation of his movements had been irresistible. It hadn't been soulless and she couldn't regret it.

'What?' she asked, although she wasn't at all sure she wanted clarification.

'Stay,' he muttered again.

'I can't,' she murmured, fervently hoping that, as she had on so many other occasions, she'd got it wrong and he was only asking her to stay here now. 'I have to go. Besides, what must your staff be thinking?'

Jack reached out and tucked a lock of her hair behind her ear. 'I don't mean now,' he said with a crooked little half smile. 'I mean, don't go to the States.'

Briefly, Imogen's heart sank at the knowledge she'd been right. And then she froze, because to her utter shock it was on the tip of her tongue to throw everything she'd worked for aside and say OK.

But no, she thought, setting her jaw as she put her hands flat on his chest and gently pushed him back. That wasn't an option. She'd let her head be turned all her life and it wasn't going to happen again just because the sex had gone back to being soulful. 'I have to.'

With a frown, Jack stepped away and fixed his clothing 'No, you don't.'

'I do.'

'Why?'

Imogen wriggled off the desk and pulled her skirt down. 'You wouldn't understand.' How could he?

'Try me,' he said flatly.

She moved away from him to give herself room to breathe and sat on the arm of the sofa, watching him tuck his shirt into his trousers. 'Do you have any idea what it's like to wake up one morning and realise how pointless everything you've done is? How little you've achieved, despite all the privileges you've had?'

Jack glanced over at her. 'I guess not.'

'Well, I do. I've had pretty much every advantage going and what have I done? Absolutely nothing.' She ran her hands through her hair and then crossed her arms. 'I messed up at school, partied my way through my early twenties, the only jobs being a bit of modelling and writing the occasional article. It's shameful.' She tilted her head and regarded him thoughtfully. 'You know, you were right when you accused me of being shallow and vacuous.'

'I wasn't, and you're not,' he muttered and stalked over to a cabinet in one corner of his office.

'I have been. But I'm not going to be any more.'

Whipping round, he held up a decanter of what she presumed was either whiskey or brandy. 'Want one?' he said.

'No, thanks.'

He poured himself a large measure and knocked it back in one. 'Fine,' he said curtly. 'So study here.'

Imogen blinked and fought back the urge once again to give in. 'I'm going to the States, Jack, where I can live and study without the scrutiny of the press.'

'Stay and I'll protect you from it.'

'You can't. You know what they're like. Over there I'm a nobody. They won't give a toss about my past or who I am. They'll leave me alone. That would never happen here.'

His jaw tightened. 'I'll think of something.'

Imogen sighed and sat up straighter. 'Look, Jack,' she said, deciding she needed to be firm, more for her sake than his, 'this has been fun, could still be fun for another couple of months if we go back to the way things were before, but I'm not going to throw this opportunity away. This may be my only chance and I'm not going to blow it. Certainly not on a whim.'

For a moment there was silence as Jack simply stared at her. He went still, his face draining of all colour so swiftly that she wondered if he was all right.

And then it was as if he sort of exploded. The glass he'd been gripping flew across the room, crashed against the wall and shattered. Imogen jolted, her heart thundering with shock.

Colour slashed across his cheekbones. Fire blazed in his eyes and waves of anger rolled off him. He took a step towards her, then stopped and thrust his hands in his pockets as if not trusting himself not to throttle her. 'You think this is a whim?' he said roughly. 'You think asking you to stay is easy for me to do?'

Imogen blanched in the face of his fury and struggled to work out the reason for it. 'Why wouldn't it be?' she said, genuinely baffled. 'Things come easy to you and you're used to getting your own way.'

He glared at her. 'Things don't come easy to me and nothing since I met you has gone my way. *Nothing*.'

At his scathing tone, through all the shock and the bafflement, Imogen felt her own anger begin to stir. 'And that's *my* fault?'

He let out a harsh, humourless laugh. 'Oh, no. Don't worry. It's all been entirely my own fault. Everything from getting involved with you in the first place to the foolish hope that you might want to stick around.'

She flinched. 'Did I ever give you the impression I would'

'No. It was stupid of me. Incredibly stupid. But then that's nothing new when it comes to you.'

The bitterness in his voice stabbed at her chest and she went dizzy with a weird need to find out why he'd wanted her to change her mind about leaving.

'Why do you want me to stay, Jack?' she asked and held her breath as if everything hung on his answer, which was mystifying because it didn't.

Or did it?

His eyes met hers and held them, the blue shimmering with something she couldn't identify and wasn't entirely sure she wanted to anyway.

'For more.'

'Of what?' Her breath caught in her throat. 'The same?'

Jack frowned and yanked his hands out of his pockets to rake them through his hair. 'Well, yes. But on a more permanent basis.'

Her heart hammered. 'How permanent?'

'I don't know,' he muttered, a rare flash of uncertainty darting across his face.

Her heart then plummeted. 'Well, that's not good enough,' she said with a shrug. It hadn't mattered that much anyway.

'Of course it isn't.'

'The university I'm going to is one of the top ten in the world,' she said, ignoring the sarcasm. 'They don't dish out places to just anyone, and I'm not giving mine up for a fling that will last who knows how long.'

Jack stiffened, then gave her a horribly sardonic smile and arched an eyebrow. 'So how many strings did Daddy have to pull to get you one of those extremely rare and highly sought-after places?'

For one long moment Imogen could do no more than stare at him as his words and the mocking tone with which they'd been delivered hung between them. She blinked, the shocked disbelief coursing through her gradually turning to deep outrage and excruciating hurt. To think that for one crazy second she'd actually considered suggesting he go with her.

'Jack,' she said, her voice cold and flat, 'you're a bastard.'

And with that she stood up, snatched her coat and bag and walked out.

# CHAPTER FOURTEEN

'OK,' said Luke, planting two pints of beer on the table a week later and throwing himself into the chair opposite Jack. 'This time I *know* something's up.'

Jack shot Luke the cool, brittle smile that seemed to be fixed to his face pretty much permanently these days. Given that inside he was as cold as ice, and had been ever since Imogen had stormed out of his office, it didn't seem all that inappropriate. 'Thanks for this,' he said and took a large swallow.

Luke shrugged and grinned. 'Winner's obligation.'

'Don't get too used to it.'

'So?'

'Nothing's up,' said Jack, setting the glass down and calmly meeting Luke's penetrating stare despite knowing that that couldn't be further from the truth.

'Right,' said Luke, evidently knowing it, too.

Jack fought back a scowl and concentrated on keeping the smile on his face. 'I lost. It's no big deal.'

'On the occasions you do lose you don't usually do it quite so dismally.'

Jack shrugged as he mentally revisited the diabolical game of squash he'd just played. 'So I'm having an off day. It happens.'

He'd been having a lot of those lately. Seven of them to be

precise. Because he'd thought that he'd had a rough time of it when Imogen had first told him she was leaving, but this… This was infinitely worse.

He couldn't stop thinking about her. About their last encounter, their last conversation, and, fuelled by the excoriating disappointment that nothing he could do would persuade her to stay, the dreadful things he'd said. The more he thought about it, the more it hurt. And the greater the guilt and shame he felt.

'You know,' said Luke, shooting him a disturbingly probing look, 'the last time one of us lost that badly was me. Just after I'd met Emily and had my life thrown upside down.'

'Was it?' said Jack, glancing around the bar of the squash courts in an effort to avoid the question in Luke's eyes.

'It was.' Luke paused, then added, 'So I'm guessing your mood has something to do with Imogen.'

Her name struck him square in the chest and he nearly doubled over with the pain of it.

Dammit, why did it still hurt? It was over. Imogen was leaving and he'd be alone once again. Which was actually for the best because it was safer that way. Besides, he was used to it, so he was fine.

Or at least he would be soon. With the intensity of a relationship such as theirs it was bound to take longer than a week to get over, but he'd succeed eventually. He had to.

Rallying, Jack sat up and took another gulp of beer. 'Seeing as Imogen and I are no longer seeing each other you couldn't be more wrong.'

Luke paused, his glass hovering an inch from his mouth as his eyebrows lifted. 'Oh?' he said. 'That's a shame. I liked her. Emily liked her.'

He'd liked her, too. More than liked her…

Jack grunted and determinedly didn't think about that. O· about the dinner out the four of them had had and the w·

Imogen had effortlessly got on with the two people he cared most about in the world.

'So what happened?'

His jaw clenched. 'I don't particularly want to talk about it.'

'Fine.'

As Luke lapsed into silence in that annoying way he had Jack brooded and bristled and then eventually gave in, the perverse urge to talk about it too insistent to ignore. 'She's leaving,' he said when he couldn't stand it any longer.

'Leaving?' Luke echoed, his eyebrows shooting up.

'Going to study in the States.'

'I see. Right. Well, good for her.'

No, it wasn't. 'I asked her to stay.' His jaw tightened and his chest squeezed at the memory of how weak he'd been. 'She said no.'

'And?'

It was a good thing he hadn't been looking for sympathy because if he had he'd have been disappointed. 'What do you mean "and"?'

'Well, what was your counter offer?'

Jack frowned. 'Counter offer?'

'Surely you didn't leave it at that? Didn't you ask if you could go with her or something?'

'Of course I didn't.' The idea of begging her to let him go with her smacked of desperation and he wasn't desperate. At least not *that* desperate.

'Why not?'

'Because she made it pretty clear that I wouldn't be welcome,' he muttered.

'Really?'

Jack scowled into his beer. 'And even if I was, I can't just leave everything here.' It was impossible.

'Why not?' Luke asked. 'Don't you have an apartment here?'

'So?'

'And weren't you looking at opening a US branch at one point?' Luke added, undeterred.

'That was years ago.'

'Could be a good move.'

Luke made it sound so easy, but Jack could still see the expression on Imogen's face the second before she walked out, and knew it was anything but. 'The whole thing is immaterial anyway.'

'Why?'

He could feel a weird kind of pressure building inside him and his head went fuzzy as the undeniable truth hit him all over again. 'Because she doesn't want me.'

And that was really what was at the heart of it all, wasn't it? Imogen didn't want him. At least not enough. He'd seen it in the set of her jaw and the look in her eye when she'd told him this was her chance and she wasn't going to screw it up for anything. Basically, she'd let him know in a roundabout kind of way that he wasn't as important to her as studying in the States, and it had nearly crucified him.

He'd come to care about her, and like everyone else he'd ever cared about she was abandoning him. The difference was that this time he couldn't seem to switch himself off and shut himself down. This time every muscle in his body ached with the pain of it.

To all appearances he'd been carrying on as normal. He'd gone to work, handled meetings and traded with his usual efficiency but inside he was a mess. Inside he was falling apart. His self-control was in bits and his grip on his sanity was fast unravelling and there didn't seem to be a thing he could do about it.

Luke shifted, then sat upright and leaned forwards and took a deep breath as if preparing to say something unpleasant. 'Right. As we don't ever do this sort of stuff, I'm only going to ask this once,' he said, fixing Jack with an unwavering stare. 'Do you love her?'

Jack's heart stopped and then began to beat triple time as his blood roared in his ears. What kind of a question was that? At some point during the last horrendous week, he'd come to the dizzying realisation that he adored her. Imogen was everything he'd ever wanted. Everything he'd ever dreamed of in the moments of weakness he'd allowed himself to dream.

He'd been in love with her for weeks. Possibly since the minute she'd told him to find some other victim to devour and stormed off. Why else would he have pursued her when she'd been—and had put up—such a challenge?

And since then it had grown and developed into something much more, which was undoubtedly why this all hurt so much.

'Does it matter?' he said tightly, because Luke might be wanting to talk, but he had no intention of expressing the tangled heap of feelings coursing through him.

'Jack, you and I have known each other a long time, and you're my best friend, but if you love her and you're not going to go after her you're a jerk.'

Jack's eyebrows shot up and he glared at his so-called friend. Luke, however, looked unperturbed. 'You can glower all you like, but you are.'

'I asked her to stay,' he said again, because this seemed to him to be the crux of the matter. 'And she said no.'

'So what is this? A question of pride?'

'No.'

'Then what is it?'

'You know what it is,' he muttered and frowned into his glass. Once, many years ago over too many beers, they'd had a brutally frank discussion about their pasts and their hang-ups. It had been a one-off, and neither of them had referred to it again.

Luke tilted his head and regarded Jack thoughtfully. 'I see,' he said. 'So is that why you sabotage every potential relationship before it has the time to develop?'

What the…? Jack snapped his head up. 'I don't.'

Luke arched a sceptical eyebrow. 'Really? Then why has no woman ever lasted more than a week?'

'I get bored easily.' It was a line he'd told himself many times, but actually it wasn't true, was it, because Imogen hadn't bored him in the slightest.

'Rubbish. You deliberately put an end to things before you can get involved.'

Jack opened his mouth to deny it, then closed it, his mind racing as his dating technique over the last ten years flashed through his head. Short-term didn't begin to describe the brevity of the relationships he'd had, the relationships—if they could even be called that—he'd been the one to end before they'd ever had the chance to get off the ground.

'And I bet you sabotaged things with Imogen, too,' Luke added.

Jack stopped and stared at Luke, momentarily rendered speechless, because that was true too. By making that hideously unfair remark about her father fixing her application that was exactly what he'd done. He'd deliberately made sure she left. She was the best thing to happen to him and he'd sent her away without even considering how they could make it work. And why? Because he'd been too weighed down by his own emotional baggage.

Luke was right. And not just about that. He *had* been a jerk. In fact, he'd been worse than that. Caught up in his hang-ups, he'd been a self-centred jerk, and that wasn't him.

Jack's heart began to hammer as the realisation of just how stupidly blind he'd been slammed into his head. Which was swiftly followed by the clamouring need to put things right. That the situation might not be fixable wasn't something he was willing to contemplate. It had to be.

'Since when did you become such an expert?' he said, his voice cracking a little beneath the onslaught of everything he felt.

'Since I married Emily. She likes to discuss you.' Luke grinned for a second, then sobered. 'She cares. We both do. Look, Jack, if there's one thing I've learned it's that your past needn't screw up your future. It nearly happened to me. Don't let it happen to you.'

Jack set his jaw, his mind teeming with ideas about how to undo the massive mistake he'd made. 'I don't intend to.'

*Scumbag*, thought Imogen, pummelling the punchbag and imagining it was Jack. He was a lousy—punch—selfish—punch—thoughtless—punch—scumbag. She gave the punch-bag a kick for good measure and then stumbled back, breathing hard. Sweat trickled down her back and her muscles ached. As well they might. She'd been a member of the gym for years but had gone so rarely that each visit worked out costing her a fortune.

Well, she was making up for that now. And how. Since the afternoon she'd marched out of Jack's office, she'd spent every spare minute taking out her anger, frustration and hurt on the pleasingly resilient gym equipment.

Not that her efforts were making a difference to anything other than her muscle tone, she thought as the adrenalin drained from her veins and misery returned. It had been a week since that horrible scene in Jack's office, but every word of it was still so fresh in her memory it might as well have been five minutes ago.

How *could* he have said that? she asked herself as his parting shot and the cold harsh tone of his voice with which he'd flung it at her slammed into her head yet again. Did he *really* think that about her? After everything they'd shared? After all the conversations they'd had about reputations and gossip and misconceptions and the nasty people who knew nothing ʾbout anything yet felt qualified to judge them?

Sighing deeply, Imogen pulled off her gloves, then picked

up her sweatshirt and headed for the showers. It had hurt. God, it had hurt.

And it still did, even though there was no point. Jack hadn't been in touch, which was just the way she wanted it, she reminded herself, stepping into the shower and switching on the water, because she had a bright new future to look forward to and she didn't need someone who thought *that* about her in her life.

No. It was a good thing that their relationship was dead in the water. An excellent thing, in fact. And besides, she'd never wanted anything long-term anyway. So why was she unable to stop thinking about him? And why was what he'd said still affecting her so badly?

Massaging shampoo into her hair, Imogen let the question roll around her brain as she tried to work it out. It didn't make any sense. It wasn't the first time someone had suggested that nothing she'd achieved had been on her own merit, and it certainly wasn't the worst accusation she'd ever received.

So why did what he thought matter so much? Why did he have such power over her thoughts? Why was he so important?

Imogen suddenly froze beneath the needles of hot water as the clouds parted in her head and clarity hit her brain like a flash of lightning.

Oh, dear God.

Her pulse slowed right down and all the blood rushed to her feet. Of course. It was obvious. So blindingly obvious she'd completely missed it.

She'd fallen in love with him.

Clutching a hand to her chest, Imogen locked her knees and made herself take a deep breath, because the last thing she needed was the mortification of passing out in the gym shower.

That was it. She was in love with him. Of *course* she was. As her heart rate steadied and her vision cleared, her mi picked up a gear and raced through all the evidence. Look at everything that had happened since the moment she'd met him. And look at the way he'd made her feel...as if she were on top of the world and at the bottom of a pit of despair and everything in between.

A series of images flashed through her head, of the way he'd sometimes glanced at her, the smiles he'd given her, the things he'd done for her, and her heart turned over. She was in love with him, all right. Deeply and helplessly. And how could she be anything else? Despite the recent blip, she loved everything about him, from the roots of his hair to the tips of his toes. She loved his constant strength and his occasional vulnerability, his sense of humour and his fierce intelligence.

When she'd found out that her application had been successful Jack had been the first person she'd thought of telling. The first person she'd *wanted* to tell, above even her family. And it wasn't just that news she wanted to share with him. She wanted to share everything with him and have him share everything with her in return, and had done for weeks.

So where did this leave her? she wondered dizzily, switching off the water with suddenly trembling hands. And what might it mean for her plans to go to the States?

Thoughts thundered around her head as for the first time her dogged determination to follow the path she'd chosen wavered. The notion of giving it all up flitted through her mind and Imogen felt her knees wobble.

It didn't upset her nearly as much as she'd have thought. Did that mean she would really give up everything she'd worked for, everything she wanted, for love? She let out a long shuddery breath as the idea took root in her head and spread. It seemed she would.

For a moment she felt her heart soar. And then, as reality snapped her back, it plummeted right down to the floor. What did it matter? Any question of giving anything up was utterly and heartbreakingly irrelevant because she wouldn't be doing anything of the kind, would she?

Feeling strangely cold, and not just because she'd turned the water off, Imogen plucked her towel off the hook and roughly dried herself.

Realising she was in love with Jack left her nowhere and meant precisely nothing for her plans to go to the States because whatever brainstorm she might have had, whatever heady conclusion she might have come to, the fact remained she'd fallen in love with a man who didn't know the meaning of the expression. Whose heart had remained intact for years and in all likelihood would for years to come. A man who'd promised her nothing, who'd offered her nothing but an extended fling on his terms.

An icy kind of numbness spread through her body as she pulled on her clothes and ran a brush through her hair. The whole thing was completely hopeless, wasn't it? Even if Jack should turn up and tell her that his offer was still on the table—which was *not* likely—it wouldn't make a scrap of difference. He'd never be able to offer her anything more than a fling, and a fling, however extended and whatever the terms, would never be enough for her. Therefore she had to get over him, because what alternative was there?

Steeling herself against the pain, Imogen shoved her things in her bag and slung it over her shoulder and left.

# CHAPTER FIFTEEN

OF COURSE it would be a damn sight easier to make a start on getting over Jack if he weren't parked outside her house, leaning against the bonnet of his car with his arms crossed, looking dark and haggard and utterly gorgeous.

Imogen stood frozen to the spot a few feet from her front door, her pulse leaping all over the place as she stared at him. Wow, she thought dazedly, if she'd needed any confirmation that she was in love with him she had it. Her heart was almost bursting with it, and she was suddenly feeling hotter and more breathless than she had during her workout. Every inch of her itched to race up to him and hurl herself into his arms, which only went to prove how very vulnerable she was right now. With her recent self-discovery—and all its implications—so fresh in her mind, she felt raw and exposed and deeply unsettled.

Why was he here? What did he want? And why was she just standing there like a lemon?

This was a situation she'd imagined a dozen times but now it was actually happening she found she had no idea how to handle it. Swallowing back the ball of panic that lodged in her throat, Imogen tried to figure out the best approach. In the absence of anything else she settled for doing nothing and willed herself to calm down. Let him make the first move, she thought firmly. She might be crazy about him but he was the one in the wrong.

After what felt like aeons, Jack pushed himself off his car and slowly walked towards her. With every step he took everything around her—the row of mews houses, the cobbled street, the faint rumble of traffic—became increasingly blurry until he stopped in front of her and everything but him disappeared completely.

'Hi,' he said, and her stomach flipped at the lopsided smile he gave her.

'Hi.' Imogen shifted her weight from one foot to the other and resisted the urge to give herself a good kick as she did so, because, lopsided smile or no lopsided smile, her stomach had no business flipping. 'What are you doing here?'

'I wanted to talk.'

'Haven't you said enough?'

At her cool, detached tone, Jack flinched and she made herself ignore it because as far as she was concerned, cool and detached was an excellent way to handle this.

'Not nearly,' he said. 'May I come in?'

And have him invading her space and scrambling her senses once again? 'I don't think so.'

He rubbed a hand along his jaw and nodded briefly. 'OK, well, I guess here is as good a place as any.'

'For what?'

'The apology I owe you.'

Imogen shrugged as if she didn't have a clue what he was talking about. 'An apology? What for?'

Jack frowned. 'What I said about your father pulling strings to get you into university… It was unforgivable.'

And despite her best efforts she couldn't help her pathetically weak heart softening a little. 'Oh, that,' she said and then jutted her chin up in an effort to counterbalance the melting that was going on in her chest. 'He didn't, you know. I ha to write three essays, take a couple of exams and get endless references. It wasn't easy.'

'I know.'

'Why would you think he had?'

Jack sighed. 'I didn't. Not really.'

'Then why say it?'

'I asked you to stay. You said no. I didn't like it.'

She stared at him in surprise. Had her refusal hurt? Had it really mattered that much? She reran their last conversation, this time from his point of view, and felt an instant stab of shame. She'd been so busy concentrating on how she'd been feeling that she hadn't considered his feelings at all, had she? In all honesty she hadn't thought he had any. But of course he did. Who didn't? So if her rejection of his request that she stay *had* hurt, then that certainly made sense of his reaction. And if that *was* the case, then what other feelings might he have?

Imogen's heart began to pound as her fragile steeliness crumpled and a kernel of hope cracked open inside her. 'I'm sorry,' she said.

'Don't be.'

'I had no idea.'

'Why would you?'

'I should have thought.'

'It was selfish of me to ask you not to go. But anyway, I overreacted.' He gave her a funny little smile that made her heart squeeze. 'As you may have guessed, I have a slight issue with rejection.'

'Why?'

'People I care about have a habit of leaving me.' He took a deep breath and shoved his hands in his pockets. 'My mother, all those nannies, and now you…'

Imogen's breath caught in her throat and her heart skipped a beat. 'You care about me?' How much? she was desperate to know, but didn't dare ask.

'Of course.' He smiled and looked so deeply into her eyes

that she went dizzy with hope. 'Which is why I've come up with a solution that I think could be workable.'

A solution that could be workable? As his words sank in Imogen blinked and her heart rate slowed right down. The phrase ricocheted around her head and rearranged itself in a dozen different ways. But whichever way she looked at it a workable solution didn't sound like the answer to all her recently acknowledged dreams and it didn't sound like the declaration of love she'd secretly been longing for.

Bewilderment and disappointment ripped through her with such force that her knees nearly gave way. 'Oh?' she said, because that she was all she could manage.

'Yes,' he said, completely unaware of the tumultuous effect his words had had on her if the dazzling smile he gave her was anything to go by. 'I've been thinking about this. You won't be studying all the time. There are long weekends. Holidays. And I often have to travel to New York on business. We might rack up the air miles and our phone bills would probably be astronomical, but we could make this work.'

For a moment all she could do was stare at him. Helplessly gaze into those gorgeous blue serious eyes as something inside her fractured.

Oh, what an idiot she was. Had she really expected a declaration of undying love? A heart-wrenching profession he couldn't live without her? How could she be so deluded? Jack might have thought he'd upped his game and presented her with the ideal solution, but really all he was proposing was a fling on *equal* terms.

Agreeing to it would be the mark of insanity. It would mean having to live with the emotional turmoil of dizzying highs and crushing lows. There'd be the rush of the novelty of it in the beginning, but then gradually when other things began to crop up—as they surely would—and they stopped crossing the Atlantic so often, she'd have to deal with the dis tressing fizzling out of it and the inevitable agonising end. And she'd be left heartbroken.

As Jack would never be able to give her what she wanted and as she wasn't prepared to accept anything less than everything, there was nothing to be done, she realised with depressing finality. The only consolation she had was that at least he didn't know how she felt.

'So?' he asked, giving her a smile that looked surprisingly uncertain.

With self-preservation now uppermost in her mind, Imogen took a deep breath and said, 'No.'

For a second he just blinked at her, as if unable to believe she'd turned him down again. 'No?' he echoed, the smile vanishing and his jaw tightening. 'Why not?'

'I'm sorry. I just can't.'

'I think I deserve a bit more than that, don't you?' he said, suddenly looking so aloof that she wished she could box away all her concerns, say yes to his suggestion, and make him smile that gorgeous smile again.

But she ignored the temptation and said coolly, 'Look, Jack, let's face it. It's a nice idea, but it wouldn't work.'

'What makes you so sure?'

'If we did embark on a long-distance affair, we'd be apart more than we'd be together.' She paused, then looked him straight in the eye and went for the easy way out. 'And I don't know if I could trust you.'

Long seconds of silence passed. 'What?' he said softly, his air of detachment vanishing as his expression turned thunderous. 'What the hell makes you think you couldn't trust me?'

Imogen forced herself not to flinch at his anger, and hardened her heart. 'Well, for one thing, you're not exactly known for your staying power when it comes to relationships.'

'I've never had one,' he snapped.

'Precisely.'

'What's your point, Imogen?'

'Do you really think that absence makes the heart grow fonder? Because I don't. Don't forget,' she continued doggedly, 'I went out with Max for months, Jack, and he was having an affair with my best friend right under my nose. With what you're suggesting we'd be thousands of miles apart for days on end and that means that there'd be even more of a risk.'

'I'm not Max,' he said, sounding as though he were gritting his teeth.

'Maybe not, but give me one good reason I could trust you.'

Even though she'd only brought up the whole trust thing as a way to hide what she really had an issue with, it now seemed of paramount importance. All she needed was one tiny glimmer of proof that he was serious about this. That he more than cared about her. That she was good for more than an extended fling and that he could be in this for the long haul.

But he blinked. Hesitated.

And in that brief nanosecond of uncertainty, as she saw the shadow that flitted across his face, everything inside her shattered.

'You can't, can you?' she said, her voice breaking beneath the pain and disappointment flooding through her.

'Do you see me demanding proof that *I* can trust *you*?' he said flatly, and then his voice turned colder, harder, infinitely more cynical. 'You know, you really need to get over the whole Max thing. It's pathetic.'

'And you need to get over your phobia of commitment,' she fired back, all the emotions churning around inside her surging up to voice what was *really* at the heart of this. 'History doesn't have to repeat itself.'

'Exactly.'

As they stood there bristling at each other it struck her that they were at a stalemate. Jack had taken as many steps forward as he was able to, and she certainly wasn't going to take any when it would achieve nothing but her own humiliation

'Well, you can rest assured that for me it won't,' she said, and then added with a bitter laugh, 'Who knows? When I get to the States, I might find a nice American who *can* give me what I want. Who I *can* trust.'

Jack's expression was stony, his eyes unreadable, his body tense. 'Then they're welcome to you.'

And with the devastating knowledge that this was it and there really was nothing left for her here now, the fight and the hope drained out of her. 'I think you'd better go,' she said dully.

He stepped back, so icy and distant that she wondered if she'd ever known him. 'Don't worry. I'm going. I must have been mad to come here in the first place.'

'Then I doubt you'll be wanting an invitation to my leaving party.'

'I can't think of anything I'd want less,' he said, and with that he threw her one last unfathomable glance, swivelled on his heel and strode back to his car.

Around the corner, and out of sight and earshot, Jack killed the engine and punched the steering wheel. Hard.

Damn it all. What had just happened there? And what had happened to his decision to put things right? Put things right? Hah. Things had imploded so spectacularly they couldn't have gone any more wrong.

With hindsight he should *never* have acted on the reckless desire to sort things out with Imogen once and for all and head straight here after his drink with Luke. He should have gone home and given himself the evening to perfect his plan.

Although, while it might have been a bit hastily cobbled together, in all honesty he didn't think the proposal he'd put forward could be much more perfect. Imogen had made it clear that despite not wanting anything permanent she'd wanted more than just sex, so his suggestion should have been ideal. So why had she turned it down? Why did he get the feeling that he'd somehow disappointed her? And how had things descended into that ridiculous argument?

Jack raked his hands through his hair and scowled out into the darkness as he tried to figure it out.

Had her objection really only been down to trust? Because if it had then why hadn't he simply told her he loved her? She'd asked for a reason to trust him, and surely that was an excellent one. Why had he hesitated? Had it simply been the fact that he'd been stung she'd even had to ask, or was it that he'd realised that perhaps she had a point because how could she trust him when, having never been in this position before, he had no idea if he could trust himself?

But that was absurd. Of course he could trust himself. He loved her. Insanely. So insanely that the idea of going off with another woman made him shudder with revulsion. Although not as much as the idea that she might meet someone else did. *That* concept made him feel as if he'd swallowed a bucket of battery acid.

A nice American who could give her what she wanted? Hah.

And then Jack's heart stopped and he froze in the darkness.

He played back what Imogen had said about her nice American word for word and his head went fuzzy. What she'd said would imply that *he* could never give her what she wanted. Which was nuts. If he only knew what it was she wanted, he'd willingly give it to her.

But perhaps he did.

He went even stiller as the look he'd seen in her eyes just before he'd told her about his workable solution, the one he hadn't been able to identify, hammered at his brain. What had it been? Resignation? Frustration? Anger? Or had it been hope?

He snapped up straight as the penny finally dropped. Hell. It *had* been hope. But for what? More? Had Imogen in fact wanted more from him than he'd assumed?

His head pounded and his heart thumped as questions battered him on all sides, followed swiftly by a thundering stream of answers. He'd been a blind, stupid fool. Imogen hadn't wanted things to be over. She'd wanted everything. And what had he done? Suggested a long-distance affair. And he was an idiot, because he'd thought he'd offered her exactly what she wanted, but in truth he hadn't offered her nearly enough.

Right, thought Jack, suddenly straightening and firing up the engine. Enough was enough. Imogen wanted more from him? She wanted a reason to be able to trust him? Well, he'd give her plenty.

# CHAPTER SIXTEEN

TAKING an eight-hour flight when she was feeling so miserable was the last thing she needed, thought Imogen numbly, stepping onto the bridge that led to the plane and the next three years.

It had been two weeks since Jack had stalked off, and time hadn't healed a thing. If anything time had simply made things worse. She missed him terribly and, even though she'd been frantically busy making arrangements to leave, she hadn't been able to stop thinking about him. She hadn't been able to stop wondering if she'd made a colossal mistake and whether she should have taken what she could from him when she'd had the chance.

As she'd expected, he hadn't been in touch—although that hadn't stopped her foolishly hoping he might—and he hadn't shown up at her leaving party. Which was no great surprise seeing as she'd stuck to her guns and hadn't sent him an invitation, but even so, she'd still harboured the secret pathetic hope that he might gatecrash it, if for no other reason than to say goodbye. All night she'd waited and hoped, the revelry going on around her a cruel contrast to the growing despair inside her, but to no avail. He hadn't come and she'd felt miserable. Since then it had only got worse.

But now she was about to board, Imogen didn't know why she hadn't just cancelled the flight altogether. Every minute of the journey to the airport had felt as if she were on her way to the gallows. Every step was like wading through treacle and she had to force herself to carry on and not give in to the urge to turn round and go home.

Even being told at the boarding gate that she'd been bumped up to first class hadn't made her feel any better, because what was the point of first class if you didn't have anyone to drink champagne with? What was the point of having plans and dreams if you didn't have anyone to share them with?

In fact, without Jack in her life, what was the point of anything any more?

Blinking rapidly against the sudden sting of tears, Imogen pulled herself together. It *would* get better, she told herself firmly, glancing down at her boarding pass and then checking the numbers above the seats. It had to. She just had to be strong. That was all.

Stopping at the seat she'd been allocated, she tightened her grip on her suitcase and hauled it up, her vision blurring at the thought that there really was no going back now.

'Would you like a hand with that?'

At the sound of the deep, dry, achingly familiar voice, Imogen froze and dropped her case, suddenly feeling so weak that all thoughts of strength evaporated.

'Jack,' she murmured, thinking dizzily that if her imagination had resorted to conjuring him up—which it must have done because he couldn't possibly be here—she was in a worse state than she'd thought.

But just in case it hadn't, he could and she wasn't, she blinked away the tears and focused on the man getting to his feet from the seat beside hers. And nearly passed out because there he was, real and solid, looking serious and gorgeous and definitely not a figment of her imagination.

With her stomach in free fall, she could only stare at him in shock as he bent his head and brushed past her, then took her suitcase and deftly stowed it in the overhead locker. 'What on earth are you doing here?' she said hoarsely.

Jack glanced at her and gave her the glimmer of a smile. 'Flying to New York, I should think.'

Her heart slowly turned over. 'But why?' Surely it couldn't be a coincidence. Surely fate wouldn't be so cruel.

'Why don't you sit down?'

Imogen stayed standing, mainly because she was so thrown by his presence she didn't know what to do. 'I'm not sure I want to spend the next eight hours sitting next to you,' she said, and it wasn't entirely a lie.

But to her astonishment Jack merely grinned and folded himself into his seat. 'No?' he said, glancing up at her and then turning his attention to his seat belt. 'Oh, well, if you want to go back to economy be my guest.'

How did he know where she'd intended to sit? Imogen frowned. 'Are you responsible for my upgrade?'

'Yes.'

Telling herself not to read anything into it because what with the way her brain was disintegrating she'd only get it wrong, she said, 'Thank you. I think.'

'You're welcome. I was hoping to have the pleasure of your company for the flight, but if you really don't want to sit here, that's fine.' He flashed her a smile. 'After all, what's eight hours when we have the rest of our lives?'

For a moment Imogen thought she must have misheard because Jack had turned his attention to a magazine and was now idly flicking through it as if he had no idea he'd just rocked her world. 'What?' she said, sinking into her seat when her legs finally gave way. 'What did you say?'

'Shh,' he murmured as a faint whirring noise came from the flickering screens embedded into the seat backs in from of them. 'It's the safety demonstration. Pay attention.'

Pay attention, thought Imogen dazedly. *Pay attention?* How could she possibly pay any attention to anything when bewilderment and shock were taking up every molecule of her brain? She'd thought that the terrible effect relentless misery had had on her heart and her appearance was bad enough, but it appeared that her reason had also suffered because for the life of her she couldn't work out what Jack could possibly mean.

Or could she?

Her heart began to thump. Did she dare hope—?

No. She could stop that kind of thinking right now because she couldn't afford to get it wrong again. He was probably flying to New York on business.

She was so busy trying to remain calm and convince herself that this was indeed the case that she was barely aware of the engines roaring into life, or the air stewards drifting down the cabin to check seat belts. And she was even less aware of taking off.

'I love planes, don't you?'

What? Imogen blinked and noticed with some surprise that they were in the air and climbing. She swallowed to make her ears pop and wished she could do the same to her brain, because what was he talking about now? 'I've never really thought about it,' she muttered.

'You should, because you know the best thing about them?'

'I can't imagine.'

'There's no escape.'

Imogen twisted round to face him, her eyebrows lifting. 'And that's a good thing?' She wasn't so sure.

'I think so. Even better, there's absolutely no possibility of anyone storming off.'

She went still. Oh. This wasn't a conversation about a love of planes. This had subtext. Her senses switched to high alert and her heart began to pound. 'Good point.'

'Thank you. In fact,' he added, turning to look at her, 'as neither of us is going anywhere for quite a while, we have plenty of time to hammer this out.'

Something about the intensely serious look in his eye made her mouth go dry. 'Hammer what out?' she said a little breathlessly.

'You and me and those assumptions and misconceptions we seem to specialise in.'

Imogen swallowed hard. 'Wouldn't a phone call have sufficed?'

'Definitely not.'

'Oh. Well. Like you said, I'm a captive audience. Hammer away.'

Jack shifted in his seat to lean closer to her, and as the familiar scent of him hit her brain, she went dizzy. 'Imogen, I'm sorry about the offer I made. It was crass and stupid. You were right. A long-distance relationship isn't the answer. At least not for us.'

Yes, it is! she suddenly wanted to yell, but clamped a lid on the urge. 'I understand why you made it,' she said instead and took pride in her mature approach.

He tilted his head, the gleam in his eye turning quizzical. 'I don't think you do.'

'No?'

'No. You know, you were wrong when you accused me of being afraid of commitment.'

Her heart thundered as the hope she'd been struggling to contain suddenly broke free. 'I was?'

He nodded. 'I might have had a few issues with rejection and abandonment and things but I'm not afraid of commitment per se. In fact,' he added with a slow smile, 'I've recently discovered I'm all for it.'

'That's great,' she said warily.

'It is, isn't it?' He paused. 'But not to just anyone.'

'No? Well, imagine what would happen to your reputation…' She tailed off because she was riddled with so much hope and longing and yearning for him she couldn't think straight any more.

'I don't give a damn about my reputation. Or my many issues. I've spent far too long focusing on both. The only thing I'm interested in right now is you.'

Imogen's stomach swooped as if the plane had plunged a thousand feet. 'Me?'

'That's right.' He took a deep breath. 'Here's the thing, Imogen. When I said I cared about you I should have been more specific.'

'In what way?' she said, but it came out almost as a whisper.

'What I should have said is that I love you.'

He looked deep into her eyes and she went dizzy. 'You love me?' she echoed, barely able to believe it.

Jack nodded and gave her the ghost of a smile. 'To distraction. I have done for weeks. I'm sorry I didn't tell you before.'

'So why didn't you?' She thought of all the misery she'd had to endure and her chest tightened.

He shrugged. 'When you said you couldn't trust me, it kind of blindsided me. I didn't know what to do.'

Guilt spun through her and Imogen knew that she'd deserved every second of that misery. 'I'm so sorry about that,' she said, her cheeks reddening with shame. 'I didn't mean it. I was hurting and it was a cheap but easy shot.'

'And I'm sorry I hurt you.' He reached out and tucked a lock of her hair behind her ear, and her pulse jumped. 'Nevertheless you had a point,' he said softly. 'This is all new for me, Imogen, and I'll probably screw up even more disastrously and more frequently than I have already. But I promise you, if you'll let me, I'll figure it out. And I'll prove you *can* trust me. Every day.'

Her heart turned over. 'Every day?'

He nodded. 'Long weekends and holidays wouldn't be enough, would they?'

She shook her head and sighed. 'Not nearly.'

'That's what I figured. Which is why I'm moving to New York, too.'

Imogen's breath caught in her throat as the love she'd been keeping at bay crashed through her defences and rushed into her. 'Really?' she said as an unstoppable smile spread across her face.

'Really. I'm opening an office there and I've even been thinking about getting in touch with my father.'

'Wow,' she said, because it was all she could manage. 'You've been busy.'

'Yes, well, both are about time. And incidental.' He paused, then said, 'I just want to be with you, and if you're going to be in New York then that's where I want to be, too.'

'Are you sure?'

'Surer than I've ever been of anything.' He shot her a smile that made her heart expand. 'Besides, you might meet that nice American you mentioned, and I can't have that.'

With all the love swelling up inside her, Imogen said fiercely, 'There's absolutely no danger of that happening.'

He arched an eyebrow. 'No?'

She took a breath, put her hand on his cheek and looked deep into his eyes. 'How could I possibly be interested in anyone else when I'm so in love with you?'

That devastating smile of his spread across his face, his eyes lit up and she nearly swooned at everything that blazed there. 'God, I hoped you were.'

'I am. Inescapably, it seems. And I'm sorry, too. For not realising sooner and for repeatedly turning you away.' She ached at the memory of how blind she'd been. 'And for wasting such a lot of time.'

Jack grinned. 'Ah, well, you see, the good thing about wasting so much time is that there's an awful lot of it to make up.'

With perfect timing the seat-belt sign pinged and before she knew what was happening, Jack had hauled her onto h lap and into his arms. 'Starting now,' he added, and pulled her against him.

Imogen laughed with delight, but when his mouth found hers and he kissed her with everything he felt her laughter died in her throat. She could feel his heart thundering in time with hers and she realised that, whatever else she wanted out of life, *this* was where she was meant to be. With Jack. In his arms. And she was never going to let him go again.

'By the way,' he murmured against her lips when they broke for air, 'I realise that you won't be wanting anything to distract you while you're studying, but, I think I should let you know in advance, the minute you graduate I'll be asking you to marry me.'

With her breathing all over the place, Imogen wrapped her arms tighter around his neck and went giddy with happiness. 'Will you?'

'It's a promise.'

# EPILOGUE

*Three years later*

ANY more of this awful tension, thought Imogen, and she'd explode. The restaurant was one of the best in New York, and the food was apparently sublime, but to be honest she'd barely taken any of it in.

And was it any wonder? How could she concentrate on food when all evening she'd felt as if she were sitting on knives?

'Well?' she said, looking at Jack and so about to burst with expectation that she was unable to stand it any longer.

Jack raised his eyebrows. 'Well, what?'

'I've just graduated,' she said, because, despite the celebratory dinner, it might need pointing out.

'And how.' He lifted his glass, clinked it against hers and gave her a proud smile. 'Top of the class. Congratulations. Again.'

'Thanks.' She nibbled on her lip. 'So... Is that it?'

Jack set his glass down and grinned. 'Only if you want it to be. If you didn't want to take up the position on the board you were offered, you'd have your pick of jobs.'

Imogen resisted the urge to give him a sharp kick under the table. 'That's not what I meant.'

He raised his eyebrows. 'Wasn't it?'

'No.'

'Then what did you mean?'

Jack looked baffled, as if he genuinely didn't have a clue what she was trying to get at, and her heart lurched.

Oh, God. Had he forgotten?

She stared at him as he gazed innocently back, her mind galloping. It had been three years since he'd made that promise on the plane, the one that had kept her going through the tough times when she'd struggled with her workload and had been tempted to throw it all in, but not once in all that time had he mentioned it again.

So what with time and the immense effort he'd put into establishing his business and working on his relationship with his father, he could well have forgotten.

Or been having second thoughts.

The high Imogen had been riding for days dipped for a moment and then she pulled herself together because, either way, she could hardly ask.

'Oh, nothing,' she said lightly, telling herself that it didn't really matter anyway. She didn't need a ring on her finger to know that Jack loved her. She had proof of it daily. 'Forget it.'

Flashing him an overly bright smile, she twisted round and rummaged in the handbag that hung off her chair, hiding her face just in case the disappointment had made its way there.

'You didn't really think I had, did you?'

At the teasing warmth in his voice, Imogen stilled. Her heart skipped a beat and for a moment she forgot how to breathe. Slowly, she lifted her head and turned round to face him. Jack was smiling the smile that melted her bones every time and suddenly everything that had been all wobbly and blurry swam back into focus and settled.

'Well, it has been a long time,' she said, letting out the breath that she'd been holding as her heart started beating again.

'Quite long enough.' He tilted his head and held out his hand. 'Is this what you were looking for?'

Her gaze dropped to the ring he was holding and she stared at the trilogy of diamonds flashing in the candlelight, her throat tightening with emotion and the backs of her eyes prickling. 'I was actually looking for my lipstick,' she said, and hiccupped.

Jack smiled gently. 'You know, your sense of humour is just one of the many, many things I love about you. I love your determination, your resilience and your patience. I love the way you put up with my flaws and make me a better man.' His smile turned wicked. 'I particularly love that thing you do with your—'

*'Jack,'* she interrupted with mock horror, and glanced round to check that no one was listening.

He laughed, then sobered. 'Imogen, darling,' he said, getting up and moving round to kneel beside her chair. 'I just adore you. Will you marry me?'

As happiness burst through her Imogen flung herself into his arms, smothered him in kisses and murmured, 'I thought you'd never ask.'

\* \* \* \* \*

# REDEMPTION OF A
# HOLLYWOOD STARLET

BY
KIMBERLY LANG

**Kimberly Lang** hid romance novels behind her textbooks in junior high, and even a Master's programme in English couldn't break her obsession with dashing heroes and happily-ever-after. A ballet dancer turned English teacher, Kimberly married an electrical engineer and turned her life into an ongoing episode of *When Dilbert Met Frasier*. She and her Darling Geek live in beautiful North Alabama, with their one Amazing Child—who, unfortunately, shows an aptitude for sports.

Visit Kimberly at www.booksbykimberly.com for the latest news—and don't forget to say hi while you're there!

Happy first birthday to James,
my gorgeous, brilliant and sweet nephew.

I have every confidence that you will
grow up to be a hero.

# CHAPTER ONE

HE'D only been gone for three weeks. When he'd left, everything for this film had been fine and in place, but a mere twenty-one days later he'd returned to find the entire project sliding into hell.

Finn Marshall sat back in his chair in the trailer that served as their temporary offices while they were on location here in Maryland and rubbed a hand over his eyes. He was jetlagged and had hoped to have a couple of hours of sleep before he had to be in D.C. for the fundraiser tonight, but that wasn't looking to be in his cards. He had to sort out this God-awful mess first, and the more he heard, the less likely it seemed he'd even make it to his brother's in time to shower first.

Dolby Martin, his partner in Dolfinn Pictures, seemed remarkably upbeat for someone who had just rammed the *Titanic* into the iceberg. "We've been filming for a week now, and we're almost back on schedule."

Finn took a deep breath and tried to remember it would do no good at all to punch Dolby in the mouth. "And you saw no reason to tell me any of this while it was unfolding?"

"You needed to concentrate on getting us those permissions to shoot, and really there was nothing you could do from Monaco, anyway."

"I could have talked Cindy down."

"After Farrell told her he'd seen better acting in low-budget porn? Sorry, Finn, not even you could have charmed that snake back into the basket." Dolby shrugged. "Personally, though, I wasn't sad to see her go. I'll bet Cindy's in rehab before the premiere, and would you really want *that* hanging over the release?"

Dolby had a point, as much as Finn hated to admit it. Cindy had been perfect for the part of Rebecca: the right looks and a strong talent, coupled with a name guaranteed to get attention without overshadowing the leads. She'd sworn that she was clean the day they'd signed the contract, but he'd seen this story too many times before.

Maybe it was for the best. Technically, Dolby and the director had done the right thing, finding a replacement quickly and getting her on the next plane to Baltimore so that production was not shut down for long. On a professional level, Finn should be pleased. He should even be personally touched that Dolby understood the importance of this film to him and had reacted quickly to mitigate the damages. But Cait Reese? He shook his head. *Focus on what's important.*

"Caitlyn has been a real life-saver and a complete pro. She had her script memorized in days and jumped straight into rehearsals. Wait until you see what we have in the can already. She's perfect for Rebecca. Better than Cindy, even."

Finn didn't necessarily agree. The Cait he remembered was too primal and wild. She'd been able to channel that into light frothy characters, but the earthy, quiet strength of Rebecca? It had been three years, but…

"Trust me, Finn. You're going to be really pleased."

"If you honestly believed that, you wouldn't have signed her to *Folly* behind my back." He picked up his phone and scrolled through the voice mail messages. "Naomi is fit to be tied. You want to hear?"

"I've heard enough, thanks. Naomi doesn't want to share her spotlight with anyone. She's a real diva."

"That's a privilege she's earned and one we'll tolerate to keep her happy on this film."

Naomi Harte was one of the biggest names in Hollywood right now, and based on star power alone she had no reason to worry about anyone stealing any of her limelight. But this was personal for Naomi, too. She and Cait had launched at about the same time, and their rivalry went back to the years when they'd both still been playing teenagers in high-school romantic comedies and slasher films. Cait had always managed to stay a rung above Naomi on the ladder, though, her trajectory seemingly unstoppable until she'd flamed out so spectacularly. Many people said that Naomi wouldn't be where she was today if Cait hadn't left town when she had—and Naomi knew that. They were probably right.

"You know there's bad blood between Naomi and Cait. Did you intend to turn the set into a battlefield?"

Dolby snickered. "It's actually working out well. Naomi's real-life problems with Caitlyn make their on-screen animosity even more realistic."

"And Cait?" She wasn't one to keep her mouth closed or her opinions to herself.

"Is being far more adult about this. Caitlyn has been very up front about her desire to re-create herself and relaunch her career. *Folly* is the perfect vehicle for her return, and she's not too proud to admit that."

*Folly* might be perfect for Cait, but Cait might not be perfect for *Folly*. He wasn't in the business of providing starlets with second chances. Especially with a project like *Folly*. He had too much invested—professionally and personally—to let this become some kind of experiment.

"I'm still not sure Cait is the smart choice here."

"I gave Farrell full directory discretion to find the right person for the role *and* make sure it was someone he could tolerate. Caitlyn was his choice, and unless she decides she wants out of her contract we're bound." Dolby shook his head in censure. "*I'm* not courting her parents' wrath because you don't want your ex on the set. I like my career, thanks very much."

Talk about having the tables turned. All his life he'd been the one no one wanted to cross out of fear of retaliation from his family. That was simply one of the perks of being a Marshall. But the Marshalls ruled the East Coast. In L.A., John Reese and Margaret Fields-Reese were the sitting monarchy. It wasn't false pride or ego to say that *he* was pretty damn influential in the business, but even he couldn't touch the power of Cait's parents. One day, maybe, but not today.

"Anyway," Dolby continued, "all reports indicate that Caitlyn is sober and stable now."

Caitlyn had never had a problem—beyond partying a little too hard—and he wasn't one to throw stones there. The press had just played it up until she'd looked like a good candidate for rehab in order to sell papers. She'd been all but set up to crash if she slipped even the tiniest bit. "I'm sure she is, but that won't stop the press from going insane with this."

Dolby's grin didn't help Finn's mood much. "The buzz is amazing. Between the return of the exiled princess and the possibility of a Naomi-Caitlyn catfight, everyone is talking about *Folly* already."

"That's not what I meant and you know it."

Dolby laughed. "You have to admit the possibility of a Finn and Caitlyn reunion will make all kinds of headlines."

"Which is exactly why you should have consulted me before you signed her."

"If we have to avoid your exes every time we try to cast a film, pretty soon there won't be an actress under thirty available to us."

*But Cait wasn't just any ex.* She was the one ex that made all his other exes look like good choices. The bitterness surprised him. "I don't want my personal life making more news than this project."

That sobered Dolby. "*Folly* will stand on its own."

Dolby was an idiot occasionally, but he, too, took pride in Dolfinn's reputation. *The Folly of the Fury* might be Finn's pet project, but Dolby was committed one hundred percent.

"I know it will, but since we just stepped into soap-opera-waiting-to-happen territory, I want everyone crystal-clear in their understanding of what will and won't fly around here. All the drama needs to be kept on camera."

"Agreed."

Finn sincerely hoped it would be that simple.

Caitlyn Reese breathed the humid night air deep into her lungs as the door swung shut behind her and the noise and lights of the party inside died as if she'd hit a mute button. She'd done well in there—she knew that—but she needed a few moments of relief from the stress of the evening. Looking around, she was happy to see that the terrace was deserted—not that she was surprised. Between the heat and the fact that anybody who was anyone was inside… The air-conditioning inside was almost worth the noise, but she crossed to the balustrade, anyway, and leaned against it as she exhaled.

She chuckled to herself when she realized her hands weren't quite steady. She'd been mingling at cocktail parties since before she could walk, so there was no real reason to let a simple fundraiser—regardless of the prestige of the guest list—to give her stage fright. And the crowd was friendly enough. Whatever they might think of her personally, no one was stupid enough to do anything that might limit their access to her parents and her parents' friends. There was way too much Hollywood money they'd like to see in their campaign coffers at stake for anyone to treat her with anything other than friendly respect.

Maybe a D.C. charity fundraiser peopled by the city's social register was exactly the right place for her to make her first official reappearance. Her plan was working out better than hoped for. She wanted to call someone and share her success, but she wasn't exactly close with anyone on this continent anymore, and it was the middle of the night in London. Her parents both happened to have releases this month, so they were on their respective junkets and she had no idea what their schedules were like. Even if she did have someone to call, she wasn't sure what she'd say. *My career may not be dead anymore?* Oh, well. She shrugged and smiled. *She* was still proud of herself.

"Miss Reese?"

Caitlyn turned to see that she wasn't alone now. The tall blond man she'd been speaking to earlier was approaching her with a cautious smile on his face. She racked her brain for his name. He worked for one of the congressmen, and he was a big fan of her parents' work, knew all of her movies... Bits of their conversation came back to her, but not his name. He'd been a little over-enthusiastic, bordering on creepy, and the fact they were now quite alone didn't sit well.

*Be nice, but not too nice.* "Hi, again."

"I saw you leaving." His forehead crinkled in concern. "Are you all right?"

"I'm fine. I just needed a little air. It's a little crowded in there."

He nodded. "It's a good turnout, so that's good for the fundraising part. But it does make it hard to really talk to people." The man stepped a little closer than was comfortable. Caitlyn eased back a step herself. "And I very much enjoyed talking to you."

She nodded slightly, not wanting to encourage him with anything more.

"In fact, I'd like to take you to dinner so we can get to know each other better."

Caitlyn kept her face neutral even as alarm bells began to clang faintly. *Don't overreact. Give him the benefit of the doubt.* She took another step back, anyway. "My schedule is quite tight, I'm afraid."

"How about tonight, then, since you're already here. There's a nice bistro not far away…"

She shook her head. *This shouldn't be happening here.* The guest list was very exclusive and supposedly kept situations like this from even coming up. "I'm sorry, but I can't."

He was not to be deterred by the gentle brush-off, though. Maybe she was overreacting, but the alarm bells rang louder as he leaned closer and she smelled the alcohol on his breath.

"Then we'll talk here."

"Actually, I was just about to go back inside when you caught me." She picked up her purse and indicated they should walk. "Shall we?"

"Miss Reese…" He didn't take the hint, so she moved past him. "Caitlyn, wait, damn it."

She was two steps past him when he caught her arm and tried to stop her with a too-tight-to-be-casual grip. At that moment he crossed the line. Her training kicked in, and a second later he was on his knees whimpering in pain from the way Caitlyn had his fingers pulled back. "Do *not* touch me. We don't know each other well enough for that, so it's quite rude."

"I just wanted to talk to you."

She tightened her grip just enough to make him gasp and understand that she was serious. "That's not going to happen. You're going to go back inside so that I don't have to have you arrested for assault and make a scene in front of all those people."

At his nod of assent she released his fingers and he flexed

his fingers experimentally. "No need to be such a bitch about it."

This was not what she'd signed on for tonight. "Go away. I'm done talking to you." She stepped away and pinned him with a stare that hopefully would convince him she meant business. The adrenaline pumping through her system left her shaky but energized.

"Caitlyn…"

"I think Cait was very clear in her instructions. I suggest you do as you were told."

The voice hit her like a brick wall. Her stomach sank at the same time electricity sizzled up her spine. *Damn, damn, damn.* This was *not* how she'd planned on seeing him again.

Maybe it wasn't him. It had been three years; she'd probably just confused his voice with a stranger's. She'd been tense about seeing him, and her mind was surely just playing tricks on her. *Because anything else would just be really unfair.* Holding on to that hope, Caitlyn looked over her shoulder as the owner of the voice emerged from the shadows.

Finn.

*Great.* What had she done to karma to deserve this? She just seemed destined to have Finn a part of all the times of her life she'd just like to forget.

At least Finn wouldn't blab about what he'd just witnessed to the papers. It was a small consolation, and Caitlyn grabbed on to it like a life raft in the swirl of emotions and memories that low, rich voice stirred up.

She could tell the guy—she still couldn't remember his name—recognized Finn, which wasn't surprising since Finn garnered almost as much press as the stars in the films he produced. And, of course, everyone on the planet knew about her past with Finn. The double whammy for her admirer, though, had to come from Finn's family ties: smart people didn't make enemies of the Marshalls. *Especially* if they wanted any kind of future in politics. They were simply too powerful a family to mess with.

But this guy, proving again he wasn't the sharpest knife in the drawer, got belligerent instead. "This is a private conversation, if you don't mind."

"Oh, I mind." Disdain dripped off Finn's words.

The men sized each other up, and Caitlyn couldn't help but do the same. She hadn't exactly forgotten Finn—how could she?—but reality was slapping her in the face now. Finn could give his leading men a run for their money when it came to heartthrob status. He had strong, aristocratic features made less harsh by a deep tan earned from his love of all things outdoors. His dark blond hair had sun-bleached lighter streaks, and, as always, it had that casual windblown look that all men who weren't Finn had to work hard to achieve. The dim light made it hard to see the color of his eyes, but she knew how their deep green could suck a girl in and melt her insides.

Finn had a good four inches in height on her admirer and, while both men were lean, he looked athletic and strong even in his suit. He might have the bluest of blue blood in his veins, but he had an edge that belied the DNA—not enough to make him look out of place in the throng of political and social elite inside, but it certainly set him apart.

It made the red-faced young man look ridiculous even trying to match up. He just fell short all the way around.

And his scowl was nothing compared to Finn's.

Which brought her nicely back to the real problem at hand. Finn had an odd gallant streak when it came to damsels in distress. At the right time it could be endearing—sweet, even—but this was not the right time for Finn to channel his inner caveman.

"I distinctly heard Cait tell you she was done talking. Do you really need to resort to assault?"

What's-his-name bristled visibly. Lord, the man was too

stupid to realize the danger lurking behind Finn's controlled cadence. *She* knew better, though, and launched into damage control before this got worse. "That was just a—"

"I know what that was, Cait," Finn snapped. He took her arm and moved her a few feet farther away, putting himself between her and the man like a bodyguard. He looked her up and down, then asked quietly, "Are you okay?"

"She's fine," the other man answered testily. "It's just a misunderstanding."

Finn's green eyes flicked in his direction. He obviously wasn't impressed with the man. "I didn't ask you."

He puffed up like a blowfish and Finn squared his shoulders. With all the testosterone in the air, this was about to get ugly.

Caitlyn cleared her throat. "I'm fine, Finn, thanks. And I would like us to all go our separate ways now so that this just remains between the three of us. There's a lot of press and a lot of people inside who don't need to be party to this."

Finn's eyes narrowed as he looked her over. "Are you sure?"

She nodded and saw Finn un-bow his shoulders a little bit as he released her arm. "Fine. No sense embarrassing you unnecessarily."

*Thank goodness.* "I'd appreciate that."

He turned to the other man, who seemed to get younger and weaker-looking as each second ticked by. "Go."

He shot them both a dirty look, then stalked away. She heard the noise of the crowd inside as the door opened, and then silence, blissful silence, broken only by the sound of the traffic on DuPont Circle, settled over the balcony again.

Caitlyn moved to sit on the bench against the balustrade and sighed as she pushed her hair back from her face. She needed a minute to get herself back together. First that guy, then Finn... It was all a little too much to process in such a short time.

"What the hell were you thinking, Cait?"

The heat in his voice hit her like a slap across the face. "Excuse me?"

Finn stood in front of her and crossed his arms over his chest. She could see the muscle in his jaw twitching. "What were you doing out here alone? Where's the damn security?"

How dare he jump on her over this? She gritted her teeth to hold her temper in check. "They're probably inside with everyone else—which is kind of the point, because I wanted a moment *alone*."

"Have you lost your mind? You don't get to decide to be 'alone' in a place like this."

"A place like this? It's a cocktail party, Finn, not a drug den. A 'place like this' should be the one place I *can* grab a minute to myself without worry."

Finn didn't seem to hear her. He was too busy glaring. "Then when some guy assaults you you try to arm wrestle him yourself instead of calling for help?"

"Like anyone would have heard me inside even if I did." Finn's eyes narrowed and the thin thread holding her temper snapped. Anger surged through her. "*I* didn't want to make a scene. And you'll please note I had the situation under control just fine before you even made your entrance." She lifted her chin. "If you want to play the hero, you might want to work on your timing."

He frowned. "You should know better."

"Why do you care?"

Finn's eyebrows went up, but before he could answer a door opened and three people came out to the balcony. They passed without speaking, but Caitlyn felt her face flush, anyway. She did *not* need to be seen in a shouting match with Finn. The list of things she didn't need was growing longer each day. Maybe signing on to this project wasn't the best idea, after all.

*No. Folly is perfect. It's a gift, so don't screw it up.* And, since Finn was running this project, she'd have to swallow her anger and pride and act like a professional.

Caitlyn forced herself to smile. "However, I appreciate your concern and will keep your warnings in mind for the future."

*There.* That was the proper thing to say to set the right tone for their future working relationship. She was pleased she'd made the effort. The look on Finn's face was just a bonus.

She thought he might be about to say something more, but Finn just shrugged, a signature movement showing that this was no longer worth his time. "So, who was that guy, anyway?"

She looked around. While more people had drifted onto the terrace, no one seemed to be paying them undue attention. She had to quit worrying so much about that. There was nothing attention-worthy about her and Finn speaking together. They had to: they were coworkers, colleagues working on *Folly*. There was nothing remotely scandalous about the two of them *talking*.

At a respectable distance from each other, of course.

"I don't know his name. All I really know is that he's a fan of the whole Reese clan and that he works for someone in Congress." The eyebrow that went up told her that Finn would be able to provide a name shortly, and she almost felt a touch of sympathy for the young man. "We spoke briefly inside. Obviously that wasn't enough for him."

"Obviously."

"I think he's had a couple of drinks, and we all do stupid things after we've had a couple of drinks, you know." Finn seemed to agree to that with a minuscule tilt of his head, and she blew out her breath in a long sigh.

"Are you sure you're all right?"

"I'm fine, Finn, really. It was a surprise, but that's all. I appreciate your rescue, but I doubt he would have pressed it much further. I probably just overreacted. Either way, I think I managed to convince him that I'm serious."

Finn chuckled and the sound rolled over her like a remembered caress. "If not, he's amazingly dense. Nice moves, by the way."

"Thanks. After that thing with Mom's stalker two years ago, she and Dad made me take some self-defense classes and work with a trainer. It's the first time I've ever had to put it to the test, though. Things were different in London. Fewer people knew who I was, so the weirdo potential was way down. It was a wake-up call I probably needed."

"Hell of a way to be welcomed home."

She swallowed as Finn came to sit next to her. There was still a respectable distance separating them, but that didn't stop her heart-rate from jumping up a notch. *Speaking of being welcomed home...* She'd thought about this moment a thousand times, planned a million witty and clever things to say that would put their past behind them, show she'd moved on and had her career firmly back on track. All those clever words eluded her now, damn it. But she had to say something or else look like an idiot.

She looked around, appreciating the dim quiet of the terrace and the view of D.C. beyond. A full moon topped the Washington Monument like a candle flame. "Beautiful view." *Well, that wasn't exactly inspired.*

Based on the slight twitch at the corner of his mouth, Finn agreed with that assessment. "Indeed."

"This is my first time in D.C., believe it or not. I'm hoping to have some time to do a little sightseeing."

"If you want tours of the Capitol or the White House let

Liz know. She can call my father's office and get it arranged for you."

She swallowed her shock. Finn rarely acknowledged his paternity, so the casual mention of Senator Marshall came straight from left field. Or maybe Finn and his father were on better terms now. Things could have changed. "I appreciate that."

This all seemed so normal. Two people sitting on a terrace, chatting. But it wasn't normal. This was *Finn*, and the proverbial gorilla sat between them, so the situation made her jumpy instead. Finn, though, seemed to be willing to ignore the past—or at least pretend that they were friendly strangers—so she was enough of an adult to do the same. If he wasn't going to bring it up, she should just thank her lucky stars and do the same.

"I didn't expect you to be here tonight." That was only partly true. She'd known there was a chance he'd be here; Dolfinn Pictures supported the summer camp program, after all. Because of that, the cast of *Folly* had come in an attempt to bring more attention to the fundraiser. But Finn normally avoided D.C. like the plague, *and* he'd been in Monaco for the last three weeks. Donor or not, the chances of him showing up had been slim. This kind of event wasn't Finn's idea of a good time. His scene was still more club than cocktail.

"Well, I have to put in an occasional appearance at things to keep the Grands happy."

Finn's grandmother sat on the board, and both she and her husband, the legendary Senator Marshall, were here tonight. Porter Marshall had held the office for decades before retiring and handing it over to his son, Finn's father.

The former senator was far more personable than Caitlyn had expected, and when she'd learned this evening that *The Folly of the Fury* was his favorite book, they'd had a lovely conversation about the importance of the book and character of Rebecca. Mrs. Marshall, though… *That* had been a slightly uncomfortable moment: although they'd never met at the time, Regina Marshall obviously recognized Caitlyn's name from before. While she hadn't been anything other than polite, Caitlyn had the sneaking feeling she was on probation with the regal matriarch of this powerful family.

Which was fine, because Caitlyn had no intention of screwing this up.

She had way too much on the line.

# CHAPTER TWO

CAIT was acting strangely, which didn't make sense—or bode well for future work on *Folly*.

He'd sought her out tonight intentionally, wanting to get a clear-eyed assessment of who she was these days and whether or not she was going to make filming a personal hell for him. Dolby was the one who'd pointed him toward the terrace. The scene he'd walked in on, though…

He'd recognized the situation immediately for what it was, but hadn't known it was Cait until she'd had the man on his knees crying for mercy. He'd recognized her voice before the man even said her name—he'd had that irritated, clipped tone directed at him too many times to forget it. Then the details had hit him all at once: that coppery-blond hair that had kept hairdressers in business recreating the color on an entire generation of women, those long legs showcased by her signature stilettos, even the newly acquired curve of her hips that showed she wasn't starving herself anymore to fit the starlet mold.

The shock of seeing her had delayed his reaction time, and it had been over before he'd recovered. That was bad enough, but his *physical* reaction at seeing Cait again didn't sit well on top of everything else, and he'd let his anger loose on her. It was only his pride that had had him pulling it together to carry on a normal conversation.

Because he was not going to let Cait wreak her special blend of havoc on his life again. He'd learned his lesson there. He would keep this casual and professional if it killed him. He could be the bigger person.

"Are you ready to go back in?"

Cait seemed to be thinking very hard about a seemingly simple question. Finally, she shook her head. "Not just yet. I think I need another minute to cool down some and get myself together."

"It might have been fun to watch you break his fingers, though."

She seemed to consider that. "No. There are too many witnesses in there, too many cameras." She shrugged casually, but there was a wry smile of resignation on her face. "I don't need that kind of publicity this soon. Plus, it's tacky to start a fistfight at a cocktail party. Believe it or not, I *was* raised better than that."

At least her humor seemed to be returning. It was a long-standing joke between them: was the child of Hollywood royalty expected to behave better or worse than a child from political royalty? Using only the tabloids as their judge and jury, they'd never been able to come to a definitive answer as to how high or low the expectations really were.

And they'd certainly tested those expectations. Repeatedly.

He couldn't help but smile at the memory. "I could hit him for you."

She wrinkled her nose. "That's kind of you—and tempting—but I'm going to think positive thoughts that he's learned his lesson. The funny thing is that I think that might have been more about my folks than me. He seemed pretty interested in their political leanings and pet causes."

He understood now. Cait's connections—and all that Hollywood money—could be very valuable to an aspiring politician, and that guy had "congressional wannabe" written all over him. "Welcome back to the business."

She shot him a pissy look. "I never totally left, you know. Just because I haven't been working in Hollywood, it doesn't mean I haven't been working."

"On the *stage*. It's hardly the same thing."

Her eyes narrowed. "Don't start. I'm not going to get into that argument with you." She seemed to catch herself and her face cleared, and a wickedly innocent smile took the place of irritation. "But I'm rather flattered to hear that you've been keeping up with my career. That's rather sweet. I had no idea you cared."

Her tone rankled. There was no way he was going to let her go there. "Just because I wasn't consulted before you were brought on board, don't think for a second that I haven't verified you can actually pull this off. This film is my responsibility, and Rebecca falls outside *your* known range."

Cait's jaw tightened. *Oh, he'd hit a nerve with that one.*

She recovered quickly, though. She always did. She stood and stepped away from the bench before turning on him. "You know, if you spent more time actually working, and less time playing beach blanket bingo in Europe, you might not have to find out what's happening with your own projects after the fact."

The disdain in her voice chased off any desire he'd had to play nice. Where did Cait get off acting all high and mighty? "So you've been keeping up with my love life? That's kind of…sad, actually."

"Oh, please. Would you get over yourself? The last thing I care about is who you're sleeping with now. I'm here for one reason and one reason only. I want my career back."

He started to answer, but stopped short as a thought crystallized. Cait had been out of the spotlight for years; she wasn't exactly a hot commodity at the moment—famous parents or not. *Folly* was a great place to prove her skills, but it wouldn't do much to restore her to the fame and glory she'd once called her "birthright." Hadn't he and Dolby *just* discussed the headline possibilities today? A bad feeling crept over him. Maybe that was part of her plan. What better way to make the cover of every magazine and have her name on everyone's lips than to work that very Finn-and-Caitlyn angle he'd just laid plans to avoid.

"Oh, I don't know about that. It seems like a hell of a good way to make your comeback with a bang, doesn't it?"

He hadn't thought it would be possible for Cait to get any stiffer, but she did. With her arms crossed over her chest, she lifted her chin again until she was practically looking down her nose at him—something she could only do while he was seated.

"What *exactly* do you mean by that?"

"Being within fifty feet of me assures you every headline you want, doesn't it?" With a casualness he didn't really feel, but would grate on Cait's nerves regardless, he leaned back against the railing and stacked his hands behind his head. "Once upon a time, you claimed I was good for your Q Score. Looking for a second bite of the apple, Caity?"

Her eyes narrowed. "Your ego is simply unbelievable, Finn. Believe it or not, this is not about *you*. In fact, the very last thing I need—or want—is the kind of headlines you bring. I've grown up, worked damn hard to improve my craft *and* cleaned up my image. I take my job seriously." She eyed him with something he could only call distaste. "Since you can't say the same, why don't you just go back to Monaco until this is in the can? *That* would be very helpful for my comeback."

Oh, he'd definitely hit a nerve. Anger flushed her cheeks, and she gripped her tiny purse until her knuckles turned white.

"Now, if you'll excuse me, I have an early call in the

morning and should probably get some sleep." With that, she stalked away, head held high, and wrenched open the door to the ballroom to disappear inside.

Cait still liked to get the last word. Blaming him and storming off in a huff was her usual M.O., so that much hadn't changed. It was practically a repeat of that last night at his place. Everything had been his fault. Never hers.

He, however, had to think about bigger issues than Cait's temper. Too many people were involved in *Folly*. Money and reputations were at stake. And he would not let Granddad's glee at having *Folly* made be dampened by Cait and her possible dramatics. He would keep this project in line even if he had to kill people to get it done.

Finn gave himself a hard mental shake. He had to be rational about this. In the long run, Cait might prove to be a good choice for *Folly*. If she could pull off Rebecca, her name and potential star power could boost *Folly*'s box office revenues and award chances.

That didn't mean it was going to be less of a hellish mess in the meantime, though.

Caitlyn closed her door against the heat and spread her arms to embrace the icy chill of the air-conditioned trailer. Yesterday she'd neglected to crank the thermostat down before she left and had come back to a trailer almost as hot as the outdoors. But today... *Bliss, cool bliss.*

Her sweaty skin felt better almost immediately, and she peeled off the dress sticking to her back and hung it in the closet. Another thing she loved about this role: the fashions of the Forties were flattering and feminine and made it easy to really embrace Rebecca's character. In this heat, she was very glad *Folly* wasn't set in an era where she'd have to wear corsets and mountainous dresses. If so, she'd be battling heatstroke about now.

In just her underwear, she went to the fridge for a bottle of water. She left the door open while she took a drink, letting the cool air from inside wash over her.

She'd been in London too long, gotten used to what they amusingly called "summer" and forgotten how stinking hot and humid summer could really be in some parts of the country.

Walter Farrell had been an assistant director under her father for many years, and had learned his philosophy about authenticity from the master. Like her father, Walter felt being in a similar setting—like this insufferable heat and humidity—would help the actors really connect with the characters, but Cait was rapidly developing sympathy for all the actors who'd worked with her father. Especially on that one film set in the jungle...

But, honestly, she didn't care how much she sweated for this part. Caitlyn lay back on her small couch and fanned her face with her script. It wasn't false pride or inflated ego to say that this was possibly the best performance of her life. She was working with a stellar cast, Hollywood's best director—or at least second-best, she amended out of filial loyalty—and a crew that blew her away.

This was the life and the career she was supposed to have. It had just taken her a while to find the right path. She'd been given her second chance, and the only thing that really mattered was where she went from here.

She'd risk that heatstroke happily.

The only fly in her happy ointment was Finn. The rational pep talks she'd given herself about being an adult and leaving things in the past had turned to gibberish within just a few minutes of actually seeing him. It hadn't been her finest moment, that was for sure, but what had she really expected? The last time she'd seen him, she'd been hurt and angry, hurling ridiculous accusations at him because she hadn't been able to analyze, much less articulate, what she was really feeling.

She yawned and closed her eyes. Makeup had had a hard time covering the bags under her eyes this morning. She'd intended to call her mom today, but a nap seemed a more prudent use of her time since she still had several hours of filming to do tonight.

A 5:00 a.m. alarm was never fun, but she'd spent a good portion of the night staring at the ceiling as she tried to sort through the morass of conflicting emotions caused by seeing Finn. Of course the few hours she'd managed to finally sleep had been haunted by dreams that left her restless. Dreams of Finn.

Damn him for being so tactless. Why couldn't he be like normal people and politely ignore topics best left to die? Oh, no… He had to bring up personal junk in a professional situation.

And *that* was what she wanted to avoid at all costs. If she could, she'd give the entire planet amnesia so everyone would completely forget what had happened three years ago.

Too bad she couldn't give herself amnesia as well.

Good times, bad times… They weren't really classifiable as either. They were just "Finn Times"—fun and exciting at the time, but in retrospect not the wisest of choices and not an experience she'd like to repeat.

The residual tingle from last night's dreams rather belied those thoughts, but Caitlyn purposefully pushed those aside. Finn was tempting—very tempting—but she couldn't risk everything she'd worked for. *Eyes on the prize.*

But she would have to come to some kind of understanding with Finn. She'd accept her fair share of the blame, but that didn't mean she could just forgive and forget. Until last night she'd thought she was over it, but it hadn't taken long for all the old hurt to come rushing back.

*Damn him.*

She'd had more than her fair share of failed relationships—both before and after Finn—so why did Finn alone have the power to make her hurt?

Wallowing in the past would get her nowhere. She had to concentrate on now. Ignoring each other or acting hostile would be just as likely to attract attention and gossip. She could get through this...

A knock interrupted her drowsy thoughts. So much for that nap. She called, "Come in!" and reached for her water bottle.

"Stunning outfit, Cait."

Her eyes flew open in surprise, confirming that Finn was, indeed, in her trailer, and it took a second for the meaning of his words to actually register. Once they did... *Damn it.* Face hot, Caitlyn jumped up from the couch and grabbed the robe hanging on the bathroom door. Keeping her back to him, she shoved her arms through the sleeves. Granted, the old-fashioned underwear covered more than her bathing suit normally did, but that didn't change the fact she was wearing nothing but underwear and Finn was in her trailer. *Kill me now.*

She took extra time tying the belt to give herself a chance to regain her composure, but the chuckle coming from behind her didn't help. "I wasn't expecting you."

"I'm afraid to ask who you *were* expecting, then."

She refused to dignify that with a response. "Can I help you with something, Finn?"

"I thought we should talk." Finn dropped a stack of papers on the table before crossing to the fridge and looking inside. Her hackles went up at his nonchalant attitude.

"Fine. If you'll just wait outside, I'll get some clothes on—"

An eyebrow went up. "No need to be so modest, you know." *It's nothing I haven't seen before* hung in the a

*That* knowledge didn't help her much at all. But then, Finn had probably seen so many women naked in his life maybe he'd have difficulty remembering exactly which bits were hers.

Not that she was having any trouble remembering *his*. Her skin heated. Oh, he was decently enough dressed today, in jeans and a simple black tee that fit snugly against his body, but memories of what lay under those clothes…

"Regardless, I'd rather you wait outside and we go somewhere to talk."

Finn pulled a bottle out and offered it to her. When she shook her head, he unscrewed the cap and took a long drink. Then he sat instead of leaving. She had to wonder if he was being difficult intentionally.

"Why can't we talk here? It's hot out there."

She pulled the robe tighter across her chest and wished it covered a bit more thigh. "I'd rather not."

Finn's exasperated look was almost funny. "What is *with* you, Caity?"

"Nothing. I just don't think it's a good idea for us to be seen meeting privately in my trailer. It's…inappropriate and might be misconstrued." *Ugh*, she sounded like a virgin schoolteacher.

Finn's look said the same thing. "You're not serious?"

"As you helpfully noted last night, my being within fifty feet of you will be enough to send the paparazzi into a frenzy. I'd rather not give them more to feed on." She went to the closet and grabbed jeans and tee shirt and waited for him to leave.

Finn ignored the hint, so she frowned at him to make her point. He gave her a look that questioned her mental stability instead, so she took her clothes to the bathroom and closed the door to get dressed.

"I'm afraid it won't take even that much," he called through the door.

"Exactly," she shouted back. "As soon as we're seen to-gether—however innocent it may be—all those old, embarrassing pictures of us are going to resurface. I can't live all that down as old news if there's speculation there's new news."

Now decent, she came out and opened the shades on every window, giving anyone who walked by a clear view of what was going on inside. She'd have opened the door, but that would have just let the heat in. She wasn't willing to go that far. Propriety would just have to be served by open shades.

As she took her seat on the far side of the table, Finn snorted. "You're taking this a little far, don't you think?"

"I'm just cautious. You may not give a damn about appearances, but I do."

"How kind of you to worry about me." The smirk told her he was deliberately misinterpreting her words.

"Only to the extent that your reputation will impugn mine. I think we've proved that you can raise hell and people will still respect you, but I can't. It's a horrible double standard, so I've worked very, very hard to clean up my act." She picked up her water and drank deeply. After two disastrous starts, she really needed to bring her interactions with Finn back to the business they had in common. And *only* that. "So, what brings you by, Finn?"

He chuckled, and it put her on guard. "That very topic, actually."

"Your reputation?"

"Paparazzi, speculation, new news…"

That was odd. Those were the top three things Finn normally didn't even deign to give five minutes of his time t He *really* didn't care about tabloid gossip.

A warning tingled up her spine, but she forced her

to remain merely curious and clasped her hands together to keep them still. "Okay."

"After meeting with Dolby and Farrell this morning, we've decided to close the set for the rest of filming. Considering our past, they agreed it might be disruptive or distracting to have to worry about uncontrolled press for the next five weeks."

She held up a hand. "Wait." Barring any disasters, they'd be finished filming here by then. They shouldn't have to close the set permanently unless… *Damn.* She tried to keep her voice just this side of mildly curious. "You're not going back to L.A.?"

"No. Dolby will head back with the second unit tomorrow."

A headache began to form behind her right eye. "But why?"

"Because."

She waited for him to elaborate, but there was only silence. The man could be so unbelievably frustrating. She rubbed her temples. *Ugh.* "So you'll be here through the end?"

"Yep. Do you have a problem with that?" he challenged.

"No," she lied. She had a big problem with that. Multiple big problems. *You're an actress. You'll just have to* act *like it's not a problem.* "Do you?"

Finn looked completely unconcerned. In fact, he seemed to be biting back a smile. "Not at all."

"Okay, then." She took a deep breath. She, too, could play this game. "I'm glad you closed the set. I'd like to concentrate on my job. Not worrying about the press will make that easier. For all of us," she added.

"Unfortunately we're a little late for that."

That warning tingle took on an unpleasant sharp edge. As ɪnn pulled a couple of pieces of paper out of the stack and ːhed them toward her, that edge cut deep into her skin.

ˑictures printed from a blog. *Oh, no.* Caitlyn's stomach

sank. He first thought was that some blogger had already dug up old pictures of her dancing on tables and being carried out of bars by Finn. Or, even worse, that one picture of her and Finn on his motorcycle, her skirt hiked up too far and Finn's hand…

She didn't recognize the pictures, but the relief that flooded in was short-lived. There *had* been witnesses last night, after all. Damn. A picture of Finn and that guy staring each other down, another of her and Finn sitting on the bench, and another of her walking away, anger written across her face and irritation stamped on Finn's. She didn't need to read the accompanying text to add to the ill feeling rolling through her stomach.

"Already? Geez."

"I'd say welcome back, but—"

"I'd have to kill you if you did." Caitlyn took a deep breath and blew it out. "Are you sure you can't swap things around and go back to L.A.? Just let me get this film done without dealing with that kind of garbage?"

"No. And it would only postpone the inevitable, anyway." He looked at her oddly. "I mean, you *do* plan to move back to L.A. and start working again, right?"

"That's the plan. I'd hoped to have *Folly* under my belt, though, first. Something for people to talk about other than just my past."

His eyes widened. "So you really *don't* want that kind of publicity?"

Finally something she'd said was sinking in. "God, no."

"It made you a household name."

That reminder was unnecessary. She'd spent the last thr years trying to change that association. "And it nearly stroyed me—personally as well as professionally."

Finn shook his head. "I don't think it was that bad

The heat had made her grouchy, he'd given her a he

she hadn't slept well, and this entire day was now sucking with the strength of a black hole.

She lost her grip on her temper. "Well, you aren't widely known for your thinking skills, you know," she snapped.

Finn didn't bite back, and his cocky smile made her want to smack him. "Admit it. We had a good time."

*Not even under the pain of torture would she admit that.* It didn't matter now. She forced herself to keep her face neutral. "That was a long time ago. I'm not that girl anymore."

"What a pity." He smirked and took another drink.

Her jaw tightened so much it ached. *I will not take the bait. He's trying to get a rise out of me.* Why, she didn't quite know—other than his perverse sense of humor. She took a deep breath. "I guess I'll just solider through, then. You're right that I'll eventually have to face it, so I might as well start now." She rubbed her palms against her thighs. "You do your job and I'll do mine, and the ensuing boring lack of anything tabloid-worthy will set me up for a return to respectability. And when this film does well I should be solidly set."

"I watched yesterday's rushes. They're great. Really powerful stuff from you."

The compliment came out of nowhere, shocking her into silence while at the same time warming her. More than it really should. It made her slightly suspicious, too. Finn had always been quick with compliments on her appearance or a new dress, but never anything deeper.

"Thank you. Rebecca is a wonderful character. My mom even said she wishes she was thirty years younger so she could have read for the part."

Finn met her eyes over the table. "I can honestly say that, in the choice between you and your mother to be Rebecca, I choose you."

Shock and disbelief warred with a strange swelling in her chest. There was nothing he could have said that would have meant more to her, and she knew he knew it. The suspicion sharpened, but while Finn might be glib occasionally, he was also brutally, unflinchingly honest when it came to the business. The air felt weighty after his statement, and the silence between them was thick.

Caitlyn managed to find her breath and shrug casually. "But after Cindy Burke, of course."

Finn's lips twitched. Then, with a speed that had her rushing to catch up, he turned very businesslike. "There have been a few tweaks made to the schedule. As you know, we're a bit behind, and don't want this to drag on forever. There are some long days ahead."

She nodded.

"We'd also like for you to make a few more appearances to drum up publicity in the right places."

The cautious edge to his voice jerked her eyes to his. "With you?"

"God, no. I said the *right* places."

Caitlyn would have been relieved if not for the horror in Finn's voice. So much for any warm, fuzzy feelings he might have stirred up. Or any other equally warm, yet not at all fuzzy ones, either. She glanced at the list Finn passed her.

One name was conspicuously absent. "And Naomi?"

"Naomi has her own schedule and agenda."

She leaned back and sighed. This was juvenile high-school stuff on Naomi's part. "In other words she doesn't want to share her headlines. Especially with me. She never did."

"Naomi isn't stupid. She has a career to protect."

"Like I could do any damage to her. Like I ever *did*. The only person I dragged down was me."

"But you still managed to overshadow her."

"For all the wrong reasons, it seems." She shrugged. "F you know, I crashed and burned, and she got what she wa I don't know why she carries a grudge."

That eyebrow went up again. "And you don't?"

There was more than one way to interpret that statement, and Caitlyn didn't want to get dragged back into a discussion of them. She chose to go with the subject of Naomi. "No. Naomi thinks this is a zero-sum game. She doesn't think there's room for us both in the papers. I know that's not the case."

A second, closer look at the schedule sent a chill down her spine. "What in the hell is *this* about?"

Finn shrugged. "The PR people want to shift attention from just you to you and Jason. Maybe get a couple of folks questioning whether you two are becoming a couple. It will shift focus nicely away from us." His lips twitched. "And a romance blooming on the set with your on-screen love is a perfect way to kill two birds."

*Ugh.* Was she destined to have to make a name for herself based on who she was—or supposedly was—dating? While Naomi got to keep the attention on the project and her role? It was degrading. It left a really bad taste in her mouth. "That's a cheap ploy."

If Finn didn't stop shrugging in that who-gives-a-damn? way she might strangle him. As it was, she was grinding her teeth into a pulp to keep from shouting at him to stop.

"But you know it works."

But Jason Elkins? He was a good actor—a big box-office draw—and they worked well together on camera but she didn't like him all that much. He was a little too egotistical and not exactly the brightest bulb in the chandelier.

She bit back each of the dozen comments she wanted to make about where they could stick this grand publicity plan. ...e had dues to pay again, and it seemed her penance wasn't ...e over, after all. "Fine. I'm a team player. Whatever's best ...he project."

..mart girl."

She stood and reached for her shoes. "Don't patronize me, Finn."

"I wasn't."

He seemed sincere and Cait felt a bit bad. She was just too jumpy around him, ready to go straight to Worst Possible Meaning.

"Those were honest words from a friend."

Something icky rolled into her chest and brought a dull pain with it. Caitlyn chose her words carefully. "We were many things to each other, Finn, but I don't think we were ever really friends. Now we're colleagues, and there's no reason why we should be enemies, but I don't think we can be friends, either."

Finn's face was impassive, but she recognized the look in those green eyes. She hadn't hurt him with her words—past experience had proved he was impossible to hurt—but he was disappointed. Whether in her or her words or his own inability to charm her, she didn't know. She'd last seen that look three years ago as she'd walked out his door.

"I'm going to go get something to eat before I have to get back to Wardrobe. I'll see you around."

With that, she left him in her trailer and forced herself to walk calmly across the lot with a smile on her face. She even managed to make small talk with the crew as she grabbed a sandwich. She was proud of herself. Not for the way she'd left things with Finn—that had actually left a strange hollow feeling in her stomach—but for the fact she'd held her ground and set her boundaries.

But now that he wasn't right in front of her, all the confusion and hurt—and, okay, she'd admit there was s residual desire and memories of good times and old fe mixed in there as well—were rolling around inside.

So while she'd claimed hunger, she couldn't fin petite.

As she sat in the makeup chair, she closed her eyes and tried to connect to the feelings so she could channel them into Rebecca later. When Martha started on her hair she opened her eyes and concentrated on acting as if everything was just fine. Normal. Same as yesterday.

Martha chatted and told jokes and Caitlyn laughed in all the right places.

Maybe she was a good actress, after all.

# CHAPTER THREE

FINN didn't need to watch the filming—in fact, he probably shouldn't, since Farrell was notoriously temperamental and quick to bite when he felt his directorial turf was being trod on—but something drew him tonight whether he liked it or not.

Cait's parting shot bothered him. Oh, he'd been well aware before that she was carrying some kind of grudge against him—which was totally undeserved, because *he* wasn't the bastard in this situation. *He* wasn't the one who'd walked out.

So she wanted someone to blame? For what? *It nearly destroyed me—personally and professionally.* That did explain a lot of the shouting the night she'd left. He'd known she was starting to get a bit of backlash from their adventures, but "personal" hadn't come into it.

Or so he'd thought.

He'd chalked it up to overreaction from not getting the chance to read for that part she'd wanted in some film, and expected her to be back after she'd calmed down. The next thing he'd heard, she was in London.

She'd left the damn country without even saying goodbye That still left a bad taste in his mouth.

London had changed her; she wasn't that fun-loving f spirit she'd been back then. She looked the same—he nored the memory of the flash of heat that had moved him when he'd walked into her trailer and found her dozing on the couch in just her underwear—but she wasn't the same. This new Cait was reserved, careful and locked down tighter than a maiden aunt—and equally disapproving. Every now and then she'd let something slip that made him think she was merely pretending to be someone new, but the mask always fell right back into place, making him wonder if he'd imagined it. What had happened to her in London to damp that inner fire that had once drawn him like a moth?

Not that he wanted to go there again.

Nonetheless, he was standing there watching, even when he had a ton of paperwork waiting for him. He could easily list a dozen things he *should* be doing instead of sitting here watching Cait prepare to make out with Jason Elkins.

His earlier compliment to Cait hadn't been empty flattery. In fact, he'd been astounded by how good she was as Rebecca. He snorted when he remembered that Cait's mother envied her the part. Even thirty years ago Margaret Fields-Reese would have been totally wrong for Rebecca, and if he wanted to be honest—privately, at least—Cait's mother couldn't have pulled it off at Cait's age. Cait might have spent the last ten years in the shadow of her parents' talent, but she was about to grab the spotlight all on her own.

That much he understood better than anyone else here, and he couldn't help but be proud of her.

Still, his brain had a hard time reconciling the Cait he knew and the roles she'd used to play with the woman now dominating each scene with quiet, heartbreaking strength. No wonder Naomi was spitting nails. Cait *owned* this film now. She would rule award season.

But even knowing Cait was simply in character, doing her while the cameras rolled and thirty people watched, Finn surprised at the strange kick that landed in his gut when s kissed her.

And it only got worse when Cait kissed him back. The passionate embrace seemed to go on forever.

Farrell finally called cut and Cait rolled out from under Elkins immediately. Two women hurried over to fix her lipstick and hair while the crew readied for the next take.

"Not jealous, are you?" Dolby spoke from behind him.

That feeling wasn't jealousy. "Why would I be?" he asked casually.

"Don't know. All I *do* know is that the second he put his hands on Cait you looked like you would like to beat Elkins into a mushy pulp."

The truth was good enough here. "I just don't like him."

"Ah, but every woman between the ages of fifteen and fifty does."

And that equaled money at the box office. Finn shook his head. He knew all too well that personal likeability had nothing at all to do with job performance. Hell, his father was a prime example of a lousy person doing a good job, so his distaste of Elkins made little sense under close inspection. He'd had a lifetime of practice in keeping personal dislike separate from professional needs. It made things much easier. It took practice to keep everything in its proper box, but it worked well—until someone like Cait came along and screwed it all up.

As Brady would say, he needed to keep the bigger picture in focus. *Folly* was the important thing, and he needed to keep his focus there and there only. "I still don't like the idea of sending Cait out with him to bait the paparazzi. He's a womanizer."

"Bit of the pot calling the kettle black, I think."

For the second time in two days Finn really wanted punch Dolby in the mouth. It was the only the third time the entire seven years they'd been partners he'd been pu like this, and Finn recalled Cait had been part of the reason that other time, too.

"The difference is that I actually like women. He's nothing but a user, and I feel like a pimp encouraging this."

Dolby raised his hands and stepped back. "Whoa, there, Lancelot. Lay off the talent. We need them. What did Caitlyn say when you told her?"

"That she's a team player. She'll do it, but I don't think she really likes the idea. I don't blame her."

"Well, she needs a big name in order to overshadow yours and point the cameras in another direction. Jason Elkins is about the only one who fits that bill. We could always go back to Plan A and put you two in front of the shutterbugs…"

"And I've already said that's not going to happen." Even if Cait were game, he certainly wasn't.

"You're so touchy about this. Three weeks ago you'd have let me sacrifice kittens on the set if it would be good for *Folly*."

"Three weeks ago we were simply shooting. Now the entire project is just a backdrop for a freakin' soap opera."

"Dude, you need serious therapy."

Finn couldn't argue with that, but damned if he'd admit it.

The director called for quiet and cued the cameras. Cait lay beside Elkins, her face buried in his neck as her hand found his and their fingers twined together. It was beautiful, powerful…and completely sickening. Cait slowly sat up, her hair falling like a curtain over her face, and when she tossed it back the seductive smile she wore ripped into his stomach, spreading remembered and familiar heat and want through his veins. He recognized that smile, knew it, had had it directed him when he… When they… Disgusted, Finn turned and lked away.

Dolby trotted beside him. Once they were safely out of

range, he spoke quietly, "If this thing with Cait is going to be a problem, I'll stay and you can go back to L.A."

Why wouldn't Dolby just let it go? Probably because he knew far more than Finn was really comfortable with at the moment. "There is no 'thing' with Cait, so there's no problem, either. I refuse to make a big deal out of this. The set is closed, Cait's going to go out and pretend to be hot for Jason Elkins and I'm going to produce this movie. If everyone will just do their damn jobs, it will all be fine."

Dolby threw up his hands in surrender. "Fine. *Folly* is all yours."

"How kind of you."

The assistant director waved them down and Dolby went to see what he needed. Finn went to the trailer housing the production office and tried to lose himself in the seemingly endless number of emails. About twenty minutes later, the subject line on one brought him up short: *Comment on Caitlyn Reese's return?*

Finn sighed. On the off-chance it was actually something worthwhile, he clicked it open. Nope. No questions about *Folly* or the role of Rebecca or anything else that might be considered anything other than tabloid-ready gossip.

Good Lord. When he'd left for Monaco, *Folly* had been newsworthy because of the importance of the project. The book had a nearly cult-like following, and was required reading at many universities, so film companies had been trying to buy the rights to the book for decades. Dolfinn's success had been hailed as the get of the year.

He wouldn't care if the attention shifted to one of the cast or the director, because that would be equally valid. In the last few days, as word had spread that not only had C been cast but that he would be on the set, *Folly*'s buzz shifted toward the tawdry. The media was circling, but n good way.

He deleted the email without responding. The invasion of his private life didn't really bother him. Hell, he'd never had much of a private life. The Marshall family was always in the news: being rich and politically connected equaled fame, and he'd grown up in the fishbowl of power politics. It wasn't personal. And if it was personal, well, he'd learned long ago not to let that faze him.

He'd built his own reputation in L.A., proving that Marshall DNA wasn't destiny, but his connections and success only increased the glare of the spotlight. Honestly, he didn't care what was said about him; he lived his life exactly as he damn well pleased and the rest of the world could shove it. That was the one lesson he'd learned from his father that had served him well. Professional success came with personal scrutiny, but enough success meant his private life couldn't outshout it. Fame, fortune and power made him blog fodder, but they also meant he didn't have to answer to anyone about anything.

Why, then, did this sudden Cait-fueled interest irritate him? God knew there was nothing about their previous relationship that hadn't made the tabloids, and he'd never given that a second thought.

Until now. And he was finding out it was something he really didn't want to think about.

It made no sense at all.

"Beautiful, Caitlyn. Absolutely wonderful. You and Jason are just magic together."

Caitlyn accepted the compliments with a smile as she waited for the crew to reset the shot and the makeup artists swooped in to fix her hair and lipstick. She reached for the bottle of water and sipped gently through the straw. What she'd really like to do was swish and gargle to get the taste of Jason out of her mouth, but that probably wouldn't go over well.

She bit back a laugh. He looked good, smelled even better, and women everywhere would kill to be in her shoes right now. If only the teen magazines knew that their current cover hottie and winner of "Best Lips" should actually take home the title of "Worst Kisser." Not that a screen kiss would ever equal a real kiss, but jeez… There were close-ups involved, so chaste, fake kisses just wouldn't do. At their last rehearsal Walter had thundered on about authenticity and making it real, and she was really doing her best. If this was the best Jason could do… Well, Caitlyn felt a little bad for the women he dated.

Out of the corner of her eye, she saw Finn and froze. *What the hell?* It wasn't that he didn't belong here—he had full run of the set and there was a good chance he had a legitimate reason for observing the filming—but something slithered down her spine at the thought of him watching her do this.

It just seemed…*icky*. As if it was wrong somehow, even though she knew that was ridiculous. *They* weren't an item anymore, and this was professional kissing, not recreational. Then why did she suddenly feel like…?

The sound of her name pulled her out of her shock, and she realized the crew was waiting for her. Clearing her mind, she lay down next to Jason and let Walter direct her into place. She closed her eyes and took a deep breath, and at that moment she realized why Jason smelled so good.

That was the aftershave Finn used to wear.

Pieces fell into place and memories rushed back at her, crowding her mind's eye too quickly for her to focus on anything else. *Damn it. Now was not the time to wander down that path.* But as Jason's hands moved across her back it was all too easy to pretend it was just part of those memories. That those were Finn's hands touching her, his breath against her neck, his lips… A shiver ran over her body.

She sat up, pushing her hair out of her face, and when sh

opened her eyes it was Finn's face she saw, his eyes hooded and glowing with desire. She let the memories wash over her and take control. Her fingers shook slightly as she reached for the buttons on her blouse, then a hand caught her hair and pulled her down against a broad chest. Only part of her mind registered the crew watching and the directions being quietly fed to her; something else was guiding her.

The word, "Cut!" finally caught her attention, and she snapped back to herself. The realization of who she was actually with sent heat to her cheeks, but she forced herself to keep her face still. Looking around, she saw the big smile on the director's face, and stunned looks from some of the crew.

Jason pushed himself to a sitting position and shook like a wet dog. Her lipstick stained his lips. "Wow, Caitlyn. Hell of a take."

Thank God this was a professional crew. They expected realism. She was the only one who needed to know what had actually happened, and as the compliments about that "magic" started again she didn't bother to correct anyone who wanted to gush about the chemistry she had with Jason.

That was way better than the truth. She felt as if she'd taken method acting to a whole different—and very disturbing—place. She felt shaken.

And something burned low in her stomach. One clear look at her co-star, though, assured her *he* certainly hadn't lit that fire. Caitlyn looked around surreptitiously, but Finn was gone. She couldn't decide it she was relieved or not. *That* had to have been one of her best performances, but maybe it was best he had not witnessed it. She wouldn't have been able to face him knowing…

And then she had to do it again. And again. Until finally—thankfully—she heard the true magic words letting her know they had everything they needed for this scene. She was done.

On slightly unsteady legs, she covered the distance to her

trailer in record time and collapsed on the couch. *That was weird.*

Even worse, something inside her had been released—as if the box she'd shoved everything Finn-related into had suddenly opened and, like Pandora, she couldn't get all the feelings back in. For years now she'd been able to disconnect from the past; the memories used to be like old silent movies, but now they came roaring back in a full Technicolor, surround-sound, 3D, hi-def experience. What had been just an old flame burning in her veins was now a brush fire fanned by all those old feelings.

And not all of them were good.

*Finn* wasn't good for her. Oh, he could be all kinds of fun—up for anything, unshockable, completely unconcerned about what the rest of the world thought. His "love-me-or-screw-you" philosophy had been just what she'd needed—then, at least. The acceptance had been what she'd needed.

Finn's attitude might come from a different place—in retrospect she could put enough pieces together to know some of it had been learned as simply self-preservation—but she'd still admired it back then. She'd needed it at the time.

But she wasn't Finn. She was living proof that his approach didn't work for everyone. Theoretically, it was a great idea. It didn't always translate well into real life. Regardless of anything else, she needed to keep that in mind.

So much for all those rational pep talks she'd given herself. *Ancient history. We're both adults. Time passes; people forget. No reason why we can't work together.* Lord, the platitudes sounded really weak now, and she realized they'd never actually been strong.

In her drive to move on and move ahead she'd let herself overlook one rather glaring flaw in her plan: Finn simply wasn't forgettable. Or ignorable.

But there was nothing that could be done now. Even if sh

weren't contractually obligated to this film, she *wanted* this part, by God. Rebecca was more than just her ticket back to Hollywood; it was her chance to establish herself as a serious leading actress in her own right. No more playing the sidekick, always being compared to her mother and always coming up a bit short. She had a legacy to live up to.

Which meant she had to get all this Finn stuff under control.

And that seemed like a monumental task.

"Not hungry, Caitlyn?" Jason put down the paper he was reading and grabbed a strawberry off her plate. He smiled at her as he chewed, and Caitlyn could only imagine the caption that would go under the cute picture of him eating off her plate.

They were having a late, leisurely Saturday morning breakfast at a sidewalk café not far from her rented condo right off the water in downtown Baltimore. It was a trendy spot, carefully chosen to maximize exposure and photo ops for passersby. And it had worked; they'd drawn plenty of attention to themselves simply by doing nothing, and Jason's popularity ensured that those photos would make their way to the blogs in quick order. After three days of them filming love scenes, rumors were already rumbling about their "amazing chemistry" that "might mean something more." This breakfast would give those rumors legs, but only she knew the truth behind that so-called chemistry.

Jason reached for another strawberry without asking, and she pushed her plate across the table to him. "I don't really like to eat for the cameras. They always manage to catch me at just the wrong moment. I'll get something later."

He obviously thought that was funny, even as he chowed down on the rest of her fruit and yogurt, and while there was some truth to the statement, there were plenty of other issues complicating it.

Jason went back to his magazine as she stared at her paper, and to the world they'd look like any other couple having breakfast. She'd drawn a hard line about any snuggling or other public displays of affection, so they were going for the "comfortable companionship" vibe. Everyone would fill in all the blanks they wanted without Jason or her offering anything more.

She really hated this whole arrangement on principle. It was deceitful to pretend to a relationship—of any sort— simply to up her popularity by tying it to Jason's. She found it insulting on a professional level and personally distasteful.

At the same time it beat eating alone. Not by much, granted, but the grind of "work all day, go back to a rental alone at night" had started to lose its shine already. She didn't know anyone in Baltimore other than the cast and crew, and after keeping hours as long or longer than hers they weren't much for socializing, either.

She wasn't bored, but she was getting a little lonely. Jason was a poor substitute for actual company, but at least he was a breathing human being.

He'd been reading a magazine and now pushed it toward her. "Good interview."

"Thanks." At least that woman had given her the chance to put some of her past in a different, more flattering light. It was a start.

"This says you went to London and took acting classes."

"Yeah, I did some workshops, too."

"Rumor had it you went there to check into rehab."

She'd gone to London because it was far away from California and still in an English-speaking country. She'd considered Australia at first, but at least she knew a few people in London. She'd gone to hide and think.

"That's why they're called rumors. They're rarely true."

"Why?"

Jason was pleasant to look at, but talking to him made her head hurt. "Why what?"

"Why take classes?"

Was he really that slow? "To improve my craft."

"You already knew how to act."

"Yes, but there's always something new to learn, right?"

"If you say so."

And that explained so much about Jason. She'd now take bets that his career had an expiration date in the not too distant future. Caitlyn shook her head as Jason went back to his magazine. She'd had the talent and connections to get her start in the business, but she'd found out the hard way that it just wasn't enough.

She'd had plenty of time over the last few years to analyze how it had all happened and where it had all gone wrong, and the disturbing return of a whole bunch of feelings she didn't want to dissect didn't change any of her conclusions.

In many ways Finn had been the perfect choice for "Caitlyn Reese, Actress." He'd been a rising power player from an already powerful family, and his reputation and prestige were being bolstered by a string of successful films. She'd been the daughter of the industry's most respected director and America's favorite actress. Their relationship had given the papers great headlines—all kinds of garbage about the merging of dynasties.

While she had been born into Hollywood royalty, it wasn't really her world and she hadn't quite found her place. Oh, she'd had all the right connections to put her on a path to live up to her parents' legacy, but she'd never really managed to get all the pieces in the right places at the right times.

Growing up in that shadow had left her lacking certain social skills, and that had led to rumors of haughtiness and self-absorption, so that by the time she'd turned twenty-three she'd had a string of great acting credits to her name but no friends and little attention outside the films.

Then she'd met Finn. Their connection had been instantaneous, red-hot and immediately front page news. Overnight, her reputation had changed completely, launching her into the public eye like a publicist's dream.

Oh, she'd launched, all right. Right into the danger zone.

Finn had understood her—or so she'd thought. Being herself hadn't worked out all that well, and that had made the hurt worse. Then things had just gotten out of hand. It had been totally accidental, but that original plan had fallen by the wayside for her, and by the time she'd realized how deep in she'd gone, there'd been no graceful way out. Within six months she'd fallen just as fast as she'd risen, becoming a cautionary tale about the young, rich and famous in Hollywood. It had been utterly humiliating—for her and her parents.

But then she'd run away to London, and things had been different. Her reputation had preceded her, but without Finn to help fuel the fire she'd been able to live a bit more quietly. Distance had given her perspective, and after long discussions with her agent and her parents she'd launched her new plan. Her name guaranteed her acceptance into the right circles, but she'd never used it. Instead, she reinvented herself and thrown herself into acting classes and workshops. With the confidence she'd gained she'd made a new set of friends, and created a new life that was the polar opposite of the one she'd left behind. She'd taken smaller roles to stretch her range, gained some respect for those performances, then moved slowly up the ladder to bigger parts in the West End.

The constant exchange between the West End and Broadway meant she'd known plenty of people in New York when she'd arrived six months ago. Mentally, emotionally and professionally, she'd managed to end up in a good place.

A true redemption story, ready to be told.

But now… She was starting to feel a little restless and alone. The feeling was familiar, but not fun. And she could feel the pressure mounting already: she needed to be "out there," making the magazines, getting her name on people's lips again… Living up to her legacy.

Thankful for the sunglasses that hid her eyes, she glanced at Jason again. Yet, somehow she'd already been reduced to this.

Four more weeks. Only a month. She could handle it.

"You ready?" Jason's voice cut into her thoughts.

"Yes." *Finally*, she added to herself as Jason paid the bill and they left, setting off a new flurry of whispers when Jason put his hand on her lower back to guide her out.

Jason had left his car in front of Caitlyn's temporary home, and they walked the few blocks back. After they turned the first corner no one seemed to be paying any attention, and she felt her shoulders relax.

"I'm not really sure I like this idea of pretending we're something," Jason grumbled.

Surprise caused her to miss a curb and stumble a bit. Jason loved the attention from the press. Courted it, even. Maybe she'd pegged him wrong and he did have a conscience when it came to stuff like this. "Really? Me—"

The corners of his mouth pulled down as he shook his head. "You and Finn were high-profile. I don't want to look like I'm taking seconds or just your fall-back plan."

Her dislike of Jason grew a little more every day. "*Or* people might think that, given the choice between you or Finn, I chose you."

"I hadn't thought of that…" He brightened considerably. "I like that interpretation."

*Of course you do.* "Honestly, though, I don't want this to be any bigger than it has to be. I don't want anything coming back to bite me later, or anything that will look like we were intentionally trying to make people believe something false."

"But we are."

He just wasn't the sharpest knife in the drawer. "No, we're not. We're just not correcting their erroneous conclusions yet. We, as colleagues, had breakfast together. We might even catch dinner one night. People do it all the time, you know. I want to be able to honestly say we are just friends and make sure they'll have nothing solid to point to that might suggest otherwise."

"Then what's the point?"

She appealed to the one thing she knew would work: his ego. "You don't want Finn overshadowing you on *Folly*, do you? The producer shouldn't get more attention than the lead actor, right?"

"You're right."

"We're really just keeping attention where it belongs, instead of letting Finn run away with it."

"Good point." They paused in front of Jason's rental car. "Want a ride in?"

*I've had about enough of you this morning.* "Thanks, but I'll drive myself."

"See you later, then."

As Jason drove away she realized she was right, and that knowledge relieved her own conscience and brightened her outlook considerably. Not only would they keep the media's attention where it belonged—on *Folly*—they would keep hers there as well. Maybe this plan wasn't the worst idea, after all.

Provided it worked.

In the half-hour it took for her to drive from Baltimore to the set on the Patapso River, Caitlyn repeated every mantr and affirmation she could bring to mind so many times th she nearly believed the plan might actually work. Her mo began to lighten, only to crash when the very first person she ran into on the set was Finn.

*Why was he hovering over the production like some first-timer who didn't trust the crew to do their jobs?*

Finn looked mildly surprised to see her, but the explanation came quickly. "I thought you were having breakfast with Jason."

*And good morning to you, too, Finn.* There was an edge to his voice, though, that kept the retort behind her teeth. "I did."

Finn raised an eyebrow at her. "So where is he?"

That eyebrow grated across already raw nerves. "I wouldn't know. I'm not his keeper or his manager."

"But it went well?"

*Define well.* "The restaurant was lovely, and plenty of people saw us. That's what you wanted, right?"

"That was the plan."

This conversation was stilted, awkward and bordering on antagonistic. There was a set to Finn's jaw that she recognized as irritation held in check, but she couldn't be the cause. She'd just gotten here, for goodness' sake. She knew the root cause of *her* attitude, though, and while Finn was to blame, she knew it wasn't really his fault. She would just have to get hold of herself and get over it. And that would best be done at a safe distance from Finn Marshall.

"I'm sure Jason will be along shortly, and if I see him I'll let him know you're looking for him."

Finn shrugged. "Don't bother."

*Okay, now I'm lost.* "Then I'll just be in my trailer if anyone needs me." *Beating my head against the wall, trying to knock the stupid out.*

He nodded once, then walked away, leaving her standing ere feeling rather foolish.

Once again, it was a feeling she was used to.

# CHAPTER FOUR

EVEN though his body clock hadn't fully adjusted to the time change, Finn was up before sunrise Sunday morning—and sunrise was not something he saw very often. At least from *this* side. He often saw the sun coming up as he made his way to bed, and the fact he was up at such a ridiculous time only compounded his bad mood. He needed a good night's sleep.

Being back in his childhood room at Hill Chase normally caused him to sleep like the dead, but the dreams that had plagued him since Cait's sudden and unexpected return to his life still kept him tossing and turning all night. The strange sensation of want—rather like a nagging feeling—circling through his blood irritated him. Old flames had never held much interest for him before, but Cait seemed to be the exception to that rule, too. Hell, Cait had never run up against a rule she couldn't break, bend or circumvent. It was one of the things they'd had in common.

He'd finally given up all pretense of sleep and gone to the stables. A long ride on Duke helped clear his head, if nothing else. Although he was accepting of the changes that had happened in his absence, he still didn't really *like* what he was now in the middle of. His project was behind schedule, hovering dangerously close to going over budget... And then there was Cait. Oh, she was definitely a wrench in the gears he hadn't been expecting.

He should have sent Dolby to Monaco instead of risking *Folly* by going himself. He was paying for that bit of bad thinking now. Still, he had to admit that Cait was the right choice—even if it wasn't the choice he'd have made. *Folly* was better for having her in it, and he needed to remember this was about the project—not Cait, and certainly not him.

His sudden appreciation for rules and the need to keep the bigger picture in mind made him feel like he was channeling his brother Brady this morning, and that didn't help his mood, either. He needed to shake it all off and think about something else before he ruined his entire day.

He and Duke were already back in the stable before the hands had made their way in to start the day. Duke snorted as Finn handed him over to finish being brushed, and Finn gave him a treat before he left.

He missed Duke—and from what the hands said Duke missed him—but it wasn't as if he could move his horse to Malibu. But he really did need to start scheduling more trips home. And not just for his horse. The Grands weren't getting any younger. They were both still spry and in general good health, but for how much longer?

He and Dolby had toyed with the idea of expanding more into television, and with the number of shows shooting in New York, it would make sense to establish something on the east coast as well. New York was far enough away to keep him sane, but only a short train ride to D.C., and he could spend more time here to keep the Grands happy.

As Finn came up the hill to the house he could see the Grands on the back terrace, enjoying their morning coffee, which wasn't surprising. Granddad liked to watch the horses as they were turned out in the morning, as over the last few years he'd finally had to admit he was getting a little too old to be as hands-on as he'd used to be.

Yeah, after *Folly* wrapped he'd talk to Dolby about possibilities for Dolfinn on this side of the country.

"Good morning, dear. Did you enjoy your ride?" Nana waved him toward a chair, and he realized the table was already set for breakfast.

"I did. Let me wash up and I'll join you. I'm starving."

"Be quick," Granddad grumped. "Gloria's been holding breakfast until you got back."

"And bring the others with you," Nana called as Finn opened the door.

Finn stuck his head under the faucet and changed into clean clothes. As much as he would have liked to bang on Brady's and Ethan's doors, just for juvenile kicks, Ethan spoiled his fun by being in the hall already, still buttoning up a clean shirt.

"You were up early." Ethan's hair was still damp, meaning he hadn't been up very long at all.

"I don't have a lovely wife to keep me up all night."

Ethan's grin confirmed his late night, but before Finn could say anything, Lily came out of the bedroom, twisting her hair up into a ponytail as she walked. Lily's cheeks were flushed pink and she wore a small smile. *Seemed Ethan had been up for a while, after all.*

"'Morning, Finn."

"'Morning. They're waiting on us to eat."

Lily motioned them forward with a jerk of her head, since her hands were now busy tucking a tee shirt into her jeans. "Then let's hurry. I'm starving."

Finn smirked. "Can't imagine why."

Lily blushed even pinker. Ethan punched him in the arm and tried to frown him into good behavior.

A musical jingle floated from the other end of the hall, announcing Aspyn and Brady's appearance. Aspyn was a modern-day flower child, all the way down to the anklet of small gold bells that was the source of the sound. How she managed to tolerate his stick-in-the-mud oldest brother was a mystery for the ages.

Neither one of his sisters-in-law were anything like who he'd expected his brothers to marry, but he liked them both— sometimes more than his brothers.

"You were up at the crack of dawn this morning," Brady said. "Did you *have* to try to wake the whole house?"

Finn made a point of looking Brady up and down. "I obviously disturbed *your* beauty rest."

Aspyn shook her head at him in censure, but there was a small smile on her lips. "You're so bad, Finn Marshall."

He grinned at her. "Just part of my charm."

Aspyn laughed as she moved past all three of them and hooked an arm through Lily's. "Bloodshed before breakfast would make me lose my appetite. Let's go before they get too worked up."

Lily and Aspyn disappeared down the stairs, leaving him to the grumblings of his brothers. The smell of bacon grew stronger, and they arrived on the terrace just as Gloria and one of her many minions were bringing out a mountain of food.

Ethan surveyed the table. "All of Finn's favorites again, I see."

Gloria swatted Ethan and leaned in to kiss Finn's head as if he was still a child. Last night's menu had been one of his top five favorites, too. He hadn't eaten that well in months.

"You, Ethan Marshall, are out here all the time, eating your way through my kitchen like a teenage locust. I don't get to cook for Finn very often."

"I'd consider that a blessing," Ethan grumbled as he pulled out a chair for Lily.

Aspyn took a seat across from him, leaving Finn trapped between Ethan and Brady.

"Just eat," Gloria scolded. "Especially you, Lily. Aspyn, that sausage is the vegetarian type you like." Gloria fussed around the table for a minute more, then patted Finn fondly before she returned to the kitchen.

"See, it's true that absence makes the heart fonder." Finn loaded up his plate with Gloria's famous French toast—so famous that the White House chef had asked for the recipe and been politely turned down. "That and an autographed picture of Pierce Brosnan gets me French toast today."

Ethan dumped a pile of bacon on Lily's plate before filling his own. Lily slid half of it back onto the platter. "I guess we're lucky she didn't kill the fatted calf," he muttered.

"Maybe that's dinner tonight," Granddad offered.

"Alas, I can't stay. I'll be leaving right after breakfast." Nana started to protest, but Finn shook his head. "I'm sorry, Nana, but I'm just covered up with work. I'll be back next weekend, I promise. And once we wrap I'll come stay for several days before I head home."

"This is also your home," Nana said pointedly.

Guilt swamped over him, just as he knew she'd intended. "I know."

Brady sipped at his coffee. "Some prodigal son you are, coming home and immediately leaving."

"You should really brush up on your allegories before you try to drop them into conversations. Prodigal would imply I'm coming home broke or in disgrace, and I'm neither, thank you very much."

Ethan leaned close. "Nor looking to reconcile with Daddy," he muttered under his breath.

Finn snorted, Ethan jumped as Brady kicked him under the table and Nana frowned at them all. Her tone cool, she said, "That much is true for the time being. It would be nice to keep it that way."

Finn knew she wasn't addressing Ethan's crack about their

father. She understood that minefield too well to go there. They would all just pretend nothing had been said at all. That was the Marshall family plan. Ignore everything you can.

"Believe me, Nana, I've got plenty of money. Ethan can vouch for me on that."

Her eyes narrowed. "That's not what I was referring to, and you know it. I'm very tired of seeing your name in the paper for all the wrong reasons."

A smart remark about not reading the papers sat on the tip of his tongue, but Finn held it back. He had no such reservations when it came to Ethan and Lily, both of whom were fighting back smiles and looking ridiculously innocent. "Oh, like you two have any room to talk."

"Ethan is one hundred percent reformed." Lily somehow managed to sound prim. "And I'm the freakin' poster child for reformation."

"There's nothing worse than a former sinner to lay on the condemnation."

Lily merely smirked at him. Ethan was obviously a bad influence on her.

"The point, Finn, is that eventually everyone must grow up and settle down." Nana leveled a look at him. "You're almost thirty. Don't you think it's time?"

Finn looked to his grandfather for help, but Granddad feigned interest in his breakfast. Brady wore his usual smug smile, and Aspyn examined the hem of her napkin. But Lily and Ethan, those traitors, were nodding in agreement, egging Nana on. Not that she needed help at any time, but after marrying off both of his brothers in a little over a year, Nana was looking for the hat trick.

Finn leaned back in his chair and glared at his brothers. "Really? You want to go there?"

They both just lifted their left hands to show wedding bands.

"Nice try. But neither one of you got anywhere close to an altar before your thirtieth birthdays, so I figure I still have a little time."

"You're missing the point, dear. While I—and your grandfather—" she waited for Granddad to nod his agreement "—would love to see you settled and happy with a nice girl one day, I'm more concerned with the situation currently at hand."

*Oh, please don't go there. I'm not in the mood.* "And that would be…?" he asked innocently.

"Caitlyn Reese."

*Yep, she had.* Nana had a knack for going right where he didn't want her to—and she could make him feel twelve years old again at the same time. Defensive maneuvers would only play right into her trap. And this was Nana, so offensive maneuvers weren't allowed at all. Playing dumb seemed his best bet. "What about Cait?"

The irritated lift of her eyebrow clearly stated she wasn't buying his dumb act. And a quick look told him that Lily and Aspyn had joined Granddad in his studious approach to eating, leaving Ethan and Brady watching avidly with get-yourself-out-of-this-one smirks on their faces. He couldn't look there for help, but maybe they wouldn't be a hindrance, either.

He could hope. But he wouldn't hold his breath.

Nana set down her fork and met his eyes evenly. "I met Miss Reese the other night at the benefit. She's not at all what I expected based on her previous behavior with you."

"We were young and just having a good time. So we made the tabloids. It's not like I'm the first Marshall to steal a headline. It's practically a rite of passage in this family."

Brady cleared his throat. "It was more than just one headline. You two tore a swath through southern California. *We* remember those days clearly, even if they're a vodka-soaked blur to you."

Oh, his memories were just fine. Working overtime, in fact.

He looked to Lily, who merely shrugged, then to Aspyn, whose nose was wrinkled slightly in apology.

"Even I remember them, Finn, and I spent most of that summer chained to a tree in Oregon."

Brady turned to Aspyn. *"What?"*

"Nothing. More coffee?" Aspyn smiled angelically at Brady's we'll-talk-about-this-later scowl. "All I'm saying, Finn, is that you two were news, and no one has forgotten it. Caitlyn may have been more low-profile the last few years, but you haven't. I saw an interview with Caitlyn's mother recently, and she's very excited about her daughter's return to their family business. Put all of that together, and you've got people's attention whether you like it or not."

"Exactly," Nana added. "Regardless of your past deplorable behavior, Miss Reese seemed to be a lovely and quite charming young woman. And from what I hear she's showing signs of reformation as well."

There was a bear trap here, waiting to snap on his foot, but damned if he could tell exactly where. "I'll tell her you said so."

"I'd like to have the same things said about you. You've already made the papers…"

"It's nothing, Nana. You know how these things go. Rest assured that I have no interest in Cait beyond her performance. This is strictly professional. In fact…" He could not believe he was saying this. "Rumor has it that Cait and Jason Elkins might be becoming more than just co-stars."

"I'm glad to hear it, and I wish them well." Nana picked her fork up again. "I'm sorry to have brought up such an unpleasant topic at the table, but I'm happy that we got it sorted out."

"Nice save," Ethan whispered behind his coffee cup. "You almost had me believing it."

"Shut up before I make Lily a lovely young widow."

Nana cleared her throat. "We're old, not deaf, you know."

Lily snickered, which earned her a grin from Ethan, but Finn could only frown at her in retaliation. So he kicked Ethan under the table instead, earning him a "what did I do?" look.

Granddad, thankfully, changed the subject. "How's my movie coming along?"

"Fantastic." Finn liked the way Granddad smiled when he spoke about "his" movie. The first Senator Marshall had been the subject of a bio-pic about his career and characters in movies about the civil rights movement and the war on terror. He'd even played himself in a comedy set in the Capitol. But *Folly* was the movie Granddad considered "his," and that pushed Finn to put up with whatever he had to in order to make it happen.

It was because of Granddad that Finn had even gone after the rights, and it was Granddad who'd finally been able to convince the heirs to agree to sell. It turned out that the author had been a supporter of Granddad's career. *Folly* was Finn's present to the man who was more his father than his grandfather, and he'd even gone as far as to cast his brothers and cousins in small cameos as an extra treat—but Granddad didn't know that.

"Are you sure you don't want to come to the set and watch? Maybe be an extra?"

"No, no. I don't want to ruin the experience by knowing what went into it. I expect excellent seats at the premiere, though."

"Done."

With that assurance, Granddad stood and extended a

hand to Nana, and they left for their morning walk over the grounds.

Lily sighed as they walked down the path. "Your grandparents are like characters from their own romantic movie."

Finn looked at her over his coffee. "Still reading those romance novels, Lily?"

Lily lifted her chin proudly. "Every chance I get. I believe in happy endings. Your Grands, Brady and Aspyn…" Lily paused to accept Aspyn's nod of agreement before smiling adoringly at his brother, who grinned back like a lovesick teenager. "Ethan and me."

"Spare me the details, please. I just ate."

Lily grinned as she pushed her chair back from the table and stood. She kissed Ethan, and then leaned down close to Finn's ear. "Your day will come, Finn Marshall," she whispered.

"Is that a threat?" He heard Brady's snort and Ethan's chuckle.

Lily shook her head. "Just faith in your happy ending. You deserve one, too." She winked before she straightened up and turned to Aspyn. "I'm going to the stable. Want to come?"

Aspyn nodded and stood. "I'm with Lily on this one—literally as well as metaphorically."

With that, both women walked away, the sound of Aspyn's anklet jingling along with Lily's laughter. That left him with only his brothers at the table, and both of them were staring at him. "What?" he finally asked when the silence got too long.

"She's not wrong, you know."

Of course Ethan would agree with his wife. "That my day will come?"

"That you deserve a happy ending."

Finn looked at Ethan carefully, but couldn't find any trace

of sarcasm. "Not you, too? I get enough of that from Nana. Just because you—"

"This has nothing to do with me."

"Or me," Brady added.

"Or even Nana's quest to get you to the altar," Ethan said.

"Then what *is* this about?"

Ethan cleared his throat and looked slightly uncomfortable. Brady sat silently and Finn knew he was about to hear something he wouldn't like.

"At the risk of sounding like your therapist—"

He was right. "I don't need a therapist."

Brady coughed. "Maybe you should reconsider that stance."

He leveled a stare at both of them. "Because...?"

Ethan snorted, sounding so much like Brady that Finn did a double-take. "The one relationship you've had with a woman that lasted longer than six weeks was with someone even more screwed up than you."

The anger that flared on Cait's behalf startled him. "Don't—"

Brady stopped him. "There's no need to jump to her defense. I'm sure she's got many fine qualities, but you two took hedonism to new extremes, and it doesn't take a shrink to see that you simply fed off each other's demons."

If anything, they'd been exorcising them. "I don't know what the hell you are talking about."

"Don't you?" Brady's eyebrow went up. "Caitlyn's background is oddly similar to yours—a famous family, the constant scrutiny by the press, the pressure of expectations. You seemed to find the one person on earth who was equally as emotionally disconnected as you—and you couldn't even make *that* work."

"Cait and I were just having a good time."

Brady lifted his coffee mug in a mock toast. "And you just proved my point."

"You had a point?"

"You barely let us—your family—into your life. You certainly don't let anyone else in. It's all superficial and safe. Easy, even. I know how attractive that feeling can be. But it's dangerous. If you can't find someone else to care about, you end up caring only about yourself. And then you're no better than our father."

"That is ridiculous."

Ethan took the opportunity to pile on. "We have always backed your decision to move to California. We, more than anyone, understood your need to get the hell out of Dodge. You were so young when Mom died. It was much harder on you, because you didn't know what an ass he was before then. Things were so screwed up after that I'm surprised you didn't end up in therapy."

The jump from Cait to his father had Finn struggling to keep up. "You think I have daddy issues? Me and half the world. The man's a royal bastard, but I'm hardly scarred by it."

"Aren't you?" Ethan asked.

Before he could do more than shake his head Brady added, "Why do you think the Grands ride you so hard? They see the signs, the pattern re-emerging."

That cut disturbingly close to the bone for Finn, but Brady wasn't done.

"Do you think they're proud of the kind of son they raised? The man he is today?"

"He's a senator, for God's sake—and a good one, too. Most parents would be pretty pleased."

Ethan waved that away. "Professional success isn't the same thing. You have that already and they're proud. Disgustingly so, if you ask me. But still they worry."

This conversation had hit too many sore spots, and Finn wanted out. "Then find them something else to worry about." He turned to Ethan. "I know—why don't you get Lily pregnant? That should distract them nicely."

Ethan smirked. "Done. But it's really too early to be telling folks."

Finn choked on his coffee and it burned all the way down. "Seriously?" At Ethan's nod, he looked at Brady, who showed no surprise on his face. It must be true, and Brady must have known already. "Congratulations. When?"

"About seven months. But we're not changing the subject just yet. Back to Caitlyn—"

Cait wasn't exactly a change of subject, but it beat their armchair therapy hands-down. "I have no interest in Cait beyond her performance in *Folly*. And it's award-worthy, by the way."

"I don't doubt it. Lily and I saw her in London about eight months ago. She made a wonderful Desdemona."

"Her acting ability has improved dramatically, pardon the pun."

"And that's your only interest in Cait?"

Finn nodded.

"Then have a little pity on the poor girl," Brady said. "Haven't you caused her enough trouble?"

Damn it, he was *not* the villain in this. In any of it. Not now and not then. Cait was not some poor, naïve girl he'd led astray. "Cait grew up in the tabloids, and she understands this business better than you think. If she didn't want to be in the headlines again she wouldn't have signed on to one of my projects."

Brady shook his head. "Make up your mind, Finn. Either it's something or it's nothing."

"It's nothing that's anything for you to worry about."

Ethan turned to Brady. "Twenty bucks says it's something."

"There's no way I'm going to take that bet. We both know it's something. My only question is how much of a something it's going to be."

*This was one of the many reasons he spent his life on the opposite side of the country from his family.* No one should have to put up with this level of interference. "I'm going to say this one last time, so pay attention. Regardless of what Cait and I used to be, our relationship now is strictly professional." His strange reaction to seeing Cait kiss Jason niggled at him, but he pushed it aside.

That statement got him disbelieving snorts from both brothers.

"Then you're stronger than I gave you credit for. Either that or you're an idiot," Ethan clarified.

He'd kill Ethan, but the Grands would disapprove. They seemed to actually like him for some reason. "Speaking of idiots, you and Lily are due on the set Friday by two for Wardrobe and Makeup."

Ethan and Brady exchanged a look that told him they were dropping the topic, but Finn knew it was probably only temporary. Their matching smirks confirmed it, but Finn would take what he could get at the moment. All this talk of Cait had churned up too much history, and he didn't need that today.

Ethan's smirk transformed to a grin. "Oh, I'm really looking forward to it."

He sounded far too cheerful and sincere for someone who'd grumbled about it from day one. Finn was instantly suspicious. "Why?"

"Because who can resist watching a slow-motion train wreck?"

Brady nodded. "When are Aspyn and I scheduled again? I can't wait."

With a glare that only caused his idiot brothers to laugh, Finn stood and tossed his napkin on the table. He didn't bother to comment as he walked away, leaving them laughing like loons behind him.

Had he really been considering a move back to this side of the continent? Where he could have this kind of conversation on a regular basis?

*Yeah, New York was going to be too close as well.*

# CHAPTER FIVE

ALTHOUGH the set was officially closed to the media at large, they simply couldn't afford to keep all the press away. Interviews had to be done; the project had to be pimped properly. So, while she'd much rather go back to her trailer for a rest from the heat and a little peace and quiet, Caitlyn put her game face on and smiled back at the over-excited reporter from *Insider Unlimited*.

The first few questions were the usual—what was it like to be back? How excited was she to be a part of *Folly*?—and Caitlyn fell back on stock answers to save her energy for the questions to come. And they did.

"So, Caitlyn…" The I'm-your-best-girlfriend tone was a dead giveaway that the next question was a zinger. "We've heard there's some tension on the set between you and Naomi Harte."

"There's always tension in any production," she interrupted with an airy wave of her hand. "We're all working very hard, very long hours, and it's really hot this summer. It makes us all grouchy." She kept her voice light. "The relationship between Angela and Rebecca is very complex and emotional, and maybe folks confused on-camera tension with real life. All I can say is that Naomi is perfect for the role of Angela, and it's wonderful to be working with her again."

The plastic smile of the reporter faltered for a moment,

but then she narrowed in. "Three years ago you had a very public and *dramatic* relationship with Finn Marshall. Does it make things awkward now?"

She'd prepared herself for this, practicing low-key answers that couldn't be misquoted out of context. "Only in that I never knew how hard-working Finn really is, and how much he cares about this project. As a producer, he has the Herculean task of making things happen. Keeping a production of this size and complexity running smoothly is much harder than people think. I never had the opportunity to work with him before now, and I'm just blown away that he's *that* good at what he does." *There—that should shut her up for a bit.*

"So there's no problem?"

"None," she lied with a shrug.

"And the rumors about you and your co-star Jason Elkins?"

She'd practiced this, too, and she knew her smile was the perfect mix of humor and censure. She'd learned the art of this dodge from Mom, the true master of misdirecting the press. "Are probably greatly exaggerated. We *are* spending a lot of time together, but that's the great part about liking and respecting your coworkers. You have someone fun to hang out with after work."

Whether it was from disappointment that Caitlyn wasn't giving the answers she wanted or something else, the reporter wrapped up quickly after that and thanked Caitlyn before moving on to her next interview.

Proud of the way she'd handled that, Caitlyn sipped at her water and pulled out her phone while she could still ride on that high.

Her mother answered on the third ring. "Caity, darling! How are you?"

*Where to begin?* She couldn't exactly tell her mother that she was caught in a melodrama that had nothing to do with the script. Not when Mom had taken her at her word that this time would be different. Without embarrassment to the Reese legacy.

"I'm okay," she hedged. "Just had a few minutes and thought I'd say hi."

"I only have a couple of minutes myself. We are actually about to board a plane for Spain."

Of course. "I forgot about that. Daddy's getting some award, isn't he?"

"Lifetime Achievement. And he sends love."

"Love back to him. I guess we'll talk when you get back."

"Is everything okay there?"

"Yeah, of course. We're a little behind schedule, but..."

"Oh, it's so annoying when that happens. You should—"

Caitlyn could hear her father in the background, hurrying Mom along.

"Look, darling, I've got to go. You know how John is. I'd tell you to be wonderful, but I know you will be. I'll call when I get a free minute tomorrow."

"Okay. Bye," she said, but the line was already dead, and she knew that "tomorrow" really meant sometime next week, when her mother remembered her again.

Caitlyn felt slightly deflated, but not surprised. Her parents were always on the move, always had been, and she was quite used to it. It came with the territory. Hell, she'd gone through this very issue with her therapist a dozen times as a child, and the mantras came back easily. John and Margaret Reese didn't belong to her; they belonged to everyone. That didn't mean they didn't love her, but they had careers that demanded so much of them she had to adjust *her* demands and expectations.

Maybe it was for the best. There was no reason to dump her problems at their feet. It wasn't as if they could do anything. She'd handle this the way she handled everything else, and if she needed advice she'd call her agent.

They'd be at the premiere, though. They never missed one of those. When she felt cynical she credited the photo op, but she knew they came because they were proud of her. And they'd be even more so when they saw *Folly*. Mom wasn't the only one a little envious right now; Daddy had gotten his nose a little out of joint at hearing one of his protégés would be directing. He'd been after *Folly*'s rights for years.

Everything would be fine in the end.

But first she had to get through filming without having the whole thing drive her over the edge. She felt jumpy and tense, and no amount of meditation could help alleviate the stress of navigating this minefield. A strong drink sounded grand.

Taking a deep breath, she headed back to Wardrobe, past where the reporter was now interviewing Naomi with over-the-top gushing. Caitlyn maneuvered behind her cameraman just in time to hear the reporter say, "So, has there been any tension between you and Caitlyn Reese over your new romance with Finn Marshall?"

Caitlyn stumbled, and Naomi shot her a sly smile before turning back to the camera.

But she couldn't hear Naomi's response over the roar in her ears.

She managed to avoid Finn for the next week. Well, mostly. It was impossible to completely avoid him on set, but she kept those interactions quick and tried to include an audience whenever possible. That audience and her determination to focus solely on business didn't stop Finn from making inside jokes that had her gritting her teeth, but it helped her hold her tongue and not say anything she'd regret.

While she could physically avoid him as much as possible,

mentally Finn was constantly bothering her. She'd gotten to
the point where she couldn't film a romantic scene with Jason
*without* picturing Finn the whole time. Method acting had
taken on a whole new meaning in her life, and she wished
she'd never even heard of it.

Most of her scenes in the film ran parallel to Naomi's, but
the ones they did have together had taken on a sharp edge that
the director loved. And, again, that came from Finn. Their
characters were supposed to be at odds over Jason's character,
but the real-life idea of Naomi and Finn added extra bite in
their performances. Caitlyn told herself that Finn wasn't her
business, but the fact it was Naomi of all people just rubbed
her the wrong way.

Thankfully, she didn't have to witness any nuzzling or
snuggling on the set—they were both too professional for
that—but the papers were full of Naomi and Finn having a
quiet dinner or seeing a movie. Even Jason started to get a
little annoyed—he didn't mind sharing the headlines with
Naomi, but Finn taking those headlines was just too much
for his ego. *Their* "quiet dinner" hadn't garnered nearly as
much attention as Finn and Naomi's. Tempers were running
high all over the place, and the heat didn't have much to do
with it.

Caitlyn felt as if she was living in the middle of a melodrama. Her countdown of days left on the set was all that kept
her sane. It would all be worth it soon enough. She could do
this.

Of course just as Caitlyn almost had herself believing this
little pep talk, the whole plan had to go to hell.

Chris, the assistant director, was a native New Yorker, and
had joined her today at a table in the shade for a snack. Their
conversation had turned into a debate over the best place to
get Korean barbecue in the city. She had just elicited a promise from him to at least try her favorite place before he re-

committed to his earlier choice when he suddenly looked up and shouted Finn's name.

"Sorry, Caitlyn, but I've been trying to track him down all day. It won't take a minute."

That gave her a whole five seconds to steel herself before Finn sat down across from her. "Hi, Finn. If you two need to talk, I'll go."

Finn gave her a strange look that said he was well aware she was trying to avoid him as he returned the greeting. She made to leave.

"No, don't," Chris said. "You're not finished eating, and it's not like we have something top secret to discuss."

Put like that, she didn't have any reason *not* to sit there while Chris and Finn went over something about the schedule. She checked her phone for messages, sent an email to her parents and quietly looked up her name on Google to see if anything had made the blogs.

She heard, "See you later, Caitlyn," and looked up to see Chris leaving, already involved in a conversation on his own phone. That left Finn at the table with her, and awkwardness settled in quickly.

For her, at least. Awkwardness of any sort just wasn't in Finn's repertoire of emotions. He seemed totally at ease. Casually dressed in a tee shirt and jeans, he looked ready to step into a music video, while she felt wrung-out and haggard and in desperate need of a trip to Makeup. And while it was comfortable enough here in the shade, and a nice breeze had finally kicked up, his hairline was damp, as if he'd been doing something in the sun to work up a sweat. The entire effect was one of ease and confidence. *How did he manage that?* It just wasn't fair. She just felt wilted.

"So how are you, Cait? I haven't see you in a few days." He picked up his sandwich and took a bite. Now she really was stuck. There was no way she could walk off and leave him to eat alone—especially since she knew how much *she* hated to do exactly that.

*Breathe.* "Good. And you?"

He shrugged. "You and Jason got the cover of *Star Track* this week."

*As did you and Naomi.* Pride kept her from saying anything, though. "That's what you wanted, right?"

Finn's over-dramatic sigh was almost funny. "*I* wanted a shoot uncomplicated by outside problems. A media circus—regardless of the cause—only makes my job harder."

Since Finn was dating his talent rather publically, that rang a little false. "Jason and I were *your* brilliant idea."

Finn shook his head as he swallowed. "Actually, it was Dolby's."

"Whatever. Whoever was responsible for starting the whispers did a good job. You'll notice those pictures are completely innocent until a heavy layer of speculation is applied."

An eyebrow went up. "So it *is* all just a rumor?"

She nearly choked. "Of course it is. How can you even ask that?"

"I've seen your love scenes." He smirked and she wanted to kick him under the table. "They're hot. And emotional."

Caitlyn felt the blood rush to her face. She hoped he'd think it was from the compliment he'd just paid her. The truth would go with her to her grave. "Thank you."

"I can see how folks might think—"

"But *you* should know better. Anyway, only people who have never tried to kiss someone when there are dozens of people watching and there's a camera ten inches from your face would ever think anything like that. It's far from romantic."

"So how do you do it?"

Finally her chance to give him a little bit of that mock back. "It's called acting. I'm sure you're familiar with the concept."

That earned her a frown. "I meant you, specifically."

"Why?" she knew she sounded suspicious and defensive, but she couldn't help it.

Surprise crossed his face. "Because I'm interested in craft."

It was her turn to be surprised. "Since when?" Never once had they talked about craft. Or business, either.

He shrugged again. It pushed her over the edge. "*Please* stop doing that."

"What?"

"Shrugging. Don't ask a question and then pretend the answer doesn't matter. Either you care about something or you don't."

"That's a lot to read into one shrug."

Only because she had a history with that shrug. It practically defined everything that had been wrong with their entire relationship. Not that she was going to tell him that. "Lesson one on craft, then. Body language matters. It doesn't matter what comes out of your mouth or what you meant. What people perceive is what they believe. And that's just as true on-screen as off."

"You sound awfully bitter about something."

"I have cause to be, don't you think? I learned that lesson the hard way."

"Poor Cait."

She would *not* let him rile her. "The fast trip from rising star to cautionary tale is fueled solely by what people perceive about what they see."

"It wasn't that bad."

"Please. The only thing that kept me from being blackballed in the industry was my parents. That and the public's never-ending interest in watching a train wreck."

"You're exaggerating. I was there, remember?"

*Did she ever.* "Finn, you have many fine qualities, but I wouldn't list 'keen powers of observation' among them."

"I'd argue I was watching you pretty closely."

She ignored the double meaning to snap, "Yet you didn't seem to notice when I was imploding personally and professionally."

"Do you actually believe your own press? If I'd thought for a second that you really had half the problems the tabloids accused you of I'd have said something."

"Beyond 'Have another drink, Cait'? You were part of my problem."

"So that's the grounds for your grudge."

"I wouldn't call it a grudge. It's just a memory of that hard-learned lesson."

"Which was…?"

She sighed. "Forget it, Finn."

"No, you're the one who brought it up. If it's the root cause of your attitude, let's clear the air."

She looked around. "I don't think now is the time or place."

"Seems like a good time to me. That way we can move on."

Wasn't that exactly what she wanted? To move on?

"Fine. The truth of the matter is that you were my drug of choice, and like any addict I lived for it and the way it made me feel." The words started out difficult to say, but then the gates opened and everything began to rush out in a flood. "And, just like any other drug, it was destructive. The more I loved you and the more fun we had, the more my world shrank to where you were the only thing. As long as I was on that Finn high I didn't have to worry about living up to my parents' or the public's expectations. I thought I could win the world over by just being me and living my life the way I wanted." She stopped for a breath, and an oddly cathartic feeling washed over her at finally saying it all out loud.

"And what's wrong with that?"

"It might have worked for you, but me… I lost the respect

of my peers, my family, my fans. And the worse it got, the more I let you convince me more of the same was the answer."

Those green eyes met hers in surprise. "I thought we were having a good time."

It was her turn to sigh. "And that's what's so dangerous. And sad. A good time was all you cared about, and I was your good-time girl back then. When it all landed on my head and the press decided I was flaming out, *your* answer was to go to Baja for the weekend."

"I thought you might need to get away for a few days."

"What I *needed* was you to realize that I was in trouble. For you to do something other than shrug it all off. Maybe for you to realize that a drunken Mexican adventure wasn't quite the right way to convince folks that I wasn't one step from rehab."

"That explains what you were ranting about that night."

"And it didn't seem to faze you at all. I'd just lost a really nice endorsement deal because I wasn't considered stable or professional enough, and you didn't care."

"I didn't *know*. There's a difference."

Her temper was burning hot now. So much for not letting him rile her. As much as she hadn't wanted to go there, now she couldn't stop. "Not when the reason you didn't know was because you didn't care enough to actually ask."

"So that's your grudge. I wasn't exactly what you wanted at that exact moment in time. The world can't always revolve around you, you know."

"But it's got to revolve around something." She crossed her arms over her chest. "You've perfected the art of not giving a damn. Somehow it seems to be working for you, but damned if I know how. So there's the root of my so-called grudge. I needed an adult, a partner—not another addict who needed me to enable his quest of thumbing his nose at the whole world."

"Oh, so everything was all *my* fault?"

"I'll take responsibility for my own stupid actions, and I've now paid the price for them."

"To paraphrase my sister-in-law, our mistakes are what make us the people we are today. You seem to be doing all right."

"As do you. And that's what's dangerous for anyone who falls into your orbit. I don't deny that I learned a lot and had a hell of a good time while the times were good. But that doesn't mean that I'm not allowed to have regrets, either."

Finn seemed oddly pleased. "I'm glad you finally admitted it."

"What? That I have regrets?"

"No, that we had a good time."

"There's more to life than a good time."

"That's what life is for."

"You know, Finn, it must be nice to have the world on a platter and no worries at all. But the rest of us aren't that lucky. And that's probably a good thing. One Finn Marshall is more than enough for this world."

"I'm glad I'm unique."

Only Finn could smile in such a way as to make a statement like that sound charming instead of completely worthy of smacking him. Oddly, it took the heat out of her anger. They were never going to fight this out to a solution, but at least she'd said it all.

She laughed quietly. "You know, in a way, so am I."

"What does that mean?"

"Honestly… I don't really know." There weren't words to describe it. "I like you, Finn. Even after all we've been through, you're just impossible *not* to like. I'm not sure I like me, though, when I'm with you. So it's a conundrum. And one that I think is best served by us staying away from each other." She swept the crumbs from her sandwich off the table and stood.

"Hey, Cait?"

She turned.

"You want to know what I remember about that trip to Baja?"

There was a deep purr in his voice that sent shivers over her skin in defiance of the heat, and the light in his eyes made her heart stutter. She swallowed hard. Thinking about Baja made her chest hurt. It encapsulated their entire relationship. For three days she'd been lost in Finn, not knowing that her life was in flames back home—and not caring to check, either. She'd decided she was in love, but that feeling had crashed into reality and she still remembered the gut-punch waiting for her. They'd rehashed enough of their past to know there would be no catharsis waiting on the other side of this topic.

"Not really."

The look on Finn's face called her a liar without him having to say a word. "The Cait that ran off to Baja on a moment's notice wasn't living her life looking over her shoulder or muttering disapprovingly. She wanted to see and do and experience it all. And she wasn't afraid of anything. That Cait was incredible. Do you ever miss her?"

That cut close to the bone, and, damn it, she had the distinct feeling he knew it, too, and had done it on purpose. She felt like a fraud, as if she'd been lying to herself with her new attitude and Finn had stripped it away to uncover the truth under it. Not only had he proved he *did* still know her with that one statement, but she was surprised to find out the urge was still very much there, if buried slightly under the ash of old burns.

*Perception shapes reality.* She just had to make sure her perceptions didn't backslide and ruin the reality she was creating for herself now.

She took a deep breath. "Finn, as delightful as these little trips down memory lane are, they're really not…pertinent to the here and now. And I'd like to stay focused on *now* and move forward from *here*."

"Then quit worrying so much about the past. Let it go. It doesn't matter now."

"Easy for you to say. I envy that ability of yours sometimes, but I actually care about things beyond my next good time."

"And you think I don't?"

"I know you don't."

There was that look again. The one she couldn't decipher logically enough to judge his reaction to her words. She felt a little bad; her words had been harsh. But how dare he try to downplay everything and forget it with one of his famous and annoying shrugs?

The silence spun out and Caitlyn couldn't figure out what she should—or could—say next. Retreat seemed the safest—if cowardly—option. "I'm going to Makeup now. Bye."

Behind her back, she thought she might have heard Finn laugh quietly.

# CHAPTER SIX

CAIT's ponytail swished against her back as she walked away. He shouldn't spar with her. She was right: it was unprofessional, and not only unnecessary to their working relationship but probably harmful as well. He should just stay the hell away from her, but for reasons he couldn't even begin to understand he couldn't. She'd ignored him for days—which had only nagged at his need to call her on it—but this wasn't exactly where he'd thought they'd end up when he had opened the discussion.

Their conversation had cleared up a lot, but it had raised far more issues, and Cait was insane if she thought she could dump all that out there and then just walk off. He'd been unjustly tried and convicted, and for the first time ever that bothered him.

Plus, he was reeling from the way Cait had almost casually mentioned that she'd been in love with him back then. He doubted she really realized what she'd said, but it had slammed into him with unexpected force. It forced him reevaluate a few things.

They had unfinished business. She might want to pretend that fact didn't exist, but he wasn't playing that game. He was self-aware enough to know she'd dented his ego three years ago, and that might be fueling it some, but he was honest enough to admit that being around her had lit a fire that just couldn't be ignored.

That in itself was unusual, as he'd never had any desire to go back to a woman once things were over. Why did Cait alone have that effect on him? Cait had called him a drug, and at the moment he felt a bit like an addict who'd been given a reminder of what he'd given up and now the craving was consuming him.

And, like a junkie, he was not going to be able to resist.

That was why she was avoiding him—that much was clear now. She, too, was fighting that pull instead of just letting it play out the way it should.

Cait might try to talk a good game, but he'd seen the look on her face when he'd mentioned Baja. She'd given herself a part to play—Caitlyn Reese, Serious Actress and Reformed Sinner—but underneath... Oh, it was still there. She'd just let the pressure and the shame try to force her to be something else. He understood the reaction, but Cait was taking it to new extremes.

And he was just ornery enough to force her to break character and face that fact. It would make things easier in the long run if they got past all of this. She wasn't going to like it, though.

*Speaking of things Cait wasn't going to like...* He looked at his watch. He needed to be in Wardrobe in ten minutes. Cait was in for one hell of a surprise, and he didn't want to miss a second of it.

An hour later, he wasn't sure he'd made the right choice. Oh, he was forcing her to face facts, but it wasn't going as expected.

"You've got to be kidding me." Cait shot the assistant director a look so dripping with venom that Chris actually backed up a step.

"Caitlyn, honey, what's the problem?"

Finn adjusted the tie of his Army uniform and grinned. "Yeah, Cait, what *is* the problem? I've got a SAG card, so I can both act and produce. It's all legit."

She barely acknowledged he'd spoken, and he could see her fighting to find words that wouldn't come across as ridiculous.

She addressed her question to Chris only. "When did this become amateur hour?"

Chris pulled Cait aside, but Finn could still hear their conversation clearly.

"It's a bit part, and Finn's done this before. I promise you won't have to carry him. He'll make you look good."

Chris thought this was a professional objection, but Finn knew it was personal. He could tell she was torn between acting like a diva or just sucking it up.

"You're trying to tell me there's no one else to do this?"

"This isn't L.A., or even New York. We don't exactly have a wide variety of actors just roaming through the woods in the hopes they'll come across a film set."

"Fine."

Cait adjusted the belt on a dress that made her waist look impossibly tiny. She took a deep breath that nearly caused her breasts to pop the buttons off her blouse. These WWII-era fashions were definitely growing on him. Well, the female fashions, at least. Cait looked fantastic, but his uniform was a bit over-starched. "Let's just do this," she groused. "It's been a very long day already."

As she walked away, Chris turned to him. "Caitlyn's usually so easy to work with. She just must be tired or something. I doubt it's personal…" Chris seemed to catch himself as he put two and two together. "Although maybe it is."

"Oh, I'm sure of it." He grabbed his hat and moved to his place.

He and Cait were pretty much live scenery for most of this scene. One of many couples dancing and chatting in the background while Jason and Naomi had their big emotional thing in the foreground.

Cait took her place across from him at one of the small tables in the pavilion. It was set up festively, like an outdoor party, with candles on the tables and paper lanterns hanging from the exposed beams. A swing band was set up on the other side of a dance floor, and extras milled about.

She kept her voice low. "What? You think you're Alfred Hitchcock now? Making little cameos in your movies?"

"Hitchcock was a director."

"I know that," she snapped. "It makes it even more egocentric to cast yourself in a movie when you're just the producer."

"*Just* the producer? What happened to how hard-working and professional I am?"

Cait bit her lip. He assumed she hadn't realized he'd seen her little interview already.

"That was before I knew you were vain enough to do this."

"It's not vanity. This is a present for my grandfather."

"You couldn't get him a tie or something?"

"The man has everything already. Except a movie."

After a brief frown, Cait ignored him while they did the light check, but she definitely wasn't happy. Maybe he shouldn't have pushed this. If her anger was going to affect her performance...

He shouldn't have worried. When Cait opened her eyes the anger was gone, proving once again she was a pro. As the cues came, she leaned in and propped her chin on her fist. A small flirtatious smile played over her lips and his body hardened. *She's only acting.* But, damn, she was good.

"We're supposed to be talking and flirting, remember? I thought you'd decided you were an actor now."

Her voice was barely above a whisper—just enough for

him to hear without creating additional noise on the set—but the challenge was there in her words and in her eyes.

He could never resist a challenge.

He leaned forward as well, letting his eyes rake over her. "I don't even have to act. I've been wanting to tell you for days how beautiful you are. I didn't think you could get more beautiful, but you did."

Cait's eyes widened and her lips parted in shock.

"It's so hard not to kiss you and see if you taste as good as you look. If it's as good as I remember." Taking hold of her hand, he let his thumb trace over the soft skin of her wrist. "Your skin…it was always so soft, so smooth under my hands, my tongue. And you loved being touched almost as much as I loved touching you." He felt her pulse jump, and her tongue rubbed over her bottom lip.

He was growing hard, uncomfortably so, and Cait was in real danger if she didn't stop looking at him like that. Her smile was frozen in place, but the heat in her eyes scorched him. This had turned into something far more dangerous than he'd predicted.

He pulled himself together forcefully. Leaning a little bit closer, he whispered, "How's that for acting?"

Cait's façade slipped the tiniest bit, but only someone paying close attention would have noticed. She swallowed hard, and the heat in her gaze faded to something else. She slid her wrist out of his hand and traced her finger over the rim of her glass instead. "Pretty average, actually."

He'd give her credit for a quick recovery—especially since he was having such a hard time doing the same. "You're a hard woman, Cait."

"And you're a—"

"Cut!"

Cait smirked, but kept silent as the crew quickly reset for a second take. When the cue came, Cait leaned in again. "You're supposed to be flirting with me, not trying to seduce me."

"There's a difference?"

"Of course. Flirting is a game. It's about the thrill of the chase. Seduction focuses solely on results."

Her scolding words were at odds with the flirtatious look on her face. It bordered on confusing. Although he knew she was playing to the cameras, there was something genuine as well. Like the smile she'd worn the other night... He remembered the reality too well to believe it was *all* an act.

"You don't play games, Cait. It's not in your nature. You look for the genuine. That's part of your charm."

She batted her eyelashes and gave him a sly smile. "I have charm?"

"Oh, definitely. That's why I'm trying to seduce you."

She faltered before she cut her eyes at him. "But I'm Rebecca right now, not Caitlyn. And you're not the hero of this story, so you don't get to seduce the girl."

The pressure against his zipper bordered on painful now, and Finn silently admitted the full truth he'd been denying. He wanted her. Badly. Their attraction had always been intensely physical, and his body was remembering that with a vengeance. It was only his big brain that continued to fight it. Coupled with the way Cait kept eyeballing him like a tasty treat... She was damn lucky there were two dozen people standing around and the cameras were rolling.

Of course maybe that was why she thought she could get away with it. She wanted the game? The thrill of the chase? Fine.

*Game on, Cait.*

Tugging at the collar of his uniform, he reminded her, "But I'm going off to war. I may never know the love of a woman again. You'd deny me one last touch? A taste? A sweet memory to take to battle with me?"

She swallowed hard. "Been there, done that."

He let his eyes roam over her again until she started to blush. "Yeah, I remember."

"Well, then, you don't need—"

"My question is..." He waited until her eyes met his again. "Do you?"

Cait looked away, but not before he saw her unguarded reaction. *She did.* That much was clear. And, for all her prim talk, the memory was a good one. *Oh, Caity,* he thought, *you forgot that I always play to win.*

*Damn Finn.* What the hell kind of game was he playing? "Torture Caitlyn" seemed an obvious answer, and he was doing a damn fine job of it.

Finn seemed to be waiting, and Caitlyn scrambled to find the proper words—or even the proper tone.

Because she remembered, all right. Hell, she couldn't seem to remember anything else these days.

"Well..." she hedged, only to be saved, once again, by the wonderful sound of the word, "Cut!"

Finn grinned, seemingly aware of her relief that she didn't have to answer right now.

Caitlyn looked away, unable to keep eye contact, only to meet Naomi's killing glare. So Naomi was feeling a little possessive of Finn? That possessiveness didn't sit well with Caitlyn, but she refused to examine it. Their next scene together was going to be fun. Naomi wouldn't have to dig too deep to find her motivation. In fact, Caitlyn wouldn't be surprised if Naomi "accidentally" slapped her for real.

With the cameras reset and rolling, she had to turn her attention back to Finn. "Naomi is not happy."

"She never is."

She happened to agree, but to do so aloud would be catty. "Then why do you put up with her?"

"Because I have to be nice to the talent."

"I meant off the set." She stirred the drink in front of her.

"Because I, too, am a team player."

It was hard to keep a smile on her face for the camera with their conversation taking such strange turns, but she was having a hard time separating what parts of the conversations were real and which ones weren't. Finn didn't seem to be having that problem. While he'd given her looks that practically melted her insides, he was doing an admirable job of pasting a camera-perfect smile across his face as well.

"What?"

"What what? She's vain and needy, but I hold up my end of the deal, same as you."

Now she was totally lost. "As me?"

"How do *you* put up with Jason's vanity and neediness— not to mention his stupidity?"

"By limiting exposure."

"Same here."

It was difficult not to react to that statement. "Lord, Finn, I know you've perfected the art of not giving a damn, but that's really…slimy, actually."

He actually looked insulted. He quickly reschooled his face, though. "What do you mean by that?"

"Naomi's not my favorite person, but it's unfair to use her like that. She seems to care for you, and it's wrong for you to lead her on like that when you don't care for her." *And I would know.*

He had the nerve to laugh at her. "You think I'm sleeping with Naomi?"

"Aren't you?"

"God, no. My 'relationship' with Naomi is no different than your relationship with Jason."

Why did that make a little happy bubble inflate in her chest? "Then I owe you an apology. But I still have to say that I don't think she knows that. In fact, if looks could kill I'd be dead on the floor right now."

There was that shrug again. "Oh, she knows it. It's just her irrational jealousy of you in general that's drawing the killing looks."

She'd adjusted—well, almost—to the idea of Finn and Naomi, so the paradigm shift took a minute to process. She didn't realize Walter had called "cut" until the camera moved closer to her and Finn to get close-ups and cutaways. The pensive looks were easy to do; Lord knew she had enough on her mind to ponder. The smiley and giggly ones were a bit harder, and when they asked Finn to take her hand again for some close-ups her insides got wobbly. Eventually Walter was satisfied, and she sent up a sigh of thanks.

Caitlyn had never felt so off-kilter during a shoot before. Between the death stares from Naomi, the sly smiles from Finn and the confused looks of the crew when she was a second too slow picking up on instructions... *Ugh*. She needed to get a hold of herself. Quickly. The sooner this scene was over, the better. She closed her eyes and searched for her center.

When she was called to her next mark, what little focus she'd found seemed to slither away. She'd rehearsed this scene with an extra, and normally it would be a piece of cake. They were supposed to dance—well, sway, at least—until Jason's character got jealous enough to pull her away. A hysterical laugh caught in her throat. It was almost ridiculous, considering their past, the fiasco in D.C. that night, and the current supposed love-tangle between Finn, Jason, Naomi and her.

She paced slowly, focusing on Rebecca until it was time. She just hoped she'd found *enough* focus as she took a deep breath to steel herself to do one thing she'd never thought she'd do again: wrap her arms around Finn and let him hold her.

And it nearly took her breath away.

She'd forgotten how solid he was. How much heat he generated. But what she hadn't forgotten was the feel of him, the right place to align herself to curl perfectly against his chest, the position her head needed to be in so that Finn's cheek could rest against her forehead. When Finn's fingers twined through hers to pull their hands against his chest, her knees wobbled from the onslaught of sensation and memory.

"You okay?" His voice came from above her head, but she could hear it through the ear pressed against his chest as well.

"Just lost my balance there for a second. It's these shoes," she added.

"Of course." But Finn laughed as he said it, and it rumbled under her cheek.

Dear heaven, the man was made to wear a uniform. She'd never known she could be such a sucker for a man in uniform, but then she'd never seen one—felt one, actually—filled out quite so nicely, either. Someone called "Action!" and as everyone came to life around them, she and Finn swayed to imaginary music.

No matter how many times she tried to remind herself that it was all just for show, Finn's earlier words were still too fresh in her mind. The slow, seductive movements were melting her insides, causing her to feel languid and liquid.

"This feels familiar," he mumbled.

"Indeed." It was all she could manage at the moment. Her throat was too tight and her insides were too jumbled. She closed her eyes and inhaled deeply, letting the scent of him fill her lungs. Memories and emotions swirled through her. This was not good. It felt good—better than good—but deep down she knew it shouldn't and wasn't.

A small ache settled in her chest. She didn't want to name it, because that would only make it worse. She bit the inside of her lip and let the pain bring her back to reality.

Or whatever the hell she could call *this* situation. If anything, it had crossed the line into surreal. The layers of ridiculousness meshed and the lines blurred. She was flirting with her real-life ex who was pretending to be her potential new love on camera, while her pretend new on-camera love, whom she didn't even like in real life, got jealous of the actions of the woman she was pretending to be. All while her ex-friend, who was pretending to be her sister, seethed with pretend jealousy over the pretend new love, while honestly seething with jealousy over her ex, who was pretending... *Ugh.* It made her head hurt when she tried to untangle it.

"It makes it easier, though."

She tilted her head up to look at Finn. Nothing about this was easy. "What does?"

Those green eyes sucked her in and held her. "The fact we've done this before. What do you call it? Method?"

She swallowed, unable to break away from those eyes. "Yeah. It's supposed to give a more genuine performance."

"It's too bad, then, that I'm not supposed to be seducing you. I could give a very genuine performance of that right now."

She could feel the proof of that statement pressing against her, and it sent a shiver over her skin as a fire sparked to life in her belly. *Oh, so could I.*

Thankfully, she heard the cue and was prepared for the hand that clasped around her elbow and jerked. Finn stiffened, but released her, and the two men glowered at each other. Then Jason was dragging her through the crowd out of the frame.

It was easy enough to act bewildered and clumsy. And, though the script didn't call for it, she couldn't help but look over her shoulder.

Finn didn't look happy. And that look was real. It shook

her insides, making her realize how dangerous this actually was.

And she still had at least one more take to do.

It was late. It had been a very long day. He was tired. Cait was most likely exhausted. If he had a lick of sense he'd be headed back to his place for a cold shower and a good night's sleep.

But, as his brothers were constantly telling him, he was an idiot. And, Finn thought, there was a chance he was about to really prove them right this time. There was no way he could *not* do this.

He parked his motorcycle a block from Cait's rented condo and walked the rest of the way, keeping to the shadows outside the streetlights' glow. While Cait hadn't mentioned any problems with the paparazzi staking out her place, that didn't mean he was totally in the clear. The last thing he wanted right now was a run-in with the press. Several others of the cast and crew were staying either in this complex or nearby, so if he was seen, the dots didn't *have* to connect to Cait. Not that a camera would put him off his mission, but he hoped he wouldn't have to deal with that. He simply didn't have the patience at the moment.

His official capacity meant he had access to the rental agreement, which included the code for the gate. He felt no guilt or hesitation at using it instead of calling up and hoping Cait would let him in. Once inside the walled courtyard, he let out at small sigh of relief he'd gotten in unobserved and took the steps up to her door two at a time.

He'd left the set only a few minutes after she had, so she couldn't have been home very long. He could see lights on inside. Finn rang the bell and waited.

He could hear movement, but the lag between the noise and the sound of the lock being flipped could only mean Cait wasn't thrilled to see him on her doorstep and had debated before deciding to open the door.

But she did open it, albeit only a foot or so. Her body blocked the opening. "It's really late, Finn," she said in lieu of a greeting.

"I know."

"And I'm tired."

"I figured."

Cait's teeth caught her bottom lip. For someone who claimed to be tired—and should be tired—she looked remarkably alert. She'd removed all the makeup from earlier, allowing her own natural beauty to glow with that girl-next-door goodness. And without all the mascara her eyes seemed brighter.

While she'd brushed the old-fashioned style out, her hair still held a bit of the curl, giving her reddish-gold waves around her face. She wore an overlarge tee shirt with the London Underground symbol on it. He could see the hard peaks of her nipples, and his hands itched to trace them. The shirt swallowed her almost to the hem of her frayed cutoffs. Those long, shapely legs were bare.

Cait shifted her weight, balancing one bare foot on top of the other, and leaned against the doorframe. "So what brings you by?"

He caught her stare and held it. "I think you know."

There was no surprise or shock, not even a trace of outrage at his statement. Her face remained still; the only indication she'd heard him was a slight hitch in her breathing. "What makes you think I'd let you in?"

"Because you want to."

She shook her head and snorted. "God, you're cocky."

He stepped closer and Cait had to lift her chin to keep eye contact. There was annoyance in those eyes, but that wasn't all that was simmering there. It had the same effect on him as a caress. "No, just honest. I've never lied to you, never taken you anywhere you didn't want to go. If I'm wrong—" and he knew now he wasn't "—just say so and I'll leave."

He knew that look on her face. She was arguing with herself, trying to talk herself into a different position. It annoyed him. He'd taken the bigger step, showing up here. She had to cross the remaining distance.

Cait dithered so long Finn began to wonder if he'd read the situation wrong, after all.

Then, in a flash, Cait's mouth landed on his.

He froze. Although this was what he'd come for—the logical outcome of the simmering tension of the last few days—the reality of Cait's lips pressed against his still came as a shock to his body.

Just as quickly, though, the paralysis broke and he grabbed for her face, holding her steady as her mouth opened under his and his tongue slipped inside.

Cait jumped as if she'd touched a live wire and her hands clasped around his biceps in a vise-like grip. It was easy, then, to walk back a step or two and move them both inside the door.

She responded by boosting herself up, wrapping her legs around his waist and using one foot to push the door closed with a bang.

Anchored against him now, Cait let her kiss turn carnal, and he could taste the desire that drove her.

It set him on fire.

*This* was what he'd tried to forget, what he'd let himself pretend he *could* forget: the sharp-clawed need that Cait brought roaring to life inside him. It blotted out everything that wasn't Cait, shrinking the universe to the woman who felt like a flame in his arms.

They weren't going to make it to the bedroom. Hell, he wasn't going to make it to the couch. Her touch robbed him of all control, went deep inside him to shine light on all his secrets and made him feel invincible at the same time. He sank to his knees, then let Cait push him back onto the carpet. She covered him like an erotic blanket, her legs tangling around his until she captured his thigh and rocked against it with a groan.

The sensation of Finn's thigh pressing against her core sent a shock wave through Cait that blurred the edges of her vision. She was already on the edge; the last few days had primed her for this moment, and it wouldn't take much effort on Finn's part to take her the rest of the way.

She could feel a similar urgency in him; the skin under her hands thrummed with energy and restrained desire, and it only fed the flames licking at her. But she also knew Finn—her body certainly did—and she knew that urgency would not translate to speed. Finn might be hungry, but he wouldn't be rushed. The thought sent an anticipatory shiver through her.

Rising to her knees, she grabbed the hem of her shirt and pulled it over her head. Finn's hands had been at her hips, holding her, but they now slid up over her waist and ribs until he cupped her breasts, his thumbs rasping over her nipples until she nearly sobbed at the sensation.

She needed to touch him, too. To feel his skin under her hands again. She tugged his shirt out of the waist of his jeans and pushed it up. *Mercy.* Finn hadn't let himself go in the intervening years. If anything, the ridges defining his torso were more pronounced. She felt a bit embarrassed over the few pounds she'd gained. But then Finn pushed himself up to peel the shirt the rest of the way off and pulled her back to the floor with him, giving her skin-to-skin contact that nearly scorched her.

She ran her tongue along his neck, and the familiar taste of his skin brought back memories of other times, other places.

The growl that came from deep in his throat only sharpened the clarity of what she was doing.

It was insane. It was stupid.

It was inevitable.

From the moment she'd learned Finn was heading this project she'd known, deep down, that this would happen. Even more disturbing was the fact she'd rather *hoped* it would happen.

Pressing her to her back, Finn captured a nipple in his mouth, and there was no room for anything anymore. Only pleasure. Pleasure that nearly overwhelmed her.

It didn't mean anything, she told herself almost desperately. She could enjoy it for what it was and nothing more.

It was hard to think, but she really didn't want to, either. Nothing really made sense, anyway. Except this.

*This was what got you in trouble last time.* It was a sobering thought, but not one that could hold up against the moist heat of Finn's mouth as he revisited all the places he knew would drive her wild. That place on her neck. The back of her knee. Everything became a sensual blur, and she bit her lip to keep from screaming. She might pay for this in the morning, but sometimes the high was well worth the hangover.

Then his head dipped between her thighs, and the touch of his tongue drove her right over the edge.

She recovered enough to open her eyes and focus in time to see Finn kneeling between her legs as he rolled on a condom. His eyes were dark as he met hers, and she knew he was getting close himself.

But his smile was a wicked promise as trailed his fingers along her inner thigh. "You still with me, Caity?"

In answer, she wrapped a hand around his hard length. A hiss escaped through his clenched jaw, and his fingers dug into her hips as she guided him into position.

Was that groan his? Or hers? It all blurred together as Finn slid in with agonizing, deliberate slowness until their hips met and he buried his face in her shoulder.

Cait could feel his heart slamming against his chest, and a poignant pang cut through the haze as Finn twined his fingers through hers and sighed deeply. The connection was complete. Electric. Perfect.

And terrifying. It stirred up too much inside her to not scare her.

Then Finn pushed up to his elbows and began to move.

And nothing mattered after that.

# CHAPTER SEVEN

"YOU'RE going to kill me, Caity." Finn spoke to the top of Cait's head. She was sprawled across his chest, breathing heavily, but he felt her laugh. She rolled off to the side, arms spread wide over the bed as she gasped for air.

"Not if you kill me first." She stretched and smiled. "But I'll die a happy woman, that's for sure."

They'd made it to the bedroom after the second—third?—time. He'd lost count, trapped as he was in Cait's erotic web. He should be sated, exhausted, but he didn't seem to have Cait out of his system yet, and the need to touch her hadn't abated. Desire still curled through him, as if he had to make up for lost time.

Cait sat up and reached for her water on the bedside table. As she did, he noticed a scar above her right elbow. It looked recently acquired, but thoroughly healed. He ran his fingers over it. "I don't remember seeing this on the set."

"Makeup does a really good job covering it." She stiffened, then twisted and tried to see over her shoulder. "Oh, hell, do I have carpet burns? I still have one more scene in a swimsuit tomorrow, and I'll never be able to explain those away."

"No carpet burns." She let out a sigh of relief that caused him to laugh and earned him a half-hearted swat. "But where'd you get this?"

"Remember that night on Sunset with the guy and the camera?"

Of course. They'd been coming out of a club—pretty trashed, granted—but it had been the paparazzo that jumped in front of them, camera flashing, that had caused Cait to miss the curb and fall. She'd landed wrong and banged her arm up pretty bad. The pictures of her flat on her back had made the papers—as had the ones of him swinging for the cameraman. He'd nearly been arrested and the media circus had been a nightmare. But... "Where did the scar come from, though?"

"It turned out I actually broke the bone, and since it was never set it didn't heal properly. It kept bothering me, until I finally went and had it checked last year. They had to go in and re-break it and put in a pin. The doc says the scar will fade eventually." She grinned and snuggled back against his side. "Remember that one blogger who kept calling us self-destructive? Well, I now have the scar that might prove he was on to something. Looking back, I'm surprised I don't have a lot more scars to show."

She was laughing, but he didn't find it funny. She'd talked about lasting damage, but he'd never thought it would be literal and physical. Guilt nagged at him. It was a new feeling that sat awkwardly on his shoulders, and he didn't like it. "I didn't know you'd hurt yourself that bad."

"I know that, Finn." She pushed up onto her elbow and the smile was gone. "And I'm not blaming you for it. Accidents happen. It's not like we were poster children for personal responsibility. We're just lucky that was the worst of it."

"Yet you still carry a grudge for everything else?"

She grinned. "Absolutely. I'll accept my fair share of responsibility, but I reserve the right to be grudgey."

He ran a hand down her back and over her butt. "And this makes sense how, then?"

"It doesn't. But, then, I've never associated Finn Marshall

with good decision-making, anyway. That's probably part of what makes you so hard for me to resist."

He understood the feeling, and as the silence stretched out that feeling warmed him. Then she sighed and pushed the rest of the way up to a seated position.

"And on that note, it's probably time for you to be leaving."

The words hit him like cold water. "What?"

"We both have to work tomorrow. I need to sleep for a couple of hours—and you do, too. But in a couple of hours the neighborhood will be waking up, and I really don't want anyone to see you leaving here."

He'd had similar thoughts, but rationality had a hard time holding up against the feel of Cait's skin against his. "You're kidding me." When she shook her head, irritation slid over him. "Ashamed of yourself, are you?"

"Just don't feel like dealing with the fallout. There's enough melodrama out there already without making this a real soap opera."

Technically, Cait had dodged the question, but he didn't call her on it. She rolled off the bed and to her feet. She found a tee shirt on the floor and pulled it over her head before disappearing out into the hallway. A minute later she returned, carrying his clothes, and dropped them on the bed.

It seemed she was serious. "You're kicking me out?"

"Not exactly." She smiled, but it was weak and slightly humorless. "Just encouraging you to leave without feeling any guilt for not staying the night."

"I suddenly feel cheap and tawdry."

She cut her eyes at him. "You're the one who showed up on my porch looking for a booty call."

"That's not…" He trailed off as Cait lifted an eyebrow at him in disbelief. "*Entirely* true."

"There was *another* reason bringing you to my door in the middle of the night?"

Damn it. He'd trade his trust fund for a good answer—if for no other reason than to remove that look from her face. He reached for his shirt instead, and heard her snort as he pulled it on.

Cait got ready for bed as he got dressed, and while she didn't exactly shove him out the door there wasn't much in the way of a proper goodbye. She had the lights off before he was even fully down the stairs.

It did feel rather tawdry—regardless of her valid reason for kicking him out.

And he didn't like it at all.

It was another hot, sticky day on the set and everyone's tempers were running on short fuses. Except Caitlyn's.

She was exhausted and distracted, but the endorphins still flowing through her body kept her temper at bay. She had too much on her mind, anyway, to get pulled into petty squabbles, and, since she really didn't want to accidentally say something she might regret later, she claimed a headache. Asking one of the production assistants to come get her when they were ready for her, she went back to her trailer to lie down.

The sleep she'd supposedly kicked Finn out in order to get hadn't come for a long while. She'd known what would happen if she let Finn in last night, but there hadn't been a way to resist the irresistible.

Was it smart? No. But then hadn't she decided their entire relationship showed a remarkable lack of good judgment? She allowed herself a tiny smile. Finn would be hard to resist even if she didn't have so many memories of how good they could be together—physically, at least. Had it been enjoyable? Oh, definitely.

But that didn't stop her from regretting it. Just a little. Sex only confused things, complicating an already complicated situation. Just when she felt she'd figured out who she wanted to be, Finn threw three years of soul-searching and planning out the window with a smile and a kiss. And that meant she hadn't really changed that much at all.

Her excuse for making him leave last night had been valid, but it had also been a much-needed out from the situation. Something had awakened inside her and she needed time to sort out what that meant. She was just glad he hadn't flat-out asked to stay, because she would have had a very hard time saying no.

And she probably would have slept much better with Finn as her pillow, because Finn made everything seem so easy. Accept something at face value for what it was and it became simple. Addictive.

She was smart enough to know that not all things that felt good—or even slightly right—were necessarily good in the long run. But even that knowledge didn't allow her to relax, and the minutes ticked by slowly as she stared at the ceiling.

"Fifteen minutes, Caitlyn." The knock on her door and the voice brought her back to earth.

She gave herself a strong shake. It probably had been inevitable, but she had it out of her system now. People went back to their exes all the time for a little relief, so she could cut herself some slack, chalk it up to the shock of being around Finn again and go back to her original plan.

Feeling resolved and more focused, Caitlyn grabbed her water bottle and went back to the set.

That resolve lasted all of five minutes, as Finn was deep in conversation with the assistant director not five feet from where she needed to be. She looked inward for focus and shrugged out of her robe. She made the mistake of looking at Finn as she draped it over the back of her chair.

His smile was appreciative, not leering, but it still had

her tugging at the bodice of the bathing suit. But there was a warmth in his eyes, too, that knocked her off balance a little.

Even more disturbing was the little glow that it lit inside her chest.

*Ah, hell.*

Finn felt a bit foolish watching Cait's trailer from the window of the office trailer. It was late, and everything shut down for the day hours ago, yet Cait hadn't returned to her trailer. Her rental car was still there, meaning she hadn't returned to the city for the night, but he didn't know where she was. Her trailer was dark, but there were lights on in some of the others, indicating she was in one of them. But short of going door-to-door looking for her…

No, he might feel foolish, but there was no reason to act foolish as well.

He glanced back to the email that was half-occupying his attention, and when he looked up, he saw the door to Cait's trailer close and the light inside come on. He shut down the computer and crossed the short distance separating the trailers.

He didn't bother to knock, and Cait merely looked up in surprise. "Oh, it's you. What's up?"

Her beautiful hair was pulled up in a ponytail that curled over her shoulder before she tossed it back in an impatient gesture. In a pair of frayed and tattered jeans, a tee shirt that hugged her curves and flip-flops, she looked like a fresh-faced college student. The battered leather backpack he remembered only completed the look, but that didn't stop the lust that had been kept simmering all day from roiling to a boil in his veins.

He wanted to pounce on her at the same time as he simply wanted to enjoy the moment and prolong it. "You're here late tonight."

"As are you," she said, then rubbed her hands over her face like she was frustrated. "There is a cold beer and a hot bath calling my name, so…"

He ignored the hint. "Why so stressed?"

"Not stressed. Just tired. I've spent the last two hours reading through with Naomi and Jason for tomorrow. It's exhausting."

He sat on the little couch. "Something not right?"

She dropped her backpack and sat at the other end, scrubbing a hand across her face. "Oh… No… I mean, it's fine. Just tense. And the tension is quite draining."

"If Naomi's giving you a hard time…"

She sighed and seemed to sink into the cushions as she leaned back and closed her eyes. "I can handle her. In a way it's funny—sad funny, not ha-ha funny. If I didn't know better, I'd feel bad. But it's her problem, not mine. And it's going to make that scene really amazing." She opened her eyes and smiled tiredly. "And that's what matters, right?"

Finn didn't know if he should feel insulted or not at her casual attitude. After all but kicking him out last night, she'd pretty much avoided him all day today. And while he'd caught at least one look thrown in his direction that defied interpretation, she was otherwise acting as if nothing at all had happened.

And these days he had no idea what was acting and what wasn't.

But something had happened. *That* had been real, and it called him back to her tonight against all good sense.

"Is this going to take long?" She pushed to her feet and went to stand front of her fridge with the door open and a pensive look on her face.

Her words collided hard with thoughts headed in a direction of what would take all night. He shook himself. "What?"

"Whatever you're here for."

What *was* he here for, exactly? Oh, he knew what his body wanted, but for the first time ever he felt oddly conflicted. This was new and disturbing—and it was a feeling he associated only with Cait. "It might. Why?"

"Then I'm going to open this." She held up a beer bottle. A bump of her hip had the door closed and she was screwing the top off. "I don't normally drink at all on the set, but I do keep one on hand in case of an emergency. Want half? I'll fall asleep on the way home if I drink the whole thing."

"Lightweight," he teased, but he nodded as well.

"I swore off alcohol for a while when I moved to London. All those people who were 'concerned about my drinking problem—'" she included the air quotes "—should be glad to hear I haven't had more than a buzz in three years."

"So the rumors about rehab..."

Cait poured half the beer in a coffee cup before offering him the bottle and keeping the cup for herself. Instead of returning to the couch to sit, she leaned against the table. "Aren't true. Once I got away from everything—my parents, the press..." She trailed off and wouldn't meet his eyes.

"Me?"

She looked up, considering, before she finally nodded. "Yes, even you to a degree. My stress levels went way down and I had less need to find solace in a bottle. I found healthier ways to deal with things—meditation, yoga..." At his laugh, she stopped. "What?"

"A California girl has to move to London to discover meditation and yoga? That's got to be a first."

That finally earned him a smile. "I even became a vegetarian for a while, but bacon tempted me back. I love British bacon. I think I gained ten pounds from bacon alone."

"It looks good on you." He let his eyes wander over her until she began to blush. "I'm serious. You used to take starving starlet to a new level."

"Just another thing I didn't have to worry about once I left." Cait finally moved back to her place on the couch. This time when she sat, she left her shoes on the floor and stretched her legs across the cushions with another deep sigh. "By the way, one of the P.A.s mentioned that your brother and his wife are going to be extras tomorrow?"

He sat the bottle on the table and lifted her feet into his lap. Digging his thumbs into the ball of her foot, he began to rub them the way she liked. She groaned and closed her eyes in pleasure. "Ethan and Lily. They're pretty much just scenery, so don't worry that it will be amateur hour."

She opened one eye. "I guess I should apologize for that crack. You did a great job." He warmed a little, because that wasn't a compliment Cait would throw out casually. "My question, though, is why has this become a family affair?"

"Like I said, *Folly* is a present for my grandfather. Putting his grandchildren in it is just an extra surprise."

"That's really sweet of you." Cait's forehead wrinkled as something occurred to her, then she nodded. "Ah, I understand now."

His hands stilled. "Understand what?"

She wiggled toes painted a garish shade of red until his fingers started to move again. "Why you've been so involved and constantly hovering over this project."

"Because the damn thing is a three-ring circus."

She shook her head as his hands moved to her calf and squeezed the muscle. "No. This is the one thing your brothers can't do for your grandfather."

Her perceptiveness caught him off-guard. He'd never hidden the fact that this film had personal importance to him because of Granddad, but he'd never said anything about his brothers. Cait had always managed to get deeper under his skin than he liked, but still… He frowned at her.

"Oh, don't do that. Probably no one else but me has figured that out. You don't give a damn about much, but your grandparents are the exception. So I understand."

"And what makes you think—?"

"You tend to talk a lot when you're drunk." She grinned at him.

"I do not."

"You do, honey. Or you did, at least. Your family was one of your favorite topics, and I can read between the lines. Your brothers live close to home, do the family business thing and they're the 'good' ones. But, no matter what they do for your grandfather, making him a film is something only *you* can do. I think it's wonderful, and I'm honored to be a part of it." She lifted the coffee cup in a mock toast. "Here's to making your family proud of their wild child."

So she wanted to dig into psyches tonight? Fine. He could play that game. "And yours," he added, lifting the bottle.

She stiffened, but didn't say anything.

"Oh, come on, Cait, you outright babble when you're drunk. You think I don't know that you're out to prove something to your parents? You always were, and I don't see a stint in exile changing that. In fact, some might say it's what's fueling your return."

Her mouth twisted, but she didn't try to deny it. "Then here's to living up to expectations. For once. May we both be successful."

"Those are two different things, Cait."

"Maybe for you," she scoffed. "I think we've established that the rest of us see the world a little differently."

"Maybe *you* established that. I don't agree."

Cait lifted her hands in surrender. "I'm too tired to fight with you again."

He gentled the massage into a caress. "That's certainly not why I'm here."

"I figured that much." She pulled her legs out of his lap

and curled them up to her chest. Wrapping her arms around them, she rested her cheek on her knees. "And it's tempting, but I don't think it's wise."

It took him a second to figure that out, and the rejection stung. It was tempered, however, by the sigh of regret in her voice. "And that's because…?"

"It's not healthy. Or fair, really, for me to use you that. Like a crutch."

He didn't fully understand her words. "I'm a crutch?"

She nodded, but her lips twisted. "Coming home is tough—tougher than I thought—but I shouldn't lean on you to make it easier for me. I think I need to stand on my own this time instead of using you to prop me up. It's wrong."

"I'm not complaining."

"No." She chuckled. "You wouldn't. But if I'm going to get my life back on track, I can't get all tangled up with you again. To be honest, you're dangerously addictive, and I don't see it ending well."

"You're over-thinking this."

"That would be a first for me, wouldn't it? Actually thinking something through before acting?"

"You're too hard on yourself. You always have been. There were expectations on you, but you let them get to you too much. And if you want to be all self-helpy about it, *that* was what nearly destroyed you three years ago. If you want your comeback, make it on your terms. Otherwise you'll end up back where you were before you left."

She snorted. "When did you get such insights into the human psyche?"

"It's not the human psyche. It's *your* psyche. Like I said, I was watching you pretty closely at the time."

Cait was quiet for a moment, but it wasn't an uncomfortable silence, so he let it spin out until she said with a soft smile, "Maybe I was wrong."

"I'll agree to that in general terms, because I like to be right, but for the sake of this conversation maybe you should be more specific."

"When I said that we weren't friends… In a strange way, I'm beginning to see that we were."

"Are," he corrected. Somehow it seemed very important to make that clear.

"Friends with benefits?" she challenged.

"I've never lied to you, Cait, and I won't start now."

"I know. And I think that's probably why you're so dangerous for me. The honesty can be brutal, but it's refreshing all the same, and it does make it easier in the long run." She laughed at her words. "No misunderstandings."

He met her eyes. "It's easier that way."

Cait pushed to her knees, and Finn wondered if he'd missed something. But when she crawled over the few feet separating them on the narrow couch and threw a leg over to straddle his lap, he assumed she'd worked it all out in her head. His hands went to her waist automatically, fitting perfectly into the soft indentation below her ribs and splaying down to the waistband of her jeans.

Her hand cupped his jaw, and the butterfly-light caress of her thumb across his lips sent lightning through his veins. "I still don't think…"

The ends of her ponytail brushed across the tips of his fingers, and he wrapped the silky strands around his fist. The light scent of her perfume tickled his nose. "Then don't think so much. Just take what you want. What you need."

He caught her smile as her head dipped to his.

The craving for her was still there, springing to the fore at the first taste, but it was tempered more than expected. The edge wasn't as sharp, and something else had filled the gap. Something that was quintessentially Cait. His hands shook slightly as they pulled her closer to him, molding her body into his.

*Take what you want.* Cait didn't know what she wanted—other than this, *now*. Right and wrong were too easily confused when it was Finn leading her down the path. Her skin sizzled to life under his hands, the nerves overly sensitive to his touch. She was fascinated by the play of muscles under tanned skin as he peeled his shirt over his head and removed hers. Those shoulders looked broad enough to support the weight of the world, and once upon a time she'd wanted them to support her. This time, that was exactly what he was offering—however temporarily—and there were no strings attached.

Finn's hands worked the snap of her jeans, releasing the zipper and letting his fingers fill the gap between denim and skin, and his mouth left shivers in its wake as it moved down her neck to the sensitive skin over her collarbone. The muscles in her neck felt weak, and her head tipped back to give him greater access. As his tongue moved to the hollow at the base of her throat, she let her hand slide down his chest to his straining zipper.

She traced the bulge and Finn's groan reverberated through her. She wanted to move closer, press herself against him... Cursing the narrow couch and the difficulties of jeans, Cait slid off Finn's lap.

His eyes were bright as he watched her wiggle both jeans and panties down to step out of them. Arching his hips, he mirrored her movements and his clothes landed on hers on the floor.

Then he settled back onto the couch and extended a hand to her. Taking it, she let Finn reposition her, her thighs framing his, as she lowered herself inch by inch. His hands splayed across her back, holding her against his heat, and the shudder that started in him ended in her.

Cait let her forehead rest on his, and his breath cooled the skin of her neck, leaving goose bumps. She held still, just enjoying the moment and the sensation. Then Finn's hands moved to her hips, and she let the sensations take over completely.

Right or wrong, this was honest. It was what she needed and what she wanted, and she was happy to take what Finn was willing to give.

She'd carried a knot in her stomach for so long, the lack of it felt strange. Strange enough that it took her several hours to identify what was different about her today.

The cynic in her just wanted to chalk it up to several toe-curling orgasms and file it away under "you just needed to get laid." But sex wasn't *that* good a cure-all. Not even sex with Finn.

No, her whole attitude was different today. Even the heat seemed more bearable today as she rested in her chair under a tent between takes. Naomi's little temper tantrums seemed more sad than anything else, and Jason's ego simply amused her. Her co-stars weren't her problem.

So she had to assume it was Finn. Late last night she'd realized that she wasn't just living down her past with the public. She was also living it down to herself, looking for forgiveness for the spectacular way she'd destroyed everything she had. Out of spite and weakness, she'd let her demons drive her almost as if she wanted to bring it all down. And deep down she probably had wanted to. Being around—and with—Finn again had rather brought her full circle, and she was ready to pick up where she'd left off.

Finn seemed to have forgiven her. She was slowly forgiving herself. Everything else had to be earned. She knew what she wanted now, and she could only earn those things the hard way. But she was in a good place to do so. She'd found herself again.

"Ms. Reese?"

Caitlyn shook herself out of her reverie to see a young, dark-haired woman approaching. Based on her clothes, the woman must be one of the extras, but the extras weren't normally allowed to roam free on the set like this. "Yes?" she answered cautiously.

"I just wanted to introduce myself. I'm Lily Marshall."

The name took a minute to penetrate. "Finn's sister-in-law?"

Lily nodded. "That's Ethan—he's mine—over there with Finn."

Caitlyn followed Lily's finger to the man laughing with Finn. For all he liked to complain about his brothers, there was a certainly comfortable vibe that belied his grouching. But, *mercy*, the two of them together were breathtaking. They had the same hair color and build, and together, they had quite a few appreciative looks being thrown their way. If the other brother was anything like that…

"Good looks run in the family, I see."

"Oh, they all look like that. You just have to get used to it. Hell on the ego, though, to have to stand next to them." Lily waved a hand, but the smile showed she was actually quite pleased with her husband's looks. "The whole family belongs on billboards. It's just dangerous and wrong for men to be so pretty."

It was a half-hearted grumble, and Caitlyn laughed. "I agree. Very disconcerting for the female population." Since Lily wasn't just any extra, Caitlyn indicated the chair next to her. "Would you like to sit?"

Lily shook her head. "I didn't really mean to disturb you that much. I just wanted to say that I was a fan. Not just your movies, either," she corrected. "I saw you do *Othello* in London. You were amazing. It made me cry."

"Thank you." There was something sincere and genuine about Lily that made her easy to talk to. "But please sit. It gets boring by myself sometimes, and I could use some company today." As Lily sat, Caitlyn asked, "How long have you been married to Ethan?"

"A little over a year. Brady—he's the oldest—got married last Christmas, so Finn's starting to feel the heat now."

Caitlyn nearly choked on her drink. Finn married? That was...well, simply unimaginable, regardless of how quickly the tabloids were to pre-plan any star's wedding. She had to assume that Finn's family would know that Naomi wasn't really in the running, but...*yikes*. Talk about stumbling into a minefield.

"Well, Finn tends to do..."

"Whatever he damn well pleases. Yeah, we know."

Exasperation and frustration tinged Lily's words. Maybe there was more danger here than she'd thought. Were there family tensions she didn't know about? He looked comfortable enough with his brother, but she knew all too well that looks could be deceiving. For Finn's sake, if nothing else, she didn't want to accidentally say anything that might make that worse.

She chose her words carefully. "You don't get along with Finn?"

Lily's eyes widened. "No! I mean, yes... I mean..." She shook her head. "I adore Finn. It's impossible *not* to."

"True." Caitlyn wanted to suck the word back once she saw the look on Lily's face. She reached for her drink. *Damn.*

"Is it difficult for you?" Her voice carried concern, not the digging-for-dirt she usually got. But this was Finn's sister-in-law...

She hedged her answer, anyway. "What do you mean?"

"Being here with Finn. Considering…"

Thankfully, she could fall back on the same pat answers she'd been using for weeks now. "We all have exes. And in this business, it's all but guaranteed you'll have to work with them at some point. You can't let all that personal stuff affect the work."

"I remember when you two were together. Just from the magazines, of course."

*Great.* She didn't realize she'd said it aloud until Lily laughed.

Patting her arm in a friendly and oddly comforting gesture, Lily said, "Believe me, I am the last person on earth who'd pass judgment on anyone for anything. I think that's why Finn and I get along. He's like that, too. As long as you're in a good place now, how you got there isn't important."

This must be the sister-in-law Finn had quoted at her with such admiration in his voice. An odd spurt of purely irrational jealousy spiked into her, but she forced it down. "You seem to know him pretty well."

"Finn was the only person to give me the benefit of the doubt when I needed it. I owe him big-time."

From the adoring looks Lily kept throwing her husband, that seemed slightly disloyal. "Not Ethan?"

"Since it was Ethan he was defending me against…" Once again she waved it away. "It's a long story. But Finn is special and I would like to see him happy."

Caitlyn's heart gave an odd stutter. "I think he is."

"Special? Or happy?" Lily challenged.

Caitlyn couldn't figure out the correct answer. "Both?"

Lily gave her a look that clearly questioned her sanity. "He's come a long way, but he has a way to go yet. Finn does a good job putting on the public face, but then all the Marshalls do. It worries me, though, and since you know him pretty well you probably know what I mean."

"I'm not sure we're on the same page. Finn and I aren't exactly—"

Lily kept on talking over Caitlyn's words, and Caitlyn realized that Lily probably knew Naomi wasn't really in the picture. Even worse, she'd jumped to the assumption that Caitlyn *was*.

"I think Finn's missing out on something, don't you? He's sheltered himself so long that I'm afraid that it's becoming the truth…"

Lily trailed off, and Caitlyn figured it had to have something to do with the confusion on her face.

"Or not."

Caitlyn wanted to press the issue more because, frankly, she was quite interested in this glimpse into Finn's psyche by someone who knew him well and wasn't romantically interested in him. But that would be out of line. It wasn't her business. And she had the sinking feeling she'd already revealed more than she should have to this woman.

Before she could regroup, though, someone called Lily's name, and she looked up to see Ethan motioning to his wife.

"I gotta run before I get in trouble. We had long lectures this morning about how we're not supposed to bother the stars. I was just so curious about you."

*That* statement seemed loaded and dangerous.

Lily slid off her chair. "I'm sorry if I bothered you, but it was very nice meeting you, Caitlyn. I hope to see you again."

"Me, too, Lily." It was unlikely, however, and Caitlyn felt a little twinge about that.

Lily went to her husband's side and he hauled her against him without pausing. It was lovely to see how attuned he was to Lily. Caitlyn could see some conversation go back and forth—and at least some of it was about her, since they occasionally glanced in her direction—before Finn frowned at Lily and Ethan shoved him. Laughter followed.

She put her headphones back on and went back to the script she was reviewing for later. The changes were minor, but she didn't want to hold anything up by not being on top of it. A minute later, though, she sneaked a peek at Finn, who had now moved to a table with Lily and Ethan.

It was interesting to watch, and she told herself her need to see was just research for future roles where she had a sibling and needed to create that family dynamic.

Lily was nice enough, but she was obviously wrong. Finn was possibly the happiest, most untroubled person she knew. He was certainly the most confident. Anything that wasn't great just got shrugged off those broad shoulders.

She sneaked another peek at Finn. So why wouldn't Finn be happy?

He had everything.

# CHAPTER EIGHT

THE loud bangs on his front door coupled with the ringing phone he'd tried to ignore could only equal one thing. Well, two, actually: Brady and Ethan.

Finn glanced at the clock as he rolled out of bed and grabbed the jeans he'd left on the floor after another late night with Cait. She might have the morning off to laze about and catch up on sleep, but he didn't. Of course when he'd dragged his carcass home like some teenager sneaking in in the wee hours of the morning, he hadn't expected his brothers to come pounding on his door just after sunrise, either.

He stretched and felt his muscles protest. He and Cait were going to have to work on actually making it to a bed. The pounding got louder as he got closer, and he could hear the two of them outside his door. Sadly, there was zero chance they'd go away, so he had no choice but to answer.

Wrenching open the door, he squinted at the light and his annoying brothers. "What do you want?"

Brady held out a cup of coffee from the shop about two blocks away. "We are taking the ladies to Cherry Hill Park today for an art something-or-another, and they thought you might like to come along."

"No." Finn started to close the door in their grinning faces, but Ethan caught it and they both walked in as if they owned the place. He rolled his eyes but accepted the coffee when Brady held it out again.

"Why not?" Ethan asked.

"Because I don't want to."

That earned him a snort from Brady. "Neither do we, you know."

"The fate of the married man is to attend art shows for no reason at all. That's your bad luck."

Ethan dropped to the couch and propped his feet up on the coffee table. Brady took the chair opposite. It looked as if they planned to stay a while, and any hope of a return to bed was disappearing fast.

"Where are Aspyn and Lily? I thought you were—"

"Shopping," Brady answered. "There's a maternity store next to the coffee shop. They'll meet us here when they're done."

He never should have given any of them the address of his temporary home. He took the other end of the couch and scrubbed his face to wake up. "So you're just going to bother me until then?"

Brady took mock offense. "So much for brotherly love. We've barely seen you since you got back."

He pointed at Ethan. "I saw you yesterday." Turning to Brady, he added, "And I'll see you day after tomorrow."

"That's on the set. That's not what we meant."

"I'm not on vacation here. I'm working, remember?"

Brady snorted and pulled a magazine out of his back pocket. A picture of him and Naomi took up a good portion of the cover. "Could have fooled me. That doesn't look like work."

Finn left it where it landed. "Obviously you've never taken Naomi Harte to dinner."

"Trouble in paradise?"

"That was most definitely work by every possible definition of the word. You two are both well aware that certain things must be done for the sake of appearances, and letting people speculate about the nature of my and Naomi's relationship is good for appearances. There's nothing more to it than that."

Ethan looked at Brady. "You owe me fifty dollars."

More betting? When had his family become such gamblers? And on his personal business, no less. It was ridiculous.

But Brady wasn't paying. "No, you're only half there."

"Are you kidding me? I was there yesterday. There's a reason why our baby brother makes his living behind the cameras—he has no acting ability at all. Even Lily noticed you could've roasted marshmallows on the looks he was giving her."

Brady shook his head. "That doesn't mean the feelings are mutual."

"Oh, they're mutual. Caitlyn is not as transparent as this one, but—"

Finn started to interrupt, but his brothers seemed to have forgotten he was even in the room.

"Then why hasn't it leaked to the press?" Brady countered, indicating the magazine.

"Finn must have better control over his people than others do. Or else he just hires blind idiots to work for him—"

Finn stood and headed toward the bedroom.

"Where are you going?" Ethan interrupted himself to ask.

"You two don't seem to need me for this conversation, so…"

Ethan waved him back. "You could end it—and make me fifty bucks—by just 'fessing up that you're sleeping with Caitlyn Reese again."

"You don't need another fifty bucks."

Ethan merely grinned. "Ah, but the bragging rights that come with it are priceless."

Brady ignored Ethan to pin Finn with the "big brother" look and tone. "Not too long ago you were swearing that you and Caitlyn were ancient history, so your attempts to skate around the topic now make me think there is something going on between you two."

Ethan nodded. "Might as well tell us, because we're not going to let it rest until you do. I might even have to hint to Nana that—"

"Enough. Sometimes I wish I was an only child."

Brady nodded. "I think the same thing every day."

He'd never been one to care what anyone—including his brothers—thought of his love life, but for some reason he really didn't feel like sharing in this instance. Letting his brothers in to this part of his life just didn't sit right. It was what it was: two people who understood each other and their needs. But there was no way that those two idiots would let it rest, and unless he wanted to be hounded endlessly he had to tell them *something*.

"Cait and I are friends."

Ethan shook his head. "Try again. You've never been just friends with a woman."

"I didn't say we were *just* friends." He suddenly felt like a teenager. "We're close friends."

"Very close?" Brady asked.

He let the silence spin out, but his brothers didn't take the hint. "Quite close," he conceded.

Brady frowned and fished out his wallet. He handed a bill to Ethan, who pocketed it with a victorious grin, then turned that frown on Finn. "You do realize you're playing with fire here and just asking to burn the whole house down, right?"

"Wow, that's a tad over-dramatic. I am not now nor will I

ever be running for office, so even the biggest scandal I could possibly hatch won't bring down my career."

"Do you really give that little of a damn about other people?"

The heat in Brady's voice surprised him. "Excuse me?"

"It's not all about you, you know."

*I never should have let them in.* "I think the Marshall legacy will be fine, regardless of what I do."

"Probably. But I was talking about Caitlyn Reese."

"Cait is none of your business."

"And she shouldn't be yours, either. Aspyn brought me up to speed on Caitlyn's side of that sorry story. No wonder she's been in exile."

"What?"

"I only pay attention to you and your messes and how they affect us, so I'd never given a second thought to the fallout for her."

"She seems nice enough," Ethan added, "but I have to question her intelligence, getting mixed up with you again."

With that Ethan had crossed the line *and* reached the limits of Finn's patience in one fell swoop. "And that's all for today, folks. I need to actually work—and don't you two have an art show to go to?"

"Not just yet. We haven't said what we came to say."

"What is with you two this morning?" When Ethan merely raised an eyebrow, Finn got his answer. "Nana. She set you two on me, didn't she?"

"You haven't been out to Hill Chase recently."

"So she sent you two to lecture me on her behalf?" The need to hit something made his knuckles itch.

Ethan chuckled. "Something like that."

"And you people wonder why I live on the other side of the continent."

"We don't wonder at all," Brady said. "In fact, I'm often tempted to join you there."

"If that's supposed to be a threat, it's an empty one. You go into political withdrawal if you get more than a hundred miles from D.C."

"And you get downright belligerent at less than that distance." That remark came from Ethan.

"Because my family conspires to drive me insane."

"It's only because we care, you know," Brady countered.

"Then can we schedule this intervention for another day? Maybe one where I don't have an entire crew waiting on me to show up and actually work?" As if on cue, Finn's phone chimed as a text came in. He pounced on it gratefully. "Duty calls. I'll let you show yourselves out."

"You can't avoid this forever, you know."

*Watch me.*

Brady narrowed his eyes as if he'd actually heard Finn say the words. "Are you really that shallow? You're dating one woman in public for appearances' sake, sleeping with another on the side—I won't even go into the fact she's your ex—and you don't see a problem with that? Much less the fact that you're practically channeling your fath—?"

Finn held up a hand. "Stop. I don't know when you two decided to take up armchair psychology as a hobby, but you suck at it. I live in L.A., for God's sake, where everyone is in therapy."

Ethan shook his head. "God, you're grouchy today."

"Oh, gee, and it has nothing to do with being ambushed by my idiot brothers wanting to uncover my deep emotional problems before I'm even fully awake."

Brady turned to Ethan and shrugged. "At least he admits he has emotional problems. It's a step in the right direction."

"You two might be living an examined life these days, but it doesn't mean I have to. Not everything has to be tracked back to a childhood trauma and 'healed.' Quit dumping your daddy issues on me. The bastard has nothing to do with me or my life. He never has."

"And there's your problem."

"No, that's *your* problem. My problem is you two."

"And Cait," Ethan added.

Only the sound of his doorbell kept Finn from going for Ethan's throat. He'd never been quite so glad to have his sisters-in-law arrive. "I'm going to go take a shower. Lock the door behind you, okay?" He left them sitting in his living room with the sincere hope they'd be gone by the time he finished in the shower. This was *not* the best way to start his day.

The pounding hot water soothed his muscles but not his mood. *Why* did his brothers have to make something out of nothing? Especially something that was none of their business, like Cait. The thought of her calmed his temper some. While Cait might be guilty of self-examination these days, too, at least she didn't try to make her hang-ups his. She might be hard on herself, but she was easy on others, thank God. Brady and Ethan—and Nana, too—could use a few lessons from her on that.

He took a deep breath and calmed himself. This was temporary. Once he went home and wasn't quite so underfoot, his brothers and the Grands would back off. His life would go back to normal, and without Cait to fuel their ridiculous outrage they'd lose steam. They might continue to shake their heads and grumble, but two thousand miles would blunt the force.

All of this would pass. Normalcy was only a few weeks away. Why, then, didn't the thought improve his mood?

A morning off was bliss. Caitlyn slept late, then went for a massage and a manicure. After a little shopping, where a few folks recognized her and asked for pictures, she went to the set for a couple of hours. Five minutes after she arrived, she was warned that Finn was being uncharacteristically grouchy, and one look at his face convinced her to keep her distance.

It was a short, easy day for her, but Finn's bad mood had rubbed off even though he'd barely spoken three words to her. She'd rather been hoping he might come by tonight, but that didn't seem likely, and it bothered her more than it should.

She'd given Finn an out, but he hadn't taken it. In fact, he didn't seem to mind the fact that she was all but using him. She didn't like herself much for doing it, but she couldn't seem to bring herself to give up this chance. It wasn't as if she could have a fling with Finn in L.A. Not with the paparazzi and star stalkers there. Thankfully, what passed for paparazzi in Baltimore wasn't exactly tenacious or on every street corner. She might as well enjoy this moment while she could. Even though it looked like she'd not be enjoying it tonight.

Caitlyn forced herself to shake off the disappointment. She had no claim on him, and there were no guarantees— not even short-term ones. It was none of her business where Finn was when he wasn't with her.

She just needed to keep that foremost in mind.

At seven o'clock that night Caitlyn tuned in to *The Catner Report*, which was tabloid cable TV at its sleaziest. As much as she hated the show, it would give her a good reading on the level of gossip surrounding her—if any—and get her up to speed on what was going on in the wider entertainment world.

Carrie Catner always led with the biggest scandals, and when her name didn't come before the first commercial break Caitlyn began to breathe easy. She felt a little sorry for Cindy Burke, who grabbed the headlines by checking into rehab yesterday. They'd done a film together seven or so years ago, and Cindy was actually a sweet girl and really talented—if a little troubled. At the same time it was fortunate Cindy didn't have her act completely together or else *she* wouldn't have the fantastic part of Rebecca. She didn't want to take pleasure at someone else's misfortune, but it had been a boon for her. She'd just have to deal with the guilt.

When her picture flashed on the screen after the commercial it wasn't unexpected—especially considering the tie-in to Cindy.

"Caitlyn Reese is a name we haven't heard much recently, but that seems set to change. Currently on location in Baltimore, Reese was a surprise addition to the all-star cast of *The Folly of the Fury* as a last-minute replacement for Cindy Burke. Reese made her name in a string of romantic comedies, then moved to London three years ago and worked in theater, only recently returning to the States for a brief—but successful—run on Broadway."

*Way to damn with faint praise.*

"But Reese is better known for her headline-grabbing affair with star producer Finn Marshall that played out, then flamed out, just prior to her London move. Many speculated the affair might have contributed to the move."

*Well, that's not, too— Ugh!* She stopped the thought as a clip of her and Finn on the red carpet was replaced with a picture of Finn doing a tequila shot out of her cleavage. *Where'd they get that one?* She had no memory of that event, but that wasn't surprising.

"Reese was spotted with her former flame at a fundraiser in D.C., spurring speculation that her return to the big screen might not be all business, but witnesses described the meeting as accidental and possibly antagonistic, even though Marshall's company is heading the project."

*That was one way to put it.*

"In an interesting twist, though, Reese and her co-star, heartthrob Jason Elkins, were spotted having a leisurely brunch at a Baltimore eatery amid a swirl of reports that the on-screen romance seemed almost too realistic. Meanwhile, Marshall has been seen escorting Naomi Harte, the film's leading lady, to several of Baltimore's best restaurants. Granted, Reese and Marshall may be over, but that's got to be one *interesting* set."

Carrie Catner grinned gleefully at the camera and Caitlyn felt herself snarl. *You don't know the half of it.*

"A spokesperson for the production company claims that Reese and Elkins are 'just friends,' but refused to comment on Marshall and Harte. I guess we'll just have to wait and see. *The Folly of the Fury* is scheduled to hit theaters next spring."

Caitlyn turned it off. Well, she and Jason had done their jobs, but it seemed strange that the company would be floating the truth in rumor form. And by not commenting on Finn and Naomi they were practically confirming a lie. *Interesting* wasn't the word she'd choose for it. Her life might carry soap opera potential, at least according to Carrie Catner, but that wasn't too bad. That one photo of her and Finn at some long-ago party wasn't flattering, but it wasn't the worst photo they could have used. *All and all, not too bad,* she decided.

Her phone chirped as a text came in, and Caitlyn had to dig through her bag to find it.

The message was from Finn: *"You busy?"*

The hopes she'd carefully kept tamped down leaped back up.

*"No. Why?"*

*"Look out the window."*

Okay, this was just a little weird. Why was he texting her instead of just calling? She went to the window and peeked through the slats of the blind. The street looked normal: just a few cars parked along the curb. Then, down to her right, she saw a flash. It happened again, and she realized it was the headlight of a motorcycle parked just beyond the streetlight. The rider was draped in shadow and his helmet obscured his features, but she recognized both the bike and Finn's broad shoulders. She could see the glow of the phone's screen as Finn typed another message. What on earth was going on?

The answer pinged to her phone almost immediately: *"Want to go for a ride?"*

Was he kidding? They hadn't been caught together yet off-set, but that would be just asking for trouble. The only reason he could come here at all was because several of the cast and crew—including the director—were living in this block of condos. If he were spotted entering the courtyard it could be brushed off as visiting any number of people.

*"Are you crazy?"*

*"It's a nice night. Perfect for a ride."*

She and Finn had used to ride down to Santa Monica or Venice Beach on nights like this. Memories rose up to greet her, but she shook them away. Sex was one thing. This tee-tered dangerously on the edge of Something Else. The fact that she *wanted* to go only confirmed it was probably a very bad idea.

Finn's next message seemed to read her mind: *"You know you want to."*

That was completely beside the point. *"No way. Too dangerous."* "Dangerous" could be interpreted many different ways, so that wasn't a lie.

*"Why not?"*

Argh. She needed a good excuse. *"Someone might see us."*

*"Lame excuse."*

She happened to agree, but it was the best she could come up with.

*"But true."*

*"No cameras watching now."*

That much was true.

Finn didn't wait for her to reply. *"Come on."*

She dithered, fighting the part of her that really wanted to go. Not just because it was Finn—as if that wasn't enough—but because this spoke to that adventurous part of herself she'd been keeping a tight lid on. If she took that lid off, even just for one night, would she be able to get it back on? And she now knew why Finn was texting instead of calling. He understood how to build drama and tension, and the texts added to that sense of adventure.

Her phone beeped again: *"Well? You coming?"*

No, she told herself. She wasn't going to go. She needed to keep things with Finn behind very clear borders. But she'd already slipped her feet into her shoes and found her hoodie.

"I'm absolutely insane," she said aloud as she grabbed her keys and bolted down the stairs.

Finn flipped up the visor to his helmet and grinned as she approached. "I knew you'd come." He held out a helmet to her.

"This is crazy." But she was already braiding her hair and tucking it down the back of her shirt.

The helmet went on easily and smelled brand-new, making her wonder when Finn had come up with this idea. He helped her fasten the chin strap and flipped down the visor, then revved the motor as she swung a leg over and got on behind him. Her thighs fit around his perfectly, and as she clasped her hands around his waist, her whole body seemed to sigh into him.

With a roar of the powerful engine, Finn pulled out into the street.

She hadn't asked where they were going, but honestly she didn't really care. Finn had that effect on her. And after three years of very studiously *not* getting onto the backs of motorcycles with men like Finn, this small act was enough to make her feel wholly alive for the first time in a long time.

Of course there weren't any other men like Finn.

She laid her head against Finn's back and closed her eyes, enjoying the feel of him and the sway of the bike and the rush of the air. The sensation immediately took her back in time.

When Finn stopped at a red light and one hand came back to rub along the outside of her thigh, it literally felt like old times.

Caitlyn lost track of how long they rode, but she wasn't concerned. Everything just felt right at the moment, and she wanted to enjoy it. She knew they were getting a distance from the city as the streetlights got farther apart and the smells of the city disappeared. Finn finally pulled off the side of the road to a stop.

She sat up and flipped up her visor as he killed the engine. "Where are we?"

"Out in the county. Look."

She followed his finger and saw the bright lights. She did a double-take. "Are those fairgrounds?"

Finn grinned at her, obviously pleased with himself. "Yep. I thought you might like to go."

She didn't remember ever telling Finn about going to the fair with her cousins during those summers when she was young, but the chances of this being a coincidence were just too astronomical. The fact Finn even remembered something as silly and unimportant as that warmed her. It was sweet, actually, but...

"We can't go wandering through the fair. Someone might see us there."

Finn shook his head. "You worry way too much. No one expects either one of us to be here, so they won't be looking. Even if they think we look familiar they'll be hard-pressed to place us. We'll be just another couple enjoying the fair. Anyway," he said, as a sly grin crossed his face, "I happen to know that Naomi made a huge deal about exploring Baltimore nightlife today in front of the people most likely to spread the news. Anyone who might be looking for either of us will be trailing after Naomi instead."

It wasn't just the fear of photographers, but that excuse still served nicely. "But still…"

"I know. That hair of yours is pretty distinctive. So I snagged this—" he reached into the small storage compartment "—from the makeup trailer."

A blond wig. "How original." She frowned at it. "Even if they don't recognize me, surely someone will recognize you. You're not exactly Mr. Low-Profile."

He shook his head. "In D.C. or L.A., maybe. At a county fair in the middle of nowhere Maryland? Not likely. Anyway," he produced something else from the compartment, "I brought a hat for me." He ran a hand over the stubble on his chin and cheeks. "And I didn't shave, either. We'll blend."

If Finn hadn't shaved, did that mean this was a planned event, not just something he'd come up with spur-of-the-moment? If so… She couldn't go there.

"I don't know…"

There were a dozen dangers lurking here, not the least of which was if they *were* spotted, Carrie Catner and her Report would have a field day.

His voice turned coaxing. "I'll buy you a funnel cake. Maybe even an ice cream cone, too, if you're really nice to me."

The temptation was extreme, but it had nothing to do with the promise of food. "Fine. If this backfires, though…"

"You can kill me." The grin said he wasn't the least bit worried either way.

"As long as we're clear on that." She took off her helmet and let Finn help her adjust the wig. The blond bangs fell to her eyebrows, but a look in the side mirror had her groaning. "I still look like me. Only as a blonde."

"But no one is looking for you." He cocked his head and studied her. "I prefer you as a redhead, though."

The helmet didn't fit quite as well over the wig, but it wasn't much farther to the fairground parking lot. Caitlyn mentally crossed her fingers as they joined the line at the ticket window.

She held her breath, but no one seemed to spare them a second glance. Most of the crowd was made up of teenagers, who were far too interested in their own groups to pay attention to two adults.

Finn had the brim of his ball cap pulled low over his eyes as he bought their tickets, and after several more minutes of winding through the crowd where no one seemed to even notice them, she began to relax into the sights and sounds and smells.

"So, is it like you remember?"

"Yes and no. I would have been about fifteen the last time." Once she'd turned sixteen and had outgrown a little of her teenage awkwardness, she'd started working more and quit spending summers with her aunt. "What about you?"

Finn shook his head as he bought an enormous cotton candy and handed it to her. "I've never been to one."

She pulled off a hunk of the spun sugar before offering it to him. "Ever?"

"Nope," he said around a mouthful. "Wait—I take that back. We stopped at a fairground during one of my grandfather's campaigns. I didn't really have much exploration time, though."

She understood that. How many places had she been with her parents without actually seeing them? "I'm sorry to hear that."

"Geez, Cait, you make it sound like I was deprived somehow."

"Maybe you were." Her childhood had been pretty screwed

up, but she'd had some periods that resembled a normal life—like the summers spent in Oklahoma. It had been the one upside to her parents' schedules. She hadn't appreciated it at the time, but in retrospect…

"Then you are the only person in the world to think my childhood was deprived in any way."

He said it with a laugh, but it brought another memory to mind. Finn's childhood had been really screwed up. Her parents were paragons compared to his, and he only spoke of them in passing, if at all. It was a touchy subject for him, and one she knew to stay away from. "If you never even went to a fair, maybe it was."

"My grandparents set one up in the grounds at Hill Chase for my tenth birthday party. There was a small Ferris wheel and a carousel. Does that count?"

Since her parents had done something similar, she could honestly say, "No, I don't think that counts. For a kid, the fair is all about the rides and the junk food, but for a teenager, it's a social experience. It's all about the boys."

That made him laugh. "Then I'm glad I missed out on that. I wasn't much interested in boys. Still not, ya know."

She tucked her hand under his arm and leaned in. "Look around. You can practically see the hormones in the air. The boys and girls travel in separate packs at first, but they'll start mingling soon enough. The girls are already hoping the right boy will ask to ride through the Tunnel of Love with them."

"That *would* hold appeal."

"And the boys will show off at the midway games to win the girls giant teddy bears. It's a very complicated and important part of adolescence."

Finn snorted. "A couple of summers spent in middle America and you're an expert on teenage courtship rituals?"

She straightened her shoulders and said primly, "The most

successful actors will look back and realize they have always been avid students of human experience."

An eyebrow went up. "Quoting your mother is cheating."

She rolled her eyes at him and sighed. "Fine. I was a teenage girl and there were cute boys around. I wanted to fit in and be like everyone else, so…"

He looked at her oddly. "But you weren't like everyone else."

"No, but I wanted to be." She struggled for the right words. "You know what it's like."

"No, I don't."

It took her a second to realize that Finn was serious. "You're telling me that you always advertised your pedigree to impress people?" Finn's unrepentant grin made her want to smack him. "You should be ashamed."

"Teenage boys feel no shame when it comes to pretty girls. We're slaves to our hormones and will do whatever it takes."

"And you never wanted anyone to just like you for you? Not because of your family?"

"Liking me for myself wasn't high on my list of priorities when it came to girls."

"That's truly shameful, Finn."

"Money and power are very attractive. You know that."

"I do. Which is why most people with money and power want to be liked for something else. They try to bring attention to their other qualities."

"But *not* teenage boys. I had no problem working that angle. Most people—regardless of age—are quite shallow."

"Well, I can't claim to be the deepest puddle there is, but that's not why I was interested in you."

"I know." His mouth twitched. "The first woman I'd met on either coast who didn't need my money or my connections."

She laughed. "Because I had my own, thank you very much."

"Exactly. That's why you were such a challenge."

"Me? A challenge?" She'd been swamped by his charm and looks and...*everything*. Finn was a force of nature, and she hadn't exactly played hard to get. *Then or now.*

"Definitely. It meant I had to actually talk to you about something, try to find common interests..." He trailed off with a shudder. "It was very difficult."

"I'm flattered."

He grinned. "You should be."

She smacked his arm half-heartedly, but the truth was that she *was*. In her world, it was often difficult to know what was real. In retrospect, though, she was beginning to realize that the Finn she'd known had been very different from the public Finn. The intervening years and layers of hurt had clouded that.

But it was heartening to see that Finn again. It was more than just flattering.

"And," Finn continued, "since you *still* aren't impressed by my money or my name, I'm now going to have to try to impress you your way." He sighed dramatically before twining his fingers through hers and leading her to the shooting gallery. "Which one of those teddy bears do you want?"

At that, this adventure seemed to morph into something that felt a lot like a date.

And it scared her more than a little.

But it wasn't nearly as scary as the feeling that washed over her when Finn finally won the fuzzy purple bear she'd pointed out. He presented it to her with flair, and her heart lurched painfully in her chest.

This was what falling in love with Finn Marshall felt like. She remembered it all too well. And that was dangerous

# CHAPTER NINE

FINN could have purchased a dozen teddy bears for the money he'd spent shooting an air rifle with a crooked sight at a stupid mechanical duck. But in the end, he'd prevailed, and Cait accepted the token with what he could only call glee. He'd seen women less appreciative of diamond jewelry.

"You can add it to your collection."

"Collection? Hardly. This is the first time anyone's ever won me one." She rose up on her tiptoes to kiss his cheek. "Thank you, Finn."

She seemed so genuinely pleased that Finn rather felt he'd accomplished something much more complicated—like dragon-slaying. He couldn't put a name on the feeling inside his chest, but he was very glad he'd decided to bring Cait here tonight.

Cait tucked the teddy into the crook of her elbow and dragged him toward something called the Scrambler. The ride looked decrepit and possibly unsafe—more like it belonged in a movie where dozens of people were about to be killed and maimed in an unfortunate carnival accident.

But Cait enjoyed it so much, they got back on for a second ride. The big surprise came when he realized he was enjoying it, too.

Cait, for all of her public glamour, was ridiculously easy to please. He'd forgotten about that. He'd forgotten how easy it was to just be with her, being Cait and Finn—not Caitlyn Reese and Finn Marshall. Cait couldn't be impressed or cowed by a famous name or a fat checkbook, and he didn't have to be anything other than himself.

Whatever reservations Cait had harbored earlier about being here evaporated completely as they made their way down the midway from ride to ride. As they reached the back gate Cait licked the last of the powdered sugar from her funnel cake off her fingers and looked around, the corners of her mouth turning down in a slight frown.

"What is it?"

"No Tunnel of Love. That stinks. I wanted to ride the Tunnel of Love."

A dozen cheesy *double-entendres* sprang to mind regarding tunnels of love, but he kept them behind his teeth. Mostly.

"You'll just have to fill me in later." But her disappointed frown only intensified. "What, Caity?"

"This was going to be my first time. I was looking forward to doing it."

"But earlier you said…"

"I said teddy-bear-to-Tunnel-of-Love was the general path. I never had a boy win me a bear *or* ask to ride the Tunnel of Love with me."

Oh, the need to say something about riding love tunnels was about to kill him. But Cait seemed genuinely disappointed. "Never? I find that very hard to believe."

"The part I didn't mention earlier was that I was a bit of a late bloomer, with a mouthful of braces and, geez, I thought I'd *never* get breasts. I was shy and awkward—particularly when I was so far out of my element—and I blended into the wallpaper. Without my pedigree on display I wasn't exactly Miss Popularity. Teenage boys can be quite shallow, you know."

She laughed, but it was slightly bitter. Obviously Cait's

experimental forays into being "normal" hadn't always been the way they worked out in the movies.

"This was going to be my do-over night. Rats."

As she sat on a nearby bench with a sigh, he had the urge to have a Tunnel of Love shipped in from wherever such things were made. He joined her on the bench. "I'm sorry."

"Don't be. I'm just being silly." She leaned back and toyed with the teddy bear. "As far as do-overs go, this was pretty awesome. I've had a great time. Thanks."

"My pleasure." And, surprisingly enough, he meant it.

"I need to tell you something."

"Okay."

"I was wrong to blame you for my problems. Then and now. I needed a bad guy—who wasn't me—and you were an easy target."

"We all do what we have to do to get through."

"Yeah, but I didn't handle it well. I thought I was fighting back, but I was really just running away. Going to London was just the literal part."

"Sometimes running away is the only way to handle something."

Cait started to say something, then stopped and bit her lip as she reconsidered. Finally she looked at him. "Like you did? You left Virginia and went to L.A."

"Pretty much."

"Do you ever regret it?"

"No. I needed to start over, away from my family and all the baggage that came with them. Do *you* regret it?"

"No." She gave him a half-smile. "The execution was a bit faulty, but overall I have no regrets."

"Good. Then accept it for what it is and move on."

"Like you do?"

"You can't change people who don't want to be changed. You can't change the past."

"So that's how you've come to peace with your fath— family," she corrected hastily. When he nodded, she laughed. "Wow, we really aren't normal people, are we?"

"Not even remotely."

That caused her to laugh again. "You know, *this* is probably the most normal thing we've ever done together—even if I include the wig. You're definitely the best-looking boy I've ever ridden on a Ferris wheel with."

Her hand landed on his thigh, and she squeezed gently. Cait's smile turned a little shy and knowing, but then she leaned in to kiss him. It wasn't the same kind of chaste kiss he'd received for the teddy bear, nor was it the hot, carnal kind that never failed to set him on fire. For lack of a better word, he'd have to call it "sweet."

At that moment Finn quit running. He and Cait made sense. They understood each other. He should have seen it years ago. He should have gone to London after her instead of trying to pretend she was just another ex. All his denials to the contrary were being proved false.

When she pulled away she looked happy and relaxed, and it transformed her face. He'd gotten used to the guarded, slightly wary look of mere tolerance she'd worn on the set for so long. This reminded him of the Cait he used to know, and he realized that even when they'd been alone recently she'd never really relaxed back into herself. Of course, they weren't exactly spending their time chatting, either. He brushed the blond bangs away from her eyes and ran a thumb across her jawline. Part of him wanted to take her back now and spend the rest of the evening in bed, putting a different kind of happy and relaxed look on her face—the sated kind. But he was oddly loath to end this. Hard on the heels of that realization came an even more shocking one. He was loath to end any of it, and *that* was the biggest shocker of all.

"Wanna ride the Ferris wheel again?"

She beamed. "Sure."

He stood and held out his hand. Cait tucked the teddy bear in the front pouch of her hoodie before she took it.

Three steps away from the bench, he heard someone shout "Finn!" He turned a split-second before he realized he shouldn't.

The flash of the cameras nearly blinded him.

The weatherman on the news predicted a near-perfect summer day of warm temperatures, low humidity and lots of sunshine—an ideal day to get outside and enjoy.

But there was no way in hell Cait could leave her house. She was trapped unless she wanted to face the cameras waiting outside. All the shades were drawn tightly shut, and only a visit from the police earlier this morning had kept the media confined to the sidewalk and street beyond.

*Ah, for the good old days, when it took longer than twelve hours to break a story.* Thanks to the internet, and the twenty-four-hour cable channels with plenty of time to fill, news spread like wildfire.

They'd sprinted out of the fair last night, but in the time it had taken them to get back to the city, the local paparazzi had been tipped off and were waiting for them outside her condo. She went and peeked out the window. *Yep, still there.*

The director was fit to be tied, gossip-hungry locusts had descended on the set, effectively shutting down production for the day. Her agent was hyperventilating. Jason Elkins was giving interviews denying that they'd ever been anything more than colleagues. Thank goodness she hadn't gone with the original idea to really snuggle up for the cameras, or today would have been very embarrassing for them both.

But the worst was Naomi, who'd appeared on TV looking beautifully woebegone, the occasional tear sliding down her cheek as she spoke of heartbreak and betrayal.

It was a disaster, and as soon as she got near Finn Marshall again she was going to kill him just as she'd promised.

Her only contact with Finn, though, had been a brief text telling her to *"sit tight."* She hadn't responded because she wasn't quite sure exactly what she wanted to say to him, and she didn't trust her temper not to say something she'd regret. Since she had no plans to run that gauntlet outside until she had a good story in place, that instruction had been unnecessary, anyway.

But it meant she was locked inside, unable *not* to watch the entertainment news shows. The rash of amateur cameramen who'd gotten Finn's attention and then followed them out of the fair hadn't been the first attention they'd drawn that evening, based on the photographic evidence. She'd let her guard down too soon, gotten caught up in the fun and forgotten to be careful. There was a picture of Finn winning the teddy bear, one of them climbing onto the roller coaster and—her personal favorite—one of them kissing on the bench.

Oddly enough, her disguise had worked; it was Finn who'd first drawn attention—the man had a bigger following than some A-list stars, for God's sake—so the first story to break had been about Finn "cheating" on Naomi with some unidentified woman.

Unfortunately it had been only a short jump to then identify the blonde.

That was when the fun had really started. And it was worse than she'd imagined. In addition to "cheating" on Jason—his protestations about their relationship were being chalked up to avoiding the shame of being cheated on—she was being painted as "the other woman" in Finn and Naomi's relationship. From the mileage being made out of that, you'd have thought Finn and Naomi were married with a couple of kids and she was a homewrecker.

And, of course, their history was being rehashed with glee

by the talking heads. And *where* had they found all those pictures? She didn't remember half of them—which really wasn't surprising, as they'd tended to party hard back then and there were several nights that were fuzzy at best. It was embarrassing, but Finn had been right about one thing: she'd been far too skinny.

She and Finn making out in the back of a limo. Finn giving her a piggyback ride out of a club—she had her shoes in one hand and her hair was a mess. There were the ones she called the "Sunset Series": three photos of her stumbling off a curb and sprawled on the ground, two of Finn swinging at the cameraman and one of them arguing with the police. *Classy.* Someone had finally dragged out the one of her on Finn's motorcycle, and her humiliation was complete.

She would never claim that their reputations were completely undeserved—but, geez, no wonder it had got as bad as it had. In the retrospective pieces on TV they both looked as if they were one bender away from celebrity rehab.

Especially her. And while there were plenty of stories of the young and famous shaving their heads, forgoing underwear when climbing out of cars and wearing electronic anklets for multiple DUIs to compete with her flame-out, somehow *she* seemed to be the poster child for all that was wrong with "Kids in Hollywood."

She should turn it off, but listening to the reporters gleefully describe her fall from grace was exactly the punishment she deserved. Lord, the public never forgot anything. Even if they did, the gossip columns were happy to remind them.

She heard an increase in the noise level outside and went to the window. Peeking through the shades, she saw Finn making his way through the crowd, ignoring the shouted questions and waving away the cameras.

*Nice of him to let me know he was coming by.* Part of her was feeling petty enough to leave him standing out there to face the press and the ensuing embarrassment alone, but that would only make the situation worse. Instead, she unlocked the door and let him in.

She slammed the door behind him and threw the bolt. "You are a brave man to show up here, you know."

"They're just reporters."

She leaned against the door. "The press is *not* who you should be scared of at the moment."

"If you'll just calm down—"

His patronizing caused her to lose her already tenuous grip on her temper. "I will not calm down. I've spent all morning trapped in here—"

"I haven't exactly been at the beach myself. I've been trying to do damage control."

"This is your idea of damage control?" She waved at the TV, where they were replaying Naomi's and Jason's clips. "It looks more like every man for himself right now. Why aren't *they* 'sitting tight'?"

"It's messy, yes, but—"

She gritted her teeth. "Just once in your life could you at least pretend to give a damn about something? Anything?"

Finn finally got irritated and lost that calm, placating tone. "If you'd lay off your pity party for just a minute," he snapped, "I'll explain how we're going to get through this mess. All of us."

"Oh, I'm all ears." She stomped over to the couch, so mad now that she was tempted to take a swing at him. The pictures flashing on the screen now—what she was beginning to call their worst hits—didn't help her mood any. She pointed at the TV. "*That* was exactly what I wanted to avoid. I was very clear about not wanting my past with you dragged out and rehashed."

"Then you shouldn't have signed on to one of my projects."

"Excuse me?"

He crossed his arms over his chest. "Not everything is about you, Cait. Your insistence that everyone try to pretend we had no past helped put us in this position."

"You're blaming *me*?" Her head might explode at any moment.

"Oh, I've saved some blame for Naomi, too, because her unreasonable demands based on her jealousy of you caused part of this, but you get your fair share."

"And you get none at all? How convenient. My apologies for coming by your apartment and your trailer—"

"Enough. I won't apologize for wanting you. I've never hidden that fact and, you're right, I don't give a damn who knows it."

"You've made that very clear," she muttered.

He continued as if he hadn't heard her. "But I have bigger issues to deal with."

"I don't know. This seems like a pretty big deal to me."

"And you're right. It seems like a big deal. To *you*."

At that moment she almost hated him. And it hurt. But that hurt was a vivid reminder of why she should have never abandoned her earlier plan not to get near him again.

"In the grand scheme of things, Caity, it's not, and it will blow over. Hollywood is nothing if not forgiving."

Caitlyn opened her mouth to argue, but Finn cut her off.

"I will not let this mess derail my project at this point. Go on camera and say whatever you want to make yourself feel better. Say we're just friends, or that you were trying to steal me away from Naomi. I don't really care. Just say something and be ready to stick by it. But think carefully about what you want to say, because you'll have to ride out whatever comes after that."

"In other words, you're not going to involve yourself? How typical of you to just remove yourself from the situation. It gives me the choice of either getting pulled into a catfight with Naomi over you or falling on my sword. Great." She collapsed back with a sigh and rubbed her hands over her eyes.

"You're overreacting. I'd recommend you take the middle path and just let it blow itself out. You only have four days of filming left before the rest of us go back to L.A. to finish up. You can suck it up for that long."

She pushed to her feet and started to pace. "Gee, Finn, thanks for the support."

"Frankly, I've had it with the whole damn lot of you. The pettiness, the egos…"

"*My* ego? You're practically asking me to wear the scarlet letter for the sake of *your* project and you have the nerve to complain about *my* ego in the same breath?"

"You're damn right. Big picture time, Cait. The project is what matters here."

"To *you*." She threw his words back at him.

"It should matter to you, too. You of all people—"

That stopped her pacing. She stepped in front of him. "Me of *all people*?"

"Your father is famous for saying it's all about the work, not the people. You know that's how it works."

"Do *not* quote my parents to me. I'm well aware what they say in public. Unlike you, though, I know what they say in private. And my father told me many times that starlets are infinitely replaceable. Why do you think—?" She interrupted herself. "Oh, that's right. You don't think about anything other than yourself."

"Says the person too focused on her own press to realize that if she'd focus on *Folly* instead of—"

He knew just where to aim the blows to do the most damage to her ego. Well, so did she. "Screw you, Finn. This isn't about the damn film. Your precious picture will be fine. Your grandparents will be so proud, and you'll outshine your brothers for once. Hip, hip, hooray."

His eyes narrowed. "Don't bring my family into this."

"Why not? You brought mine into it."

"Because it was relevant."

"Here's relevance for you. Go to hell."

"Oh, grow up, Cait. This kind of garbage just comes with the territory."

"No, this kind of garbage comes from being with *you*. Once again I'm getting dragged down, and you won't lift a finger to help." There—she'd said it. It had been simmering under her anger all day.

"I am trying to help."

"Lord, I'd hate to see what you do when you do nothing. Oh, wait—I already know. Maybe I should just pack my bags and head back to London."

"Don't play the martyr, Cait."

"I'll play whatever part I damn well want. It's well within my range. Rest assured, though, that I'll make sure that *Folly* is everything you want it be. Can't let your grandparents down again, can we?"

"Well, just realize that there's no project in the world that will make your parents proud enough to actually pay attention to you."

She saw red and heard the slap reverberate around the room. Only when the painful sting started crawling over her palm and up her arm did she realize she'd actually slapped him. It had been hard enough to turn his head, and his cheek was turning red from the impact. She'd never been mad enough to hit another person before. Guilt battled with the elation of vindication as the silence grew heavy between them.

Finn rubbed his fingers over the mark. "The A.D. will be in touch about call times tomorrow. After losing time today, we'll be rearranging the schedule."

Caitlyn was still breathing hard, and the anger and adrenaline rushing through her blood had her shaking. The sinking feeling in her stomach, though, came from something else entirely and bordered on pain.

"I'll be there."

A curt nod was Finn's only response, and he was out the door before she could say anything else. She heard the shouts of the crowd outside, then the roar of Finn's motorcycle.

That hadn't gone as planned.

She went to the fridge in search of wine.

Five hours later Caitlyn was comfortably buzzed, but it wasn't enough to take the pain away. In fact, it was simply making it easier to be depressed and cranky. She should have known better than to seek solace in a bottle again. It wasn't helping any more this time than it had in the past.

The throng outside her door had thinned a little, but not enough for her to brave going out. Not that she had anywhere to go.

And she didn't have anyone to call, either.

So instead she got to sit here, alone, and think. And thinking was the very last thing she really wanted to do, because the more she thought, the less she liked her conclusions.

Funny how everyone had used to say she was a happy drunk. Today she was just a maudlin drunk, steeping in her own pity.

Finn had been partly right. It galled her to admit it, and it disgusted her that she'd been so far off-base before as to not see it herself. She'd spent her whole life trying to prove something to her parents, and when that hadn't worked she'd bounced the other way and made sure she had their—and everyone else's—attention. From then on, it had just been a vicious circle.

Funnily enough, Finn was the only person who had genuinely seemed to accept her back then. She snorted. *Because he hadn't cared.*

But he had to have cared a little bit. Maybe? At least back then? Or not. It was very hard to tell because he cared about so little. Especially now, damn him.

She'd locked up all her inner parts to keep them safe and under control, and then she'd given the key to the last person on earth she should. Why on earth was she surprised to end up right back here again? It would have been insanity to expect a different result.

Caitlyn leaned back on the couch and closed her eyes. At least Finn was consistent. And he seemed happy enough. Maybe she should take his advice.

Why did she care what people said about her? The tabloids contained no truth at all, so why let it bother her? Why *not* just do as she damn well pleased and at least make herself happy?

*Folly* would guarantee her entry back into her career. It wasn't Finn who'd made her look like such a loose cannon that no one wanted to work with her. So as long as she kept the partying to a minimum she'd still have her job. The rest of it… Well, she'd just have to hold her head high and act like she didn't care.

It wasn't as if she didn't have a shining example to follow. Finn was certainly the master, and she could simply emulate him.

It had to be easier than this.

"Do you need me to find you a local dentist?"

Finn looked up to see Liz, one of the P.A.s, looking at him oddly. "No. Why?"

"You keep rubbing your jaw like it hurts or something. Do you have a toothache?"

"I'm fine." His jaw was a little sore. Who'd have known Cait had such a strong right arm? He fully admitted he'd deserved it, though; that crack about her parents had been uncalled for and he was honest enough to admit it. But her accusations and blame-throwing had pushed him to retaliate in kind, and he'd gone directly where he knew it would hurt most.

And he felt bad about it. That wasn't his style or usual M.O. He just hadn't decided how—or if—to apologize for it.

Because, honestly, he was still pretty damn angry over the entire mess. It had little or nothing to do with the media circus playing out around them; he'd spent his entire life jumping from one ring of the circus to another, and he knew that eventually the circus would pack its tents, move to another town and someone else would grab the spotlight.

Right now, he'd just like to finish this project with a minimum of headaches or disasters. That would be lovely.

It was also highly unlikely.

He was in an evil mood, and he felt bad about what happened at Caitlyn's the other night. He hadn't spoken to her since then, figuring they both needed some time to cool down. He still wasn't fully there and wouldn't be until he'd had a chance to sort out her warped thinking.

According to her, *everything* was *always* his fault. And her constant fall-back argument that he simply didn't care was growing old, not to mention insulting. If he didn't care about her he wouldn't have taken her to that stupid fair in the first damn place. Maybe going to the fair wasn't the best idea he'd ever had, but that didn't warrant him getting branded the villain *again*. Either she was unbelievably shallow or completely self-absorbed. Possibly both.

Evil wasn't a strong enough word for his mood, actually.

The crisp, disapproving email from Nana had just about pushed him right over the edge. His brothers he could ignore. Their calls went straight to voice mail to be deleted. The crew...they were professionals and would get the job done. The cast—well, they could just suck it up and act like adults.

Naomi was getting all the mileage out of this that she could, and Jason was just an idiot who could also be ignored. Nana, though, was not ignorable, and she had the irritating ability to make him feel like a naughty child.

She *was* avoidable, though, and for now he was avoiding both her email and voice mails. It wasn't as if she could get more upset over this "deplorable and embarrassing" situation.

Cait was also avoidable—and she was avoiding him—but that would soon change. A glance at the activity outside showed that the crew had broken for lunch, so he sent a text to Cait: *"Meet me in your trailer so we can talk."*

A reply came back a few minutes later. *"Now is not a good time."*

Finn was sorely tempted to text back *Tough*, but Cait's next message came through before he could.

*"I have a long day ahead and talking to you now will only throw me off. I need to concentrate."*

Had it been any other excuse he'd have searched her out at the catering trailer whether she liked it or not. But Cait was doing exactly what he'd asked her and everyone else to do: sucking it up and getting the job done.

She'd even made a statement to the media from the stairs of her condo: "Finn Marshall is a colleague and a friend, but that line got blurred the other night. We all know how dangerous trips down memory lane can be. My apologies go to Naomi for my behavior, but only she and Finn can decide where they will go from here. You can all be assured it was a one-time mistake. Now I'd just like to focus on finishing this film."

He'd told her he didn't care what she said, so why did that tick him off? Obviously he was just going to be in and stay in a foul mood all day.

At least until he got to talk to Caitlyn and get this sorted out.

# CHAPTER TEN

HURRY up and wait. That was the mantra of all productions. Usually Cait didn't mind; she enjoyed watching the crew—the attention paid to every detail, the work that went into making the magic. The actors' parts in the production almost seemed superfluous sometimes, like an add-in at the last minute.

But today she had no patience for the hanging around. This was her last scene on her last day of filming. Unless something went wrong, or a problem was discovered at a later date, her part was done. And, while she felt some sadness at putting aside Rebecca and moving on, Caitlyn couldn't ignore the itching feeling between her shoulderblades. Freedom seemed just a short distance away.

The last two days had given her time to think, to focus on what she really wanted and what was really best in the long run. Now that she knew, she was ready to move on and put this behind her.

It was big talk—if slightly repetitive at this point—but she had a *real* plan now. Just because she was now on Plan Q because Plans A through P had gone up in flames, that didn't mean it wasn't a good plan, nonetheless.

She sat in her chair, waiting for the director to quit arguing with the script supervisor, and fiddled with her phone for lack of anything better to do. The upcoming scene would be a relatively easy one: awkward moments with Jason and

Naomi's characters and a stilted goodbye. It was perfect for her mood. It would barely count as acting.

When a shadow crossed over her she looked up with a start.

It was only Naomi, but the relief was short-lived. While she'd been avoiding Finn the last two days, she'd been tense because Finn might decide he wanted to talk, anyway—whether or not it would throw her off her game—but Naomi wasn't exactly who she wanted to talk to, either.

With a cold, smug smile, Naomi took the seat next to her. Caitlyn went back to her phone, determined to ignore her, regardless of how childish it might seem.

Naomi opened with a dramatic sigh. "Well, I hope you're happy, Caitlyn."

Pretending to misunderstand her meaning seemed the best idea. "I am." She forced herself to sound cheerful and relaxed. "It's been great working on this project, but I'm looking forward to having some time off."

Naomi's eyes narrowed. It wasn't a good look for her, especially with all the makeup she had on. "I meant, I hope you're happy that you've managed to make this entire production all about you."

The scold in her tone only raised Caitlyn's hackles. She wasn't in the mood for this. "I know what you meant, Naomi. I was just giving you the chance to *not* act like an immature bitch."

Naomi's jaw dropped slightly, but she recovered quickly. "I can be an immature bitch. It's one of the perks, you know. I'm America's Sweetheart at the moment, and you're just a has-been who can't keep her legs together around Finn Marshall."

*So that's how it's going to be? Fine.* "Stings, does it?" Sarcasm dripped off her words.

Eyes wide and innocent, Naomi played dumb. "What?"

"The fact he doesn't want you."

Naomi huffed. "At least I have some pride. Finn may want you, but he sure doesn't love you. Not then, not now. You're just a convenient playmate."

Naomi's words stung, but Caitlyn was a good enough actress not to let it show. "It still doesn't change the fact that, given the choice between me and you, he chose to play with me. Losing out to me again has got to suck."

Oh, she'd hit a nerve with that comment, but after a brief stutter Naomi shrugged. "Only if I really wanted him. Which I don't."

"Then you're a better actress than I gave you credit for. Because you're sure acting like you're jealous. Everyone—especially the press—thinks so."

"Better to be thought jealous than a drunk slut," she fired back.

Caitlyn pretended to consider the statement. "You're right. It's a bit of a bummer I spent all that time trying to rebuild my reputation only to come home and pick up right where I left off." Naomi started to smile at her seeming victory, so Caitlyn went in for the kill. "Unfortunately for you, though, I *am* home. And I'm here to stay. Even though every tabloid is dragging my name through the mud, at least they're spelling it right. 'America's Sweetheart' is just a nice way of saying 'pretty but boring.'"

Heat flashed in Naomi's eyes. "Big talk from the person who started this whole disaster just to try and make everyone forget what happened three years ago."

"That was my mistake. I should have been wearing my past proudly to show how far I've come. So, while I may have fumbled this pass, I guarantee I'll be doing my touchdown dance soon enough."

"You think you're that good? You actually think this will be the time you'll step out of your mother's shadow?"

"I *know* I'm that good. And if anyone's worried about shadows, it's you. *I'm* not the one who had to get Finn to take me on a couple of 'dates' in order to make sure no one forgot I was working on this picture. And once it's released—"

"I'll have top billing," Naomi interrupted smugly.

"Well, there's a first—and a *last*," she emphasized, "time for everything, isn't there?"

If it were possible, steam would be pouring out of Naomi's ears. Caitlyn watched as Naomi clenched her fists and knew she was itching to smack her. "Now who's being an immature bitch?" she snapped.

"Caitlyn? Naomi?"

Caitlyn looked up to see one of the P.A.s approaching with a wary look. And it wasn't just any P.A.; Liz worked directly for Finn. Her little snipe-fest with Naomi had not gone unnoticed, and while Liz wouldn't spread tales unnecessarily, it would definitely make it back to Finn.

She forced her face into a neutral smile. "Yes?"

"They're ready for you."

"Wonderful. Thank you." She stood and brushed at a wrinkle in her dress. She felt amazingly calm and centered, which was odd since she should be all tangled up after that conversation. Naomi, however, looked as if her head was about to explode. "Your face is a little red, Naomi. Maybe you should go back to Makeup and see what they can do for you."

She left Naomi sputtering.

"I've never seen anything like it, Finn." Liz was wide-eyed as she gave him the rundown on the showdown. "I mean, I was expecting hair-pulling and scratching to start at any minute."

*At least they'd waited until Cait's last day to get into it.* "Do you know what it was about?"

She shrugged. "Something about billing and bitchiness."

"Personally, I'm surprised they didn't go at it before now. Did everything go okay after?"

Liz nodded. "Perfect, actually. They got it in one take. They're still finishing up with Jason, though."

"Good. We can wrap this up and go home. I've had enough of this place. How about you?"

"Definitely. It's so humid here." Liz slowed down as they approached the trailers. "I'll...um...go pack up some more stuff. I'm pretty sure Caitlyn's in her trailer."

Finn let her go ahead and angled off towards Cait's. Her door was standing open, and as he approached, a duffle bag landed at the bottom of the steps. He stepped over it and entered without knocking.

Cait seemed to be sorting through a stack of papers on the table. With a sigh, she just scooped them all up and shoved them in her backpack. When she stood and saw him she froze. Then she sighed again. "By all means, come on in."

The trailer was stripped of all personal items already. "You seem to be in a rush."

"I've been ready to go for two days now. I don't have much here, or at the condo so I'll be leaving in the morning."

"For New York or L.A.?"

"New York, actually." Her voice was falsely friendly. "I left so quickly that I left some things unfinished. Then I'm taking a short vacation, and I'll be back in L.A. in a couple of weeks. If you need me—for something *Folly*-related," she clarified, "my agent will know how to find me."

Cait was cold and distant, and all but telling him to forget her phone number. Her attitude hadn't improved over the last two days. But then, hadn't Cait already proved she could carry a grudge?

She zipped up the backpack and hiked it over her shoulder. "I would like to thank you and Dolby and Walter for this experience. It's been a great opportunity for me." She lifted her chin, seemingly proud of herself.

Since she wasn't going to bring it up, he was going to have to. "About the other day…"

Her shoulders dropped a fraction of an inch. "Yeah. I guess I should apologize for slapping you."

"You were stressed."

She snorted. "Don't make excuses for me, Finn. I said I *should*, I didn't say I was going to. You deserved it."

This was a change. He hadn't expected her to be so adversarial about it. He didn't know what he *had* expected, but whatever he'd planned to say escaped him now.

Her attitude changed and her voice became crisp and irritated. "Do you need something? I have a lot to do before I leave."

"I just wanted to see how you were holding up."

"Just fine." She smiled and lifted her chin, but the smile was plastic.

"You're a good actress, but even I'm not believing that."

"You're right. I'm not fine." Her face softened and, eyes downcast, she closed the space between them. "This is such a mess."

"It's blowing over already. By the time you get to L.A., something else will have taken its place."

"I was talking about us."

The sudden change threw him. And when her hand came up to rest on his chest and trace over his heart, the muscles twitched involuntarily.

"You know, I missed you so much when I left. I nearly called a dozen times."

Her voice was husky, longing, and it brought out a similar feeling in him. "Why didn't you?"

"It was hard, but I'd been kicked around so much by the press—and you were all tangled up in that—and I was hurting. I figured a clean break was best. You know, leave it all behind." Cait's voice was low, and her eyes followed her hand as it moved over his shoulder, his arm. "I thought I'd moved on, but I guess I'm a little like the media. Unable to forget." She fell silent, but her hands continued to move, stoking the fire. Finally, she spoke again. "Do you want to know why my love scenes with Jason were so hot? Because he wears the same aftershave you used to. I could smell it and picture you. Picture *us*."

His skin tightened.

"Some memories are just burned into your soul, you know? I thought I was over it, that I'd be able to resist, but I was wrong. I told myself I could have one small taste without danger. I was so wrong. You're my drug, Finn, and I simply can't resist. Even when I know it's bad for me. So it got me thinking..." She lifted her eyes to his then, and he nearly recoiled from the anger and bitterness there. Her hand came to his nape and she pulled him closer. "Why resist?"

He grabbed her shoulders and set her away from him. A smirk played at the corner of her mouth. "What the hell is wrong with you?"

"Nothing, Finn. I'm actually feeling quite right, and I owe that to you. So if you want one more for the road..." Her face was a picture of innocent confusion, but her words hit him with the same force her slap had. "What? Isn't that why you came here to see me? What you wanted?"

So much for understanding her. For thinking they somehow made sense together. He felt foolish, and he didn't like it. "Silly me. I came to check on you. I was worried."

"Ah. No need to worry about me." She moved away and perched on the edge of the table. "Why the face, Finn? I'm doing exactly what you told me to do. You've been right all along."

"About...?"

"Not giving a damn what other people think. It's very... liberating." There was something dangerous in her voice.

"I've always thought so."

"So I've decided to quit fighting it. Every town needs a bad girl who tries but never quite gets redeemed. It gives them someone to root for and feel superior about at the same time. I think I've found my niche."

He could see the anger and frustration radiating off her, but it was the determination that worried him. "What happened to your great redemption story?"

"Eh." She waved a hand. "I shouldn't try to play outside my range. People can tell when it's false. You certainly saw right through it. I hope you'll understand, though, when I say that we're kind of played out as well. I'm only looking to you for inspiration, not participation."

Finn didn't know what to say. He needed to say *something*, but this Cait seemed like an entirely different person, and he had no idea where to even begin with something that wouldn't make this entire farce even worse.

She seemed to be waiting for him to speak, and when he didn't, she pushed to her feet and rubbed her palms on her jeans. "So, I think that's a wrap. Are you here in your official capacity as producer?" She waited for him to shake his head. "And you're not here for sex, so I guess we're done."

Cait grabbed her backpack and slung it over her shoulder. "I'm sure I'll see you around."

"Cait…"

She sighed. "You've got some talent, Finn, but you're really not *that* good of an actor. Don't try to pretend you care. It's beyond your range."

Finn was speechless, and the feeling didn't sit well.

Caitlyn felt as if she was choking. Her throat felt closed and tight and it was nearly impossible to inhale. She'd been running on anger and outrage and frustration for days now, but the pain was finally starting to break through.

That had been the performance of her life. Definitely award-worthy. But, damn it, she would *not* let Finn toy with her like that.

She hadn't being lying, though, about the addiction. She'd been foolish enough to think that a taste of Finn would be safe. That she'd be able to put him behind her again.

She'd been horribly wrong. And the withdrawal symptoms were killing her. She loved the big jerk, but Finn wasn't capable of returning the feeling. Hadn't he proved that three years ago? Why had she gone and put herself back there again?

Because she was an idiot. A glutton for punishment. Even now, as much as she was hurting, she wanted him. If he hadn't pulled away, she'd have happily…

She had to give him some credit, though. Finn hadn't misled her; he'd been upfront from the start. He wasn't the one changing the rules mid-game and then crying when the other side didn't want to play.

No, this was her mess. Because the same things she hated about him were the same things she loved about him. The acceptance. The freedom. The lack of pretense. It was honest, but without more it felt shallow.

She laughed at herself. Oh, the irony. Looking for depth in Hollywood was a fool's errand. Unfortunately, after a lifetime in that puddle she really wanted something in her life that had some depth.

And Finn wasn't it.

Of course she had to accept the fact that maybe she wasn't that deep, either, and that bothered her. For now, at least. If it were true…well, she'd learn to accept it. Maybe embrace it even. It wasn't defeatist; she simply needed to find her strength and play to it. Even if there wasn't much to that strength.

With a sigh, she started the car and looked up to see Finn standing in the doorway of the trailer, watching her. It was impossible to read his face. Possibly there simply wasn't anything there to read.

She took a deep breath and was glad to feel the constriction in her throat loosen at bit as she realized she'd accomplished more than she thought.

She'd faced down Finn and survived, after all. She could face down Hollywood, too.

Finn tossed his cards on the table and Brady reached over to flip them faceup. When he saw Finn's hand, he sighed and nudged Ethan. "The idiot went all in on a pair of absolutely nothing."

Both his brothers looked at him as if he'd lost his mind. Finn shrugged.

Granddad's game room at Hill Chase was decorated to evoke old-fashioned gentlemen's clubs: dark woods, leather chairs, muted lighting. From the bar and dartboard at one end of the room to the pool table by the balcony doors, it was a masculine space, perfect for brotherly games of poker at the card table in the middle. The rest of the main house was quiet—the Grands, Lily and Aspyn had retired long ago, leaving them to beer and cards.

Brady had the "Disappointed Big Brother" look down pat. "Is there nothing sacred to you?"

"What? It's poker, Brady."

"Exactly. I thought you at least still took poker seriously."

He could happily punch Brady for that crack, but Nana disapproved of them destroying her furniture. At the same time, a knock-down-drag-out with his brothers might just make him feel better. He certainly wanted to hit something, but they'd wake the house if he did.

"It's just a game."

"Which I just won, by the way," Ethan reminded him, raking in the pot with glee.

Finn lifted his beer in a toast. "Good for you."

Ethan pushed back from the table and crossed his arms. "Okay, what the hell is wrong with you? Your mood is just... foul."

"Well, we can't all be a constant ray of sunshine like you."

Brady nearly spat his drink. When he recovered, he grabbed Finn's beer and moved it to the other side of the table. "I think it might be time to cut you off. You've obviously lost grip with reality."

"Hey, they call L.A. La-La Land for a reason. Reality isn't necessary."

Ethan looked at Brady and spoke as if Finn wasn't even at the table. "He *is* in bad shape."

Finn knew they weren't referring to the amount of alcohol he'd consumed. He was nowhere near done drinking them under the table. While none of them had mentioned their visit that other morning, he knew his brothers hadn't forgotten the topic entirely. He'd love to know what they reported back to Nana, though, because the lecture he'd expected had never come.

It was rather disturbing. Disturbing enough for him to broach the subject. "Am I a bastard?"

Brady snorted. "Well, I can't say with certainty, because I wasn't at your conception—thank God—but you do look a lot like the rest of us. So, I'll go with no."

"I should really know better than to try to converse with you two."

Ethan's face rearranged itself into honest curiosity. "Tell us what's on your mind, then, little brother. We're all ears."

He debated for a moment, then decided that if he could go all in on nothing once tonight, he might as well do it again. "Cait."

Ethan reached for his wallet and handed Brady a bill.

So much for thinking his brothers could be serious about

this. "Good God, what is it with y'all and this need to bet on my life?"

"It keeps us from getting too invested in the idea you might actually get your life straightened out."

"I have fame, fortune, success... What more do you want from me?"

Ethan looked at Brady, who merely shrugged. "At the risk of sounding maudlin, which I will blame on too much alcohol, we just want you to be happy."

"I *am*, damn it." He slammed his hand on the table, causing poker chips to jump.

"We can tell."

"Bite me." Finn went to the fridge behind the bar for another beer.

Brady turned in his chair to face him. "So if you're so happy what's all this about?"

Finn sorted through several answers, and when none of them seemed right, shrugged instead.

"Did you see that?" Brady nudged Ethan. "Aspyn was right."

Ethan nodded. "I thought it was just an annoying habit, but I'm going to go with her on this one."

He was going to regret asking, but... "What?"

"Your answer to everything is a shrug," Brady said. "You really don't seem to care. No wonder Caitlyn keeps leaving you. No matter what happens, you shrug it off."

"Because there's very little in life that's truly life or death. Everything else will sort itself out in time."

"And it makes you look like you really don't give a damn."

What had Cait said? *People believe what they see.* Now his brothers were piling on, too. "I care when it's worth caring about."

Ethan nudged Brady. "I like Caitlyn—"

"You don't even know Cait," Finn interrupted.

"I know she's got guts. Most people wouldn't have the courage to try to redeem themselves and make a comeback. They'd just slink away into obscurity."

Brady nodded. "True. That does show guts."

"And she probably would have done fine if I'd left her alone."

"Then why didn't you?" Brady asked.

Finn started to shrug, but caught himself. "Because I wanted her." He came back to the table and sat.

Ethan leaned forward and propped his elbows on the table. "I think she's proved she wants you, too."

"She says I'm a drug."

Brady's eyebrows pulled together. "That's new."

Ethan was nodding, though, as if he agreed with Cait. "I'd believe that. The allure of drugs is the high. It feels good. And you two certainly seem to have a hard time staying away from each other."

"Then I just don't understand her. Life is short. Do what feels good."

"Sure," Brady added. "But how many people do you know that went into rehab?"

"A few. But Cait isn't an addict."

Ethan rubbed his eyes. "I've had too much to drink to play with metaphors, so let me explain this to you in small words. If she says you're a drug, it means that as much as she wants you, she doesn't think you're good for her."

Finn fiddled with his poker chips. "She's made that much very clear. And look—it seems she's right. Her life seems to spin into hell every time she gets near me."

"Then you have to show her that you are good for her. That you can be good for each other."

"And how exactly do I do that?"

"By offering her what she needs."

"I don't know what the hell she needs. I don't think she

does, either. One minute she's planning her great redemption story—which doesn't star me—and the next she's deciding she'd rather play the tragic heroine. Also without me, I might add." He rubbed a hand over his face. Once again, Cait was the great paradox of his existence. There were scores of people lined up to tell him what he could do for them, what they needed from him. But not Cait. She didn't want or need anything he had to offer. "Lord, if anyone is a drug it's her. She's messed with my brain enough."

Ethan rolled his eyes. "Then suck it up and quit acting like an idiot."

"Gee, thanks."

Brady flipped a poker chip at him. "Ethan's right. And he knows from experience. So do I, actually. You're certainly carrying on a family tradition."

Ethan laughed. "It must be in the DNA. You know, we *do* suck at psychology. We were doing an intervention for the wrong thing."

"I don't have a clue what the two of you are talking about."

"The great Marshall failing is arrogance," Brady explained. "Taken to the extreme, you'll end up like our father. It makes for good politicians, but lousy people. We were trying to save you from that."

"We were totally barking up the wrong tree." Ethan shook his head sadly.

"Well, I'm glad you admit it." The conversation had taken a wrong turn, and Finn was having a hard time following along. "I still don't see what this has to do with me."

Ethan leaned forward. "Do you want Caitlyn?"

"Yes."

Brady held up a hand. "The more important question is do you love Caitlyn?"

Finn hesitated. How many women had told him he was incapable of that emotion? It certainly wasn't one he was familiar with. He certainly felt *something* for Cait, but was it love?

Ethan saved him from answering. "For the purpose of going forward—and because I really don't want to be at this all night—the judges will accept that as a yes."

"And…?"

Brady went to the bar and got two more beers. He returned to the table and handed one to Ethan. "Then pay attention, little brother, 'cause your big brothers are about to teach you something very important."

"And what would that be?"

Ethan grinned. "How to grovel."

# CHAPTER ELEVEN

FINN had never been so happy to hand something over to the post-production team. And he didn't realize how much *Folly* had been weighing on him until he did so. He wanted to be in the editing room, but he was honest enough to admit that editing was not his forte, and he'd be more in the way than anything else. Both Farrell and the editor, Paul, shared his vision for *Folly* and he had confidence in their work.

But he'd check in in a couple of weeks, regardless. Just to be sure.

He sat on his balcony, watching the waves lap the Malibu shore. Once back in the controlled setting of a studio, the last weeks of filming had gone quickly and without catastrophe. Without Cait around, his stress level had decreased substantially, mainly because Naomi had chilled out as well. As expected, the hoopla had died down as soon as Cait left for New York. Almost immediately, there'd been something else to take its place, and while Finn knew it wasn't forgotten, it was no longer hot news.

The last few weeks had been successful and easy, yet oddly boring.

Three scripts for potential new projects, a preliminary plan for a New York expansion of Dolfinn, and a budget for the next project lay on the table next to his chair. He was studiously and deliberately ignoring them all.

Because, according to the buzz, Cait was finally back in town. Which meant it was time for him to make a decision. He had to put up or shut up. And, since he was utterly miserable, it was looking more likely like he'd have to put up. Possibly even tonight, because tonight was *Folly*'s wrap party.

He had no idea if Cait was planning to show or not.

Contrary to her statement before she left Baltimore, Cait was remaining rather low-key at the moment: shopping on Rodeo Drive, lunching in all the proper spots and slipping back into her birthright as if she'd never left. She wasn't flying under the radar, but she wasn't calling undue attention to herself, either. She was just letting it be known that she was back. While she was currently staying at her parents' house in Beverly Hills, she'd been spotted house-hunting not far from here, making the statement she was back to stay without saying a single word.

Especially to him. *He* had to get his news on Cait from the media, the same as everyone else. It was frustrating.

Her agent was also letting it be known that Cait was actively seeking a new project, but when a casting director for Dolfinn's next picture had sent over a script perfect for Cait, he'd been turned down.

Finn wasn't sure if that was personal or not.

And it bothered him that it might be. She was certainly avoiding him. He'd remained cautiously optimistic that Cait would get in touch once she'd had some quality time to think and cool down. That hadn't happened. Now she'd arrived back in L.A., he figured they were bound to run into each other eventually, and he could let things happen naturally, but *eventually* was taking way too long and his patience was at its end. He was going to have to make the move, and for the first time in his life he wasn't sure how he was going to handle it.

His evening with Brady and Ethan had resulted in a painful hangover the next morning, but it was the hard truths that bothered him the most.

Brady had asked him if he loved Cait. He'd hesitated at the time, but now he was sure. He missed her. There'd been a hole in his life the last three years, only he hadn't known it. Or hadn't admitted it. Now he not only admitted it, he knew the cause. He needed her to feel complete.

And when he'd nearly thrown a punch last week at that stupid reporter who'd hounded him about Cait he'd known for sure. He didn't care what they said about him, but he cared what they said about her. And not only because she cared so much. It was the first time he'd worried about what the press was going to say about him. About them.

It was a giant mess. He and Cait were destined to live out their lives in the tabloids. They'd made that choice when they chose their careers. And since they'd be in the press separately or together, he'd rather it be together. The trick would be convincing Cait that it wouldn't be the worst thing ever.

So much for those people who thought he didn't give a damn about anything or anyone.

He gave a damn about Cait. And it was killing him.

One way or the other, *something* had to give. And if Cait didn't show tonight—well, tomorrow he'd turn stalker and go find her. The stalemate had gone on long enough.

Caitlyn took a deep breath as she smoothed out the shimmery fabric of her dress. Julio had done them both proud with this creation. It draped perfectly off her shoulders, showing plenty of collarbone and just a hint of cleavage. Nipping in at her waist and somehow managing to make it look several inches smaller, the dress stopped just short enough to draw plenty of attention. With a pair of simple black stilettos and her hair twisted into loose curls, she hit the sweet spot between dressy and casual, landing perfectly between look-at-me! and low-key.

Julio was a genius, and, even more importantly, had welcomed her back with open arms, calling her his muse. The truth was that Julio had many muses, but he knew that anything he put on Caitlyn would get plenty of attention. He made her look her best, and she guaranteed him more free advertising than anyone else. It was a win-win situation.

Caitlyn certainly needed the boost of a fabulous dress if she was actually going to attend the wrap party for *Folly*. Everything had been going so well since her return to town that she really hated to revisit the disaster. But she was damned either way. If she went, everyone would speculate there was more to the story, and they'd replay everything from Baltimore to remind the public how juicy it all was. If she didn't go, they'd *still* replay everything from Baltimore, only this time it would play out as being so scandalous she didn't dare show her face at the wrap party.

She really wished there was a very good, very public reason she needed to be elsewhere tonight. Honestly, it seemed rather anticlimactic to attend a wrap party now, weeks after her involvement with the film had ended. But it would be rude to the rest of the cast and crew not to go. Plus, it was well-known that Dolfinn threw some of the best parties in the industry. If she wanted to be seen as a major player, she needed to be at the parties with the major players.

Even if one of them was Finn.

She'd spent a lot of time recently very studiously not thinking about Finn. It wasn't helping all that much; her chest still hurt and her arms still ached. Like everything else, that would pass in time. *I have to keep telling myself that. Pretty soon I'll believe it.*

She wasn't asking for the moon. She just wanted to come first with someone for once, before the film and the press and everything else that shouted for attention all the time. Years of therapy had given her acceptance as far as her parents were concerned, but she wanted more than that from Finn. She couldn't live with anything less.

Dolfinn had rented out one of the clubs on Sunset, and the band of paparazzi and fans staking out the doors turned *en masse* as her limo pulled to the curb. She checked her hair and put a smile on her face as the driver opened the door.

Several photographers shouted her name, and she turned to pose and wave at the cameras. She even signed an autograph or two. Yep, this was her life. She was home.

Why did it leave her feeling rather flat?

Walter Farrell caught her in a hug as she walked inside. "Good to see you, Caitlyn." He tucked her arm in his. "It was absolutely wonderful working with you. I've got a script I want you to read."

"Have your assistant send it over. I'd love to look at it." *Score one point.* The director not only wanted to work with her again, he already had a project in mind. Enough people had overhead Walter's words to ensure that info would make the rounds quick enough. Maybe her comeback wasn't going to be as rocky as she'd imagined.

Then someone was pressing a champagne flute into her hand, and the atmosphere became party-like. This was the part of wrap parties she really liked: the chance to actually meet the people who made it all work while they weren't all busy *making* it work.

When a rep from the distribution company pulled her aside to talk about a couple of opportunities beyond her normal press junket schedule, her personal disaster seemed to be paying off professionally. It hadn't been fun, but maybe it had been worth it.

Even Dolby seemed happy to see her. "I've sneaked a peek,

and it's fantastic. Make sure that new house has a mantel for all the trophies."

"I'll do that."

"And I'm glad you came tonight. Some people seemed to think you wouldn't."

She'd bet Naomi—who was on the other side of the room, pretending she didn't know Caitlyn was even there—was one of those people. Oh, she was glad she'd come, after all, if for no other reason than to tick off Naomi. It was juvenile, but she'd get her thrills where she could.

"I wouldn't have missed it for anything."

Though she kept the smile on her face, Dolby's comment had dampened the pleasure of the evening for her a bit. While the hoopla in the press had died down, it *did* bother her that her peers and colleagues might still be gossiping about her behind her back. She could handle the changing opinions of the public, but professionally she didn't want the taint and the awkwardness.

The crowd was dense, the sheer number of people responsible for this project showing the scope and difficulty of getting this story to the screen. Thankfully, the crowd kept her busy and away from Finn. She couldn't fully enjoy herself because the tension of knowing he was there and that she'd have to run into him eventually put a knot in her stomach.

"Eventually" came a little quicker than she'd have liked. She was chatting with the armorer, who she'd worked with years ago on another film. Since the battle scenes had been filmed on the studio's back lot in L.A., this was the first she'd seen him since. Mid-sentence, she saw Finn out of the corner of her eye.

In black pants and a casual gray shirt, he looked like the star of the film instead of its producer. His hair had the perfect casual tousle that other men had to work to achieve, and the overhead lights caught the blond highlights. His tan was deeper; obviously he'd been back on the beach since his return. She couldn't quite see who he was talking to, but he laughed at something and the smile nearly weakened her knees.

All in all, he looked good enough to eat with a spoon in slow bites, and something inside her ached. It was beyond unfair to want something she couldn't have so badly. And it *hurt*. She had the sudden urge to go back to London. It was much easier to get over someone when they were five thousand miles away—it was like ripping off the bandage quickly. The fact he looked so completely unaffected just rubbed salt in the wound.

Being back here in the same town was just going to drag out the pain and make it even more difficult.

She knew the second Finn spotted her. She could almost feel his eyes on her. But she would be safe for a few more minutes. She'd have time to prepare herself. It wasn't as if Finn could just stop what he was doing and come over here—

"Cait."

*But I could be wrong.*

Very aware that everyone was watching and trying to listen, even as they pretended they weren't, she forced herself to smile. She even managed to lift her cheek for the mandatory air kiss next to her cheek. "Finn. It's good to see you. Dolfinn throws great parties."

He started to say something, but stopped, his eyes cutting to the crowd that was only just managing to pretend to be uninterested. She could almost see Finn change his mind about what he was going to say. *That was a first.*

His jaw was tight, but his words were casual enough. "Are you enjoying being home?"

"Yes, I am, thanks. I'm still figuring out where the best new restaurants are, but it's good to be back."

"Try Intaglios on Santa Monica. You'll like the fish."

She nodded, but the sheer inanity of the conversation had her biting her lip so as not to laugh. Finn noticed, and his jaw loosened a little as well.

"And how are your parents?"

It was a loaded question, but one she was prepared for. "They're happy to have me home, of course, and looking forward to the premiere. They're quite proud, actually."

Finn nodded in understanding. "Glad to hear it."

Their audience had noted their boring small talk and moved back to their own conversations once she and Finn didn't deliver fireworks immediately. The noise level began to return to its earlier level.

Finn dropped his voice a notch. "You look good, Cait. One of Julio's creations?"

"Of course. *He's* certainly glad I'm back."

"You're keeping a low profile these days."

She sipped at her champagne casually. "I'm trying to get settled. You know, get my bearings again."

"Planning your big splash?"

Oh, she knew exactly what he was referring to. "I'm keeping all my options open at the moment."

"That seems like a wise decision."

"I have been known to make those occasionally. I try to learn from my mistakes." She hadn't meant that as a jab, but Finn seemed to receive it as such. She wasn't going to take it back or try to explain, though. Retreat, however, seemed to be a viable and smart option. "I think I'll go refill my drink."

"I'll go with you."

"I don't think that's wise."

"I don't care."

"Why am I not surprised?" she snapped, and Finn had the gall to look offended. She quickly adjusted her smile and attitude so as not to attract attention. "Look, this really isn't the time or place. There are too many people, too many cameras. I don't want to—"

"Come on." Finn stepped to his left, out of the main room into a side hallway. When she didn't follow, Finn's mouth tightened and he returned to bend close to her ear. "You know I don't care one way or the other who witnesses what, but I know *you* do. I want to talk to you—alone—and I have no problem carrying you out of here if I have to. Your choice."

It certainly wasn't much of a choice. She was well aware Finn would do it, too, if she pushed him. *Might as well get this over with.* She'd let him say whatever was so God-awful important and then go about her merry way.

She sat her drink on a table and squared her shoulders. "Fine," she conceded, following him into the hall. "Let's just get this over with."

Finn pushed open a door directly to her right and nearly hauled her inside. She was sputtering with outrage as he flipped on a light and she realized they were in a storeroom of some sort. He closed the door behind him and stood in front of it, blocking any chance of escape.

Getting her feet under her, she adjusted her dress back into place. "I swear, Finn, you are *this* close to getting slapped again."

"If it will make you feel better, do it." He lifted his chin in a dare.

Caitlyn suddenly realized how small and quiet this room was. Facing Finn while surrounded by a hundred people had seemed an impossible feat, yet she'd managed. But here...? There was barely two feet between them because Finn's big body took up most of the space. She could smell him, feel the body heat radiating off him... She took a step back and found herself against a shelf.

Trying to act casual, even if she didn't quite feel it, she leaned against it and crossed her arms over her chest.

Indicating the liquor bottles around them, she shook her head. "I'd end up breaking something if I took a swing at you, and I don't want to add property damage to this fiasco. But it would serve you right if I did."

His voice and face softened. "Are you ready to talk to me now?"

*Stay strong.* "There's nothing to talk about, Finn."

"I disagree."

"Of course you do." She'd meant it to sound snappy and sarcastic, but it came out tired instead. *Damn.* "There seems to be very little we agree on anymore."

Finn's response was to kiss her. There was no warning, no time to think, just a flash of movement and then Finn's mouth was on hers, his body pressing close. It was like throwing a match on a stack of kindling: a moment of stillness followed by a *whoomph* as it caught and burned.

This was what haunted her dreams. The feel of Finn's lips, the way the energy moved from him through her and back again. She could taste desire and want, but beyond that there was a feeling of calm and *rightness*. Which was wrong.

Caitlyn broke the kiss and fought for control. "The last time someone tried that I brought him to his knees."

"You frequently bring me to my knees."

Finn rested his forehead against hers as she tried to process his words. His hands moved from her arms to grip the shelf on either side of her shoulders. She could easily duck under and escape, but for reasons that she didn't want to explore too deeply at the moment, she stayed where she was.

"And it was a risk I was willing to take," he added.

"Why?"

"Because I wanted to remind you why you should listen to me." He lifted his head from hers and grinned as he tucked a lock of hair behind her ear. "And because I like kissing you. I've missed that."

"You are an arrogant, conceited—"

"And you are stubborn, frustrating and..." he paused as he traced a finger over her jaw, causing her breath to hitch slightly "...perfect."

She'd done dozens of scenes where the hero said or did something that melted the heroine's heart—and she'd pulled them off—but now she knew what it was *supposed* to feel like: a warm squeeze that tapered off into a shiver, leaving her heart in her throat and her eyes burning.

She wanted to say something snarky and snappy, putting him in his place. The words wouldn't come. "I don't think I can do this, Finn." Her hand was cupping his jaw. Once she realized it, she let her hand drop and looked away. "We've struck out twice already."

"Then we still have one more try."

"I can't go through it again. It's too much. Too hard." Her voice cracked a little. "And it hurts too bad to walk away from you."

"Then maybe you should quit walking away."

She looked up and stared him down. "You've never given me a good reason to stay."

"I love you."

Caitlyn felt slightly faint.

Finn watched the color drain from Cait's face as her eyes widened. She even swayed a bit before she steadied herself. Maybe he'd gone a step too far. Maybe he'd misread the entire situation and gone all in on an empty hand.

Either way, Cait wasn't exactly showing joy at his spontaneous declaration.

But she'd kissed him back, and was currently standing in his arms instead of bolting for the door, so that had to mean something.

At least he hoped so.

"Cait?"

She blinked and blew out her breath. "That's…new."

Between what he'd expected to hear and what he'd hoped to hear… Well, that was neither. He couldn't say he hadn't been warned, though. Brady and Ethan were being proved right, damn it.

"It's not a new feeling, Cait. I just figured out the words."

"You can't be in love with me."

Another answer he hadn't expected. "Why not?"

"You don't let people get close to you. Not like that."

He toyed with a lock of hair that fell over her shoulder. "You're right. You're definitely the first."

She sighed and her shoulders dropped in defeat. "I can't."

"Because…?"

"Love is… Love is… It's supposed to be comfortable, easy."

"I can't decide if you've watched too many movies or not enough of them."

Her lips pressed into a thin line. "I'm serious. We have a good time together, but I'm not sure we're really good for each other. It's like we're—"

He tightened his fingers on the shelf to keep his temper under control. "If you bring up drugs and addiction one more time—"

"But it's true."

"No, it's not. An addiction shows a weakness for something you shouldn't have or don't need. Finding someone to lean on isn't an addiction."

"Well, it's not exactly healthy, either."

"That's ridiculous. I love you for you. It's simple. I *want* you to lean on me."

"But before—"

"You think I don't know that you thought being yourself wasn't good enough for your parents and that ridiculous idea of a birthright? I have a legacy, too, but DNA is not destiny. We've both proved that. The more you beat yourself up over it, the more you needed to escape the disappointment. It became a self-fulfilling prophecy. But I wasn't the cause. I was just the outlet." He paused to rub a hand over her hair. "And I'm okay with that. Whatever you need, I want to be that for you."

Cait's eyes widened with each word, and when they couldn't go any farther her mouth dropped open as well. He'd laugh, except his own response was rather similar. He'd surprised himself with that little impassioned speech.

Closing her mouth with a snap, Cait cleared her throat. "That's a really sweet, wonderful and…" her mouth quirked "…kinda cheesy thing to say."

"I obviously spend too much time with bad scripts. But the sentiment is real." He cleared his throat. "And one you haven't reciprocated. Yet."

"I've always loved you, Finn." She said it quietly, without meeting his eyes, and he didn't realize he'd been holding his breath until she finally said the words. "Which is why it's been so hard to be back. To be around you. I thought you didn't care."

"There are a lot of things I *don't* care about. But I do care about you. If you want me to sue the tabloids for slander and invasion of privacy, I will. There are plenty of attorneys in my family with nothing better to do than keep the media tied up in lawsuits for decades. I'll have my father call Congressional hearings if it will make you happy. If you want me to buy billboards or skywrite, I can do that, too. Whatever it takes to prove it to you. Honestly, I don't give a rat's ass what anyone thinks of me or mine, because it's a waste of energy I could use on something far more fun or important, but whatever is important to you is important to me. And if that means I have to take on the media or whoever, I will. Hell, I'll buy all the damn magazines out if you want."

"You'd do that for me?"

"More, actually. Just tell me what you want."

"But why?"

"Because I need you. We may not be good for each other in the normal sense, but we're not normal people. We don't live in a normal world. You are the one thing that really matters to me. Nothing else. And I'll be happy to prove that however you want."

Cait swallowed hard. "Wow."

"You keep saying that."

"Because this is a whole new Finn."

"Same Finn. I'm just making a few things clear to you this time around."

Her smile was blinding. "I appreciate your efforts. That's all I really needed to hear."

"And?"

Cait ducked under his arm and reached for the door. That was not what he'd expected, and he grabbed for her elbow. "Cait, wait—"

As she opened the door the sound of the party intruded. "I can't carry you, but I will drag you if necessary. It would be easier if you'd just follow me."

She extended her hand and he took it. At that moment, his world finally righted and made sense. "Anywhere."

Every head turned in their direction as they exited the closet, but Cait merely grinned at the crowds parting in shock in front of her as she walked toward the front doors of the restaurant with him dogging her heels.

The paparazzi were still four deep behind the roped-off entranceway, and his and Cait's sudden appearance brought a barrage of shouted questions and blinding flashes.

Without a word, Cait threw herself into his arms and planted her lips on his.

And he totally forgot the cameras were there.

Not that he cared, anyway.

# EPILOGUE

"HERE we go." Caitlyn grabbed the remote and turned up the volume, nudging Finn until he put down the script he was reading.

"I thought you hated Carrie Catner."

She dropped down beside him on the couch, settling in to the corner, and draped her legs across Finn's lap. "I do. With the heat of a thousand suns. I just want to know if she's going to hatchet me to death again tonight."

"She wouldn't dare."

She appreciated the show of loyalty, but Carrie Catner seemed to live to criticize her these days. Oddly, though, it didn't bother her all that much. She still wanted to know what was said, though.

"Self-appointed fashion police annoy me."

"You looked amazing last night, and even she couldn't say otherwise." He leaned over to give her a kiss.

The intro to *The Catner Report* played and Carrie's overly perky face filled the screen. "Last night's Los Angeles premiere of the much-awaited World War II drama *The Folly of the Fury* was a star-studded event. Fans of both the book and the stars were lined up around the block. Even some of Washington's VIPs were on hand to honor former US Senator Porter Marshall, to whom the film was dedicated, and who was instrumental in getting the much-loved book to the screen."

"Aw, your Grands look adorable."

Finn nodded, a small smile playing around his mouth. His hand smoothed along the outside of her thigh.

"The film's stars, Jason Elkins and Naomi Harte, seemed on friendly enough terms, calling into question recent reports that the two had a falling out shortly after filming."

Caitlyn was livid. "Nothing about *her* dress? Naomi's stylist must have been high to put her in that sack. Even I felt bad for her."

"Of course star-watchers know that the true trouble on set was between Harte and supporting actress Caitlyn Reese over the film's producer, Finn Marshall."

Caitlyn stuck out her tongue at the screen. "Yeah, yeah, we all know. Old news."

Finally the clips of her and Finn began to roll, and Carrie's voice picked up urgency. "Reese and Marshall arrived at the premiere in the company of her parents, director John Reese and actress Margaret Fields-Reese, and Senator and Mrs. Marshall. The continuing romance between the children of both Hollywood's and Washington's most powerful and influential families have positioned the pair as a rising power all their own. While the couple makes regular appearances around town and are sharing a Malibu beach house, they've kept quiet on any future plans. However, Marshall was recently spotted at Harry Winston on Rodeo Drive—"

Finn cursed and grabbed for the remote. Caitlyn smacked his hands away and turned the volume up another notch.

"—and an anonymous source claims he was examining engagement rings. While a purchase *was* made—and we can't say for certain it was a ring—careful examination of Reese's hands last night showed no sign of anything large and sparkly."

Finn grabbed for the remote again, and this time she let him have it. Not that she could have stopped him in her semi-shocked state. He silenced the TV as her heart seemed to stutter in her chest. She kept her cool, though, and merely looked at him expectantly. He looked distinctly uncomfortable.

She finally had to break the silence. "You were shopping at Harry Winston? After a new watch or something?"

Finn sighed. Lifting her legs with one hand, he arched his hips and reached into his jeans pocket. "It was supposed to be a surprise, you know. With some flowers and wine or something."

She swallowed hard as Finn resettled and balanced a box on her knee. "I'm still quite surprised."

Finn cracked the box and the sides opened like wings.

*Whoa. Holy...* Caitlyn knew her eyes had to be popping out of her head, but she kept her hands in her lap. "Wow. That's certainly *not* a watch."

Finn's eyebrows pulled together. "Cait..."

"But it's beautiful."

He removed the ring and held it with his fingertips. From the look on his face, Finn seemed to be having a hard time choosing his words. Finally he sighed. "Do I have to ask?"

"It would be nice." She bit back a laugh at his discomfort. "Just so that we're clear, you know?"

That earned her a frown. "*Clearly*, I'm hoping that you'll marry me."

She frowned back at him. "I can't say yes unless you ask."

"You don't get the ring until you do," he teased.

"Then we're going to be here a while."

Finn grinned. "Do you have something better to do?"

She shifted a little closer and ran her hand over his chest.

She felt the muscles jump and his heartbeat kick up as she pressed a kiss to his neck. "Maybe."

"That's cheating."

She shrugged. "I don't really care."

* * * * *

# THE PRICE OF FAME

BY
ANNE OLIVER

**Anne Oliver** was born in Adelaide, South Australia, and with its beautiful hills, beaches and easy lifestyle, she's never left.

An avid reader of romance, Anne began creating her own paranormal and time travel adventures in 1998 before turning to contemporary romance. Then it happened— she was accepted by Mills & Boon for their Modern Heat series in December 2005. Almost as exciting; her first two published novels won the Romance Writers of Australia's Romantic Book of the Year for 2007 and 2008. So after nearly thirty years of yard duties and staff meetings, she gave up teaching to do what she loves most—writing full time.

Other interests include animal welfare and conservation, quilting, astronomy, all things Scottish and eating any-thing she doesn't have to cook. She's traveled to Papua/ New Guinea, the west coast of America, Hong Kong, Malaysia, the UK and Holland.

Sharing her characters' journeys with readers all over the world is a privilege and a dream come true.

You can visit her website at www.anne-oliver.com.

# CHAPTER ONE

NIC RUSSO always planned for contingencies. The volcanic ash cloud from Chile sweeping across southern Australia had already disrupted air travel and any moment all flights out of Melbourne's Tullamarine would be grounded.

His instincts were always spot on and Nic didn't intend being one of those passengers caught up in the chaos.

In line at the airline's business check-in, he speed-dialled Reception at the airport hotel, heard Kerry's familiar, but somewhat distracted voice on the other end and smiled. 'Hey, babe. It's Nic.'

'Nic, hi.'

'How's it going there?'

'Hectic.'

'I bet. Reckon I'm going to need that reservation after all.'

'You're not the only one. There's a waiting list a mile long.'

'Ah, but they don't know the receptionist like I do.' He grinned. 'Connections, Kerry babe.'

'Are everything. Right.' He could hear the clatter of her fingers flying over her keyboard. 'So…that's for one guest?'

'Depends…' He deepened his voice and drawled, 'What time do you get off?'

The muffled cough was laced with friendly amusement. 'You're incorrigible, Nic.'

'So you keep telling me.' He could envision the humour in her eyes and knew Kerry and her partner, Steve, would have a laugh over it later tonight. 'If I'm still grounded when you get off, do you want to come by for a thank-you drink?'

While he talked, his attention was drawn to the slim brunette in line ahead of him. She'd been a passenger on his flight from Adelaide earlier in the day. He'd noticed her perfume then and he noticed it now—French and expensive but cool and light and refreshing.

Was it only her perfume that captured his interest? Neat and conservative weren't his type but there was…something about her. Something timeless.

The notion tickled him for a moment. But only for a moment, because Nic didn't do that nostalgic sentimental nonsense where women were concerned. In fact, he didn't do sentimental, period.

But it was exactly how she made him feel, and that was weird. He could imagine standing behind her just this way on the edge of a still lake and watching the stars come out. Flicking aside her single strand of pearls and the glossy hair that had escaped its knot and putting his mouth right there, on that slender neck—

'I'd love to catch up,' he heard Kerry say, jolting him back to the noisy, overcrowded terminal, 'but at this point with everything so uncertain I don't know how long my shift's going to be.'

'No worries. You're busy; I'll let you get on with it. Maybe I'll see you shortly. *Ciao.*'

He disconnected, his eyes still focused on the back of the woman's neck. Shaking away the odd feeling she'd invoked, he studied her from a purely objective viewpoint.

Who wore pearls these days? Unless she'd dressed for a royal garden party.

His gaze wandered over her shoulders, covered in a slippery-looking fade-into-the-background jacket, then down to a matching knee-length skirt over a well-rounded, caressable bottom. A sexy little handful. Warmth flooded his palm—and other places. He could do a tea party if it meant taking her home after...

Tea party? Pearls? Hell, if that turned him on, his libido needed some serious attention. It had been a dry couple of months, after all.

She'd been in the aisle seat one row back and across from him, plugged into her music player, eyes glued shut every time he looked, fingers stiff on her lap. No rings on her left hand, he'd noticed, but a heavy chunk of bling on her right. Maybe she suffered from the same affliction he did? But the suffocatingly claustrophobic effect of being hermetically sealed in a flying tin can was a tedious necessity in his life.

Whatever the reason for her tension, she'd been an intriguing distraction. Her apparent lack of interest had given him the opportunity to glance back every so often and wonder whether that peach-glossed mouth would taste as luscious as it looked. How she'd respond if he put his theory to the test. The expression he'd see if she opened those eyes and saw him watching.

He grinned to himself—yeah, that was more like him. The excitement of the chase, the inevitable conquest. And temporary. None of that timeless sentimental rubbish.

He shuffled forward with the line.

So she was also travelling to Fiji and flying Tabua Class. She didn't look like a businesswoman; not in that insipid suit that whimpered 'don't look at me', but she didn't look like a tourist either. Maybe she'd have the seat next to him and he could spend the next few hours finding out what colour her eyes were and whether or not a hot-blooded woman lay beneath that drab, conservative exterior.

Assuming the aircraft got off the ground.

She stepped up to the counter and slid a high-end brand-name suitcase onto the conveyor. A moment later, he watched her walk away, those mystery eyes hidden behind a pair of supersized sunglasses. A celebrity or a wealthy socialite? he wondered, swinging his own travel-battered bag onto the conveyor and reaching for his documents. Whoever she was, he didn't recognise her.

He proceeded to Immigration and Customs, unable to keep his eyes off the enticing sway of her backside a few metres ahead. *Forget it, Nic, she's not your type, remember?* Except his body didn't want to listen. So he deliberately stopped, shrugged off his jacket and stowed it in his cabin bag and studied the departures board a moment. He was supposed to be using the flight to brainstorm the ins and outs for his current computer game, not lusting after some unknown woman. Who wasn't his type.

He'd not gone far when he caught sight of her again amongst the milling crowd. And all casual, carnal thoughts vanished. A reporter he recognised from one of the local gossip rags stood in her way. She was shaking her head and attempting to move on, but the guy, easily twice her size, was blocking her progress, shadowing her steps as he towered over her. Intimidating her.

Nic's gut tightened reflexively as his own childhood images charged back. And now, as then, not a single person intervened or came to her assistance. No one cared, no one wanted to get involved.

*No way.* He swung his cabin bag over his shoulder and moved fast, the hand on the strap jammed into a fist. No

way would he stand by and allow the bully to get away
with it.

'Leave me alone,' he heard her say as he neared. She
was standing her ground, one palm thrust in front of her,
then she shook her head again, trying—and failing—to
pass. 'I've already told you, you've mistaken me for someone el—'

'There you are.' Nic said the first thing that came to
mind. 'I've been looking everywhere for you.' Keeping
his hands easy and non-threatening, he touched her rigid
shoulders and turned her to face him.

Beneath her flawless complexion she looked pale and
stunningly fragile, a vanilla rose facing the dawn of summer's first heatwave. Up close her skin-warmed perfume
was even more sensuous. Damn, what were her eyes saying behind that sunglass shield?

He didn't take his eyes off her face, willing her to give
him a chance to show he meant no harm, and said, 'Clear
off, mate, she already told you, you've got the wrong
woman.'

Charlotte blinked. One moment she was trying desperately
to deny her identity, the next, she was being swept against
some dark-shirted stranger with abs of steel who seemed
to think she was someone else.

Large hands held her in place and a deep voice against
her cheek murmured, 'Trust me and play along.'

She froze, her already hammering heart tripping against
her ribs, her insides trembling. She couldn't have freed
herself anyway; she was gripping the handle of her cabin
wheel-bag in one hand, her documents and handbag in the
other, and his arms were like prison bars. Well, not quite,
because they were big and warm and somehow protective
rather than restrictive.

As if he knew she'd had a recent run-in with the press and was desperate to avoid another. But he didn't appear to recognise her so she grabbed the lifeline he seemed to be offering with a vengeance, met his eyes and forced her lips into a smile. 'And here I am… *Honey Pie*.'

His brows lifted a fraction at that, then, nodding once, he returned a co-conspiratorial grin, his hands sliding off her shoulders and down her back.

And before she could draw another breath, his mouth touched hers. Tender yet firm but not hard and controlling. *Trust me and play along.* His words played back to her in that wholly masculine rumble that still echoed in her breasts, making them swell and throb with a tantalising heat.

For an instant, a whole other 'play along' scenario scorched the backs of her eyeballs as his lips teased and toyed with hers. She was vaguely aware of the voices around them blurring into one meaningless hum. This guy could *kiss*. Somewhere an inner voice warned her that she didn't know him…except instead of easing away as she should be doing, she *kissed him back*.

He pulled her closer, dived deeper and took complete possession. Of her mouth, her senses, her…everything. It was like falling and flying at the same time. She'd never experienced anything like it. Somewhere in the dim distance she was aware of an announcement over the PA system but the part of her brain that processed rational thought had already shut down.

She could feel his hands sliding lower, fingers playing over her spine and settling on her hips, beneath the hem of her jacket and against her skirt so that she could feel every pressure point his fingers made through the thin silk. His warmth soaked clear through her underwear to shimmer on her skin, coarse denim rasped against her skirt as his thighs came into contact with hers.

A moan rose up her throat. He was hard as rock. Everywhere. It made her feel soft and feminine and totally boneless and she found herself sagging against him.

He changed the angle of the kiss, bumping her glasses with his cheek or nose and tilting them sideways. She felt the pressure of his lips lessen and wanted to cling a moment longer—wanted *more*, *deeper*, *hotter*—but he lifted his head and straightened the glasses on her face and grinned. An intimate we're-sharing-a-secret kind of grin. 'Missed you too, *babe*.'

'Uh-huh.' She felt as if she were waking from a trance. She realised she'd stopped breathing and drew in some much-needed air. A whiff of some unfamiliar spicy fragrance teased her nostrils. The intimacy of the moment lessened, but her pulse was still stammering, colour and commotion and movement swirling all around her as she stared up at him.

His eyes...the deepest darkest brown, she noticed now. Mesmerising, compelling. The kind of eyes you could lose yourself in and never find your way back... She tightened her slippery grip on her belongings. 'I—'

He touched a long tanned finger to her lips, glanced over her shoulder and gave her a look alerting her that the media pest was still watching, then said, 'We'd better get moving—pandemonium's about to break out.' Curling a hand around her upper arm, he began to guide her towards the exit.

'Hang on!' She stopped. This was suddenly moving way too fast. 'Where are you taking me? What is *going on*?'

'Shh.' His warm breath tickled her ear, making her toes curl inside her shoes. 'Didn't you hear the announcement?' A flicker of barely there humour crossed his gaze—as if he knew she hadn't. 'All flights are grounded until tomorrow morning at the earliest.' Tightening his grip, but not so much that it felt threatening or uncomfortable, he propelled her forward. 'So we're going to the airport hotel.'

Of course she hadn't heard any announcement. She'd been otherwise occupied. Blind and deaf and mute to everything but him. His hands resting with familiar ease on her waist, his lips moving expertly and intimately over hers as if they were long-term lovers...

She didn't even know his name.

She jerked to a halt as warmth flooded into her cheeks. 'Wait. Just wait. I don't—'

'You'd rather stay here and take your chances?' He glanced at her, one eyebrow raised, his dark eyes assessing.

No. Definitely not. Wise or foolish, she'd take her chances with Mr Expert Kisser.

He tugged on her hand, giving her no further time to consider her options. 'Your stalker's following us—don't look back.'

A shiver ran down her spine as she struggled to keep up. Difficult when her knees still felt like clotted cream. 'How do you know?'

'I know how the guy's mind works.' They were approaching the terminal's glass doors, being swept along with the tide of noise and people. 'He's watching to see if our impromptu display of affection continues. Waiting for us to slip up.'

'But my luggage...'

'Has been checked through. You'll have to make do with what you've got.'

They walked out into a dull winter's late afternoon. Passengers who hadn't heard the news were still arriving, others were diving into taxis as fast as they pulled into the kerb and disgorged their load.

She accompanied him towards the sky bridge that led to the multi-storey car park and hotel. 'I'm sure we convinced him,' she murmured, yanking her wheel-bag up over the kerb and onto a strip of grass. Heavens, this guy had convinced *her*—introverted scene-avoider, Charlotte Dumont. And in more ways than one.

'Convincing, you reckon?' He stopped, looked down at her, lips curved into that devastatingly intimate-secret grin again. His eyes were twinkling. Or maybe it was just the sun momentarily peeking out from behind the clouds. 'I think we should give it another try,' he said. 'To be absolutely certain.' Before she knew what he was about to do, he slipped the glasses off her face. 'Ah,' he murmured.

She jerked her chin up, daring herself to meet his gaze. 'You were expecting brilliant blue or moss green? Violet maybe? I appreciate your help,' she hurried on before he could pay her some smoothly delivered yet empty compliment she didn't want to hear. She bent to unzip the side pocket of her bag, slid her documents inside, then straightened. 'Really. Thank you. But was all that…' she waved a hand, trying to find the right words to express the almost orgasmic experience and failing '…necessary?'

*Orgasmic?* One kiss? Oh, she so needed to get a life. A *new* life. And wasn't that why she was taking this trip? Time away to ponder her future and decide what she wanted to do? Which could, just maybe, include spicing up her non-existent sex life?

'Absolutely it was necessary.' His eyes remained on hers as he dumped his cabin bag at his feet. 'Subtleties are lost on guys like him.'

'Okay.' She nodded. 'Right. But I don't think we need to repeat the performance.'

He glanced towards the terminal. 'Think again, *babe*.'

'Oh, no.' She didn't look, snatching at her glasses instead, but he shook his head, holding them out of her reach. He stood so close she could feel his heat all down the front of her body.

He caressed the side of her face with his thumb. 'He can't be sure you're who he thinks you are—he's too far away to see the colour of your eyes. And that's his loss because they're enchanting.'

*Oh, please.* Flynn had been a smooth-talking charmer too. 'They're *grey*.' She resisted reaching for her glasses again because that was exactly what he was expecting her to do.

'Is there a reason you hide them behind sunglasses?' he asked, studying her closely. Curiously.

No way was she spilling her family history. 'I woke up with a headache, if you really want to know.'

'Sorry to hear that. How is it now?'

'Better. Shall we get this over with, then?'

One eyebrow rose. 'You liked it well enough a moment ago.'

And she had. She sure had.

He touched her face again. 'You should make the moves this time. Persuade him you're hopelessly besotted with me.'

A stiff breeze ruffled his hair. Black hair too long to call tidy, dark brows and olive skin that told her he was of Mediterranean descent. He had a square masculine jaw and prominent cheekbones. Lines crinkled at the corners of his eyes, as if he enjoyed life in the outdoors. His sensuous mouth curved easily and told her he also enjoyed more than a little indoors activity.

*Hopelessly besotted?* How could she be? She'd never laid eyes on him before. And yet she couldn't have said it better herself. And that should worry her because she wasn't going to be lured and seduced by another man's suave talk and good looks ever again. A man who undoubtedly knew exactly what he was doing, and did it often and well. 'I don't even know your name...'

Amusement touched his lips. 'It's Nic. Yours?'

She shook her head, rolled her lips together, then said, 'I should tell you he didn't have the wrong woman and he's probably an expert lip-reader.'

His gaze immediately dropped to her mouth and those dreamy brown eyes darkened. 'All the more important to head him off, then, don't you think? Kiss me.'

His husky demand stroked her skin and she rubbed her jacket and the goose-bumps that sprang out on her arms beneath her sleeves. 'I...' *Don't kiss men I don't know.* Except she already had.

'Say my name first if it makes you more comfortable.'

As if he knew her concerns. 'Nic.' She liked the way it sounded on her tongue. She liked the fact that he was doing his best to put her at ease. That he'd just saved her from public humiliation. That he was possibly the most stunning-looking guy she'd ever laid lips on. 'Nicholas...?'

'Dominic.'

'Dominic.' Reaching out, not quite able to look him in the eye, she placed a tentative palm on his chest. His shirt felt warm and smooth against her fingertips. Hard muscle shifted beneath her hand— Her fingers jerked away instinctively.

But what had Flynn said when he'd ended their engagement? She wasn't outgoing enough, not glamorous enough, not confident enough to be any aspiring politician's wife. That after twenty-four years as the daughter of a socially distinguished couple, she should be used to being in the public eye.

Since then she'd made a decision to work on her shortcomings. Hence this trip. To relax, regroup and refocus on the new direction her life had taken. To work on improving her confidence. She so wanted to prove her ex wrong. Then she could move on. And hadn't she already proved with that horrible reporter that she could be confident when it counted?

'Hey,' he murmured, catching her hand and putting it back against his shirt. 'Just shut your eyes and go with it. If it helps, pretend I'm someone else.'

No way. If she was going to do this, she was going to enjoy it, and that meant giving him her full attention. Her new life's direction could afford a little side-trip along the way. Then she'd book herself a room for what was left of today and this evening. She wouldn't have to see him again—all flights out of Melbourne did *not* go through Fiji.

So she took a deep breath, then boldly moved her hand over his shirt, taking her time, enjoying the sensation as she let herself relax and acquainted herself with the rugged unfamiliar terrain. Her other hand joined in—there was…so much of him. This excursion could take hours.

Disgruntled passengers trailing baggage and bad language flowed around them, as if they were an island in a flood-swollen river. Heavy exhaust fumes and the odour of jet fuel from aircraft not going anywhere clogged the air but all she could smell was Nic's spicy fragrance and warm masculine skin.

'Nic.' She met his direct gaze and said, 'Is there some woman out there somewhere who's going to want to scratch my eyes out?'

His lips curved boyishly. 'I could ask the same of you,' he said. 'It's a no from me.'

Charmed against her will—and wickedly turned on by that sexy mouth—she smiled back. 'And it's a no from me.'

'So no more procrastinating.'

She moistened her dry still-tingly lips. 'Is he still watching, do you think?'

That kiss-me-I'm-gorgeous smile continued playing around his mouth as he toyed with the button on her jacket, knuckles grazing her chest, eyes locked on hers. 'Does it matter?'

Her nipples tightened beneath his barely there touch and the corner of her mouth curved up. 'No.' Not one iota. Right now it *so* didn't matter. Give Stalker Man something to gawk at and enjoy herself at the same time, right? Meanwhile, the pest would get the message, find someone else to harass and she'd be free to reclaim her anonymity. All perfectly public and safe.

'Nic.' She rose up on tiptoe and planted her lips on his. *Not* tentatively this time. Winding her arms around his neck, fingers playing with the tips of his silky hair, surprised and amazed that she could let herself and her inhibitions fly away so easily.

Nic's wasn't the smooth, close-shaven jaw she was accustomed to and the unfamiliar masculine texture tickled her chin, sending reverberations all through her body. Which hadn't happened in a really long time.

Her mouth softened and parted without any help on her part. He swallowed her sigh and quickly took the lead, his tongue sliding against hers as he shifted closer, his hands sliding over her bottom, tucking her against him. Outrageously intimate and a long way from publicly acceptable.

She didn't know and she didn't care how long they stood there, locked together until she heard a man mutter, 'Get a room,' as he trudged by.

Nic broke away; his head came up. 'Sounds like good advice.' His voice sounded a little hoarse and husky. He slid her glasses back on her face, then picked up his bag, hefted it onto his shoulder. 'Let's go.'

'Wait…'

He glanced back at her and Charlotte saw that his eyes had changed. Not just amused now, but…surprised? As if she wasn't what he'd expected. And hungry, as if he'd like to devour her at the first opportunity. A delicious little shiver shimmied down her spine.

She looked about at the passengers already swarming over the sky bridge towards the hotel. A curious mix of disappointment and relief threaded through her system. 'Looks like we might already be too late.'

Grinning, he caught her hand. 'Then it's lucky I booked a room earlier.'

# CHAPTER TWO

LUCKY for *him*, she decided when they arrived in the congested lobby. Because now she thought about it—rationally—no way was she going with him to his room, no matter how expert a kisser he was. She'd filled her quota of daring, uncharacteristic behaviour for...oh, the next ten years or so.

'Wait here,' he told her as they entered. And as if the crowd parted for him, he made his way to the desk and spoke to one of the busy staff. But Charlotte shuffled to the end of the queue. There had to be *something* still available.

He returned moments later holding a couple of swipe cards. 'Okay, we're set.'

She shook her head. 'Thanks for everything, but I want to book my own room.'

Quirking an eyebrow, he grinned. 'You don't trust me after all we've shared?'

And that was the thing, wasn't it? She'd shared *all that* with a stranger. 'So why *did* you kiss me?' she murmured as the crowd milled around them.

He grinned. 'You can ask me that when you called me *honey pie*?'

There was that. 'You could've just stopped at "get lost"...'

His grin vanished. 'I don't like bullies.' He shrugged but she saw the tension in his shoulders. 'I just reacted.'

And she knew right then that he'd had firsthand experience with harassment. Something in his own past had triggered his Good Samaritan act. 'Thank you,' she said quietly.

'If I—'

'Please don't apologise.' *I enjoyed every memorable mind-numbing second.*

'Why would I apologise?' The grin was back. 'I'm not the least bit sorry. Are you?'

*Not at all.* But it was over. 'Thanks for your help but I still want to get my own room.'

'With this crowd?' He shook his head. 'There's someone I want you to meet.' He guided her to the business side of the desk, a light hand at her back. 'Kerry, this is…?'

'Charlotte.'

'Charlotte.' He said her name like a caress, his eyes lingering on hers as he said, 'Is there anything you can do for my friend here?'

Kerry, an attractive blonde with cornflower-blue eyes, barely looked up, her fingers busy on her keyboard. 'Sorry, Charlotte, we're fully booked. But Nic spoke with me and we're happy for you to share at no extra cost.'

Their earlier performance played in front of Charlotte's eyes like some hot romance movie. A public kiss was one thing, sharing a room with a guy she knew next to nothing about was something else, no matter how chivalrous he seemed. 'It's okay.' She tightened the grip on her bag and prepared for a long evening ahead. 'I'll buy a book or magazine and find somewhere else to wait.'

Kerry flicked Nic a look, then motioned Charlotte aside. 'My partner, Steve, and I have known Nic for years. He's an okay guy. You've got the chance to spend the next twelve hours or so in comfort; I'd take it if I were you.'

Charlotte nodded. 'Thanks, anyway.'

'Your decision.' Kerry inclined her head. 'Excuse me...' She was already moving away to deal with a woman who had one hysterical child attached to her leg.

'Look, you take the room.' Nic pushed a swipe card into her hand. 'I'll use the gym, catch up on some work at the business centre, then chill out in the terminal. I'll let you know when they're flying again.'

'Oh, no. That's very generous but I can't accept.' It just wouldn't be right. '*I'll* wait in the terminal.'

He frowned towards the lobby's entrance. 'What if our friend turns up again? The jerk's persistent enough. And sneaky enough.'

Charlotte's skin crawled and she couldn't help glancing towards the crowded entrance. 'Then I'll just come clean with him and maybe he'll leave me alone. About that... I should probably explain...'

'But you don't want to. And that's okay, I don't need to know your business. Here's what we'll do.' He curled his hands around her upper arms. 'We'll check into the room together, then I'll park my stuff and leave you to it. Okay?'

There was an openness and honesty in those dark eyes. So attractive, so alluring. And something she hadn't seen since that last time her father had kissed her goodbye and called her his princess. Right before her family had climbed aboard the doomed helicopter...

Her father had been the one man she'd always been able to count on. To trust. Somehow she imagined Dad would approve of Nic. That he'd tell her she could trust him too.

She nodded once, but for the life of her she couldn't make her voice work.

'Right, then, that's settled.' He took charge of her bag and they walked towards the elevators.

They didn't speak in the crowded lift. Nor as they walked down the dim, thickly silent corridor to their room.

Nic swiped his card in the slot, motioned her through, then followed with their hand luggage.

The clouds had rolled away, leaving a hard blue sky. Blinding late afternoon sunshine flooded in, reflecting off the distant tarmac where scores of stranded aircraft waited for the ash cloud to lift. Her temples throbbed with the light's intensity and the memory of a dull headache from earlier echoed at the back of her skull. She drew the heavy drapes closed. And with the imprint of their kiss still hot on her lips, she realised immediately how her action might be misconstrued.

The room was plunged into semi-darkness and the intimacy wasn't lost on Nic. Shadows softened Charlotte's features but he could see the puckered brow, the tense stance as her fingers twisted on the edge of the curtain. She wasn't comfortable with the situation.

Nor was he, but for entirely different reasons. He'd been in a painful state of arousal since he'd discovered she tasted even more luscious than he'd imagined—and he'd imagined quite a lot. He indicated the closed drapes. 'Headache still bothering you? Do you want to take a nap?' *Do you want me to join you?*

'No to both, but thank you.' Something flashed across her eyes, as if she shared his let's-get-naked thoughts. But maybe her tension wasn't the anticipation he hoped for because she only said, 'I might watch TV awhile. If that's okay with you?'

'Fine. Make yourself comfortable. I'm going for a run.'

Without looking at her, he yanked a pair of shorts, a T-shirt and running shoes out of his backpack and went to the bathroom to change. He needed to release some of his own tension and a dose of cold Melbourne air would cool his blood. The colder the better.

He splashed water on his face and checked himself out

in the mirror. A smear of her lip gloss glistened on his lips. He smiled at his reflection as he rubbed it away. Now he knew. Ms Neat and Conservative on the outside wasn't so conservative on the inside. Perhaps they could—

He shook the images away, ran his fingers through his hair and glared at himself. He'd offered her refuge. And that changed the rules. It was entirely her call if she wanted to take it further. Still... He shook his head and turned away from the mirror. Absolutely not.

He considered taking a cold shower but decided against it. Getting naked and knowing she was probably spread out on that bed watching TV wasn't going to do him any favours.

When he returned from the bathroom, she was standing right where he'd left her. The big screen was still blank, the room was still silent. But the atmosphere had changed. Her fragrance and the scent of her skin smelled sharper, warmer. Damper. She must have turned up the thermostat on the air conditioning because it felt a damn sight hotter in here than it had moments ago.

Her eyes skimmed down his body and he felt as though a thousand fiery pinpricks had blistered every square centimetre of skin.

Then she snatched up the TV remote. Put it down. Drew in a sharp breath as if she'd come to a decision and was wondering whether to let him in on it.

'Everything all right?'

'Look, I don't want to kick you out of your room. Please. Stay. I'm fine with it.' Her gaze shifted to the double bed, then snapped back to him and he swore the air around them crackled. 'In fact, I'd feel a lot better if you stayed.'

Yeah? He smiled—so would he. 'Okay...' That glint in her eyes... Hot. Wary too, but definitely hot. His whole body tightened, stiffened, and a bead of sweat trickled

down his back. In a deliberately casual move, he laid his
discarded clothes on the back of the office chair at the
desk. 'So what's your real name? Or aren't we going to
get into all that?'

'I told you, it's Charlotte.' She slid her palms down her
skirt as if they were sticky. 'But no surnames, no talking about ourselves and swapping life histories. We'll be
gone tomorrow.'

His thoughts precisely. So…she wanted to play…
Nothing personal, nothing complicated. One night. This
had to be his lucky day. The surprise of it, and of her, was
like a mid-winter's heatwave. 'Fine by me.'

'I'm going to take a shower now,' she said, suddenly
and randomly, as if plucking the words from the increasingly sultry atmosphere. 'Alone.' She moved to her bag,
unzipped it, then tossed him an I-mean-it look over her
shoulder. 'I'll see you shortly.'

'Right.' So she wanted time to get ready; he didn't mind
waiting. 'I'm off for that run, then. When I get back…' at
the door, he looked her over the way she'd looked at him—
though he might have lingered a tad longer '…we'll see
how we get along.'

He took the stairs down to the lobby two at a time. He
saw Kerry amidst the carnage, sticking a sign on the door
advising alternative accommodation, and stopped.

'Is your friend okay?' she said, giving him a quick
glance as she smoothed the sign in place.

'She is.'

She shook her head on her way back to the desk. 'And
by that glazed look, I'm guessing the drinks invite's off
the board now. How do you do it, Nic? You're like honey
to a bee.'

'My magnetic personality, babe. And it was a mutual
decision to share the room, under the circumstances.'

'Of course it was,' she said, amused. 'You're obviously her hero. I'd hate you on behalf of all women if I didn't know you better.' She waved him off. 'Now go away. I'm too busy and too married to be sidetracked by a charmer like you.'

He grinned—charm had nothing to do with it. Fate had played right into his hands. Man, he had to love volcanoes. Even lousy reporters.

'And if you're not careful, Nic,' she was going on as she resumed her seat in front of her computer, 'one of these days you're going to find yourself charmed right back and life as you know it now will be a distant memory.'

He gave her a wave as he moved off. 'Not gonna happen.'

Kerry didn't look up from her screen. 'Uh-huh.'

He took the elevator, jogged across the sky bridge and onto grass, dodging passengers, following the arrivals road and outdoor car-parking, his mind reliving their up-close and the way Charlotte had responded. As if she couldn't get enough. He grinned to himself as he waited at the kerb for an airport bus, then crossed a median strip and headed for a line of bushes. Who'd have thought? Charlotte whoever-she-was was one hot babe.

And she was waiting in his room. *Their* room.

So what the hell was *he* waiting for? Why was he out running in this cold blustery wind when he could be getting better acquainted on that big wide bed with a woman who, if he was reading her right, wanted the same thing?

Because he'd already decided to run before she'd given him the hot look. Then chosen to take a damn shower—alone. She'd made it abundantly clear. She'd needed time. Fair enough. And now he thought about it, he wanted to give her that time to mull it over and be sure. Because *he* was sure he didn't want her backing out once they got started. In fact, he was so ready to get started, his body so tightly wound and hot, it was a wonder he could move at all.

In his experience conservative types in silk suits and pearls weren't compatible with one-night stands. But dress sense aside, she'd not played the distressed damsel card. The guy had been seriously hassling her but she'd held her own—like the strong heroines he portrayed in his computer games. He liked that about her. She wasn't afraid to stand up for herself even though he'd seen the flicker of panic in her eyes. So if she changed her mind, he reckoned she'd let him know.

Testosterone surged through him, tightening his muscles, pumping through his blood, and all he could think about was getting her naked and exploring the abundantly curved body he'd held against him. With his eyes, with his hands. With his mouth. Hell—he hoped she wasn't the type to change her mind.

He checked his watch. Time enough to have finished that shower. And if not…well, he'd just have to finish it with her. He turned back towards the hotel, making a detour via the terminal's food court on the way.

Since she'd already told the guy, and she'd needed the time to *breathe*, Charlotte took the shower. With no change of clothes available, and not wanting to crease her suit any more than it already was, she put the terry bathrobe provided by the hotel on over her underwear.

She swiped the mirror and stared at her reflection. Her mouth looked plumper, fuller. Her eyes looked bigger. More slumberous. *Bedroom eyes*. Oh, God. She rubbed a hand over her heart, which still hadn't settled into its usual rhythm. She'd never had a one-night stand before. Never been with another man before; Flynn had been a part of her life since her mid-teens.

Part of her life? *Huh*. She picked up her brush, dragged it through her hair with hard, swift strokes. Their relationship had been over less than two weeks when she'd seen him and the glamorous daughter of a wealthy businessman in the newspaper's social pages.

So she was getting on with her new life, starting today. She'd never met a guy's gaze—so full on and meaningful—the way she had Nic's just now. And he was coming back to *see how they got along*.

And with that look in his eyes it could mean only one thing: sex. Hot and fast and uncomplicated. Spontaneous. Frivolous. Happy. And wasn't that what she wanted too? Just for tonight. Then she'd never have to see him again.

Oh. My. Was that really Charlotte Dumont thinking those thoughts?

Swinging away from her unsettling image, she gathered her things and tentatively opened the door. Hearing no movement—so Nic hadn't returned yet—she walked into the bedroom.

Nic's backpack sat next to hers on the luggage rack; his spicy scent lingered on his discarded clothes on the back of the chair. He wasn't here yet he was all around her. She noticed some glossy brochures he'd left on the desk. She didn't want to get personally involved with him, wasn't ready for another relationship, but they were…just travel pamphlets. Nothing personal, nothing private. She couldn't resist picking them up.

The Hawaiian Islands. Brochures on deep-sea fishing, golf, whale-watching expeditions. The best surfing spots. He'd marked off some, made notes she couldn't decipher and crossed out others. He was on his way to Hawaii for what looked like a full-on guy vacation. No wonder he looked so fit. Bronzed. Well…nourished. He obviously knew how to chill out and have *fun*.

The word conjured up all sorts of scenarios; not the outdoor kind, but the intimate indoor kind involving him and her and that big bed with its soft white pillows. Her whole body burned. It wanted to burn alongside his. It wanted to know what it was like to be made love to by a man with Nic's expertise because one thing she was sure of was his ability to pleasure a woman. And then he'd be off to Hawaii and she'd be totally satisfied.

But it had to be her way. Her rules. No talking about themselves and their lives beyond what happened in this room. No swapping phone numbers and email addresses and promises to catch up. She didn't *want* him catching up. She wanted one night to prove to herself that she wasn't the girl Flynn thought she was.

Anticipation raced through her body. To calm herself, she made a cup of the complimentary coffee provided and slid the curtains back as the afternoon faded and the sky took on the early evening hues of orange and lavender. She sat on the only armchair and flicked through a women's magazine she'd bought earlier but she soon tossed it onto the nearby desk, too frazzled to concentrate on some superstar's private life exposed to the world.

And if it hadn't been for Nic, her private break-up with the popular candidate for the upcoming state elections might have been public fodder too.

She really, really owed Nic. So she could have just bought him a bottle of wine or a meal to show her appreciation, couldn't she? They were here until tomorrow morning at the earliest so it wasn't too late to suggest catching a cab into the city and finding some cosy candlelit café…

Except then they'd come back to this room and that bed

with a few glasses of happy in their systems and it would still be here—the amazing attraction.

She tucked her bare feet up beneath her, pulled the pins out of her hair and teased her fingers through it, enjoying the new feeling of being feminine and free. Why eat out when you could feast on something much more pleasurable right here? Like hot masculine skin and lips and tongues and… Her mouth dried, her skin frizzled. She couldn't help it; she giggled like a schoolgirl at the wicked thoughts running through her mind.

She was still giggling when he walked in.

# CHAPTER THREE

Nic heard the feminine laughter as he pushed open the door. Husky with a hint of wicked. He grinned. Until he caught sight of her sitting on the chair, her face in profile as she stared out of the window, her dark hair aflame in the sun's reddening light and his amusement shifted beyond a simple *Wow* to something approaching awe. Unbound and auburn, the glossy mass rejoiced around her shoulders like a celebration of freedom.

She'd turned the TV on to a radio channel. Something soothing and blue and jazzy and she obviously hadn't heard him come in, so he absorbed the moment with all his senses. The fragrance of her recent shower, the delight in her laugh, her sheer and glorious abandonment.

And he realised he was witnessing something he doubted many people saw when they looked at Charlotte. The woman's inner beauty. And an innate sexuality that he found irresistible. He had a feeling she didn't show that side of herself often, much less share it.

He hoped she'd share it with him.

She'd swapped that seriously awful suit for the hotel's robe. Was she naked underneath? His groin tightened. She still wore the pearls; their iridescence reflected the sun's vermilion rays. He imagined lifting them, warm from her body, and sliding his fingers beneath to explore her creamy throat.

He couldn't be certain she'd changed into the robe as an invitation or prelude to sex. It made sense that she'd wear it since their luggage was checked in at the airport. But that was about the only thing that made sense right now because for the life of him he couldn't remember ever being this captivated by a woman before.

Again the sense that this was different—*she* was different—slid through him like a ripple on a millpond. He shook off the shivery silvery sensation and discreetly cleared his throat to announce his presence. 'Anyone for soggy gourmet pizza?'

She swung to face him and a thousand different emotions flitted over her expression before she settled for happy-to-see-him. 'Yes, please.' She uncurled herself and stretched out a pair of long shapely legs in front of her. 'Where did you find pizza?'

'The airport's café. The last one. Or the last half of one. I had to fight off the hungry hordes.' After setting the box on the desk, he switched on the lamp, then reached for the bottle of wine on the shelf above the bar fridge.

She rose, smiling and shrugging the lapels of the robe closer. 'My hero.'

His hand jerked a bit at that as he upended two glasses. 'You want wine?'

'Thanks.' She lifted the lid on the cardboard container. 'Yum, I love artichokes.' She peered closer. 'It *is* artichoke, isn't it?'

He grinned. 'I think so.'

She reached for her handbag on the coffee table, pulled out a linen napkin embroidered with her name, then proceeded to polish up the motel's cutlery.

Swallowing his surprise, he opened the bottle, then set

a couple of paper plates next to the pizza box. 'You like Italian?'

'I do, but seafood's my favourite.' She scooped up the slices with a knife, set them on the plates. 'There's a fabulous seafood place at Glenelg, on the Marina Pier. Their King George whiting is to die for.'

'I know the one.' He didn't tell her his apartment overlooked said pier as he splashed a generous amount of the ruby liquid into the glasses. 'And I agree with your review. It's one of my favourite food haunts when I'm in Adelaide.'

'Mine too.' A little hitch in her breath as she stared up at him. 'Seems we have something in common.'

'I'm hoping that's not all we have in common.' He couldn't resist stroking his knuckles lightly down the side of her face. Testing her, tormenting himself. Her skin was smooth as silk and smelled like flowers.

Her eyes turned glassy, like a still ocean on an overcast summer's day, and she pressed her lips together, then said, 'We weren't going to talk about ourselves.'

'Who said anything about talking?'

Their gazes clashed, but he didn't act on the hot fist of anticipation gripping the lower half of his body and the impulse to show her the alternative option. Plenty of time. A girl like Charlotte definitely needed slow. And he'd already made up his mind to give her a chance to decide whether she still wanted to act on that hot look he'd glimpsed earlier.

So he only lifted the glasses, offered her one and said, 'Let's eat before this sloppy offering gets any colder. Cheers.'

'Thanks. And cheers.' Taking her plate, Charlotte returned to the armchair while Nic sat at the desk. She took a sip, then set her glass on the coffee table in front of her. Her cheek was still tingly and warm from his touch. Other parts were tingling too, with a wickedly wanton need like she'd never experienced.

But he was giving her space and she appreciated that. Even if she was having a full-on fantasy around him and what they could get up to on that office chair...

'Hawaii's nice this time of year,' she said to take her mind off her fantasies, determined to keep the conversation on neutral topics.

He glanced at his pamphlets then at her, his gaze thoughtful. Unreadable.

'I know we agreed on nothing personal but they were just there...'

He smiled, all trace of whatever she'd seen in his eyes gone in one mischievous twinkle. 'All good, Charlotte, it's not personal. And yeah, it's the best time of year. Get away from the cold.' He bit off half his slice in one go and chewed, then washed it down with a mouthful of wine.

She sliced a corner off her own piece, watching the man's enthusiasm over the very ordinary food. He had a strong tanned neck and prominent Adam's apple, which moved as he swallowed. Oil from the pizza glistened on his upper lip... She wanted to jump up, lean down and lick it off. She really needed to slow her thoughts down to warp speed.

'You've been there before?' she asked, keeping to the script.

'I try to make it every couple of years. Hanalei Bay on Kauai. The surf's great there. How about you—have you ever been?'

'Once. To Maui. It was a family holiday to celebr...' She trailed off as the memory of her parents' tenth wedding anniversary surfaced. The little twinge in her heart had her rubbing her hand once over the area and caressing the pearls at her throat. 'But that's against the rules.'

'Sure—if you say so.' His eyes probed hers and his voice gentled. 'You okay?'

'Fine.' Her smile relaxed as she finished the last bite, patted her mouth then popped the fancy napkin back in her bag. 'You know, you're a very nice man.'

'*Nice?*' His brows rose. 'That's a bit of a worry.'

'I mean honest. Considerate…' Totally gorgeous.

He chuckled and popped the remainder of his pizza into his mouth. 'You sure you're not a rebellious princess on the run from some minor European nation somewhere?'

'What? Oh, the napkin?' She grinned back. 'I'd carry my own cutlery if the airlines allowed it. I have personalised soap too. Somewhere…' She searched the bottom of her bag unsuccessfully, then shrugged. 'Call me eccentric.' Or a product of a privileged and traditional upbringing. If her folks could see her now and knew what she was thinking…

She bet Nic had a string of women in his life. She wondered how old he was. Around thirty? She reminded herself she didn't want to know because then she'd want to know more. Like where he lived and what his work was and…how he liked to make love.

'"Sex Fact or Fiction".'

She almost spluttered into her wine. 'Pardon?'

'The quiz.' He was looking at the cover of the magazine she'd left on the desk. 'You haven't read it yet?'

'I must've missed it. Obviously you didn't.'

'I'm a guy. I saw the word sex,' he said, amusement in his voice as he flicked through the pages. 'Okay, test your knowledge. Sales of condoms decrease when a recession hits—fact or fiction?'

She took a moment to compose herself and consider. 'Fiction. Definitely. Too expensive to go out and too expensive to have kids.'

He nodded. 'Correct. How about this? Humans are the only species to have sex for pleasure.'

The way he said 'pleasure', all virile and velvet and promising, made her skin rupture with heat. She took another sip of wine. 'Yes.'

'Not so.' He studied her with inscrutable eyes. 'Apparently we're not the only creatures on the planet wanting to get it on.'

'Oh?' But was she the only one in this room right now wanting to get it on? He was as relaxed as if he was discussing the weather, one arm slung over the back of the chair, whereas she was as tense as strung piano wire.

'How about this, then? Men's sexual organs are designed for more pleasure than women's.'

'Um…' She trailed off at the hot promise of that pleasure. Her own feminine places dampened and she had to resist squirming on the chair. 'Fiction.'

'Yep. Women have it all over men in this department. According to the quiz, the clitoris is the only known organ that exists for the sole purpose of pleasure.'

Oh. Her cheeks felt as if they were on fire. Had she ever had such a bizarrely intimate conversation with a guy before? 'Um…sexual organs aside…' she bit down on her bottom lip '…surely it would depend on who's giving the pleasure?'

His head came up and he looked at her through lazy-lidded eyes. 'You're a woman—you tell me.'

'For me…' She struggled for composure and sophistication. 'It definitely depends on the partner.'

'Wouldn't this partner's expertise have something to do with it? Besides liking the guy.'

'Ah…'

'I mean, you could be totally hot for him but if he doesn't know how to do it for you… Ever had a guy like that? You really like him, the connection's there, the spark, the desire, but then you're left hanging. So to speak.'

'Uh…hmm.' *Flynn*. The earth hadn't exactly moved with him. Ever. She'd told herself that was okay because she'd loved him, and love and affection and common goals were more important than physical fulfilment.

Maybe she'd been wrong, because there'd been a shifting of tectonic plates happening beneath her feet since she'd kissed Nic. She knew instinctively that he wouldn't be the type to leave any woman unsatisfied.

'What's this non-committal "hmm"?'

'It's a yes, okay?' she snapped out, hating to admit it. Hating that he knew already. 'I've had guys like that.'

A slow and sexy, won't-happen-if-you're-with-me look drifted across his expression.

If he ever decided to make a move.

And why was this all about her? His focus was entirely too…focused. She deflected with, 'But a guy can enjoy sex with anyone because it's all about basic drive or need, right?'

His gaze drifted over her like slow-moving lava. 'Personally speaking, I like to connect with the woman I'm with. Enjoyment has to be about more than satisfying a basic urge. I feel a connection with you, Charlotte. I'm pretty sure you feel that connection too. I'd like to see where it takes us.'

*To heaven and beyond?*

His eyes had darkened as he spoke and she felt a shifting and thickening of anticipation in the air. But he didn't move. Not so much as the flicker of an eyelash.

Ah. 'Are you waiting for me to give you the green light?'

'Your call.' He remained ostensibly at ease, legs sprawled in front of him, arm still relaxed on the back of the chair. Only a muscle tic in his jaw betrayed his tension. 'You need to be sure this is what you want. But for pity's sake, make it soon.' His voice thickened and he looked down at his crotch. 'Because you're damn near killing me.'

She'd deliberately kept her eyes above his waist, but now she followed his gaze to the impressive bulge in his shorts. And swallowed. Her whole body went weak, except for her galloping pulse. She also noticed his thighs were as tanned as his neck, sprinkled with dark hair and heavy with muscle as if he worked out. A lot.

She wanted to touch. She wanted to feel those thighs rub against hers. She wanted that magnificent masculine part of him inside her.

But she didn't want entanglements. No morning after, no getting to know each other beyond the physical. 'Only tonight.'

'Fine. Should I take a shower first?'

'No.' She smiled. 'Told you you're considerate.' She liked the way he smelled: warm and slightly sweaty but not unpleasant. A primal masculine smell that beckoned and aroused her feminine instincts. 'I want it—I want you—as you are. I want to feel your sweat on my skin. Now.'

He smiled back. 'First move's all yours.'

'Mine?' Her trembling fingers tightened a little on the soft terry lapels. She knew how to initiate sex…but with a man like Nic? Except she didn't know Nic, not really. So what did she mean: 'a man like Nic'? What did Nic-who-she-didn't-know want or expect?

'You could start by taking off that robe,' he suggested after a few seconds of silence ticked by. 'Or you could come over here and let me do the honours.' Still he didn't move. 'I'll leave that decision to you.'

Eyes fastened on him, she pushed up off the chair. The few steps she took seemed like miles while her blood drained to her legs. She was glad of the background music because it covered the sound of her heart thumping its way out of her chest. Not with fear but with the illicit, dizzying prospect of having sex with a man who was, by anyone's standards, a stranger.

She was the one in control—because Nic had given it to her. She was the one with the choice. And she wanted this night with this man.

Coming to a stop in front of him, she loosened the looped tie just enough so that the robe's front edges parted slightly. As she was standing, his head was tilted back a little, eyes focused on hers, and it was her first chance to look down at him. She reached out and smoothed a strand of his hair off his brow. 'Decisions, decisions…'

He slid his fingers behind the loop in her belt and drew her closer, between hot, hard thighs, and she had to drop her hands onto the chair's metal arms either side of him to keep her balance and stop herself from collapsing onto him.

His breath, his scent and his heat mingled with hers as they continued to stare at each other. 'You like being on top, then.'

She started to laugh but her throat was dry and it came out husky and low and slightly desperate. 'I like being any way.'

Oh, my God. Had she really said that? And was that smoky, seductive voice hers?

'So…' he untied her belt and slipped his hands inside to lightly circle her waist, surprise in his eyes when he found bare flesh '…swinging naked from the chandelier's a possibility?'

Her breath hitched at the feather-light brush of skin on skin and she arched forward, her breasts aching to be teased and stroked. 'No chandelier here…' Only recessed lighting and a desk lamp…

'Pity.'

'But whatever we get up to, do you have protection?' Her mind was hazy, but not that hazy.

'We'll get to that. Eventually. Or are you in a rush?'

'I thought *you* were. Didn't you just say—?'

'I'll survive a little longer.'

She wondered if she would. Spot-fires were breaking out all over her body; it was a miracle she wasn't glowing. Or perhaps she was but right now she was too distracted watching Nic. His expression: part pain, part pleasure and all for her. 'Nic…'

'Charlotte…' he teased back and his tone left her in no doubt he was as turned on as she. But he withdrew his hands from her waist, put them behind his head. 'What are you hiding under all that towelling?'

She pushed up off the chair's support and straightened, then, with a boldness she'd never felt, she shrugged off the robe. Its coarse texture tickled her bare skin on the way down.

Nic watched, his breath snagging on a growl of approval. Who'd have thought? Conservative Charlotte liked sexy underwear. Skimpy shimmery panties and bra, spattered with starbursts of silver rhinestones and so sheer she might as well have been naked. But so much more erotic with her dark, peaked nipples pushed up against the fabric, her breasts spilling over the top like an offering of abundance. The strand of pearls still luminescent at her neck.

'Aren't you full of surprises,' he murmured in absolute appreciation. 'Gorgeous.'

But not too voluptuous. Not too slim either; just long, strong, clean lines and curves. Perfect. Exquisite. It was a crime against mankind to hide such beauty.

But she wasn't hiding it from him.

She resumed her earlier position, hands on the armrests, leaning over him. Her breasts were at eye-level and with any other woman that was where he'd be—mouth busy right there on that creamy skin, teasing the fabric aside with his teeth, tongue exploring.

But, as delectable as they were, it was her eyes that captured him most. Wide and aware with smoke and secrets shifting like shadows. Her fragrance, the cool, light signature perfume, drifted over him like evening mist. And in his mind's eye he saw that calm lake at sunset. If he believed in enchantment, he imagined it would be like this.

Behind his head, his fists tightened. He put them on his thighs to stop himself from reaching up and pulling her mouth down to his and plundering. He sensed her willingness but this wasn't the moment for fast. Rather a moment for reflection.

She hadn't admitted it, but Nic knew this wasn't something Charlotte did casually and often. He didn't linger on the reasons why she'd made an exception for him. 'You're not used to this, are you?' he murmured, and heard her quick exhalation, felt the tension thrum through her body.

'What do you mean? Sex?'

'One-night sex.'

'Is it that obvious?'

'No, no.' He kept his voice low and slow and soothing. 'I mean that in a good way. Keep doing what you're doing—you're fantastic.'

He shook away the unsettling thoughts and concentrated on what he knew well. How to enjoy no-strings, uncomplicated sex. And the easy pleasure of having a woman initiate it.

Smiling, she lowered her lips to his, a slow sultry kiss that soothed and smoothed and seduced. Her hair was a curtain of silk around them and the bluesy pulse of the music beat a lazy syrupy rhythm. He thought of languid afternoons by a pool and hot skin and cold, creamy sunscreen.

He lifted his arms then, fingers spread to mould around her slender shoulders and draw her closer. Her fingers stroked through his hair, then cupped the back of his head. Still watching his eyes. There was a glide of silk as she parted her long, long legs and slid them over his thighs to twine herself around him. She hooked her feet behind the back of the chair, the sultry heat of her feminine core snug against his burning erection.

Still holding his head, she leaned forward and kissed him again, her sparkly bra snagging his T-shirt as she settled closer. A groan erupted from deep in his gut. Her smile was smug as she found the worn jersey's hem and tugged upwards. Suddenly his T-shirt was gone, flung somewhere over his shoulder.

Her fingers danced over his chest, twirled around his nipples, then slowed to a gliding waltz and headed south, dead centre. To the waistband of his shorts. Hands diving beneath, she rocked once against him, her fingers tightening on their captured prize. 'Nic…'

'Okay, now you're playing dirty.' He reached behind her, snapped the catch on her bra and peeled it away. Creamy flesh, dark, ripe peaks. Greed hazed his vision but she didn't give him time to feast, surging forward to rub the hard little nubs against his chest as she watched him.

'I like playing dirty, don't you?' Her laugh was low and sexy as she massaged and squeezed. 'Fast and dirty even better.'

He tried to laugh too, but it snagged in his throat. His control was fraying, his whole body one throbbing ache. 'You're a wicked woman.'

'Too wicked for you?'

'Not possible.' He cupped her damp heat and watched

her eyes smoulder, her playful smile fade to serious. Her hands stopped being busy and he grinned. 'Pay-back time.' He slid a finger along the edge of her panties and felt her shudder. He slipped beneath to stroke her slick flesh and heard her moan. Arousal heightened, breathing quickened.

Somehow he managed to reach over his shoulder and drag his trousers off the chair, fumbling for his wallet and a condom in the rumpled folds while he thanked the stars his clothes were within reach.

Impatience, desperation and demands and needs. He freed himself, rolled on protection. A quick tug and her panties shredded beneath his fingers. No laughter now, no teasing wordplay. Just pure passion and dark desire and every fantasy he'd ever had. He plunged deep, thrusting up into silky heat and willing delight.

He held her silvery gaze long enough to see that her response matched his own. He gripped her hips, her hands fisted in his hair. They found their rhythm. The world evaporated leaving only speed and greed and heat.

The chair rocked beneath them. He thought he heard the tinkle of a glass as it toppled and rolled but maybe it was the sound of his sanity shattering.

She came on a stunned gasp, her inner muscles clamping around him. He gave himself up to glory and followed.

# CHAPTER FOUR

SHE hadn't been able to get enough of him, Nic thought hours later as night moved inexorably towards dawn. Nor he her. And why not? Making the most of the time limit she'd imposed. He turned his head to watch her sleep. Hair in disarray around her face, over the pillow. The gentle sound of her breathing as her breasts rose and fell. Her cool blue fragrance was going to tease his nostrils and his memory for quite some time.

He felt entirely too relaxed to worry about the curious little niggle that it had never been quite like this with anyone before. That *connection* he'd so casually mentioned to entice her? It had been…well…more than he'd expected.

He shifted onto an elbow for a better look at her bathed in the gold of dawn. His fingers itched to stroke the side of her face, her lips, her hair. He wanted her again. Wanted to feel her tight, hot wetness clench around him as she came… Wanted to look into those haunting eyes she had and— He frowned. Maybe he wasn't as relaxed as he'd thought. But it would pass, he assured himself. Of course it would. And she'd made it clear enough: one night. He'd been happy with the arrangement. More than happy.

Okay, he decided on a slow breath of relief, sanity still intact after all. They'd shared a fantastic few hours but it was time to make a move towards getting out of here.

Careful not to disturb her, he rose and went to the bathroom, checked his mobile for updates to flight schedules, then showered and left her sleeping while he went in search of breakfast.

Charlotte woke to the hum of air conditioning and the sound of water running in the bathroom. She didn't move for a long moment, reliving the night and all she and Nic had done together. She'd lost count of how many times he'd made her come.

But his side of the bed was empty now, the sheets barely warm to the touch. She felt a vague disappointment that he'd not woken her earlier, then stretched. Aah... She'd expended more energy than she'd realised, she thought as her eyes slid open on a clear dawn sky, steadily lightening with gold and aqua. She should include sex in her exercise regime.

'Rise and shine.' Nic appeared freshly shaved and dressed. 'The ash cloud's shifted. Flights resume in an hour or so. We need to get moving.'

'What time is it?' she murmured, *without* moving. She was way too naked beneath the sheet, and her underwear—she had no idea where it was.

'Six-thirty.'

She groaned into the pillow.

He had a way too cheery wide-awake voice. Obviously he was raring to get to Hawaii and begin his surfing vacation, that basic sexual drive they'd talked about last night satisfied for now.

And he'd satisfied her too but it was finished.

In one way she mourned the fact, in another, she was so, so relieved. Because last night Charlotte Dumont's body had been invaded by a nymphomaniac. In fact, now she was almost too embarrassed to look him in the eye, and a warm blush suffused her entire body.

She tried her best to ignore it. 'Is that coffee I smell? *Real* coffee?'

'Cappuccino or latte?' Still managing to look crisp in yesterday's clothes, he lifted a couple of paper cups with lids from the desk. 'I didn't know what you liked so I bought one of each.'

'I'd love the latte, please. You've been out already?'

'Organisation, babe.' He moved to the bed, held out a cup and a small plastic shopping bag from one of the terminal's tourist shops. 'You might need these too.'

Propping herself up on one elbow, she peeked inside. She glimpsed a pair of lolly-pink panties with a map of Australia imprinted on the front. Oh, dear. And the reason she was going to be wearing tacky nylon souvenir undies for the rest of the day spun through her mind like hot-pink candy floss. 'Um. Thanks.'

'It's for my own peace of mind as much as yours. I'd go nuts with the mental image of you buck naked under that skirt all day and not being able to take advantage.'

The candy-floss colour bled into her cheeks. She sat up, winding the sheet up around her torso as she did so. 'Oh…well, then…'

Head on one side, he studied her a moment. 'There's something intriguing about a woman reclining naked in bed wearing only pearls. You've got me wondering: why pearls?'

'They were my mother's. And I'm not reclining. Now.' Sentimental secrets were not up for sharing. Setting the cup on the night stand, she scrunched the sheet higher. 'Um…'

He must have known what she couldn't ask because he picked her bra up from the bottom of the bed and tossed it to her. The glint in his eyes dissipated as he studied her. 'Everything okay?'

'Yes. Fine. Why wouldn't it be?'

'You look—'

'I'm going to take a shower,' she said, all casual and carefree. But she didn't move. Her fingers couldn't seem to let go of the sheet. She'd not given a thought to the morning after the night before. Whatever would he be thinking of her?

And why did it matter? In less than an hour they'd say goodbye and that would be it. She just had to get through this awkward time, then she could relax and enjoy her holiday.

'Better make it snappy.' Checking his watch, he rose, picked up his bag and headed towards the door. 'See you in the lobby in fifteen minutes.'

She was grateful for his sensitivity to her unspoken need for privacy despite the fact that he'd seen, touched and tasted nearly every naked inch of her, but the blush still hadn't cooled when she found him downstairs amongst the swirl of people. Her hand dived into her bag for her sunglasses.

He swung his pack onto one shoulder, setting a cracking pace across the sky bridge with a trail of other passengers and leaving no breath for small talk.

They arrived inside the terminal. 'Thanks for everything,' she said, well before they reached her check-in desk. 'Um…I meant rescuing me and all…' She trailed off. All, indeed.

'My pleasure.' His dark eyes twinkled in the harsh down-lights.

*Mine too.* She rolled her lips together before she said too much. 'So…I…guess it's…goodbye, then.'

'Let's just say *au revoir*, babe.'

He bent to brush a chaste kiss across her lips. There was something about his expression when he straightened that sent a little shiver down her spine, but then before she could look into his dark velvet eyes one more time he turned and walked away, disappearing into the crowd.

Biting down on her lower lip, she fought an urgent impulse to call him back. Memories of his heat-slicked body against hers, their fevered moans and air ripe with passion swarmed through her mind. But more than that, he'd come to her assistance when she'd needed it, no questions asked. Why was she letting this man walk out of her life with almost no possibility of finding him again?

She started after him, but a couple of steps on she realised it was too late. The terminal was teeming with chaos and commotion; she'd never find him and she ran the risk of missing her flight. And even if she caught up with him, what could she say? What *was* there to say?

They'd shared one fantastic night. But the probability of him wanting more wasn't a probability at all or he'd have tried harder to get her contact details. If he'd wanted to, he'd have persisted, found a way—men were like that. But he'd not asked her once. Not once. Happy to walk away. She told herself she was *not* disappointed.

Charlotte was grateful for the comfort and relative privacy of the spacious Tabua Class window seat at the front of the aircraft. She didn't have to look at other passengers, and the seat next to her was vacant. She plugged in her music player, closed her eyes and drifted…

*Cold*… Charlotte rubbed her arms against the aircraft's air conditioning, fighting sleep and the images that had plagued her for the past six weeks.

Flynn in her kitchen, impossibly handsome, and telling her, 'I've decided to stand as a candidate for the next state election.'

'You what…? Politics?' She struggled to process his announcement. 'I thought you were just networking at the electorate, volunteering your skills. That it was part of your business plan for our wine and cheese place…'

'There's not going to be a place, Charlotte.'

A chill swept down her spine. 'But your viticulture course…'

'I switched courses last year.'

*'And you didn't tell me?'* Everything was spiralling away. 'You didn't bother to tell *your fiancée you were considering a career in politics*?' Who was this man she'd thought she knew? 'What happened to sharing? How could you shut me out that way?'

'I know how you feel about being in the public eye.' He shrugged. 'And frankly, being married to a little grey mouse isn't going to work for a future politician.'

And she felt herself shrivel beneath his critical scrutiny. The guy who'd seduced her at sixteen with his flashing green eyes, his smooth words and good looks stared at her now with chauvinistic intolerance.

'Take a look at yourself, Charlotte.' His gaze crawled up her body once more. 'Take a good look at this place.' He waved a disparaging hand around her kitchen. 'You're living in a damn time warp. I need a wife who'll stand by me into the future. A woman who knows how to make a fashion statement. One with some backbone who's not afraid to speak up in public.'

The utter betrayal of everything she'd ever believed in about him. About *them*.

She jolted awake as the aircraft hit turbulence. Or maybe it was her stomach still tying itself in knots over his harsh words. So she concentrated on watching the twisting ribbon of surf along the coast as the aircraft began its descent into Nadi. Flynn had used her position in society to build connections, then tossed her aside.

*Little grey mouse.*

She ground her teeth together as a patchwork of different greens came into view. Last night she'd proved she was confident and capable of being whoever she wanted to be. She should thank Flynn for the wake-up call.

She watched the brown river snake below them—palm trees rippling in the afternoon breeze, hazy smoke spirals towards the bony ridges of distant highlands—and drew in a deep breath. New horizons and some time to blow away the cobwebs.

She stepped out into the moist tropical air and followed her fellow passengers across the hot tarmac and into the terminal. Four locals in bright shirts with hibiscus flowers behind their ears welcomed them with white smiles and their pretty yellow banjos, dreamy island harmonies blending.

*'Bula!'* Welcome.

*'Vinaka.'* Thank you.

Smiling at the pretty ground staff member in her *Sulu Jaba*, the traditional long skirt topped with a bright fitted dress, Charlotte headed for the baggage carousel and collected her luggage. She loved Fiji already. A place where she knew no one and no one knew her…

That thought vanished with a sharp inhalation when she caught sight of a pair of broad shoulders encased in a familiar dark shirt near the carousel. Her heart jumped into her mouth and every muscle seemed to melt. She watched him pull his bag off the conveyor, bronzed forearms, muscles twisting.

Nic.

She couldn't move, and against her will her eyes drank in the sight. His tall, tanned, testosterone-packed body, the long lanky stride as he walked towards Customs. What was he doing in Fiji? A connecting flight? Except he'd collected his luggage already.

Conflicting emotions tore through her like a summer cyclone. The swoon effect of remembering that body naked and stretched over hers and the chill factor of realising he'd deliberately misled her about Hawaii. Heat flared like a furnace, burning her cheeks.

She didn't *want* to see him again. But her body had other ideas and called her a liar. Her breasts tingled with remembered pleasure, her inner thighs quivered with the memory of the warm dampness of his mouth there.

*No. Yes. No.* She really tried to look away but it was as if her eyes were pre-programmed to follow him. The one-off fantasy man she'd allowed herself to indulge in.

Hadn't he indulged in her too? Seemed, like her ex, he was also one of those smooth-talking rogues who knew how to seduce a woman and make it seem as if it was all *her* idea. She didn't know how he'd managed it but he had.

She proceeded through Customs keeping well behind him but damned if he wasn't standing smack bang in front of the exit doors talking on his mobile when she emerged. How was she going to get past him? Or was that his intention?

Then, as if sensing her watching—condemning—he looked over his shoulder and met her eyes, and she wished she'd turned away already because now it was too late, she was powerless against the pull.

Not taking his eyes off her, he spoke to whoever he was talking with on the phone and disconnected. He started walking towards her.

Was he *smiling* when he knew she didn't want anything more to do with him? They'd had an arrangement, they'd said goodbye… No—she'd said goodbye, she remembered. He'd made a point of saying *au revoir*. She didn't know how he'd found out her intended destination, but he'd *known* and he'd said nothing.

Her head spun. Was he a reporter too and she'd just been totally made a fool of…?

She was ready when he reached her. She was strong. She was cool. 'What are you doing here?'

He slung his backpack to the floor, all charm and smiles. 'What one usually does here in Fiji—relax and enjoy.'

'You lied to me.'

His brow furrowed, those eyes all innocence. 'Lied?'

'You said you were going to Hawaii.'

'No. You *assumed* I was going to Hawaii.'

She tried to recall the conversation but right now her mind wasn't operating at full capacity because it was too busy looking at the way his gorgeous lips curved ever so slightly. Teasing her. Or was he mocking her? 'And you let me,' she clipped out. 'We talked about it, you let me believe—'

'You asked if I'd been there before. I said I try to get there every couple of years. Just not this year, as it happens.'

'You knew exactly what I meant.' She frowned. 'You didn't tell me you were travelling to Fiji when we talked about Hawaii.'

'Why would I? No exchanging personal information. Your rules, Charlotte, remember?' he said softly. Seductively. The way he'd whispered how good she felt and what else he'd like to do to her.

'I didn't see you in the airline lounge in Melbourne or in Customs…'

'That was my intention. You were adamant you only wanted one night, no further services required.'

She felt herself colour at his crude assessment of the evening. Obviously it would seem that way to him and why should he believe her if she tried to explain? But rather than special, he made their night together sound cheap and sordid and ruined the memory and she resented him for that.

'I'd have been better off facing up to that reporter,' she said tightly.

He gave her a grin that twisted her insides into a tight little ball again. 'Charlotte, come on. Loosen up a bit.'

She could read it in his eyes—*the way you were twelve hours ago*. Her chin lifted. 'What about now? You're not trying to avoid me *now*. In fact you're making it your business to catch up with me.' Her eyes narrowed. 'Maybe you're a reporter too and you were in on this together.'

'You don't really think that.' He blew out a breath, looked about them. 'Why don't we find somewhere more private to talk—?'

'No more private.' She would not give in to the temptation and tightened her fingers on the handle of her suitcase. 'Right here's fine.'

'Okay.' He raised a hand as if to touch her face, then changed his mind, lowered it again. 'I've been thinking about you for the entire flight. And I wondered if maybe you've changed your mind. Because I'd really like to see you again while we're both here.'

'I didn't come to Fiji to meet someone. I came here to be alone.'

'A shameful waste of romantic sunsets, don't you think?'

'No.' She could enjoy sunsets; she didn't need a man for that. And she refused to think what she did need a man for… So she didn't think about how hard and hairy his forearm would feel if she reached out and touched it. She ignored his familiar masculine scent, arousing now in the humid air wafting through the exit doors. And she totally didn't think about the dark, drugging taste of his kisses, the way his eyes had glittered down at her in the dark, jaw clenched as he came inside her.

'Admit it, Charlotte, you enjoyed our time together as much as I did.' His voice was deep velvet and pure seduction. 'It could be even better on a balmy tropical night with the windows open, the breeze wafting over hot damp skin…'

'Yes,' she snapped, not allowing herself to be tempted by the images he conjured. 'Not the bit about *better*—' she waved a jerky hand in front of her '—I meant last night. I admit it, okay? But that was last night.'

'And you're thinking how much you'd like to do it again.'

'You…you're way too sure of yourself.'

'You prefer a less confident man?'

'I prefer to be *alone* as I already told you. Men are not on my agenda right now.'

'Yet you made an exception for me.' He grinned. 'I'm flattered.'

'Don't be.' She pushed the words out. 'You were available, you were convenient and I used you. I used you *shamelessly*. A one-off. Nothing more.' She forced herself to look into his eyes and not crumple into a mindless mess. She even managed a smile—not too difficult when escape was just beyond those doors. 'I hope you enjoy your vacation. Goodbye.'

'I've got a car waiting. At least let me give you a lift to your hotel. Where are you staying?'

'I've organised for a car from the resort to collect me. In fact, he'll be wondering where I am.' She started walking, made a show of looking at her watch while noticing most of the passengers from their flight had already left the terminal.

'I'll walk you out.'

Trailing her suitcase, she headed for the exit, not looking at Nic walking beside her. While she scanned the area
for her ride, she saw Nic signal a shiny limo, which immediately drove to the kerb. The chauffeur who stepped
out was middle-aged and wore smart traditional clothing.

He grinned, teeth white against his dusky skin. 'Hey,
Nic. *Bula vinaka!*'

'Malakai, *bula.*'

Charlotte watched on, surprise mingling with confusion
as the pair clasped hands and greeted each other as if they
were old friends. 'Another resort guest on your flight is
riding with us,' she heard the chauffeur say, looking about.
'I don't see her yet.'

Nic looked her way and said slowly, 'Vaka Malua Resort
by any chance?'

Oh, no. She couldn't believe it. Then she noticed the
colours of the hotel's logo in the man's attire—turquoise,
black and ivory. Of all the resorts she could have chosen...
She nodded once. Fate was truly punishing her.

Nic said something to the other man in a low voice, then
stepped up and took her bags, swung them into the limo's
boot and said, 'Charlotte, this is Malakai.'

Malakai flashed his wide smile for her and opened the
car door. '*Bula*, ma'am. Welcome to Fiji.'

'Hello. *Bula.*' She forced a smile for him but her mind
was scrambled as she walked towards the vehicle.

Maybe she'd make some sense of it when she could finally close the door to her suite and block out the rest of the
world. Vaka Malua was a new luxury resort and, according to its website, spacious and private. She had her own
personal plunge pool and a view overlooking the sea. If she
chose, she could avoid the other tourists. Nic, for instance.

Nic waited until she'd climbed into the vehicle, then
made a snap decision and slid in beside Charlotte, en-

suring plenty of space between them. She was giving off vibes that would have most fellow passengers diving for the seat next to the driver, and under normal circumstances he would have enjoyed catching up with Malakai. But he knew it was all a front designed to keep him at a distance when what she really wanted was for him to touch her again.

As they headed south from Nadi towards the Coral Coast and Natadola Beach he carried on a running conversation with Malakai, but his mind was on the passenger sitting stiffly beside him.

He didn't believe Charlotte's talk about a convenient fling for a second. He knew women and she wasn't the type. He'd manipulated the situation to his advantage. So she was understandably annoyed with him, but even behind her invisible shield he could feel the pull between them.

Unlike him, she obviously came from old money. A rich babe with something to hide? He'd seen the emotion cloud her pretty grey eyes when she'd talked about her mother's pearls and the family holiday in Hawaii. Family was obviously important to her.

She claimed she didn't want anything to do with him. He had forty minutes or so to work on that. He pressed the button and the limo's window slid partway down, letting in the welcome fragrance of the tropics. 'Have you been to Fiji before, Charlotte?'

'No.'

He laid an arm across the back of the seat and angled himself so he could see her better. 'First impressions?'

'Friendly. Relaxing…I hope.' She sniffed the inrushing air. 'What's burning?'

'Sugar cane. They burn off before harvesting.' Her hair was tied back but strands were escaping and twirling around her temples. He only had to lift a finger and he'd be able to touch it but she was just starting to relax. 'Is the breeze bothering you?'

She shook her head. 'You know the driver,' she murmured.

'I'm a regular visitor to Fiji and Vaka Malua. Malakai's worked there since the resort opened.'

'Okay…so what does *Vaka Malua* mean?'

He looked into her eyes and said, 'It means to linger, or stay awhile.'

*Of course it did*—he could read the scepticism in her eyes. She held his gaze a split second longer, then turned away to let the air blow on her face.

He smiled to himself and turned to watch the Fijian green slide by before looking back at her. 'Do you travel a lot?'

'Not for the past couple of years.'

'How long are you here?' *How long do I have to convince you to change your mind?*

'Two weeks.'

'Well, I hope you find what you're looking for.'

She didn't reply.

Sensing she wasn't going to open up, he used the rest of the journey to provide a running commentary of the area they were passing through. Large cream dwellings set back from the road amongst encroaching vegetation, purple and red flamed bushes and stands of banana palms. The regular abundance of locals walked along the side of the road.

The resort came into view, a cluster of steep-pitched grey roofs in the traditional way of Fijian architecture, the Vaka Malua Club's deluxe bures perched on the top of the hill, the rest of the resort sweeping down to the beach.

Malakai pulled under the portico and the wide open-air reception area. 'You getting out here too?' he asked Nic.

'No.' He turned to Charlotte as Malakai slid out to open her door. 'Here we are. I have something to take care of elsewhere.' He nodded towards the staff approaching with smiles and banjos and shell necklaces. 'Looks like the welcome party's ready to cater to your every wish and command.'

She looked quickly at him and her eyes flashed hot—as he'd intended them to with his mention of wishes—before her gaze darted away to her handbag, which she'd strategically placed on the seat between them. 'I hope you enjoy your visit,' she said, climbing out.

'You too.' He watched her departure, unable to stop his gaze from wandering. She had the sexiest backside he'd ever come into contact with.

She was going to be here two weeks.

'Wait.' Flipping open his wallet, he pulled out an Aussie fifty-dollar note and scrawled his phone number across the bottom. He jumped out, came around to her side of the limo and tucked it in the top of her handbag. 'In case you change your mind.'

Without waiting for her response, he climbed back into the limo and shut the door. 'Take me home, Malakai.'

Smiling, he wondered who'd give in first.

# CHAPTER FIVE

'THE new furniture arrived safely?' Nic talked freely now they were alone and heading for Nic's residence adjacent to the resort along a private road crowded with lush vegetation.

'*Ni mataka,*' Malakai told him. Tomorrow. 'It was sent to the resort by error this afternoon. They promised to come back in the morning.'

'And the artwork's finished?'

'*Io.*' Yes. 'Tenika likes the paintings very much.' Malakai spoke with shy fondness of his wife. 'We hung it like you said. Very nice.'

'I'm looking forward to seeing it.'

Nic was also looking forward to catching up with the couple who occupied a separate wing of his home, keeping the whole place spotless and liveable whenever he was down south, which was often weeks at a time. It was so satisfying to be in a position to provide two people he cared about with employment and accommodation. He knew how it was to live in poverty.

Moments later they drove through the high gates and onto the property. His contentment rubbed alongside pride as his luxury white home with its timber-louvred shutters open to the afternoon breeze came into view. He'd bought it several years ago as part of an ageing hotel. Then he had negotiated with the owners to bring the whole resort into the twenty-first century by becoming a silent partner.

It had been a gamble, sinking his first million into something he knew little about, but it had paid off, providing an ongoing income for locals. He hadn't done too badly out of it himself. He didn't get involved with the day-to-day business but he spent time at the resort when he wasn't working, knew the staff, attended festivities, checked on its overall efficiency.

But his private home was a sanctuary he guarded fiercely with high walls and monitored security. He didn't entertain here and no woman ever came within these walls. Not since Angelica. If he wanted female company while he was in Fiji, he found it elsewhere at another resort, preferably away from the main island.

The car stopped and Nic stepped out, leaving Malakai to park it undercover and bring in his luggage as he always insisted on doing as part of his job.

Luxuriant foliage and tropical flowers lined the path. He noticed a couple of recently planted hibiscus bushes and one of Tenika's personal touches—a Fijian carving, the equivalent of a garden gnome.

Over the next few hours he caught up with Malakai and Tenika over refreshments, admired the new kitchen garden they'd planted in his absence.

Later, refreshed from a swim and a shower, he checked his computer. Twilight settled over the bay with purple and vermilion hues. The smell of the resort's kerosene torches wafted through the window. The nightly traditional *Meke* on the lawns down by the sea was in full swing. Distant singing and drumming throbbed on the air. Nic sat back, satisfied the five massive screens reflecting a three-dimensional wrap-around image of the Utopian world he'd created were ready to work on.

*Utopian Twilight* had been his first major success, written—inspired—after The Angelica Incident. It had taken three years in the courts to reclaim the earlier works she and her lover on the side had plagiarised. Retreating from real life's raw deal into his alternative world had saved him.

*Chameleon Twilight* had followed a couple of years later. *Chameleon Council*, the final in the trilogy, was almost finished. He needed a break to revitalise his creativity, but online gamers were clamouring for more of the Onyx One's adventures. So… Leaning back, he tapped his fingers on the edge of his desk… Bring in an unexpected new love interest for the Onyx to keep the female players on board…?

From his upstairs office window, his gaze drifted to the exclusive club bures. Maybe his last-minute heroine would be a woman with a quirky penchant for personalised accessories…with a mysterious past…

After checking in to the resort, dinner in her room and an early night, Charlotte spent the first day lazing by her pool and catching up on a novel she'd been meaning to read for ever. She also enjoyed the warm tropical air on her winter-pale skin, the wide blue Pacific view from her balcony, the friendly room service.

It was because she needed some alone time—not because she didn't want to bump into Nic.

In fact, she didn't think of Nic at all. And she did *not* look at that fifty-dollar note burning a hole at the bottom of her bag. It was illegal to deface money, wasn't it? She ought to report him.

He was reminding her that he was here somewhere. Available. A phone call away.

On the second morning she threw back the sheets at six a.m. She would not allow him to dictate what she could and could not do on her first precious vacation in more than two years. Why should she feel like a prisoner in such a luxurious resort with the balmy breeze tickling her skin and beckoning her outside for an early morning walk?

So after a quick breakfast in her room, she pulled on a pair of skinny white pants and a shell-pink T-shirt. She piled her pad and pencils and a bottle of water in her holdall, plonked her sunhat on her head and ventured out.

She breathed in the salty beach smell. Breakfast aromas from the open-air restaurant. Freedom and relaxation.

The thick, scented air stroked her skin as she set off past the bures and along tidy curved paths flanked with Fijian Fire Plants and their brilliant red and gold and chartreuse leaves.

She passed the early risers heading towards the pools and other water activities. She could hear the distant splashes and laughter over the soft murmur of the sea. It sounded like fun.

But, for today at least, she wanted alone time with no distractions. She headed for a clump of scraggy casuarinas and Screw Pines not far away.

Three weeks ago she'd sold her parents' winery where she'd always worked. It had been a close-knit family business and she'd managed the office. The new owners had invited her to stay on but she didn't want to work with strangers who might want to change the way her family had operated the business for generations.

She didn't need paid employment—she had her inheritance—but she had to do *something*. The charities she and her mum had put so many hours into weren't enough of a challenge or distraction.

Until she came up with that elusive something, she'd continue with her lingerie designs, which she'd played with over the past few years. Only a hobby, but she loved the whole process—the designing, the construction and, most of all, the wearing of them.

Underneath her plain outerwear, she could indulge her secret passion for sexy and be that sensual woman she wanted to be. The way Nic had made her feel for those few special hours…

*Get that thought out of your head.*

As she approached the pines she saw colourful bougainvillea trailing over a high cream wall. She noticed a wide break in the foliage and walked through. A bright umbrella provided shade for the wooden table and chairs. There were a couple of recliner chairs covered with striped matting for those who wanted to sunbathe, but it seemed the guests were more interested in the water because there wasn't a soul around. Perfect.

She opened her sketch pad and spread it on the table, pulled out her pencils and let her hand wander over the paper, experimenting.

The Pacific Islands. Vivid colours and bold designs. Sexy playful styles that spoke of fun and summer. But with her libido still so highly charged, she could still feel the sparks and her ideas soon turned to more erotic designs. Crotchless knickers. Hmm. They'd have come in handy the other night…

Her hand moved quicker over the paper as ideas formed. She'd just finished designing an idea for a bra with a starburst radiating from a peek-a-boo cut-out in the centre of the cups when she heard the sound of heavy footsteps approaching.

'Hey, there. You.' The deep male voice shattered the peace like a volley of gun shots. Stern, annoyed. And familiar. She jerked her hat lower, pushed her sunglasses further up her nose and peeked beneath the brim.

Nic was striding towards her in a pair of short white

shorts. The rest of him was naked, showing off his well-defined abs and a washboard stomach glistening in the sun. He'd been swimming or working out. More like swimming by the way his shorts clung to his thighs. Her breath caught and her pulse did a crazy happy dance.

She ordered it to *stop*. 'Are you stalking me? Bec—'

'Stalking *you*?' he snapped out. 'You're on private property.' He came to an abrupt halt a few metres away, squinting and shielding his eyes against the sun's early morning rays. 'Charlotte?'

Spreading her trembling hands over her sketches to hide them, she managed to flip the cover down and stood up to minimise the difference in height. 'I—'

'What are you doing here?'

'It's a free resort,' she said, lifting her chin. 'And what do you mean private property?' A not-so-funny feeling slid through her stomach… He'd not checked in to the resort with her… 'I had no idea this part was private property. What are *you*—?'

'The sign on the gate gave you no clue?'

'What gate?' She looked back to where she'd come from. 'Oh. That gate.' That big double gate with 'Private Property, No Guests' on it in big black letters. She swung to face him. 'If you leave it open so wide that no one knows it's there, one can't be blamed for not seeing it.'

He exhaled sharply and muttered, 'The furniture movers must have left it open.'

Mind brimming with questions, she stared at him, then at the surroundings. Her eyes flicked over his shoulder and now she noticed glimpses of a thatched structure—probably a pool shade—through the heavy bushes. 'You live here?'

He moved a step closer, his gaze curious and drawn to her sketch pad. 'What are you doing?'

'Nothing.' Snatching her pad off the table, she slapped it against her chest. 'Just sketching. The flowers. Leaves. Shapes. Nothing really.'

'How do I know?' His dark eyes captured hers. 'It could be *you* stalking *me*. I don't know you, after all, do I, Charlotte? How do I know you're not here to—?'

'Who *are* you?'

'Nic Russo. And I live here.' He gestured with his chin. 'Show me what you're working on.'

Sketches of scantily clad female anatomy? 'No. It's private.'

One brow lifted. 'So is this garden.'

'And it's beautiful.' She said the first thing that came into her spinning head. 'Stunning. And I love those masks on the wall…'

'So are you—beautiful and stunning.' His voice slid over her senses like honey. 'Are you wearing a mask too, Charlotte? Hiding who you really are?' He resumed walking towards her. Predatory male with his prey cornered.

She slid one foot ever-so-slightly backwards, mentally calculating the direction of the gate behind her. Trying to figure how long it would take to get there if she ran very fast. 'No. I'm a private person, that's all.'

'So am I when it comes to guarding what's mine. Maybe that reporter was onto something,' he continued slowly, as if enjoying himself. But she couldn't be sure. 'Maybe you're an undercover spy. Out to steal my next project.'

'*Spy?*' she sputtered, incredulous, but, for heaven's sake, now he looked *serious*. 'Steal?' She took another step back. 'Are you living in some alternate reality or just plain crazy?' She shook her head, kept walking backwards. 'I refuse to have this ridiculous conversation.'

He followed, quickly gaining on her. 'Alternate reality. Interesting you should say that. A coincidence?' He was so close now she could see his long black eyelashes. Every pinprick of dark stubble. The *almost* smile tucked away at the corner of his mouth. Maybe.

But maybe not.

'I apologise for trespassing,' she went on, 'but I'd appreciate a straight answer before I leave.'

'And if I give you that answer, will you let me see what you're working on?'

She tightened her grip on her work. 'No.'

He spread his hands. Resigned? Somehow she didn't think so. She tapped her finger against the pad. 'Straight answer, please.'

'I write computer programs. Very lucrative computer programs.'

'Oh…' She'd figured he was more of an outdoors job kind of guy. 'Like accounting software, that kind of stuff?'

'Not quite.' He sounded amused. 'Do I look like an accountant?'

She grinned, amused right back despite herself. 'Not quite.'

'I build alternative worlds and create characters to live there. It's interactive. Anyone can visit so long as they pay and log in online. But some people think it's okay to steal work that's taken another person years of blood, sweat and tears to write.' There was a cold, implacable calm of personal experience behind the brown gaze.

'Okay. I understand. I'm sorry, I just saw the garden and no one was around…'

'Or maybe you couldn't stay away.' His voice deepened, his eyes changed. Tempted. 'You asked about me around the resort and came to tell me you wanted to continue what we started for a few more days.'

'No…Nic…I…' *need to think.* Except she couldn't remember what about when he was looking at her that way.

He closed the gap between them. She could smell the sharpness of salt water on his hot masculine skin. 'No...'

The breeze had strengthened and his hair blew around his face as he said, 'You could clear everything up if you prove you're actually working on something here and not just lurking.'

'I wasn't lurking, I was—'

'Hoping desperately that I'd come out and find you,' he murmured silkily. She heard his words but it was their smooth, deep cadence that captured her. She remembered how it had sounded when he'd laid her down on the bed and told her what he was going to do to her, and how.

He took her hat off, tossed it on the table. His hands moulded firmly around her shoulders and he pulled her closer, his lips a warm whisper away from hers. She swayed towards them, couldn't wait to feel them on hers. When he pulled the pad out of her loosening grasp and laid it on the table beside her, she didn't attempt to stop him.

'Because if *I* found *you*,' he continued, 'you'd not be giving in first.' He tightened his hold, eyes dancing. 'And that's okay. I don't mind letting you win. This time.'

Before she could object to that—did she even care?—his mouth swooped on hers. Smoothly, expertly, confident that she couldn't resist.

Instant addiction. She felt herself being swept up in the tastes and sensations as a stiff breeze swept across her sweat-damp skin and rustled the palm fronds. Unable to stop herself, she slid her hands upwards over sun-warmed skin exploring all the different textures while his mouth worked magic on hers.

But if he was just proving a point and he'd meant it to be light and easy, the emotions rushing through her were any-thing but. Distant alarm bells rang a warning. She wasn't ready for these feelings and this thing with Nic would only end badly for her. She'd stop…any moment now…

The muscles in her legs turned lax, her arms coiled around his neck and she hung on, her toes curling inside her sandals.

Nic lifted his lips a fraction. 'I hate to interrupt this, but your work…'

'Work?' she murmured, craning her neck to recapture his lips.

He licked her bottom lip with a lazy stroke of his tongue. 'Whatever you were doing. When I interrupted you. Remember that private thing you didn't want me to see?'

She pulled back and swivelled her head to see her precious designs scattering like giant butterflies across the garden. 'Oh, no!' Yanking out of his arms, she stumbled across the lawn and into bushes, grabbing what she could. 'I've got them,' she yelled in case he followed. 'Do *not* look…'

But when she turned around with the crumpled pages in her hands, he was regarding her with telling interest. He didn't say a word but a smile played around his lips.

'I'm leaving now,' she told him, her face burning. Stuffing her papers and everything she could lay her hands on into her holdall, she grabbed her hat and backed towards the gate. 'Stay away from me. I mean it,' she said through clenched teeth when he only kept smiling that know-all smile. 'You're bad for me.'

She turned and fled, knowing he was watching. Bad for her peace of mind. Bad for her will power. Bad distraction.

Bad, bad, bad.

Still grinning, Nic watched her go. He waited until she'd disappeared past the gate, then retrieved a loose sheet that had snagged under the table. He couldn't *not* look, now, could he? Smoothing out the page, he stared at the erotic image.

Flowers, hmm? His grin broadened. But he looked closer. This was a skilled artist's work. She'd added notes on the construction, fabric details, colour combinations.

And his initial response to finding her in his garden had been to shoot first, ask questions later. Good God, he'd all but accused her of espionage. He hoped his quick manoeuvre to kiss her instead had distracted her thoughts elsewhere.

It sure as hell had distracted *him*.

He folded the paper in half. The perfect excuse to see her again. Not that he needed one. He closed and secured the gates, his thoughts filled with his unexpected visitor. Naturally she'd want her design back. It was only right that he returned it. Tonight was soon enough.

He went straight to his computer, sat down and studied the screens alive with characters going about their quests in their fantasy world. Tapping the mouse, he got back to work. He had a full day's adventures to finish before he could turn his thoughts to other pursuits.

Closing her door safely behind her, Charlotte shut her eyes. Images danced behind her eyelids. Images of losing control. *Hoping desperately that I'd come out and find you,* he'd said. Huh. Like he'd know. Except he did. And she couldn't fool herself—desperate was exactly how she felt, which was why she'd told him to stay away. The only sensible thing she'd said to him. And the bit about him being bad for her.

Because she knew his type—he could charm the knickers off a nun with a single tilt of those lips—and that wasn't the type of man she wanted to get involved with. Nic was a great—perfect—one-night kind of guy, but that kind wasn't the sort of man she wanted to share other things with. Like confidences and dreams and hopes and interests. Like building a life and a home together. Like sharing his family to help compensate for the loss of hers.

Nic was so not that man.

Crossing the room to gaze over the rooftops, she picked out his palatial two-storey home amongst the trees. 'Oh, Dad, what would you say about me?' After her behaviour, she was hardly his princess any more. Her fingers touched the pearls at her neck. Mum would be appalled.

Nic *Russo*... Turning away from the view, she opened her notebook PC and switched it on. Thirty seconds later she was looking up the name and checking the social-networking sites. But the Nic Russos she found on the Internet didn't match anyone who created computer games and obviously made millions doing so. Not even a Dominic Russo turned up anything.

Her fingers clenched over the keyboard. As soon as she'd calmed down, when her mind was less cluttered and she'd thought things through, she'd find Nic Russo or whoever the heck he was and demand more answers.

If he didn't find her first.

# CHAPTER SIX

AT FIVE-THIRTY Nic showered and went downstairs, Charlotte's paper in his shirt pocket. Tenika had ironed him a Fijian shirt—crimson with a white hibiscus print—and laid it on his bed along with a fresh white hibiscus. He knew she expected to see him wearing both.

She was in the kitchen washing the vegetables he'd seen her pick earlier from his window. These days her wiry close-cropped hair was tinged with silver. The patterned hot-pink blouse over her black *sulu* complemented her dusky complexion; her hands were busy pulling leaves off stems.

He reached for a banana. 'How's your day been?'

She turned from the sink and smiled, teeth white against her skin. '*Bula*, Nic, you want *kakana* already? Eat vegetables today from the garden with fresh fish.'

'*Vinaka*, but don't cook anything for me this evening.'

'Ah, you have a pretty *marama* waiting for you.' She looked him up and down and nodded approvingly. '*Totoka*. Very handsome. She is lucky. A guest at the resort, Malakai told me.' Her eyes danced with matchmaking delight.

Nic had to smile. The pair of them never gave up no matter how often he told them he was more than happy with his bachelor status. 'Malakai's jumping to conclusions.'

She shook her head, put the leaves in a colander and turned on the tap. 'He doesn't jump—he is too old. He said you and the pretty *marama* were talking in the car yesterday. Very close.'

'Charlotte was on the same flight. I have something I need to return to her.'

Tenika made a *pfft* sound and sloshed water about in the sink. 'You like her—Charlotte. You want Malakai to bring the car around?'

'We're not leaving the resort. We're just going to watch the *Meke* then maybe have a meal.'

'You bring her here tomorrow so I can meet her and see for myself if she is good enough for you. I can cook good *kakana* for you and her.'

'I don't think so.'

She strained off the leaves, dumped them in a bowl. 'You never bring the pretty *maramas* here. To your home.' She pursed her lips, her coal-black eyes pierced his. 'Maybe you like this one more than the others—you bring her.'

'Tenika…'

'Maybe you marry her. Make babies.' Wiping her hands on her apron, she nodded to him. 'Fijian people like babies. I can help.'

Tenika and Malakai had never had children of their own. Nic saw the emptiness in her eyes sometimes but Tenika would have to look elsewhere for surrogate grandkids.

'I know you can,' he said softly. He took the hibiscus from behind his ear and slid it behind hers. 'I'll see you tomorrow.'

He took the back route through the gate to avoid running into staff who'd expect him to stop and talk. He'd planned his time and didn't want those plans disrupted. The *Meke* started at dusk. This evening was perfect—still and warm, with a multi-hued sky and the charcoal aroma from the open-air barbecue.

He had access to all areas of the complex and it had been a simple task to learn that she was staying in one of the resort's most exclusive bures.

He knocked, and a moment later she cracked open the door.

'Good evening.'

She opened the door wider. 'I've been expecting you to show up.' She wore a black sarong spattered with electric blue and white frangipani flowers, giving him an unob-structed view of her neck and shoulders—his gaze low-ered—and obviously no bra. Her glossy hair was piled on top of her head.

'It was only a matter of time.' He leaned against the door frame with a smile.

'Guess you'd better come in.' She walked away but looked back at him over one of those bare shoulders. 'Did you work your charm on the girls at Reception too?'

He stepped inside, closed the door behind him. 'Didn't need to. I'm a silent partner—finding one Charlotte Dumont on the books was easy peasy.'

Her shoulders tensed before she continued across the room. 'I see.'

'Your name was on Malakai's airport's pick-up sheet.'

'And, of course, you couldn't help noticing.' Those pretty grey eyes were clouded with worry when she fi-nally stopped and turned to him. 'So I guess you know all about me now.'

'If you mean did I do a computer check on you, the an-swer's no. I respect privacy. But if you want to tell me a bit about yourself, that's fine too. I was hoping it might be tonight.' He saw her notebook PC on the desk and gestured with his chin. 'You won't find me on any social-networking sites.'

She blushed. *Guilty.* 'I wasn't… Much.' She crossed to the desk quickly and switched it off. 'You said you write computer games. I'd've thought you'd want a link so your fans could contact you.'

'I use a pseudonym.'

'That's convenient.' Her tone was sceptical, like her expression.

'Isn't it.' Walking towards her, he dug his wallet from his back pocket and flashed his driver's licence in front of her eyes. 'Read this. Aloud.'

'Dominic T. Russo.' She nodded. 'Okay.'

'And…' he took out her sketch, unfolded it and held it out '…I thought you might be wondering where this was.'

She took one look at the page, closed her eyes and folded it again and muttered something short and unexpectedly earthy.

'Charlotte, you just keep on surprising me.' He loved the way her cheeks coloured, the vulnerability she couldn't hide. It stirred up his protective side, amongst other things. 'Your secrets are safe with me.'

Her eyes darkened and sparked at the same time and he knew she was thinking about their one night together. Her fingers tightened on the page. 'I didn't even check them… You flustered me this morning.' She fanned her face with it. 'You're flustering me now.'

'Am I?' He assumed an expression of mock concern. 'Anything I can do to help ease that?'

'I refuse to answer on the grounds that it might cause me to break out in a rash that would prohibit me from leaving this room for the rest of the evening.'

'Tell you what, why don't you answer and we'll deal with the rash together if it happens?'

'Why don't I?' But she only slid the page between the covers of her sketch pad. 'Thanks for hand-delivering it.'

'I didn't think you'd want it floating around the complex. It looks important,' he prompted.

But she only said, 'It could be,' without elaborating and slid her notebook into its leather bag. 'I was just going to change and go down to watch the dancing.'

'That's handy because I came to ask you if you'd like to accompany me and maybe get something to eat after. But don't change, you fit right in as you are. The resort's casual, and loads of tourists wear their swimming costumes and sarongs.'

'Not me.' She crossed to the cupboard, pulled out a long white dress.

He shook his head. As stunning as he imagined she'd look in the slim sheath, he wanted to see her in those vibrant colours for a change. They accentuated her eyes and made them come alive. 'When in the islands, do as the islanders do. Keep the sarong. Please.' Besides, he wanted the chance to take it off her later.

She drew in a deep breath as if giving it some thought, then slid the dress back in the cupboard and said, 'Give me a moment to freshen up at least,' and disappeared into the en-suite bathroom.

He sat on one of the roomy saucer-shaped bamboo chairs to wait. Her suitcase was open on the bag stand. His gaze wandered over the contents. Underwear. Every colour, every fabric, every fantasy. If he had his way, he'd enjoy watching her dance instead, wearing his choice of garments. Then peeling every one of them from her body. Slowly.

But he put those carnal thoughts on hold. Tonight was about getting to know her in a social context. It was about discovering more about Charlotte the person.

To start with, at least.

Walking to the window, he stared out at the sunset reflecting off the ocean. They'd get to know each other a little better, enjoy a few more nights together, then she'd be gone. He didn't even have to make some excuse to call it off and leave.

Perfect.

Charlotte's fingers trembled slightly as she pulled the elastic out of her hair. She ran a brush through the tangled mess. Seeing Nic hadn't made her shaky—if you discounted the quiver of desire running the length of her inner thighs the instant he'd appeared in her doorway—it was the knowledge that he'd seen her risqué bedroom designs.

She adjusted and retied the sarong's knot between her breasts. She hated drawing attention to herself but maybe Nic was right. If she went casual, she'd blend in with the rest of the crowd. She left her hair down, scooping one side behind her ear.

So much for telling Nic to stay away. She knew exactly how the evening was going to end if he had his way. And she wouldn't fight it; she knew that too.

She was also looking forward to watching the traditional dance with him, sharing some time over a drink or a meal. Finding answers. As long as she treated him with the caution one usually reserved for dangerous animals, she'd be fine.

It was a perfect outdoors evening. The still water reflected the last sliver of sun. Coconut palms were silhouetted against an ocean of red and an orange sky. Someone was lighting the kerosene torches and cauldrons; the warm smell wafted on the sultry air.

'The younger kids from the local village school are performing tonight,' he said as they walked towards the

sounds of tribal drumming. There was an almost possessive note to his voice.

'You know these kids?'

'I've been involved with the school's computer literacy
programme for a couple of years now, so yeah. The older
kids help the younger ones. One big family, no one's excluded. It's the Fijian way.'

From his tone, Charlotte had a feeling Nic had missed
out on those things while growing up.

They sat on benches with other guests to watch the
show. A troupe of male dancers entertained them first, burnished bodies gleaming in the firelight. Then the women,
festooned with flowers, their grass skirts alive with movement. The kids joined in last, to the audience's delight and
applause.

As the crowd dispersed to find their way to one of the
complex's half a dozen restaurants, Nic signalled one of
the dancers. 'Kas!'

'Nic!' she called, with a smile, and hurried over, her grass
skirt rustling. '*Bula*. You're back!' They bussed cheeks. 'The
kids have missed you.' She tapped him lightly with her palm
fan. 'Hope you're going to remedy that soon.' She turned
her wide smile on Charlotte. '*Bula*.'

'Charlotte,' he said, with a light touch at her back. 'This
is Kasanita Blackman, our dance teacher—just one of her
many teaching skills. Charlotte's a friend visiting here for
a couple of weeks.'

'*Bula*. It's nice to meet you.'

'Welcome to Fiji, Charlotte. I hope you enjoyed our
special performance. We've been practising for a month.'

'It was fantastic. The kids seemed to be enjoying it as
much as the audience.'

'Ah, yes, they're so excited.' Kasanita groaned. 'I don't
think we'll get any serious school work done tomorrow.'

Charlotte grinned. 'I bet.'

'Why don't you come and visit us while you're here? Get Nic to bring you when he comes. That's assuming you like kids and noise.'

'I love kids and noise…I think. I haven't been inside a classroom in years.'

'Okay, then. I hope to see you soon. Nic?'

'How about tomorrow? Charlotte?' He turned to her. 'Does that suit you?'

She smiled. 'I'm looking forward to it already.'

A chance to see a little of the real Fiji that other tourists might not. But more than that, she was looking forward to learning more about Nic and the support he gave the school. She admired guys who supported charities, especially when there was nothing in it for them personally—unlike Flynn who only did it to further his political ambitions.

They chatted with Kasanita a few moments then said their goodbyes.

'She's lovely,' Charlotte said as they walked towards one of the outdoor restaurants. 'English surname—did she marry an Aussie?'

'Her father's Australian, her mother's a local. He came here for work, they met and he never left.'

He led her to a quiet candle-lit table away from the rest of the diners and she knew he'd reserved it for them in advance. Right on the sand with the water lapping a few metres away, spotlights throwing up an amber glow on coconut palms, a candle in a frosted glass on the table.

A waiter appeared, his black *sulu* topped with the resort's black and aqua shirt. He set a couple of fancy fruit cocktails in front of them. Nic ordered a shared plate of local Indian delicacies and spoke with Timi for a few moments—he seemed to be on a first-name basis with all the staff—then they toasted the evening with their drinks. Something deliciously smooth and frothy with coconut, pineapple, fresh lime and alcohol.

Nic waited until Timi had gone to get closer to his dinner companion. Her hands were resting on the table as she leaned back on her chair to admire the stars and he couldn't resist running a finger lightly across her knuckles.

'So, Charlotte,' he began, capturing her eyes as her gaze snapped back to him. 'We've seen each other naked. I think it's time we got acquainted on another level, don't you?'

She made some kind of strangled sound in her throat and sucked deeply on her cocktail straw. He'd never seen such beautiful eyes. Even in semi-darkness they shone with an inner luminescence that only drew him closer. *A moth to the flame*.

He leaned in, his forearms on the table. He didn't mind the heat, and he wasn't averse to taking a risk. Taking risks had got him where he was today, but he waited a moment longer to let her settle. 'Ask me something.'

'Okay, I have a question,' she said slowly. 'Kasanita mentioned you've not been back in a while, yet you said you live here—how does that work?'

'I have an apartment in Adelaide. I divide my time between the two.'

Her eyes flickered. 'You're from Adelaide too?'

'Originally from Victoria. I moved to South Australia more than ten years ago. So there's a possibility of seeing you wandering Adelaide's Rundle Mall some day?'

'I live in the Barossa Valley, but the mall's a favourite haunt, yes.'

'You're not related to Lance Dumont by any chance?' He was a society big name in South Australia and royalty in the wine industry. Dumont owned the award-winning Three Cockatoos Winery. The man was worth a fortune.

She nodded and her gaze dropped to the table. 'He was my father.'

'So you *are* a princess after all.' Then he remembered that Lance and his wife had died in an aviation accident some time back, and his casual grin vanished. 'Hell, Charlotte, I'm sorry... I didn't mean to bring up painful memories.'

'It's okay.' She looked up again with a watery sheen in her eyes and a determined brightness to her voice. 'It's been a couple of years now. But I do miss them. And Travers.'

'Travers?' A boyfriend? A *husband*?

'My brother. I lost my whole family in one crazy afternoon and my safe little world crashed as surely as that helicopter. It's never been the same since.'

'That's tough,' he murmured, and meant it. He didn't know how it felt to have a family—at least not a family where people loved and cared for each other—but he could empathise with those who did when he saw the pain of loss in their eyes. Even though he didn't need or want that connection himself. 'Do the authorities know what happened?'

'Dad had a heart attack at the controls. We had no idea he had heart problems; he was always so fit and full of life. Dad loved to play up to the media.' She smiled a small private and poignant smile that tugged at his heart. 'He'd have been chuffed that he made the front page of the newspapers in three states.'

Their platter came. Charlotte set her linen napkin beside her plate and they ate for a few moments while they enjoyed the flavours of the food.

'You must be used to the press, then,' Nic said, choosing a coconut-covered melon ball.

'I've always avoided it whenever possible.'

'Why was that idiot reporter giving you a hard time?'

'I…' She trailed off on a sigh, and studied her wine glass as she twirled its stem between her fingers.

'You should tell me about it. That way if it happens again—'

'If it happens again, you won't be there to rescue me.' She met his eyes with a fierce finality and he knew it was the simple truth. She was leaving in two weeks. He wasn't.

'My fiancé and I broke up six weeks ago. He's in the public eye. The guy was chasing the story behind it. I thought, stupidly, if I denied my identity he'd leave me alone.'

'Did you love him? The fiancé.' His question surprised him. The reason behind it and the knot that tightened around his heart in response surprised him more.

Of course she'd loved the man, he thought. He was beginning to understand Charlotte's close ties to family. And he comprehended something very clearly: when she committed to people—whether it was her family or a man— it would be for keeps. So he figured she hadn't broken it off; her ex had.

In any case, she sidestepped his question, asking one of her own. 'What about your family, Nic?'

He never talked about his background. And with someone like Charlotte Dumont, society princess? He might as well be from the other side of the universe. She'd planned to marry and no doubt start her own family; he was a confirmed bachelor who lived for his work. Lived *in* his work; in a world where he ruled absolutely. They'd never find common ground.

Except in bed.

And wasn't that all that really mattered here? 'No siblings,' he said. 'I never knew my dad. My mother died twelve years ago.' He set his fork down carefully and reached for his glass. 'That's about it.'

'No.' She hesitated before placing her hand over his, and her eyes filled with compassion. 'That's the short, sharp and shiny version you give to anyone who asks. But I'm not anyone and I'm here and I have all night…if you want to talk?'

'I don't want to talk.' He turned her hand over, linked it with his. Slid his fingers slowly between hers, letting the tension build, watching her eyes change from sympathetic to wide and aware. Taking the focus away from his past. 'Are you still hungry?'

Shaking her head, she slipped her napkin in her bag. 'If I was, you just made me forget.'

With any other woman, he'd have smiled at the ease with which she'd surrendered, but the feelings Charlotte invoked were suddenly too strong for such trivialities. He rose and pulled her up, saw an answering flash in her eyes and tightened his grip. 'What I *really* want to do is unwrap you, lie you down and make you forget you ever had a fiancé.'

## CHAPTER SEVEN

LEAVING the lights and music and chatter behind, Charlotte half walked, half ran, her hand in Nic's, urgency rushing through her veins like a waterfall after rain. They headed for soft sand and cool shadows and the eternal shoosh of the sea. As soon as they reached the shoreline she kicked off her sandals, swiped them up, laughing like a crazy woman.

Maybe it had something to do with near hysteria and never having experienced such urgency with a man. Flynn had been her only lover and it had been nothing like this.

Nic glanced down at her but didn't loosen his hold. 'What's funny?'

'This.' She waved her sandals in the air. 'Not so much funny as unexpected. I feel like a different person, I keep expecting to wake up and...'

Her laughter died and she trailed off and looked at him as he slowed his steps. His jaw was clenched, eyes fierce. A strange tight feeling clenched around her heart. 'What?'

He didn't answer, just pulled her further along the beach. The instant they were hidden from public view, he stopped and yanked her to him with both arms, so that she was pressed flat against his chest. 'Charlotte, what you make me want to do to you,' he muttered. He loosened his hold but only so that he could mould his hands around her skull. His fingers twisted in her hair as he crashed his mouth down on hers.

Demanding, desperate. She tasted the richness of his lips and tongue, the darker flavour of his desire. His grinding need against her belly. He was not the casually suave and charming man to let a woman take the lead tonight. He was that dangerous animal she'd warned herself about.

And she abandoned her caution absolutely. Gave herself up to him without reservation or hesitation. Her senses were so attuned, she felt every tremor: his and hers. The soft skitter of night air over her arms, the cool sand squishing between her toes. The heat flowing between their tightly pressed bodies.

She heard the mutter of appreciation as he kissed her, his groan of reluctance as he pulled away. He dragged his fingers down through the length of her hair, then let it fall softly to her shoulders. 'You were made for the night, Charlotte. That hint of the mysterious about you that makes me want to discover your deepest secrets.' He looked down at her, eyes as dark as the ocean. 'Do you still want to be alone?'

She knew it couldn't last, but right now she felt as if she never wanted to be alone again. 'I'd rather be with you,' she said, and reached out her hand for his.

'Come on,' he said, tugging her forward again. They followed the curve of the beach in silence, starlight guiding them, creating silvery streaks across the shallow pools between the thin ribbons of sand. No words were necessary, both knew where they were headed.

His home came into view, blocking out a slab of the night sky; she recognised the louvred windows and the scrawny pines spearing skywards behind the stone wall.

But instead of heading towards it, he led her further along the beach and up where the sand was soft, and coastal bushes provided protection. The air was pungent with marine life and rotting leaves.

'Here,' he said. 'No one'll find us.' He sounded out of breath, as if he'd been running a marathon.

'You sure?' They were both breathless and it wasn't only the rush to get here.

'Sure I'm sure.' A thread of that familiar teasing tone wound through the urgency. 'The bushes are adequate cover.'

His fingers fumbled a bit as he untied the knot between her breasts and she plain forgot about whether they could be seen. The silky material slithered away, leaving her naked but for a pair of sheer black lace panties threaded with red satin ribbon...and two red bows covering her nipples.

'Man, you are something else.' Appreciation darkened his gaze, molten chocolate desire as it skimmed over her body. 'Wow.' He fingered the bows, peeled them off with care, exposing her taut nipples to the cool air.

'These are designed for moments like this,' she told him and took his hands, placed them on her hips where the side seams were held together with matching bows.

Humour touched his mouth. 'You're a clever girl.' He tugged on the ends of the ribbon, watched the panties fall apart. 'And a little bit wicked.'

She knew she surprised him, that he'd prejudged her, and took pleasure in the fact as she unbuttoned his shirt with quick fingers, then reached for the snap on his jeans. 'I'm not what you expected, am I?' she said between breaths, sliding her fingers between the denim band and hard masculine abdomen. 'I'm not what I expected either—not with you. You turn me into someone I hardly know.'

His seductive hands were busy too, and a moan caught

in her throat as he flicked his thumbs over her nipples, the electric charge zapping straight to her womb. 'I think it's you who's wicked, Dominic Russo.'

'I think you talk too much,' he muttered, and shut her up with a long, drugging kiss that turned her blood to quicksilver and left both of them speechless.

Her head spun with his taste and the hot, arousing scent of his skin. He'd reduced her body to a quivering mess of need. Any moment her knees would give way. She gave up on trying to undress him and lifted her now useless hands to clutch at the sides of his open shirt. 'Hurry.'

A glint of a smile in those dark, dark eyes, and the sharpness, the intensity, the confidence of a man who knew his own sexual power. 'You'll need to let go of my shirt.'

Ah. Her arms fell limply as he shrugged it off. Grabbing a condom from his pocket, he shoved his jeans down long powerful legs, kicked the denim out of the way.

And then they were both naked, the night's soft light bathing them in silver and black. The stars seemed to spin closer as he spread her sarong on the sand and tumbled her down with him.

He was hard as steel and inside her in seconds, mouth and hands greedy, devouring her demands as if they were his own. Just what she needed, fast and frantic and so, so hot.

Clever man. He knew just what she wanted. What she craved. Dizzy delight, unimaginable pleasure—they pounded through her system the way a storm surge crashed onto the beach, bringing her to peak and leaving her swamped and stunned and ravaged. Not in pain, but in breathless, glorious delirium.

No time to recover, he took her up again, driving her to the crest of the highest wave and over, then dragging her under with him to some deep airless place where sanity vanished and passion ruled.

Finally spent, she coasted with him into calmer, shallower waters where touches grew languorous and kisses turned lingering. Time now to drift like the tide and think only of this moment and this man.

'You're not what I expected either,' she murmured a few moments later. Or it could have been hours—time no longer seemed relevant.

He shifted so that he could pull the ends of her sarong around them. 'What *did* you expect?'

'Not this.' She snuggled closer as the cooler air wafted over her skin. 'I didn't expect this. Us.' The instant the word was out she knew she'd made a mistake.

'Us...' he said, carefully. 'Babe, I don't do "us". I'm not that kind of guy; you should know that up front.'

He was blunt to the point of being curt but at least he was honest and she knew exactly where she stood. Which was where she told herself she wanted to be. Casual. No disappointments. But she'd given him the clingy female impression—a big no-no.

'I meant the "us" as in being together again here kind of us.' Embarrassed, she struggled for words. 'After all, it was only supposed to be one night.' She raised her head and forced a casual smile. 'Don't get the wrong idea.'

But he had got the wrong idea because he didn't smile back, just went very still and looked up at the sky.

He'd made it obvious he wasn't looking for anything more than temporary. Neither was she. She couldn't. Not now, not yet. Maybe not ever, because she suddenly didn't want to imagine being with a man who wasn't Nic in this way ever again.

And how self-destructive was that kind of thinking? She let her head flop back too, beside his, and stared skywards at the drifting stars. 'I'm leaving soon anyway so whatever we have is brief. If you still…' She trailed off. She had no idea where his thoughts were.

'Two weeks. My hours are flexible and you're on vacation. We could spend that time together, if you'd like.' His fingers touched hers but his gaze remained fixed on the stars. 'What do you say?'

'A holiday romance?' Could she do that? Could she be romantically involved with a man knowing there was an end point? She'd never had a fling…

'Why not?' He shifted closer. 'Perfect location for romance. A man who wants to please you when you want to be pleased and who'll leave you alone when you want space. It'll do you good.'

'You think so?'

'It'll do us both good. I'll be your part-time tour guide with benefits, you'll be my muse.'

'Part-time tour guide with benefits.' She turned her head to look at him. 'Does that sound romantic to you?'

He looked back at her and smiled, and all the stars seemed to fall into his eyes. 'Trust me, I can do romantic.'

She bet he could. Problem was, could she let him do romantic and walk away unscathed?

After he'd seen Charlotte safely to her room and made arrangements to collect her for their school visit in the morning, restlessness drove Nic onto the balcony with a can of beer. He ripped off the tab, chugged down half the contents while he watched a ship's winking lights skim the horizon.

Anywhere else, he'd have invited himself to a woman's room to spend what was left of the night with her, but he had to consider his position at Vaka Malua. Which was why he never got involved with the resort's guests. He knew Charlotte had expected him to bring her back here. He'd seen it in her eyes when, instead of taking the quick route to his gate, they'd retraced their steps along the beach.

*Us.* She'd coupled them together and it had triggered that familiar sensation that the walls were closing in around him. It spelled long-term and commitment.

Not for Nic Russo. And he believed in being upfront and open about it. No false expectations. He drank deeply, paced to the end of the balcony and back. At least he was honest and Charlotte said she admired that about him.

So a couple of weeks… Romantic didn't have to mean complicated. Hell, no. He knew what women liked and it was a matter of pride that he'd never left a lover unsatisfied. They always understood his rules going in and were only too happy to play the game his way.

Of course, there were those few who hadn't played by those rules; those who'd tried to insinuate themselves into his life with home-cooked meals and gifts and, sometimes, in desperation, tears. Nic was immune to those tricks.

But Charlotte was unlike any other lover. She was fun and witty and sensual, but she was *more*. More than the sexually vibrant woman she'd allowed him to see. He'd glimpsed an inherent shyness and insecurity she worked hard to hide. She'd just come out of a serious relationship, which made her vulnerable to no-strings guys like him.

She'd tried to get him to open up about his past. And she'd wanted to soothe. To share. To understand. And for one unguarded moment he'd found himself strangely tempted.

But there was that thorny issue of trust. The brilliant, beautiful and devious Angelica had taught him people weren't always as they seemed and his fingers tensed on the can.

Just because he and Charlotte had a deeper than usual

rapport going didn't mean he wanted to book the resort's wedding chapel. A couple of weeks would be enough of an indulgence before getting back to what he did best. Work.

Stretching out on the wicker sofa, he breathed in the garden's damp night fragrance and concentrated on the soothing sound of the sea and the evening breeze on his skin.

Maybe she wouldn't be sleeping yet either. He punched the sofa's cushion into shape behind his head. Maybe she'd be spread out on that big bed, those pearls around her throat, reliving their passion. Would she touch herself, remembering how he'd touched her…?

It was a long time before he slept.

# CHAPTER EIGHT

CHARLOTTE inspected her holiday wardrobe the following morning. She didn't want to fade into the background today. She wanted to dress the way she was feeling—sunny and happy. She wanted to fit in with the island culture.

She wanted Nic to notice.

With an hour before she was due to meet him, she headed for the central facilities and shops. She chose half a dozen picture books and jumbo crayons for Kasanita's class. Then she tried on clothes, finally settling on a bright tropical print dress in lime and hot pink. It reminded her of the way Nic's eyes had all but set her sarong on fire last night. Before he'd taken it off her.

Not her usual choice, she thought, staring at her reflection back in her room. And she liked it: being someone different. Here in Fiji she didn't need to worry about being recognised. Here she wasn't a big name's daughter or a politician's partner. She could be herself. She wasn't entirely familiar with the freedom of anonymity. Feeling as if she were dancing on air, she reached for her hat.

She was walking along the cool elevated breezeway towards the concierge desk on her way to meet Nic when she saw him on the lawns below chatting with a couple of female staff members. She paused at the balustrade. He wore khaki shorts and a white T-shirt with a black turtle motif, his slightly dishevelled hair catching the breeze, his smile blinding, even at this distance.

Like Flynn, he was a people person, charm and charisma personified. Another pretty girl joined them. Nic hugged the new arrival's shoulders, she smiled back and said something and they all laughed. Unlike Flynn, he wasn't using his charm to further any agenda. It was professional courtesy and respect and friendly interest all the way. Also unlike Flynn, Nic made time for people because he genuinely cared about others. And he was utterly, utterly gorgeous with it.

Her heart squeezed tight, then seemed to detach from her body and took off on a journey of its own.

Oh, no. She rubbed a hand over her chest and mentally dragged her heart back where it belonged and waited the longest time for it to settle.

She was no expert on men. Apart from co-workers and a forgettable couple of adolescent crushes, her experience was limited to her father and brother who'd loved her and an ex-fiancé who had not. Falling for Nic wasn't an option. This was a holiday romance, nothing more.

She turned and continued towards the concierge desk at the end of the open-air structure, taking her time to feel the salty air drifting through the covered walkway while her pulse returned to normal.

A colourful array of beads caught her eye and she paused to talk to the local women who came in from the nearby village daily and sat in the shade, their handcrafts spread on tarpaulins in front of them.

By the time she'd chosen a bracelet of tiny lime green stones to match her dress, Nic was waiting, watching her as she approached. She felt as admired and breathless as she had last night.

'*Bula*, Charlotte.' He looked her up and down. 'Don't you look bright and cheerful today.'

'Thanks.' She smiled. 'I *feel* bright and cheerful.' She saw the appreciation in his dark eyes and was glad she'd decided to buy something different.

As they drove inland and away from the coast in his luxury car she asked Nic about the education system.

'Here they lack the funds for equipment Australian schools take for granted, particularly in the rural areas.'

'Tell me about this school we're visiting.'

Nic overtook an ancient, rusted pick-up truck overloaded with workers on their way to the sugar-cane fields. 'It caters for children from five to twelve years, with two classrooms, two teachers and sixty kids. Kasanita teaches the kids up to the age of eight.'

'So how do they afford computers?'

'They don't.' He slowed for a bus stopping to pick up passengers.

'Oh?' Of course. 'You donated them.'

He shrugged a shoulder. 'It's a good cause.'

She nodded. He was a *cause* man. She loved causes. So often she'd found it to be women who put in the time and effort. 'How often do you visit?'

'When I'm here, I try to make it every couple of weeks. Early intervention's important, so I spend most of that time with Kas's class.'

'How do you know Kas?'

'Her father owns a yachting business and takes charter cruises around some of the local islands. But we've not talked much about you yet.' He glanced at her; more specifically at her breasts. 'I take it you're a fashion designer.'

She ignored the heat his gaze invoked and tried not to think about the underwear she'd chosen specifically in the hope that at some stage he'd take it off her. 'No. That's just a hobby.'

'A hobby.' His tone suggested he thought she lived on her parents' wealth. 'What do you do, then?'

'I worked at the winery, in the office.'

'Not any more?'

'I sold the business three weeks ago, so I'm out of a job at the moment.'

He didn't reply and maybe she was being oversensitive but she got the feeling he thought she was satisfied with her unemployed status. She hastened to explain she wasn't some rich chick with nothing to do but take exotic vacations. 'My ex and I were going to open a cheese and wine cellar door place there until he changed his mind and decided to give politics a go. And now...'

She looked away, at the green mountains in the distance, and thought how far away her problems seemed on this island paradise. How she had so many things to tackle on her return. How unready she still was to tackle them. 'I decided I couldn't, not on my own.'

He was silent as they drove past fields of banana palms and more jungle. Charlotte watched blurred walls of creeping green vegetation skim by, corrugated iron structures and primitive thatched roofs.

Finally he said, 'You could turn your designs into a business if you wanted to; they're unique enough.'

'No.' Her designs were her private indulgence and a solitary pursuit. She'd given it a lot of thought since Flynn had left and decided she needed work that involved social interaction if she wanted to avoid becoming a total recluse. 'Something'll turn up.' The charities her mother and she supported could keep her busy in the meanwhile.

The school was part of a village, quaint and old and basic—a single louvred building painted bright blue with a maroon roof and a wide porch. The playground's grass surface was patchy and devoid of shade or equipment and adjoined the ubiquitous village rugby field.

But it didn't lack vitality because the moment they pulled up at the door the children spilled outside, Kas following, and suddenly the car was surrounded with friendly faces.

'*Bula! Bula!*' The kids swarmed around them, hands on the car's windows, their laughs loud and happy.

She and Nic climbed out into humidity and hot sun, crushingly different from the car's air conditioning. A couple of chooks scratched at the ground and unfamiliar bird calls echoed in the trees.

Kasanita welcomed them. '*Bula*, Charlotte, Nic.'

After being presented with garlands of kid-made paper flowers, shells and bits of silver paper, they followed the noisy class inside like a couple of royal visitors. Children's colourful artwork more than made up for the room's sparse aspect, with one exception—the six computers along one wall.

Kas offered them fresh coconut milk, then quietened the children with her guitar. Charlotte and Nic sat on rush matting amongst the children and joined in. An interactive time followed, the children free to choose activities and show off their learning to their special visitors. There was an encore of the previous night's dance.

The visit gave Charlotte a further insight into Nic. He interacted with the children naturally and knew how to reach them on their level, whether it was explaining how to use a computer program or sharing a joke or peeling a tiny girl's banana.

'What do you say to fresh grilled fish for lunch?' Nic asked as they drove away, heading towards the coast once more. 'I know this little place.'

'Yes, please. I'm starving.'

'Did you enjoy yourself?'

'I loved it. Thanks for inviting me along.' So much sharing and caring and learning in such basic conditions was a contrast to her own privileged upbringing. 'The playground could do with some climbing equipment. Maybe some shade sails.' She turned to Nic. 'I'd like to help.'

He glanced her way. 'How do you mean?'

'Funding. One thing I do know is how to raise money.'

He looked at her a moment, eyes unreadable, then back at the road. 'You're not what I expected, Charlotte Dumont.'

She stiffened, staring back. 'Reverse snobbery, Nic? You think because I was born into a privileged family that I don't see what goes on around me? That I don't care? You're a self-made man,' she said slowly. 'What happened in your past that makes you think I'm less because my wealth came to me naturally?'

He shook his head, clearly unwilling or unable to talk about that past. 'You're being overly sensitive, Charlotte. I don't think that at all.'

She remembered the darkness in his eyes when she'd asked why he'd rescued her from that reporter. He had a deep-seated animosity towards bullies. Had someone treated him as less because he came from an impoverished background? He gave her nothing with which to draw any conclusions.

She didn't ask. Some secrets were best left undisclosed, especially with someone who was a temporary figure in her life.

'Maybe a fashion show,' she said a few moments later. 'My best friend has her own bridalwear business. Or I could model my lingerie,' she joked, to clear the air of residual tension that had sprung up.

Nic grinned, his fingers tightening on the wheel at the thousand and one images that stole like seduction into his mind's eye. 'Count me in.'

'I was kidding, Nic. As if that's going to happen,' she muttered.

'Why not?'

'Forget it.' Her voice lost its humour.

'No can do. I've got the image in my head now.' He turned off the main road. 'So I insist you model some of your creations for me this afternoon. A private showing.'

From the corner of his eye, he saw her hug her arms across her chest. 'Putting myself on display for a roomful of people is just not me, no matter what I'm wearing.'

'I'm not a roomful of people,' he said, looking at her briefly before turning his eyes back to the road.

She was staring at him behind her sunglasses. 'I'm not even sure I can do it for you.'

'Sure you can. Remember Melbourne?' He could. His groin tightened at the memory of her mindless abandonment.

She made a noise that could have been amusement or it could have been pain.

'You can let yourself go when you want to.'

'Maybe I'm afraid to,' she said quietly as he pulled up at 'Inoke's Catch of the Bay', one of his favourite out-of-the-way places. 'Maybe I'm afraid of this new person.'

'Don't be,' he said, just as quietly. He killed the engine and turned to her. He reached out to take off her glasses so he could see the silvery flecks in her wide, wide eyes. The bright tones of her new dress highlighted the light tan of her skin and lent colour to her cheeks. 'I like this person. I like her a lot.'

Her eyes remained huge and she chewed on her lower lip. 'And maybe I'm afraid of that too.'

Her words eerily echoed his own thoughts. 'It's okay, babe,' he said, as much for himself as for her. 'You don't have to change.' He combed his fingers through her hair, traced the fine curve of her jaw. 'But explore another side of yourself and you may find you like what you discover. Maybe it'll help you look at life differently when you go home.'

She nodded slowly. 'Maybe.' She seemed to shiver, then came out of her pensive mood as if by sheer determination and opened the car door. 'That's a lot of maybes.' She breathed deeply, the rich aroma of the grill wafting in. 'I'm starving.'

It was perfect—the food, the warm overcast weather, her company. They spent a leisurely hour eating, then Charlotte excused herself to freshen up in the restroom outside while he paid the bill. He spent a few moments chatting to the owner, a friend, Inoke, then spotted Charlotte further up the beach collecting shells that littered the bay's coarse sand.

He headed after her, admiring the carefree way she moved, long legs flashing in the sun. Her hair was tucked up under her hat. Those creamy shoulders were going to burn. Should've brought sunscreen, he thought, but his attention was snagged by a man approaching her.

Damn. As Nic picked up his pace he watched Charlotte stop and speak with the reporter—what else could he be with that long-range camera slung around his scrawny neck? Too far away to hear what they were saying. Sensing Nic's evil eye spearing his way, the reporter glanced towards Nic, then began retracing his steps to the car park. Nic changed direction.

'Hey, you!' Nic skidded to a halt in front of him, his feet throwing up sand, and glaring at the jerk through narrowed eyes. 'If I see you anywhere near her again, I'll sue you for harassment.' Tension simmered along his jaw and he spoke through clenched teeth. 'I might sue you anyway, just for the hell of it.'

'Hey, man, what's your damn problem?' The scrawny-necked reporter glared back. 'Ms Dumont's public property—' he looked closer '—*Mr* Russo. And I never forget a face.'

'Right back at you, mate. She's on a private vacation so back off or you'll have me to deal with.'

The man's eyes sparked with interest as they flitted towards Charlotte, then Nic. 'Private, eh?'

'Yeah, private; so get lost.'

'Like that lover of yours a few years back? What was her name?' He smiled—unpleasantly. 'Never pays to be on the wrong side of the press, *Mr* Russo.' Skirting Nic, he resumed walking.

Nic waited until the reporter climbed into his car and drove off before turning his attention to Charlotte, who hadn't moved from her spot and was watching on, her expression serious.

'You okay?' he said as he approached her. Concern slid through him. He shouldn't have goaded the man; he didn't want his threat to impact on Charlotte.

'Fine. He was harmless, Nic.' She shrugged, then smiled. 'Seems I can't avoid the press here after all.'

'What did he ask you?' he demanded. 'What did you tell him?'

'That I was enjoying Fiji very much.'

She ran a finger over the smooth shell she was holding then looked up at him from beneath the hat's brim. Even from behind her sunglasses her eyes shone, telling him he had a lot to do with how much she was enjoying her vacation.

'Thank you, but you don't have to fight my battles for me. I'm okay.'

From out of nowhere, a sense of possessiveness rose up inside him like a rogue wave—and everyone knew rogue waves were dangerous. 'Let's go, babe.' Shaking off the unnerving sensation, he grabbed her hand and started jogging back up the beach.

'Hang on.' She stumbled a little as he tugged her with him towards the car park. 'What's the sudden rush? The guy's gone; you scared him off good and proper.'

'You promised to model for me. I want to make sure you don't change your mind.'

'I never said…'

He turned and grinned at her. 'And in return, I promise you'll enjoy it as much as I will.'

'Oh.' She smiled back. 'Okay, when you put it like that what are we waiting for?'

They ran all the way back to the car.

'What shall I start with?' she said when they closed the door to her room behind them.

'Surprise me,' Nic said, tossing his sunglasses on the bed.

'But I don't know what you like.'

He touched his lips to hers, but didn't linger; he wanted to watch her show off her work first and draw out the anticipation. 'I guarantee I'll like anything you want to show me.' He helped himself to a bottle of water from the minifridge, poured half into a glass for Charlotte and set it on the shelf. 'Any colour that's not beige.'

'I don't have beige lingerie.'

'Thank God for that.' He took a long swig from the bottle.

'But I do have skin tone.'

'No skin tone. The only skin tone I want to see you in is the real thing. You're a girl who should breathe colour.'

'Okay, I'll start with what I'm wearing now.'

He didn't look at her as he walked to the louvred panel that closed off her balcony, slid it open. 'When you're ready, come out here.' Moist tropical air wafted in, scented with salt and foliage. The bure was perched on the hill, the balcony private and overlooking the sea. He stripped down to skin and set his clothes within reach on the edge of the pool.

The palms cast dappled shade on the water as he lowered himself into the pool and leaned back against the edge, spreading his arms along the tiles. He needed the water's bite to cool his blood and lend him restraint if he wasn't going to drag her in with him straight off and have his way with her.

To his relief, he didn't have long to wait.

She appeared in the doorway like a fantasy come to life and he quickly realised it wasn't relief, it was a form of torture. And he'd been the one to suggest it.

He held his breath, then let it out with a growl at the back of his throat as he took in the sight of her breasts spilling over a slash of hot pink and brilliant aqua. A tiny glimpse of dark nipple in the slit where pink met blue. The panties were kept together at the back with a cheeky blue shoelace.

'You were wearing *that* while we were in a classroom full of children?'

'Um…' She grinned, lips pressed together. 'Just lucky it wasn't gym class while we were there, wasn't it?'

He swallowed. 'I'm glad I didn't know. So that's your usual day wear?'

'Yes.' She ran the tips of her fingers inside the waistband of her panties. 'These are new. I've been working on a different line since I became single again. It's fun.'

'I'm sure it is…' He surged forward. 'Come here.'

With a mock stern look, she held up a finger. 'Not yet. This was your idea, remember.'

'Okay.' He just might last a few more moments, he thought as she disappeared again, leaving her tempting fragrance behind her. Then again, he might not.

Less than a minute later she was back in a black and white number. A skinny white lace thong. The string of black pearls at the back disappeared between firm, round buttocks.

His mouth watered and his eyes followed her as she circled the pool, keeping just out of reach. 'You're a naughty girl.'

She laughed lightly, her hands clasped behind her back, which had the arousing effect of pushing her breasts forward. Her nipples stood erect against the black lace like bullets. 'And the best part is that no one knows.'

'*I* know.'

'In which case, I may just have to kill you.' She crouched down, swished a hand through the water. 'But before I do, I think you'll like my wet look. Shiny black—'

'Come here.'

'Or my lotus butterfly…'

Frustration gave him agility and he surged forward, grasped a slender ankle. 'Later,' he told her, his hand moving higher, over her calf where her skin was hot and smooth and firm.

'But I'm just getting started,' the voice above him complained. 'And I've never done this before. Indulge me.'

He looked up, past lace and curves and bare flesh. Her eyes reflected the water's ripples, making them dance and sparkle with light and fun. She knew exactly what she was doing to him.

'Oh, I'll indulge you,' he promised, every cell in his body on fire. 'In the water. Now.'

'Oh, well, if you insist. But first, we need…' reaching for his trousers on the tiles beside him, she felt in the pockets and pulled out a foil packet '…one of these.'

With the condom packet between her teeth, she slid slowly down into the water beside him, inch by excruciating inch, the bra's lacy texture rasping against his chest. Her legs twined around his like electric eels, sending sparks shocking straight to his groin.

Fire and ice. Cool water swirling over hot skin. He slid his hand between her shoulder blades and down, over each vertebra, the pearls between her buttocks. Then he turned her around so that he could feel the erotic sensation of the tiny baubles against his erection. Groaning with the pleasure, he bit into her shoulder as he slid the lacy garment down her thighs with his hands, then his toes.

She tasted of the beach and the sun and freedom. 'You're gorgeous.' He unclasped her bra, then pulled her back against him and filled his hands with her womanly shape, feeling the tight, water-chilled buds against his fingers. 'Refreshing and gorgeous.'

Leaning back against him, she let her legs float to the surface in front of her. 'You're not half bad yourself.'

It was a languid moment at odds with the way his body craved and his mind reeled—because it wasn't just the physical intimacy he whispered about against her ear. He wanted more, and he wanted to tell her. How she blew him away on so many levels. How he'd never met anyone like her. So it was as well she broke the calm with a quick fluid movement.

When she turned to face him, he saw the same emotions in her eyes before she blinked them away with a sparkling smile.

'That's enough,' she said with a laugh. She dangled the foil packet above her head. 'You have to work for the rest.' Jerking out of his grasp, she ducked beneath the surface and shot away like a fair-skinned dolphin to the far end of the pool, elegant and sleek. Then she dived deeper and only her legs broke the surface, perfectly shaped calves, feet arched, toes pointed like a ballet dancer's.

Seconds later, she reappeared, swiped her hair from her face and waved the packet in front of her. 'Hey, you're supposed to come and catch me.'

'Where did you learn to swim like that?'

'Synchronised swimming classes at school for a couple of years.'

'Is harp playing on your list of accomplishments too?'

'Piano.'

He nodded. Naturally she'd have gone to a private and exclusive school, he thought, watching her careless smile. Taking such extra-curricular activities for granted. A school with its own private and exclusive pool. Halls of learning, where that learning was valued. The best education money could buy for the Barossa wine princess.

He thought of the school he'd attended in one of Melbourne's seedier districts. Neglected buildings. A cramped, pot-holed playground where kids were bored and turned their attention to other activities. Like making life a living hell for those younger and smaller than themselves.

She stared at him, her smile fading. 'Something wrong?'

He shook off the old taunts with a grin. 'What's wrong is you're too far away.' Then he dived under the water towards her.

# CHAPTER NINE

SHIVERS chased over Charlotte's skin as Nic closed in, his tanned, muscled torso streamlined and swift. He seemed so predatory that instinctively she backed up, bumping against the pool's smooth tiles.

He surfaced right in front of her, water sluicing off his face and hair. 'Gotcha,' he murmured, snatching the forgotten condom from her nerveless fingers, then placing his arms on the pool's rim on either side of her.

Trapped. And right where she wanted to be.

Her breath caught in her throat. Her heart pounded. His eyes had lost the sombre expression she'd noticed seconds ago but what she saw there now was no less acute. Desire and intent. His gaze didn't leave hers as he ripped open the foil packet and sheathed himself.

Gone was the light-hearted banter, the teasing, the sexy foreplay. Something deeper emerged, like fresh water from a hidden spring. Mystifying and mysterious. As they watched each other an unspoken intimacy surrounded them like the heavy scent of the tropical blooms off the balcony.

She could hear the sounds of children splashing in the resort's family pool some distance away, the palm fronds flapping in the afternoon breeze. Nic's breathing. Her own. She was falling for him the way she'd never fallen for anyone before. Because he was unlike anyone she'd ever known.

And he wasn't the kind of guy she should be falling for. She needed stability, someone who'd be there for life. But she was powerless to resist him as he slid his hands over her breasts.

'Nic...'

'Shh.'

The heat of his tongue combined with the cool water, a mingling of stunning sensations as she leaned back on the edge of the pool, gave up trying to reason it all out and surrendered.

After the poolside chase and inevitable capture, she'd expected a fast and furious encounter, but this was lazy, almost luxurious. The long, slow pull of his mouth on her nipple. The glide of her legs between his. The sluggish swirl of water as he pushed slowly and deeply inside her.

Moaning with the pleasure, she slid her hands over his damp, water-cooled back, then across his shoulders, loving the hardness of him, her movements in slow motion while her mind drifted like organza ribbons in an idle draught.

He withdrew a little and raised his head to look at her. Then plunged deep and slow and true, filling her. *Ful*filling her.

Through heavy-lidded eyes, she watched him. The afternoon sun danced through the leaves and stroked his face with bronze. Luxuriant black lashes framed his eyes; hues of amber gleamed in the ebony irises. Once again she was the prey and she couldn't look away. Powerful, penetrating, persuasive, he drew her inside him until she no longer existed outside his aura. And the deep, dark places in her soul brimmed and overflowed with the emotion she was coming to realise only he could wring from her.

\* \* \*

The days passed too swiftly. Nic took Charlotte on a yachting expedition to a nearby island where they enjoyed seafood and champagne on board, then went snorkelling in the aquamarine shallows and lazed on the golden beach. There were a couple of occasions when she felt the paparazzi's presence but they didn't approach and she didn't let it bother her. She loved the open-air farmers' markets alive with aromatic spices, greens of every description, pineapples, taro and yams.

They attended the resort's traditional *lovo* and kava ceremony. A whole pig, wrapped in palm leaves and surrounded with taro and breadfruit, was cooked in an earth oven filled with hot volcanic rocks. They enjoyed every sunset together. Whether it was sipping cocktails from one of the resort's restaurants, or making love on the private strip of beach near his house or enjoying a barbecue on board a schooner, Nic made every occasion unique.

She discovered new things about him. He liked having his ear lobes rubbed but vehemently refused to submit to the silk scarf blindfold she'd teased him with. There was a scar over his left hip from a surfing accident.

He sent fresh frangipanis to her room every day, took her on a midnight picnic, organised a candle-lit massage for the two of them on the beach and made love to her as if she were the only woman in the world, tenderly and fiercely and everything in between.

He couldn't have done much work unless he was a freak of nature and didn't require sleep. But he didn't sleep with her. Each night he returned to his house on the hill. She believed it was his way of maintaining that one-step-back rule he had.

He'd been straight with her from the start—*part-time tour guide with benefits*—giving her no reason to build a fantasy future around them. But it didn't stop her from lying awake at night by herself and imagining.

She wasn't a good muse after all. Nic leaned back in his chair, scowling at his computer screens. Stupid o'clock in the morning and nothing he tried was working. Every time he thought he knew where the game was heading, he hit a dead end. Charlotte—*Reena*, he corrected himself— his game's new heroine, blocked Onyx One's movements at every turn. Tugging at Onyx with her bewitching eyes and throwing him off balance. Charlotte's eyes.

*Ridiculous.* He forced the notion away, re-evaluated his last idea, then deleted it. He'd hit a snag, that was all. Just because his hero refused to cooperate and the plot wasn't panning out the way it should, didn't mean Charlotte had anything to do with it.

Or did it?

He swung his chair around and stared through the open doors where starlight painted the palms with silver. Maybe he should make the dark-haired Reena a blonde. Or a fiery redhead. Even a silver-haired temptress. But then, why allow his obsession with a woman to dictate the most important thing in his life—his work?

He'd end this thing with Charlotte now, and reclaim his creativity, which had mysteriously dried up. Shoving a hand through his hair, he glared at his screens. His modus operandi with women had been the same for years. Enjoy the fun and romance of it all but never let them too close. Never allow himself to forget Angelica and the lesson he'd learned. Work was his life, he didn't need anything or anyone.

But for the first time in for ever, his cyber world wasn't doing it for him. He wanted to spend what was left of Charlotte's time here with her. Preferably in bed.

He assured himself that, like all good endings, their

final goodbye should be a satisfying resolution. Then he'd be able to put it behind him and get on with what mattered in his life.

And what the hell was it about his predictable life that mattered so damn much? On an oath, he shut down his computer and paced to the window to stare at the black-roofed bures. White ribbons streaked the dark sea beyond, its gentle omnipresent sound soothing.

It wasn't only Charlotte's sensuality that had him burning and reaching for her over and over again. Beneath the hot-blooded goddess she had a vulnerability that tugged at his heart and made him want to protect her while at the same time coax her out of that shell he'd glimpsed when she thought he wasn't looking.

With Charlotte there was empathy—for himself and for others, both in her words and her actions. She had a wicked sense of humour he suspected she rarely allowed others to see. Deep down she was a private person, and, more, she recognised and *respected* that facet of his own personality.

Charlotte had made him realise that not all women were like Angelica, out to get whatever they could. He'd found a woman he not only enjoyed physically and socially, but one he could trust enough to allow a glimpse into his world, and tonight was his last chance to invite her into his home.

The next morning, instead of the usual bouquet of frangipani Charlotte had come to expect, a single white orchid arrived in a vase along with a gilt-edged envelope.

Her whole body turned to stone. Flynn had sent her a single white rose the morning after he'd ended their engagement. There'd been a little envelope and, inside, a card that said, 'Thanks for the memories.'

Palms sweating so hard she thought she'd drop the vase, she carried it outside to the table on the balcony and sat down. She stared at it for a long moment, a giant fist clenched around her heart. No matter what the message said, this was a timely reminder that her holiday fling with Nic was almost over.

She was still staring at it when Nic's special knock sounded on the door. Bracing herself, she went to open it.

He looked as fresh as the morning's orchid. As sexy as midnight on black silk sheets. 'Hi.' She gave him a smile and struggled to keep her voice free and easy while that fist tightened around her heart. 'Come on in. I'm nearly ready.'

He waited until she'd shut the door before kissing her thoroughly. She clung to him a moment before reminding herself she'd be gone in twenty-four hours, and deliberately stepped away first.

She swung away from the gorgeous sight of his well-honed body and walked to the balcony. 'The orchid's beautiful, thank you.'

'I saw it by the back door and thought of you.'

'You grow orchids?' She turned back to study him, head to one side. 'You just don't look the domestic gardening type.'

'Malakai does most of the work, actually.' He jiggled his brows. 'Want to come up and see my collection?'

A grin tugged at her mouth. 'Don't you mean Malakai's collection?'

'Whatever gets you there,' he said with an answering grin.

Surprise lifted her brows. 'To your house?'

Still grinning, he walked towards her. 'So you haven't read the note yet.'

'I haven't got around to it.' She hugged her arms, then recognised her insecure action and reached for the un-opened envelope on the table. 'Actually, I was thinking of giving the market a miss this morning. I need some time...

To pack.' She stared at the table, preferring the orchid's beauty to the look she'd see in his eyes. The look that made her as helpless as a butterfly under glass.

'Fine.' He was suddenly there beside her, smelling of his familiar spicy cologne. He touched the side of her face. 'It's fine if that's true. But I know you better than you think. Something's changed.'

'Nothing's changed.'

'We've always been up front with each other, Charlotte. At least, I have.'

She bit down on her lip before deciding maybe it was time to give a little. After all, what did it matter now? 'It's weird, the timing—Flynn left me a white rose and a note when we…when *he* chose his career in politics over me.'

He studied her through narrowed eyes. 'Why did he have to choose? Why couldn't he have both?'

'Because I was an embarrassment to him. A liability for any potential politician.'

His brows lowered and his voice was hard as nails when he said, 'Then he's an idiot and you're better off without him.'

'Forget him. I have. The whole thing's a reminder to me that I'm leaving tomorrow.' *And you said it yourself, there is no 'us'.*

'So…have you got plans for when you get home?'

'I have tickets for the opera at the Festival Theatre to look forward to. It's "Carmen", my favourite.' Even if she'd more than likely bump into the press, who'd ask her all about the break-up.

But over the past couple of weeks her confidence had lifted. She'd not even felt out of her depth when the guy on the beach had approached her. Just a brief friendly exchange. Nothing to be alarmed about. She realised maybe she could—no, she *would*—face the public without the old insecurities.

'Tickets?' he was saying, dragging her back to the present. 'As in more than one?'

'Flynn was supposed to go with me. I bought them months ago. Do you like opera?'

'Never been.'

She nodded. 'It's not for everyone.'

His jaw tightened and she knew she'd offended him. That he thought she thought he wasn't cultured enough. Whatever the heck that meant.

She smiled to dispel an awkward moment and told him, 'It wasn't Dad's cup of tea either. Wild horses wouldn't have dragged him there.' She slid the envelope back and forth between her fingers. 'You'll be glad to get back to work, I bet. You've been neglecting it to entertain me.'

'It's been worth every moment.'

His eyes seemed to melt into hers and for an instant something dangerously like hope rose up inside her. Futile hope.

Then he swiped the envelope from her hand and screwed it up. 'Bad idea, this,' he said, tossing it into the waste-paper basket. 'So I'll just say it instead. I want you to join me for a popular Fijian meal tonight. And I'm going to cook.' He grabbed her hand and began tugging her to the door. 'Which is why we're going to the market.'

She tried to grab her bag on the fly. 'Hang on…'

He stopped and his eyes searched hers. 'Unless you really do want to be alone?'

*No.* She saw something in his brown-eyed gaze that had her heart stuttering. She picked up her bag and a hat. 'I'll pack this afternoon.'

Nic's waterfront home was airy and spacious, with white marbled floors and panoramic views of the coastline.

They'd barely set foot in the modern kitchen—vibrant red with stainless-steel appliances—when Nic's housekeeper appeared in the doorway with a wide flat basket of fresh-picked vegetables under one arm.

'Ah, there you are.' Nic smiled at the middle-aged woman. 'Tenika, I'd like you to meet Charlotte. Tenika's agreed to let me loose in the kitchen this evening.'

Charlotte nodded. '*Bula*. It's a pleasure to meet you, Tenika.'

'*Bula vinaka*.' Tenika's deep voice seemed to resonate through her ample body, her eyes livened with interest as they flicked between the two of them.

Nic's mobile rang at that moment and he excused himself and moved away to answer it.

'So how long have you worked for Nic?' Charlotte asked.

'Seven years. When he come here, he give me and my husband work. Very kind man.' She set her basket on the black granite counter top, nimble fingers picking off the few wilted leaves. 'You like Fiji?'

'Very much.'

'You come back again. Nic alone too much after that bad one gone.' She tossed the discarded leaves into the sink, the action as eloquent as any words.

'Bad one?' Charlotte's curiosity soared.

'Angelica,' Tenika muttered. 'Bad.'

Charlotte was dying to ask more but Nic was already ending his call.

Tenika lifted a couple of ripe mangoes from the bottom of her basket and turned on the tap. '*Ni mataka*, you go back to Australia?'

'Tomorrow, yes.'

'You and he had a friendly visit here, *io*?'

Nic exchanged an intimate glance with Charlotte that told her exactly how friendly her visit had been.

Charlotte was so caught up with watching Nic and controlling the sudden heat rushing up her neck, she barely noticed Tenika walk to the door.

'You come back again soon,' she said, smiling at the pair of them. 'I go now. Enjoy *kakana* together. *Moce.*'

'*Moce.* Goodnight.' Charlotte and Nic spoke in unison.

'Friendly, huh?' Charlotte said, slinging an arm around his neck as soon as they were alone. 'I assume *kakana* means a meal and not hot sex?'

Grinning, Nic gave her a casual kiss, then moved to the fridge and began taking out ingredients. A large fillet of fish, a plate of chopped cherry tomatoes and onions, a bowl of coconut milk. 'With Tenika, I wouldn't be too sure. Fijian women are born matchmakers.'

*Best to leave that one alone.* 'Anything I can do to help?'

'You can slice this lime if you want.' He set it in front of her with a knife.

Charlotte settled herself on a bar stool across from him. 'What are you cooking?'

'Fish in coconut milk. A special Fijian dish.' He sliced the fish into steaks. 'This is *paka paka*—fresh snapper.'

He set the pieces sizzling in a pan, then arranged the spinach and ginger leaves Tenika had picked on aluminium foil on a shallow dish and added the tomatoes and onion. The sharp, piquant aromas filled the kitchen.

'Taste this.' He dipped a spoon in the coconut milk and held it out. 'Freshly squeezed.'

'Oh, my.' She licked the thick substance from her lips while Nic placed the seared fish on the bed of leaves. 'That is rich, rich, rich.'

'Now we pour it over and add your lime.'

While Charlotte arranged the slices, she imagined how

it could be—the intimacy of being a couple and sharing the ups and downs of their day while they cooked the evening meal together.

But Nic wasn't that man and her heart faltered. What was she doing, thinking those thoughts? He was never going to offer any woman commitment. Was the woman called Angelica the reason?

'We seal the foil and let it bake while we drink cocktails and I give you the grand tour… What is it?'

She pulled herself back and realised he was watching her, a groove between his brows.

'Just thinking how much I'm going to miss…' *you* '…being here.'

'That's good to hear because it means I've been successful in my job as tour guide.' He rinsed his hands, then pulled two cocktail glasses brimming with something red and blue and exotic from the fridge.

'That looks interesting.'

'I like to experiment. I call this one Fijian Sky.'

She took the proffered glass, then walked to the balcony, held the glass up against the vermilion-streaked sunset. 'Perfect.' Nic followed and she turned, clinked her glass to his. 'To a tour guide extraordinaire *and* magical cocktail maker.'

He nodded. 'To muses.'

'Mmm.' She let the potent alcoholic flavour work its way down her throat. 'Speaking of muses, are you going to show me your work?'

'I've not been very productive of late.'

'My fault. But I'm not going to apologise.' Since he didn't offer any further information, or offer to show her around, she prompted, 'You have an office somewhere, I assume?'

'Upstairs.'

When he didn't move, she leaned closer, dragged a finger down his chest to his belt and stared up at him. 'You've seen mine, it's only fair you show me yours.'

An answering smile touched his lips and his eyes turned molten. 'Fair enough.' He rubbed his lips over hers before leading the way through the spacious living area.

The sound of water was everywhere, from the fountain to the salt-water infinity pool to an indoor garden in one corner with miniature waterfall.

Charlotte admired the Fijian décor throughout, raked ceilings and mahogany louvred panels open to allow air circulation, casual furniture around locally inspired carved tables. 'This is a beautiful home. Did you have a hand in designing it?'

'I had an interior designer come in and renovate,' he said as they climbed the stairs. 'It was pretty run-down when I bought it.' He flicked a switch and the room was filled with a cool ethereal glow.

'Wow.' She stared at the vast yet cluttered work space. A jumble of cables and computer paraphernalia took up half the room. Fantasy posters of alien landscapes covered every available wall surface. Metallic statues of mystical unearthly creatures with gleaming eyes of amber and blood-red stared at her from an array of bookshelves. A living vine of some sort grew in a pot by the window and wound its way across the ceiling.

'Dom Silverman,' she murmured, studying the multitude of awards above his computer. 'Your pseudonym?'

She noticed he hesitated at her mention of Silverman. Without comment, he switched on a computer and several screens lit up to form an almost 3-D landscape, alive with creatures and humans.

She leaned closer, eyes narrowed. 'Who's that girl?'

*Damn.* Nic had no idea how she'd persuaded him to

show her his office, his work, so easily. His alter ego, Dom Silverman. Yes, he did—with one finger and a hot look, it seemed she could make him forget everything, including caution. 'That's Reena.'

Charlotte peered closer. 'She looks like me…'

'Now that you mention it, she does. How about that?' He clicked a button and Reena wrapped herself in a silvery cloak and promptly disappeared.

'Well, bye bye, Reena,' Charlotte murmured and sipped from her glass, still watching the screens. 'So what's happening in Reena's world at the moment?'

'Nothing much lately. I've been playing around with some ideas for turning the games into a book when I've finished.' He gestured to the laptop he'd been working on for the past several evenings after seeing Charlotte to her bure. 'I've been working on computer games for eighteen years. I'm thinking maybe it's time for a change.'

'With your game's success, a publisher's bound to snap it up.'

'I'm not sure I want to publish it. Maybe it's more of a hobby. Like your underwear.'

'*Lingerie.*' She smiled. 'How did you get involved in computers?'

'When I was thirteen, the school ran a contest to design the school's website. I don't want to sound as if I'm blowing my own trumpet, but a teacher saw my potential and arranged for me to work in an office off the staff room outside of lesson times.'

'Darling, you can blow your trumpet any time you like.' She did that erotic thing with her finger again, except this time she didn't stop at his belt.

Eyes fused with hers, he gripped her hand and pressed it against his burgeoning erection. 'The prize was a computer.'

'And naturally you won.'

'Naturally.' He set his glass on the desk so he could run his other hand along the tops of her full breasts. 'I love when you wear this sarong…'

'I know.' Her voice was a husky purr, tempting him to unwind it and— 'But…I think I smell our dinner burning.'

'Damn.' It wasn't the only thing burning.

She stepped back, laughter mingling with the heat in her eyes. 'I'm so looking forward to it.'

He was too, and it wasn't dinner he was thinking about. But then, she already knew that.

# CHAPTER TEN

THEY ate on the balcony with tea lights flickering in red glasses and fluorescent purple fairy lights strung along the balcony. The flames from the kerosene torches on the beach soared in the distance, the songs from the evening's *Meke* drifted on the air.

The fish was delicious, the wine chilled and fruity, the company perfect. Charlotte stirred sugar into her after-dinner coffee. The tropics would soon be a world away and, as much as she loved it here, her home was amongst the vineyards and close trusted friends. She craved the familiar and comfortable. Nic didn't fit into her cosy picture.

With his islander shirt and golden tan and idyllic lifestyle, Nic belonged in this place he'd made his home. Who could fail to be lured by the South Pacific's magic?

'You love it here, don't you?' she said, picking up her cup.

He leaned back on his chair, arms behind his head, an ankle resting on one bronzed thigh. 'I love the freedom and lifestyle. I can leave the windows open, come and go as I please. Sleep when I want or work all night. No one bothers me here.'

She noticed something dark flicker in the depths of his eyes at his mention of the last. 'You enjoy your solitude?'

'Sure I do.' His lips were set in a smile but his facial muscles tensed in a subtly different way.

She sipped slowly, watching him over her cup. When he was around people he was charming and attentive, romance was his forte. But when it came to anything deeper there was a barrier he wasn't ready or willing to lower.

She wanted to know why. She needed to know that there wasn't something inherently wrong with *her* that men didn't want to get involved. Or was she being overly sensitive? Because Nic couldn't have been more explicit about where they stood relationship-wise on their first night together here.

'You don't want a special someone to share your life?'

Any pretence at a smile he'd had, faded. 'I thought I made that clear.' He pushed off his chair and walked to the railing where the evening breeze fluttered his hair and a bamboo wind chime.

She remained seated but followed him with her gaze. Given a choice, how could anyone not want the comfort of loved ones around them? Seeing his solitude had made it so clear to her how much she missed her family. How much she wanted that feeling of connection and closeness again in the future. 'Ever?' she asked.

'We've been through all that.'

She heard the warning tone but she couldn't let it go. 'That's just sad.' She saw the tension stiffen his shoulders and said softly, 'Was your family life so b—?'

'That's enough.' He swung to face her. His eyes were dark, impenetrable.

'No. You know about mine. Why are you so defensive? Why do—?'

'It was only Mum and me, okay? When she bothered to come home.' He looked stunned, as if he hadn't intended to spill that information.

'Oh…' She trailed off, unable to imagine such a scenario and unsure how to respond. 'Working…?'

His mouth was a flat line, his jaw tight as a fist. 'Yeah, she worked, she worked damn hard. Then spent it playing poker and who knows what else, forgetting she had a son waiting at home for her.'

Charlotte wanted to hug the little boy he'd been, to comfort the man he was now, but she knew those were the last things he'd want from her, so she remained where she was. 'That must have been difficult.'

Nic shrugged. Then sighed. Charlotte was right. He'd fought to keep his past where it belonged but those defences were crumbling, the memories flashing back as if it were yesterday. He wanted to bury his face in her neck until it passed.

With Charlotte he found himself sharing things he'd never told anyone. 'I learned to cope. Even when she was alive, I was travelling solo. I guess at the very least you could say she taught me independence.'

'Were you living at home when she died?' Her tone was tentative.

'Technically, yes, but it was more the other way around—*she* was living with *me*. I hit the big time with my computer games when I was still in my teens. Money was no longer the problem.'

Charlotte's eyes filled with sadness, clouds on a soft rainy morning. 'Oh, the poor thing. Was she ill for a long time?'

He stared at her a beat before he realised she didn't get him at all. 'Save your sympathies—she wasn't sick a day in her life. She came out of the pub one day and stepped in front of a bus. Too busy counting her winnings—or more likely her losses—to pay attention to road rules.'

She blinked, obviously shocked. 'Oh. I'm sorry.'

'It's okay. I can't honestly say I missed her because I never saw her. From as far back as I remember, her life's routine never changed. Gone first thing in the morning, back at midnight.'

'Even when you were a kid?'

His mother was one thing but the dark days of his childhood were *not* up for discussion. He looked away, focused on the empty blackness of the sea and found it entirely appropriate. 'As I said, it taught me to rely on myself, by myself.'

He turned back to see her eyes still soft and sad, and, clenching his fists at his sides, he fought the mad impulse to reach out to her. Mad because she was trying to replace that loss with herself. She was a family girl looking for a family; something he couldn't give her. 'I don't know how to be any other way, babe.'

'Maybe that's because you've never tried.' She stood up and walked over to him, laid a hand on his arm. 'Maybe that's why you created the fantasy world,' she murmured. 'To compensate for what's lacking in your life.'

His lungs constricted at her perceptive insight into his innermost self. 'My life's just fine, thanks.'

She leaned back against the railing so that she could look him dead in the eye. 'What happened with…Angelica, was it?'

'How the hell…?'

She flicked a hand. 'Tenika might have mentioned her name. And the word "bad". In the same sentence.'

'God, a man can't leave two women together for less than a minute—'

'Nic. She cares about you. And you may not want to hear this, but I'm going to say it anyway so you'll just have to deal with it. So do I.'

Her eyes were wide and clear, her voice strong and determined yet at the same time filled with an offer of comfort, or at the very least a willingness to listen, whether he wanted to accept it or not. And he realised she'd risked his displeasure or worse. *Because she cared.* Something warm and unfamiliar slid through him. She deserved something of him in return.

'Remember that first morning here I accused you of spying in my garden?' He looked away, out to sea. 'You can blame Angelica for my paranoia.' Even the name still sent a shudder down his spine. 'The woman had beauty and brains. Enough intelligence to steal my work and enough audacity to pass it off as hers.'

'Oh, Nic, that's appalling.'

'Make no mistake, I got it back through the courts.'

'How did you meet?'

'At a conference in the States. She was a computer programmer from Sydney.'

'You were lovers?'

He glared at her. 'What do you think?'

'I wondered only because I can't imagine anyone doing that to someone they cared about.'

'That's just it, she never did—care, that is. It was all about the games, and how she could use me. That's when I decided to take another name and write my Utopian trilogy. Nic Russo no longer exists in online gaming.' Pulling out his mobile, he rang through to Reception.

'What are you doing?'

'Arranging for your luggage to be brought up and checking you out.'

'But—'

'You're staying here with me tonight.'

Moments later, in his bedroom, his fingers rushed to peel the sarong from her body as he'd been itching to do all evening. But as he looked into her eyes, the need for speed was replaced by a new demand that was no less urgent. The need not only to claim, but to possess.

Passion rose as haste slowed. Time to absorb the drift of silky skin against his palms, the warmth of her breath mingling with his own, her lush curves that melted against him like sun-warmed honey. *Just a woman*, but the sensations shivered through him like quicksilver over smooth onyx.

Charmed.

The glow from the fairy lights outside his window bathed her in the mysteriously alluring shades of indigo and magenta, making him willing to forget why he'd never had a woman in this room since Angelica.

Her eyes were clear as still water, reaching inside him and touching the secret places in his heart that no woman had ever come close to. Understanding, accepting.

'Charlotte…' His murmur was low and heartfelt as he skimmed his hands over the slope of her breast, the flare of her hips. It wasn't for ever, but for tonight—one last night—he would take everything she offered.

Charlotte didn't want Nic to take her to the airport. Saying goodbye to this magical island was hard enough, saying goodbye to Nic, effectively ending their time together, all but impossible.

So she slid out of his bed before dawn, dressed quickly in the dimness, then rang for a taxi downstairs and slipped back to the resort's reception area a two-minute walk away. She'd send him an email or text to let him know she'd arrived home safely. And that would be the end of it.

A few hours later, in the airline's business lounge at Tullamarine, ten minutes before her flight to Adelaide was due to board, she tapped in Suzette's number on her mobile. 'Hi, Suz, I'm back. Or in Melbourne at least.'

'Well, it's about time.' Charlotte heard the smile in her best friend's voice. 'You did tell me not to call so I didn't.'

'And I appreciate it.'

'I know you needed the time to think about everything, but I thought about *you* while I froze through two of the coldest weeks this winter. Those golden beaches and hot tropical nights. Please tell me you had a wild romantic fling with some gorgeous guy and you've forgotten all about that creep who didn't deserve you.'

Charlotte knew Suzette wasn't entirely serious because the Charlotte Suzette knew would never have done such a thing. 'Uh-huh.'

There was a stunned pause. 'What? *What?* Fill me in *now*,' she demanded. 'What's his name and what does he do?'

'Nic Russo.' Just saying his name made her heart skip a beat. 'He writes computer games; the interactive, out-of-this-world kind. If you look up *Utopian Twilight* you'll see what I mean—amazing. *He's* amazing and—' She realised she was talking too fast, gushing in fact, and pressed those wayward lips together.

'*And...?* Where's he from? Are you seeing him again?'

'He...' *Reality check, Charlotte. He doesn't want what I want. There's nothing for us.* A band tightened around her chest and her eyes blurred suspiciously. 'No, I'm not seeing him again. It was a fling, Suz. That wild romantic fling thing.'

'Yeah, but...'

'It's over. Finished. Isn't that what you told me to do? Forget *the creep* and enjoy myself and come back a different woman? I took your advice.' And would live with the consequences. 'I'll be home by tonight if you want to come round. I've got an idea for a fashion show to raise funds for a Fijian school I visited.' *And I could sure use the company.* But she didn't say it because it would make losing Nic more real when he'd never been hers to lose.

'Love to, Charlie, but I'm still in the Riverland at the bridal fashion seminar. I'll be back soon. I'll let you know as soon as. In the meantime, email me some details on the show. I'd love to be involved.'

'Okay.' Charlotte caught the downbeat tone in her own voice and forced a smile, suddenly desperate to end this call before she spilled her guts. 'Catch up with you then.'

As Charlotte disconnected a young woman in a business skirt and white blouse rose from a nearby seat and approached with a smile. Charlotte recognised her instantly from Adelaide's social events. Great, the press; just what she didn't need.

'Ms Dumont, welcome back. I was sorry to hear about your recent split with Mr Edwards. What—?'

'Our lives took different directions.' Charlotte concentrated on sliding her phone into her bag. 'Changed priorities. That's all I have to say on the matter.'

'How did you enjoy Fiji?'

'It was great, thanks.'

Bright blue eyes gleamed with speculation. 'What are your plans now?'

'I really don't have... Wait...' Maybe she could use the press to her advantage for a change. 'I intend hosting a charity event soon, to raise money for a Fijian school. I'll be making an announcement to the Adelaide press soon.'

'Any particular reason for your ch—?'

'That's all for now.' Gathering her luggage together, she began walking. 'I have a flight to catch.'

Nic frowned at his black computer screen while he fiddled with a miniature paper dragonfly on his desk. Charlotte had left without a word. Walked out of his life without a backward glance. Hadn't even left a note—just the imprint of her head on the pillow and her lingering fragrance. He sent the dragonfly soaring across the room.

So what was wrong with that scene? Why did his morning seem heavy with cloud when the sun was shining cheerfully on the palms outside his window? After all, wasn't he habitually guilty of the same casual morning-after behaviour?

*It was wrong because he'd not been the one with the final say.*

So he told himself he'd taken a long-overdue break. He'd enjoyed the company of a beautiful woman, now it was time to get back to work. He clicked keys, waited impatiently for his world to load. The screen lit up, the familiar scene appeared and he was home. In control. Supreme Commander of his Universe.

Scene: maroon sky, blood-red moon, splinters of obsidian thrusting skyward. Onyx One, chained to the sheer cliff. Screaming wind blowing up from the volcano's fiery furnace below. Reena to the rescue on a winged amethyst creature, hair flying behind her, golden sword held high in one hand…

Charlotte.

Swearing, he shoved at the desk, his chair rolling back over the parquetry floor. He ploughed his hands through his hair and ordered himself to cool it. But all he could see was Charlotte in his bed, her beautiful body spread across his sheets like liquid gold, her gaze intense, her hands all over him wielding her signature brand of charm.

And last night he'd let his mouth run away with his common sense and told her things about himself he'd never told anyone.

Work, he reminded himself, pushing all erotic thoughts

and bad judgements and trust issues away. He had a program to write and by God he was going to do it.

His determination paid off and he worked solidly for the rest of the day and well into the night, only rolling into bed for a couple of hours' sleep before doing it all again.

Late in the afternoon on the following day, he rewarded himself with a swim, then sat in the shady surrounds to catch up with the real world in the day's local newspaper.

But on page three, his own face stared back at him, beside a large graphic that could have been plucked from one of his games. The caption read, *Dom Silverman: The Secret World of Nic Russo?* Included in the article was a small photo of him and Charlotte on board a yacht and speculation about their relationship.

He didn't bother to read it. Betrayal stabbed at him, its black stain spreading like sin in front of his eyes as he wrenched upright and snatched up his mobile.

When her phone rang and Charlotte saw Nic's number, her heart stopped, then began pounding. How many times in the last twenty-four hours had she started to ring him before reminding herself Nic didn't want anything more meaningful than what they'd had?

Then remembering how she'd left him without a word, she pressed the connect button with a mix of excitement and apprehension. 'Hello, Nic. Did you get my text—?'

'Why, Charlotte?' The words weren't what she'd expected, nor were they spoken in that sexy tone she'd grown so accustomed to hearing; they were tight and remote and filled with such cold anger a chill shivered down her spine.

'I'm sorry.' Her hands started to tremble; she pressed her free hand against her heart. 'I thought it was the best way, under the cir—'

'Was it for the money? Your inheritance not what you expected?' His sarcastic tone tore at her sudden fragility.

'What are you talking about?'

'That reporter on the beach,' he said in frigid tones that burned and froze at the same time. 'You told him about me. About Dom Silverman.'

'No! That's not true.' Her legs turned to water and she sank to the floor. 'What happened?'

'An article in the newspaper *happened*. Interesting co-incidence, wouldn't you say, that it appears the day after you skip off back to Australia?'

He made it sound as if she'd done a moonlight flit with his life savings. 'Oh, Nic, no...' Charlotte's fingers clutched her phone tighter, pressing it to her ear as if will-ing the words to convince him. 'Please, Nic. Believe me. I'd *never* do that to you.' She closed her eyes. 'I swear on my parents' graves that it wasn't me.'

A long, tense silence followed. Surely he knew her well enough to understand that she'd never use the memory of her parents in such a way if she didn't mean it?

'How the hell, then, did they find out?' He spoke each word as if chewing on leather.

'I don't know. Oh...' Unless that reporter at Tullamarine... Could she have been listening in on her conversation with Suzette? Charlotte tried to recall what she'd said, then wished the floor would open up and swallow her. 'Oh, no...'

'Okay, let's have it.'

She tried to explain, tripping over her words. She'd referred to Nic by his real name...but she'd mentioned *Utopian Twilight* in the same breath. A couple of mouse clicks and anyone would have the knowledge at their fin-gertips.

'You still don't know how to deal with the paparazzi, do you?' She could practically hear his teeth grinding together. 'Never, *never*, say or do anything in public that you don't want the world to know about.'

'Nic…' She willed herself not to cry. 'I don't know what to—'

'Tell me your address and I'll send a car for you tomorrow at five p.m. He'll make sure you're not followed and you'll meet me at Montefiore Hill at six.'

North Adelaide's Montefiore Hill overlooking the city was a favourite spot for snogging and lovers' trysts.

Not this time.

She heard the abrupt click as he disconnected. He was flying back to Adelaide tomorrow. Not for a close reunion but a confrontation.

# CHAPTER ELEVEN

WHEN the car ferrying Charlotte cruised into Montefiore Hill's car park during a rain storm, she knew the red sports car parked alongside had to be Nic's. She got a quick glimpse of him as he exited with an umbrella and opened the passenger door for her.

He didn't waste time with rain-drenched greetings, bundling her inside and rounding the car while the rain drummed on the roof. The cab drove off and he slid in beside her, smelling of winter and wet wool.

Black jumper, black jeans, black eyes. A formidable contrast to her vibrant island lover and her heart thundered with apprehension—and desire. Even under such circumstances her body seemed to have a will of its own.

'Nic…' she began, then trailed off beneath his gaze. To escape its intensity she looked at the city lights through the blurred windscreen.

He shifted closer, his warmth invading her space, but he didn't touch her. 'I'm not happy with you, Charlotte.'

'I screwed up big time, didn't I?' When he didn't reply, she went on, 'I hope you trust me enough to know I'd never do anything to hurt you. I understand you don't trust easily after everything you've told me, but I—'

'I've decided you were telling the truth.'

She let out a slow breath. 'You don't know what a relief

it is to hear you say that.' Even if his words were clipped and remote. She allowed herself to relax against the soft leather seat for the first time in what felt like a life sentence.

'So now we deal with it. Together.'

She turned to him, incredulous. Droplets of water still shimmered in his hair. 'I'd've thought you wouldn't want anything more to do with me.'

'I've given it plenty of thought over the past twenty-four hours. We all make mistakes.'

'That's very generous of you but I don't deserve it. Because of me, you've lost your writing anonymity—'

'It's not the worst thing that's ever happened to me.' Watching her, he stroked the ends of her hair with light fingers. 'Maybe it was the universe's way of telling me it was time.'

'And now our names will be linked and splashed all over the gossip columns and—'

'The name Nic Russo is known in Fiji but it doesn't have the same media exposure in Australia.'

'Until now.'

He acknowledged that but smoothed the hair behind her ear and drifted his fingers to her cheek. 'I'm more concerned about the Barossa wine princess; I know how you hate publicity.'

'I can handle it. I'm getting better at it.' Her breathing stalled at the barely there caress and she leaned into his touch, drew in his familiar scent. 'You didn't have to come all the way to Adelaide to hold my hand.'

'True. But maybe it's not only your hand I want to hold.' His voice dropped to its husky low register as he reached over her and the back of her seat reclined smoothly. He fused his mouth to hers, swallowing any reply she might have made, and his taste—warmer and smoother than the best whisky and all the sweeter for its familiarity. One hand slid beneath her jumper and up beneath the edge of her bra to cup her breast and tease a nipple.

'Nic…wait…' she managed when he finally lifted his lips to tug on her ear lobe. 'We're in a public place.'

'Relax. No one's around.' He leaned back slightly to look at her, those sensual lips curved, his eyes twinkling with the city's reflected light. 'You've never been parking in a Ferrari before?'

'Um…no.'

He unsnapped the top stud on her jeans, slid his hand down her belly and inside her panties. 'About time you did, then…'

Urgency pummelled Nic as she arched against him, her moans echoing his. He plunged his fingers into her wet heat while the rain continued to lash the roof. A few frantic seconds and he had her jeans down to her knees, his own jeans unzipped and—at last—he was ruthlessly riding her where only she could take him. No patience, no control, no finesse. Just blind, searing passion as they flew together over that mindless pinnacle.

They readjusted their clothes in silence. Nic had been fooling himself into thinking this thing with Charlotte was finished. He wanted more—just a few days, a couple of weeks maybe, get her out of his system, then he could focus on work. 'Come back to my apartment.'

She was finger-combing her hair but paused to look at him, her eyes wide, her lips plump. Ravished. Adorable. 'I'll drive you home tomorrow,' he told her, then leaned across to smooth those lips with his and murmured, 'I want to make love with you again. All night.'

'Me too,' she murmured back.

Moments later Nic swung out of the deserted park and headed for Glenelg. Probably faster than he should, considering the slippery road conditions but he couldn't wait to get her fully naked, to feel her body pressed up against his again.

'I guess you'll be going straight back to Fiji, then,' she said as they cruised through an amber light. 'Especially with this cold weather.'

'I'm here now; might as well stay on a bit.' He glanced her way. Her hair was temptingly tousled, her hands clasped tight on her lap. 'Are you still planning to go ahead with the fashion show idea? I could stick around if it's not too far away, give you some support. If you'd like.'

'Yes, I am, and I'd love for you to be here for it. Suzette's supplying the bridal gowns and formal wear and the models and I'm going to contact the attendees with money to burn. Shouldn't take more than a couple of weeks to organise.'

'Bridal?'

'Suzette's speciality.'

'No *lingerie*?' When she didn't answer, he flicked her a grin. 'Brides want something special at the end of the big day to wow their grooms with, don't they? You make a stunning model—I've seen you firsthand, remember.'

'I know what you're thinking, Nic, and you can forget it.'

'Pity.'

'Since you're here,' she went on, switching topics fast, 'those opera tickets I mentioned are for tomorrow night, if you'd like to join me. If you're not busy…'

'Guess I could give it a try.' He squeezed her thigh. 'On the condition that you come home with me after.'

'Deal.'

The following morning, Charlotte slid out of bed before Nic woke. In their hurry to get naked last night, she hadn't given the apartment more than a glance, but she took note of the bathroom now as she coiled her hair on top of her head and waited for the water temperature to rise.

Black. Masculine. No pretty-smelling soaps—and why would there be?—just a shelf stocked haphazardly with the usual generic bottles and shaving gear. Glass and chrome gleamed in the sunlight slanting through the frosted window, the lack of colour relieved by a couple of thick red towels. It was spacious enough with a deep spa and a shower stall big enough for two.

Ignoring the supermarket-brand gel dangling from one of the twin heads, she lathered up with her own tiny 'Charlotte's Meadow' travel soap, glad she'd had it in her handbag.

The cheery voice of a radio announcer was her first and only clue that she was no longer alone. She glanced up and noticed twin speakers mounted on the wall, catching a shadowy blur of movement beyond the steamy glass screen as she did so.

'Mind if I join you?'

Just hearing that husky morning voice turned her knees to jelly as the screen door opened and Nic stepped in behind her.

'I…ah…' She bit back a moan as his hands slid over her shoulders to tweak her nipples into tight little buds. 'I thought…you were asleep.'

'I was.' He nipped at the side of her neck with his lips. 'But then I smelled this perfume and had to investigate.' He leaned further, took the soap from her hands. 'It's been driving me mad for the past two weeks.'

'You can thank my emergency soap supply, then.'

'Of course,' he murmured. 'On every princess's travel essentials list.' His big body was pressed up behind her and he was obviously ready to get on with things.

'Laugh if you like,' she said, primly. 'I'm not going to change.'

'And I wouldn't want you to. It was made for you, this scent,' he murmured, nipping her ear lobe, his breath mingling with the steam that rose around them, closing them in, shutting everything else out.

'As a matter of fact, it was.' It was hard to concentrate when his erection was nudging her backside and his hands were busy drawing soapy circles around her breasts. 'Exclusively… In Paris… Years ago.' It had cost a bomb but she still imported it on a regular basis.

'So what can I smell… Jasmine?'

'And honeysuckle, sweet mandarin, black rose… amongst other things…'

'It reminds me of a lake at sunset with mist swirling low on the ground and the sky burnished with colour.'

'You should be a writer…'

'And you're there, facing the water, in something long and smooth and glowing like fire to match the sky. Then I come up behind you and kiss your neck like this…' His lips nipped and pressed across her nape. 'And the dress dissolves like gold dust under my hands.' Those hands glided over her skin, and every dip, every curve he touched sang his praises.

'Your perfume was the first thing I noticed about you,' he murmured against her ear.

'It was?'

'You were in front of me in the check-in queue at Tullamarine.'

'Oh…' How could she not have known? How could she not have felt this connection between them that had become as much a part of her as the air she breathed?

An arm reached in front of her and he set the soap on its dish, nudging closer. She spread her legs in invitation, or maybe it was surrender, as he pushed inside her, holding her upright with his strength and warmth.

'And I fantasised about doing this…' he said, pushing deeper, harder, his hands sliding over her belly, and lower, between her thighs where she wanted him with the most desperate of wants.

And Nic couldn't imagine a better way to start the day than with a fantasy come to life. 'I have to tell you, the back of your neck's an obsession of mine.'

He played light fingertips over her nape, worked slowly up from the base of her skull and into her silky hair. And she responded like a harp carved and tuned exclusively for him, her sweet sighs like angels' music to his ears. Working his fingers higher over her scalp, he felt the shiver that moved through her.

'That feels…amazing.'

'So do you…' He thrust once more—deeply—and her slick heat tightened like a glove around him. 'So do you.'

They ate breakfast overlooking the ocean. The rain had passed but it was still cold outside, the wind hurling itself against the glass and whipping up white tops. Charlotte studied his apartment, minimalist in the extreme, compared to his Fijian house, which felt like a home. Miles of glass, stern black and chrome furniture—not even a cushion or house plant to soften the austerity. A typical bachelor pad.

Munching on a slice of toast, she wondered if he brought women here, but was beginning to realise his privacy was paramount. No doubt he graced the bed of many a woman's boudoir, however. 'You have an office here too?'

He indicated a closed door on the far side of the living room. 'It's pretty basic but the light and the view make up for it.'

'Loads of inspiration, then.'

He poured himself another cup of coffee. 'I do my most creative work in Fiji. Adelaide's mainly where I work on the programs.'

Charlotte rose, carried her dishes to the dishwasher, loaded them. 'Since I'm at Glenelg, I might take a stroll down Jetty Road before I leave, if you're not in a hurry.'

'Fine by me.' He rose too. 'I'm going for a run on the beach.' He stretched, giving her a glimpse of tanned taut abdomen beneath the hem of his windcheater. 'If I know women at all, I'll be back before you but just in case...' He walked to the fridge, took a key off a hook, handed it to her.

Not wanting to disturb him if he was working, Charlotte let herself in an hour later. When she didn't see Nic, she called softly and knocked at his office door, turned the knob.

Locked.

Her buoyant mood slipped a bit. More interested in spending time with Nic than browsing boutiques, she'd cut her trip to the popular shopping strip short, and beaten him back. The locked door in his own home was also a surprise. Was that his habit or was it to keep her out? Did he still not trust her? No, it was an added security measure, she told herself. His work was valuable, and after what Angelica had done who could blame him?

On the positive side, having the place to herself gave her time to arrange her purchase of four plump red cushions along the sofa before he returned. She set the happy plant on the glass coffee table. A nice welcome home, she decided, pleased with the effect, and the cushions would be a reminder of their time together every time he sat on the sofa to admire the view.

She spent the time tidying his bedroom and en suite, then progressed to the kitchen. She was wiping down the benches when he blew in looking wild and windswept and bringing with him the scent of the sea.

She used the tea towel to wipe her hands. 'Hi.'

'Back already?' His expression told her he wasn't used to coming home to company. 'What woman cuts short a shopping expedition?'

'This woman.' She reached up on tiptoe to kiss him. 'I was beginning to think you'd run back to Fiji.'

He tucked his hands in the back pockets of her jeans to pull her hips closer but his eyes held a hint of reproach. 'Not without telling you, I wouldn't.'

'Okay, message received and understood.'

Nic kissed her again, still somewhat distracted by the newness and surprise of having someone waiting for him in his apartment. 'I didn't expect you back yet so I stopped in at that café down the beach a bit...' He trailed off at the sight of his cushion-festooned sofa, the greenery on the table, and heard the first alarm bell clang. 'What's all this?'

'I thought they'd make it a bit more homely.'

'I don't need cushions.' Or homely. Cushions were women's work; they did *not* suit a bachelor's apartment. 'I hardly ever sit here.'

'Well, you should,' she said, behind him. 'You shouldn't be chained to your desk all day...'

'It's what I do. And I won't be here long enough to fuss over any plant.'

'Oh... I didn't think of that. Jeez, I'm an idiot.'

He heard the confusion and embarrassment and felt like a jerk, but it didn't change the fact that she'd altered their relationship. Did she think he was staying on indefinitely? Did she think she could persuade him with little gifts of domesticity? How many women had plied him with similar gestures? A pot of home-made soup, a towel embroidered with his name, hoping to lure him to the altar and set up a joint bank account.

'It's not that I don't appreciate the thought,' he said, 'but—'

'Don't worry about it—give them to charity. It's fine.'

Nic knew from experience when a woman said 'fine' in that tone, it meant anything but. 'I'm going to take a quick shower, then I'll drive you home.' Maybe he could smooth things over on the way.

'No need, I've booked a cab.' She spoke crisply, her expression devoid of emotion, and glanced at her watch. 'He'll be here any minute now. I'll go downstairs and get out of your way.'

'Charlotte…' *Wait.* An odd panic worked its way through the annoyance. 'I said I'd drive you, just give me a damn m—'

'The opera ticket.' She dug into her bag, pulled it out and slapped it on the kitchen bench, eyes sparking now. 'This way you can suit yourself whether you come or not.'

Charlotte waited in the foyer for Nic to show, pacing the thick carpet, ignoring the subtle glances of recognition cast her way. She'd not been out in public since the break-up and knew there'd be gossip in tomorrow's paper. It would have been so satisfying to have had a partner to flaunt tonight and not to have to climb into a cab sad and alone at the end of the evening. Not that she wanted to *flaunt* Nic, especially since she'd revealed his identity to the press.

*I just want to be with him.*

Biting back a sigh, she checked the time. Did she really expect him to show after this morning's debacle? She'd done what he'd made clear he didn't want from her; she'd gone domestic on him.

The last bell rang. Most patrons had already disappeared into the auditorium. She should go home. There was no way she could enjoy the performance under the circumstances.

As she turned to leave she saw Nic approaching and her heart wanted to weep and dance at the same time. This gorgeous sexy man in a snappy dark suit and tie was here to meet her. She had to force herself to walk sedately across the carpet and not to fling her arms around his neck.

'Traffic was heavier than I expected,' he said, smelling freshly showered as he tucked her arm through his and walked towards the auditorium doors, which were already closing.

'You're here now.' That was all that mattered.

'Charlotte.' He stopped, looked down at her, eyes troubled. 'I shouldn't have reacted that way this morning.' He shook his head. 'Everything about you, everything with you... It's different.'

'I know.' And it scared her too.

'So what's the verdict on opera?' Charlotte watched the street lights flicker over Nic's face as he drove them back to his apartment.

'I was too busy watching you.'

Always the smooth talker, was Nic, and she basked for a moment in the glow. But only for a moment because this morning's exchange was still recent and raw. 'Seriously though, did you enjoy it?'

'I think I'm with your father on this.'

'Okay... In that case, thanks for coming with me and giving it a try. You can chalk it up to a new experience.'

'It was an experience watching you in your familiar environment.'

'Yeah. Lady Mitchell's probably on her phone right now, spreading the word.'

'Does that bother you?'

'No.' Knowing that Mum's circle of friends would gossip and speculate as a result of bumping into Grace Mitchell no longer mattered.

They parked beneath Nic's building, then took the stairs to the ground floor and walked the long way round to the entrance so they could see the ocean roll in.

'This has been a *wonderful* evening,' she said, hugging her upper arms against the chill blowing off the sea.

The wind combed Charlotte's hair so that it streamed behind her like ribbons and Nic couldn't resist running his hand through the silky strands. 'It's not over yet.'

'Nic…' She turned, her eyes as silvery soft as sea mist with a fragility that tugged at something deep within him. 'This…thing…'

'It's okay,' he told her softly, and realised he meant it. 'Different is okay.'

She smiled slowly and it was like watching the sun coming out at midnight as she took his hands in hers and led him towards the lift. 'Yes. It is.'

Wholly absorbed—*charmed*—with the vision in front of him, Nic followed. The doors slid closed, shutting off the sounds of the sea and enclosing them in stainless-steel walls as it began to rise.

Dragging off her scarf, she wound it behind his head and pulled him close. The lift jolted and the lights dimmed for a second or two before the lift resumed its ascent. 'Uh-oh,' she murmured against his chin. 'Ever been stuck in a lift?'

Nic's pulse skipped a beat and adrenaline spiked through his system. 'No.' He didn't tell her he always took the stairs.

'So do you want to be?'

'Be what…?' He was finding it hard to concentrate on

her words when his vision was turning dark and his pulse was drumming and he *couldn't breathe*.

She flicked the buttons of her coat undone. 'Stuck in a lift…'

'Not particularly.' A bead of sweat trickled down his back.

Tugging on the ends of her scarf, she pressed her body hard up against his. 'Are you sure? Lifts have a stop button somewhere, don't they? I imagine it could be—'

'Don't even think about it.' Did his voice sound too harsh, too loud? *Stop!* he yelled silently, using his self-help technique. Forcing his breathing to slow, he watched the number for his floor wink on and let out a private sigh.

'Too late, you've just lost your chance.' She danced out ahead of him, her heels tapping on the polished boards, her scarf trailing behind her. It gave him a moment to suck in air.

Shrugging off her coat, she tossed it over the sofa then turned, eyes bright and playful. She slid the strap of her black dress off one shoulder and flicked him a sultry look beneath her lashes. 'Want to see what I'm wearing underneath?'

'Later.' Self-disgust was a dark and lonely place. 'I've got some urgent matters to attend to. I'll be in my office.' He kissed her bare shoulder to take the sting out of what she'd see as a rejection, but he wasn't up for sharing his shortcomings. 'You warm up the bed for me, I'll be along in a few moments.'

Charlotte awoke in the darkness, disoriented, and aware that something had disturbed her sleep. Some sound of distress? Turning her head on the pillow, she saw the empty space beside her. She vaguely recalled Nic coming to bed at some stage. But now the sheets were twisted and thrown back. It was four-twenty a.m.

She slipped out of bed, pulled on his shirt from the bottom of the bed, then made her way carefully along the unfamiliar hallway till she reached the living room. She saw Nic on the balcony facing the sea, *naked*, his overlong hair blown back by the wind. Solitary. Lost. Alone.

*I love him.*

The knowledge—its dazzle and the dismay—ripped through her, body and soul, and she stumbled backwards. No. Not now, not with him: a man who'd made it quite clear he was happy with their temporary relationship. A man who'd told her he didn't know how to be anyone but that lonely figure standing on the balcony.

Because her legs were trembling, she sank onto the nearest available chair. *Count to five. Breathe. This is not allowed to happen—he's a friend, a lover. That's all.*

She wasn't aware how long she sat in the dark, watching him, listening to the hum of the fridge, the sound of her heart drumming in her ears and convincing herself it was hero worship. He'd rescued her, right? When he went back to Fiji it would fade. She just needed time and distance.

He must be freezing his butt off out there.

Her heart shivered in empathy, and she hesitated, torn between offering support in whatever way might be appropriate and afraid he'd not welcome it.

Maybe he liked to plot when inspiration struck. Maybe he worked best at night and naked. She was hardly familiar with his sleeping habits.

He turned so that his face was in profile. From a few feet away on the other side of the glass, she could see the lowered ridge of brow, the tight flat line of his mouth, his hands fisted on the glass balcony. He didn't look contemplative, he looked disturbed, yet he'd been fine until they'd got to his apartment.

She thought of going back to bed but she simply could not walk away and leave him to the cold winter's night. She picked up her coat that she'd left on the sofa earlier.

He turned, surprise crossing his gaze when she opened the glass door.

'Nic…?'

A guarded wariness smothered the surprise, then a hint of that playboy grin flirted with the corner of his mouth. It didn't reach his eyes. 'Hey, babe, that shirt looks better on you than it does on me.'

'Nic, it's freezing out here.'

He shook his head. 'Go back to bed, Charlotte.'

'You'll catch a chill.' She held out her coat.

'Don't give me that mummy routine.' But he took it, shrugged it on. 'Happy now?'

'Not really. And sorry about the "routine"; that's the way I am. Would you like something warm to drink?' She bit her lip. *Stop. Now.*

'I'm right, thanks.' He lifted the brandy bottle from the table beside him, splashed liquid into a tumbler with a clink of glass on glass.

'Bad dreams?' she ventured. 'I thought I heard…' She shook her head once—a man like Nic would die before he'd admit it.

'I'm working.' He took a healthy gulp of his brandy, then studied the bottom of his glass. 'Dreams give me a different perspective. Hero's got himself in a bit of a tight spot.'

'Are you sure that's—?'

'Inspiration strikes at the oddest times.' He didn't look at her. 'I do my best work at night.' His gaze lifted skywards. 'There's something about the stars at this time of the morning. They look closer somehow. You feel connected to something bigger than yourself.'

Maybe. But one thing was abundantly clear—he didn't want or need her company. She gritted her teeth against the chill and the hurt at being shut out and stepped away, both literally and figuratively. 'I'll leave you to your inspiration, then.'

# CHAPTER TWELVE

For what was left of the night Nic found refuge in his office and distraction in his cyber world. Hours later, as dawn lightened the sky, he watched the surf roll in over an indigo sea. The never-ending horizon cut the sky, sharp and precise as a blade.

He breathed in slowly and deeply, until his lungs were full and his mind clear of the suffocating darkness that had plagued him since childhood.

His personal and private hell had obviously disturbed Charlotte's sleep too. Had he cried out? By God, he hoped not. Bad enough that he'd barely got out of the damn lift without making an ass of himself.

He'd hurt her. He'd seen it in her eyes when he'd not taken her to bed, craving her comfort even as he did so. *Because she cared.* She was falling for him and that hadn't been the plan.

And against all his rules, he'd fallen for her too. *Big mistake, Nic.* What woman would want a guy with his baggage and his secrets and his phobias? Charlotte Dumont was a long-term, commitment-driven, family kind of girl, and he didn't know how to do family. Nor did he need mothering, for pity's sake. He'd done okay without it his entire life.

And she was one of those women he avoided—the kind who liked to discuss *feelings*.

Not Nic. He hadn't discussed feelings since he'd told his mother he was scared because it had got dark while she'd been gone and he couldn't reach the light switch. Had talking about it changed anything? Not a whit. Had talking about it made the dark seem more real, more menacing, more stifling? You bet.

But in his Utopian world, he wasn't confined, he was free. He could be anyone he wanted, do what he wanted.

Not with Charlotte. So with what was left of their time together, he'd be that fun casual guy she'd met at the airport. Decision made, he got back to work.

She must have slept, because the next thing Charlotte knew, Nic was dressed and alert and suggesting breakfast in one of the little cafés downstairs.

As they ate she saw no trace of the man she'd left on the balcony, just the usual carefree, flirty Nic. *That* man she could deal with and keep her true feelings hidden.

'Red kitchen, red towels, red car,' she said as she settled into the passenger seat for the drive home.

'A Ferrari's gotta be red.' He glanced at her jeans and mushroom-coloured top. 'I'd like to see *you* in red. Fire-engine-red silk… Hoo, baby, you'd look hot.'

'Red's not a colour I wear. Unless it's lingerie.'

His eyes flicked to her breasts and he jiggled his eyebrows as he turned the ignition. 'So are you going to model any of that red *lingerie* for me some time soon?'

'Maybe.' Persuasive, he was. Seductive and irresistible.

As they cruised out of the underground garage and onto the main road, he said, 'Just because you don't wear red, doesn't mean you can't try a change now and then.'

Oh, but she *had* changed. Maybe he didn't realise he'd brought about change in her and in so many ways. Good changes. She'd left the woman Flynn had known, and rejected, behind. Nic had forced her to look at life in a different way and she was going to miss him terribly for that.

Not only that.

She rubbed a hand over the ache in her heart that was growing every day, every hour, every minute. She saw many things differently now. What she'd had with Flynn was a pale imitation of the real thing. Like comparing beige sack cloth with red silk.

The eighty-minute drive to the Barossa Valley gave her time to ring around for attendees for the fashion show and take her mind off Nic. Yesterday she'd locked in her first choice for a venue, available in two weeks due to a late cancellation.

She tapped in the first name on her list. 'Lady Alexandra? Good morning, it's Charlotte Dumont.'

Nic tuned out as Charlotte made her endless list of calls. *Lady Alexandra, Sir William Beaumont, Mrs Hartford-Jones.* This up-scale event with South Australia's landed gentry was going to be a new experience for him.

They were driving into the Barossa now, the road flanked with bare vines. Low hills the colour of porridge rolled along the horizon. They passed a winery, its cellar door doing a thriving business in the middle of the week with a couple of tourist buses parked outside.

Would Charlotte use her inheritance to set up something similar as she'd originally intended? She knew the wine industry and he could see her interacting with people. But her expertise in fashion design was marketable and more unique.

Eventually he followed her directions down a private road, which widened into a circular drive around a smooth emerald lawn big enough to play a round of golf on. Bright spring bulbs danced in the breeze at the base of a two-tier fountain directly in front of the massive front door.

The home itself was a rambling two-storey blue-stone. White pillars supported a wide wrap-around veranda on both floors.

'Come on,' she told him, excitement bubbling through her voice as she climbed out. 'It's my turn to show *you* around.'

He followed her up the shallow steps and waited while she decoded the security. Inside, the house was no less impressive. A Scarlett O'Hara staircase, stained glass, Persian rugs. It smelled of floor polish and a hell of a lot of old money.

He stared up at the foyer's enormous chandelier. 'How many rooms does this place have?'

'Twenty-two. That's including the cellar, which has its own chandelier,' she said, following his gaze.

'A chandelier in a cellar?'

'Not just a cellar, it's also a place for entertaining. I'll show you later.'

*Not if he could help it.* 'And you live here alone?' He looked down at her and the flush of excitement faded; sadness clouded her eyes.

'Suzette stays over sometimes. Since Flynn left.' She seemed to shrink in stature. 'I can't sell it,' she said quietly. 'It's all I have left of my family.' She turned away and started walking towards the back of the house. 'Go for a wander—I'll put on some coffee.'

He suspected her snappy departure didn't have as much to do with refreshments as the unwillingness to look him in the eye. And it shouldn't be that way, he thought, climbing the stairs. He should be offering support. Coming back to an empty home under such circumstances had to be tough.

But how could he when he didn't believe her decision to stay here and dwell on the past was in her best interest? He knew that to tell her selling up was a better option would not go down well.

He ambled down the wide hallway, past bedrooms and guest suites filled with antique furniture, then paused at the doorway to what was obviously her parents' bedroom.

'I've left it exactly as it was,' she said behind him. Her shoulder brushed his as she slipped into the room. She walked to the bay window, fingered a tapestry on one of two French-polished chairs facing each other over a round matching table. 'Mum's cross-stitch that she was working on.'

Nic saw a half-finished jigsaw spread out on the table and a pair of men's spectacles set neatly to the side.

'They used to sit here together in the evenings. They believed in having at least an hour every night to talk to each other without the distraction of TV.'

'Charlotte…' He walked towards her slowly, the back of his neck prickling as though the room's occupants were still there. And to Charlotte, they were. 'This isn't healthy, sweetheart. You need to move on.'

He lifted a hand and might have touched her cheek but she sidestepped out of reach, her posture stiff, arms crossed like a shield, lips a thinned white slash in a whiter face.

'And what the hell would you know about it, Nic?'

*Yeah, Nic, what the hell?* His hand fell to his side, curling into a fist as a tide of dark emotions ripped through him. This world—Charlotte's world—was an alien landscape to him. His teeth clicked together audibly and he stepped back. And kept backing all the way to the door. 'You're right. I don't. I'll get going. I've got some work, and—'

'Nic.' Her hands swept up to her face. 'Nic, no. I'm

sorry. I didn't mean that. I just…just snapped.' Shaking her head, she hurried towards him, eyes as huge as saucers.

'But we both know it's true.'

'No.' Light fingers touched his arm. 'Please… It's just… I've not been away, not even for one night, since they… left.' Her eyes brimmed with unshed tears. 'That's how it feels—like they just went on a trip and they'll come through that door any moment now, bursting to tell me all about their Alaskan cruise, and I need to be here in case—'

'It's okay, Charlotte.' He gently but firmly lifted her hand away. *I'm trying to understand.* Their Fiji fling suddenly seemed like a distant memory, and this girl wasn't the same girl he'd made love to every night for over two weeks. 'You should…get some rest. You didn't sleep much last night.'

'But you've just driven me all this way. Won't you stay for coffee at least?'

'It's best if I go. I'll see you soon.'

'Soon?' Her brow creased and her clouded grey eyes searched his face.

He knew it sounded vague. Damn, he was trying to get his head around all this. Because he had the urge to smooth that worry and hurt from her forehead, he stuck his hands in his pockets.

'Come for dinner.' She spoke as if she expected a refusal. 'I owe you a dinner, don't I? Tomorrow night.'

'I'll let you know.' He began walking down the hall towards the stairs.

Charlotte followed. 'Seven o'clock,' she said, her voice stronger as he turned to her at the front door. 'I'll do something special. Please, Nic?'

How could he resist those eyes? 'Okay. See you then.'

He drove with the window down and the wind screaming past his ear. He couldn't get the image of her standing in her parents' room out of his head. The pain, the grief still so bright and sharp. *Two years?*

She'd made the house a shrine to her family. From the little he knew of her life since her family's deaths, her decision to go to Fiji had been her best decision in those two years.

But now she was home would she build on her new experiences or slip into reverse and be satisfied existing on memories for the rest of her life? That wasn't living; it wasn't even close.

# CHAPTER THIRTEEN

CHARLOTTE moped the rest of the day while she finished unpacking and restocked her groceries and tried to get on with things. The night was an endurance marathon, spent tossing and turning and regretting her defensiveness. Nic had been trying to help and she'd turned on him in the most unkind, hurtful, arrogant way possible. She'd accused him of not understanding *because of his background.*

And she'd realised it the moment the words were out of her mouth. She couldn't take them back. Could never take them back. She'd not meant it in a judgemental way, but how could he possibly understand family?

Through her bedroom window, she watched the night fade from grey to pink to day. Nic had been honest, his motivation purely based around concern *for her*, and the truth sliced like a blade. For a couple of weeks he'd made her forget, but coming home had been like taking a step backwards.

And he was right. Living here surrounded by reminders of the past was no way to live. The memories would always remain but she knew her family would be the first to tell her to move forward. They'd be cheering Nic on. It had taken getting away from everything familiar and comfortable—and Nic—to show her.

Her phone vibrated across her night stand. She was

only marginally disappointed when it was Suzette's voice and not Nic's.

'I'll be home this afternoon. I'll drop by around five,' Suzette told her. 'I've got some samples for the charity show ready for you to look at.'

'Ah, Nic's coming for dinner tonight.' If he hadn't changed his mind, that was.

'Oh? I thought it was over?'

Charlotte closed her eyes. 'Suz, have you got a few minutes? I need to talk…'

After the phone call, Charlotte got busy on the meal preparation. Fresh oysters, a lamb and potato hot pot and a sherry trifle. Easy cook, easy serve, would give her time to enjoy Nic's company and hopefully dispel the bad feeling they'd parted with.

She loved the cellar with its blend of rustic charm in the rough red bricks and the elegance of the eighteenth-century walnut dinner table and chairs. After setting the table with the best cutlery and china, she chose the wines for each course and set them aside.

Suzette was running late and she arrived with her sample pieces ten minutes before Nic was due.

Charlotte glanced at the clock. 'Can we bring them up to my room?' She did not want to face him surrounded by bridalwear.

'You are over Flynn, aren't you?' Suzette asked, a moment later, watching Charlotte carefully as she pulled a dress bag from her stash on the bed.

'Who? I've never been more over anyone or anything in my life.'

'Good. Still, I hope this won't upset you.' Suzette unzipped the bag. 'What do you think of this for the star attraction?' The hand-worked beading and cream pearls on the bodice winked like stars in the light. 'It would look amazing with your figure.'

Charlotte's heart clenched, but only for a moment. 'It's stunning,' she said slowly. 'But I'm no model. Anyway, I'll be busy making sure everything runs smoothly and people are buying.'

'And that's fine. I'd never ask you to do anything you're not comfortable with. I thought perhaps it might exorcise a demon or two.'

'Demons exorcised already. I feel better than I've felt in two years.'

'I can see that.' Suzette laid the garment on the bed. 'But be careful with this Nic guy, Charlie,' she warned, softly. 'I don't want to see you hurt again.'

Still hugging her arms, Charlotte looked away. 'I know, and I'll be careful. It's just…sometimes I think maybe, if he knew…'

'Knew what?'

*That I love him and I can't imagine not being with him.* She shook her head, made her voice brisk. 'Never mind. What's in this box?' She lifted a lid and pulled out a froth of tulle with diamanté tiara attached.

'From what you've told me, he sounds like great fling material but anything else…'

Charlotte wouldn't argue, not when her emotions were so close to spilling over. 'You're absolutely right. As usual. This is gorgeous.' She spun the headpiece around so that the tulle floated. 'Can I try it on?'

She didn't wait for an answer, putting it on her head and letting the tulle settle lightly over her face. A screen to hide the moisture that welled in her eyes.

Suzette adjusted the tiara from behind, then stepped back. 'I only finished it this afternoon—which is why I'm late—and I wanted to see how it looks from all sides

in any case.' She twitched at the tulle. 'Good job, if I do
say so myself.'

Charlotte turned and saw her misty reflection in the
night-darkened window. And for just a heartbeat out of
time, she dreamed the impossible dream.

Nic arrived a few moments early. He'd seen a car ahead
as he turned into the drive and had killed the lights and
stopped. A tall, leggy blonde in the highest heels he'd ever
seen had got out with a load of stuff; the two women had
hugged then gone inside. Suzette?

They probably had loads to discuss. He had a feeling
he was about to feel his ears burning. He stared up at the
house where light spilled from an upstairs window.

He inched the car forward and parked behind the woman's SUV as Charlotte appeared in the window. Something
white and filmy and nuptial covered her dark hair. She
fluffed it out, obviously watching herself in the glass. *That*
was precisely why he and Charlotte wouldn't work long
term.

But his gut tightened nevertheless. And if he sat here
much longer he might see more than he was supposed to.
Definitely more than he wanted to. Charlotte was expecting him ten minutes ago. How would it look if they came
outside and found him sitting in his car like a Peeping
Tom?

Grabbing the armful of daffodils, he walked to the door
and rang the bell.

A moment later, the door opened and the blonde smiled
at him. 'Hi. You must be Nic. I'm Suzette.'

'Hi, Suzette.'

She motioned him inside. 'Charlotte'll be down in a
moment. Gorgeous flowers; she'll love them.'

'I've caught her at a bad time.'

'Not at all. It's me who's in the way. I just dropped by to leave a few things here for the show.'

He shifted uncomfortably and ran a hand inside the neck of his jumper. He knew when he was being sized up for a wedding suit. Or possibly a coffin if he did anything to hurt Charlotte, because something in Suzette's eyes advised him to proceed with caution. 'You're a successful designer, I hear.'

She smiled. 'I like to think so.'

'What do you think of Charlotte's designs?'

'She's shown you?' Then she laughed lightly, blue eyes twinkling. 'I guess she has. I love them. I'm hoping she'll let us use some of her pieces at the show.'

'Good. Because I think she could make a go of it, if she decided to get serious.'

'I totally agree. We'll have to join forces and talk her into it.'

Her smile was friendly enough but he could tell it came with a warning that if he broke rank she'd crush him with her stilettoed heel.

She glanced over her shoulder. 'Here she comes now.'

Charlotte descended the stairs, wearing a fluffy jumper the colour of melted butter and black leggings that showcased her legs.

'I told you that colour suited you years ago,' Suzette said as she swept out. 'Nice to meet you, Nic.'

'Yeah.' He didn't notice her leave. He was too busy looking at the woman he'd come to see. 'New jumper?'

'I decided I needed something that reminds me of sunshine. Maybe it'll hurry spring along.'

'In that case, I chose well.' He handed her the matching flowers, then bent forward to kiss her lips.

'They're gorgeous. Thank you.' She smiled up at him

but there was an awareness of yesterday's scene in her soft grey eyes.

'I'll just get some water… Come through.'

The warm and enticing aroma of herbs and lamb filled the hall as he followed her to the kitchen. She arranged the daffodils in a vase, then picked it up. 'This way. Everything's ready.'

She led him down a narrow flight of stairs off the kitchen and his pulse picked up its pace as the walls narrowed and leaned towards him. He knew it was only his perception.

'The cellar's one of my favourite places,' she said as they descended. 'It's intimate without being confining.'

And to some extent she was right, thank God. If the ceiling weren't quite so low, it'd be even better. Haunting classical guitar drifted through hidden speakers, a crystal chandelier tossed rainbows over a long table set for two at one end. There were delicate pink wine glasses and polished silver.

How was this for a turn-around—Nic being romanced by a woman? A woman he cared deeply about. More than cared about… The knowledge and his instant refusal to accept that knowledge threw him off balance for a moment. For once in his adult life he wasn't the one in control. In more ways than one.

'Do you mind leaving the door open?' He scratched at the itch around his neck. 'I'm feeling a little warm.'

'Of course.' She moved to the table as she spoke. 'But it's always a constant temperature down here. I'm sure you'll be okay.'

She positioned the daffodils in the centre next to an ornate silver candelabrum, then pressed her palms together. 'Perfect.' She smiled at him, the chandelier's lights sparkling in her eyes like stars.

He smiled back. 'How could it not be? You went to all this trouble for me.'

'Nothing's too much trouble for you.'

*Careful, Nic.* 'This is great,' he said to the room in general, wandering over to study what looked to his in-experienced eye to be an original and highly prized piece of Australian art. 'Where's the wine? Shouldn't a cellar have wine?'

'Through there.' She gestured to a slim archway almost obscured by a wrought-iron grille. 'I'll show you later. For now, have a seat,' she said, withdrawing a plate of oysters au naturel and a bottle from a bar fridge. 'Wine?'

'Allow me—'

She whisked it out of his reach. 'I'm the hostess—I'm quite capable of pouring wine. We'll start with a char-donnay.' She paused, the bottle in mid-air. 'If you'd like?'

He sat where she'd indicated. 'I'm in your capable hands.'

She shot him a smouldering look. 'Let's just eat first. This is one of our best.' She poured the amber liquid, then sat down herself and raised her glass. 'I hope you like it. It has a tropical fruit flavour I think you'll appreciate and pairs up well with seafood.'

'To good wine.' There was the tinkle of delicate glass on glass as he touched his flute to hers.

She nodded. 'And hopefully good food.'

'Nice.' He savoured its crisp and sweet taste on his tongue a moment, then scooped up an oyster. 'You grow any other varieties?'

'We're mainly into Shiraz, which the Barossa's famous for. Three Cockatoos Winery has won barrelfuls of awards over the years. We'll try some with our main…' She trailed off, her eyes clouded and staring into space.

'What's wrong?'

'I forgot the winery's no longer a part of my life.'

He stretched a hand to hers across the table. 'Tell me about it. The winery, your family.'

With apparent effort she turned her focus on him. 'My mother's ancestors were among the first German settlers in the nineteenth century. My father's three times great grandfather migrated from France during the gold rush, made his fortune, then came to the Barossa and grew grapes. The Dumonts have always been here. And I sold them out.' Her voice dropped to a near whisper.

'No.' He turned her hand over and caressed her palm with his thumb and stared into her troubled eyes. 'You have a heritage you can be proud of no matter who owns the winery now.'

Her gaze clouded further and he knew she was thinking about his manifestly vast *lack* of background and heritage because hadn't she made that quite clear yesterday? The princess and the boy from the back streets? He withdrew his hand.

'Nic. About yesterday. I—'

'Don't. There's no need.'

'But there is, I—'

The world plunged into darkness. Black. Totally, blindingly, unfathomably black. Nic closed his eyes so he couldn't see it while his mind shut down and shrivelled into survival mode. *Breathe. Breathe. Breathe.* He concentrated only on reciting the word in his head and tried unsuccessfully to visualise a cool lake. All he could see were pin spots dancing on his eyelids.

'That damn cellar fuse must have blown again,' he heard her say through the thickening air that pressed in around him.

He didn't even attempt to speak. To do so would make him appear an idiot and, besides, his throat had closed over.

He felt the vibrations as she shuffled and bumped her way along the edge of the table towards him. A hand brushed his arm. 'Stay put. I'll be back in a jiff.'

Sweat broke out on his brow, his back. His worst nightmare. She was going to leave him here alone underground in the dark. *Scaredy cat, scaredy cat, scared of the dark.* Old pleas, old taunts. *Leering faces circling him, closer, closer till he couldn't breathe. Holding his schoolbag like a trophy, too high for a young boy to reach. Waving a blindfold in front of his eyes. Let's teach him a lesson he won't forget.*

'Stop!' He hadn't realised he'd spoken his mantra aloud until he felt her jolt. 'You'll trip; I'll come too.' He managed by sheer terrifying necessity to get the words past his quivering tonsils.

'I'm okay,' she said cheerfully. 'I know my way around, you don't.'

'I insist,' he gritted out, jerking off the chair. It tipped over with a clatter of splintering wood. *Antique wood.* He took a step, stumbled over it.

'Hey.' She laughed lightly. 'I should be the one helping you.'

He felt her hand and clutched at it like a damn lifeline. 'Fine. I'm fine.'

'No, you're not.' A pause. 'You're trembling...' Another pause—concerned and amazed.

*She knew.*

'Come on,' she said softly and led him to the stairs. 'Fifteen steps; count them.'

It gave him something to concentrate on as he felt his way, the rough bricks catching on his jumper, his shoes scudding against the stairs.

Finally. Fresh air was a cool relief on his sweat-soaked brow and he could make out the shape of the fridge, the old sideboard with its stained-glass frontage and Charlotte's eyes glinting in the kitchen's dimness. She flicked a switch and he blinked in the flood of light and pulled his hand out of her grasp.

'What just went on down there, Nic?' she asked quietly, her gaze searching his.

He scrubbed his hands over his jaw. 'What are you talking about?' He backed away on legs that felt like reeds in a wind. 'I'll be outside. I forgot something in the car.'

'Nic.' She reached for him, caught hold of his arms and stepped in front, barring his way. 'You have a fear of confined spaces?'

'Don't be ridiculous.'

'*I'm* not being ridiculous.' Her hold tightened. 'Typical man—your worst fear is admitting that you *have* a fear. Fear isn't weakness, and I want to help.'

He stood stiffly, his jaw clenched. 'If you want to help, you can terminate this conversation.'

Her eyes were resolute and full of compassion. 'My nurturing side won't let me.'

'I don't need nurturing, for God's sake.' He flicked his gaze to the ceiling, away from her soft grey eyes that seemed to plumb the depths of his soul.

'Okay, not nurturing, then. I'm talking support. Even the toughest guy needs support now and then. The trick is acknowledging and accepting it.'

He wouldn't know how. He'd been on his own so long he'd learned to live without it. He'd forgotten how to lean on another, but suddenly he yearned, desperately, to bury his head at Charlotte's breast and draw on her comfort. Worse, he was afraid if he did, he'd never let go.

Instead, he played to one of his key strengths and dropped his voice to a seductive murmur he was far from feeling. 'Support's not what I need from you, babe.'

Running his hands over the sides of her breasts to the slim curve of her waist, he leaned in to kiss her but she pushed him away hard and her eyes flashed with impatience.

'So I'm good enough to have sex with but not good enough to lean on and confide in and be *someone who matters*.'

He cursed himself when he recognised it wasn't only impatience he saw, there was hurt too. 'Damn it, Charlotte, that's n—'

'When you love someone you want to help that person any way you can. Why can't you see that? Why *won't* you see that?'

That shocked both of them into silence. *Love*. Such an overrated, overused word. But why did that single word sound so right—so complete, so *perfect*—coming from Charlotte's lips? Why did it wrap around his heart so tight he wondered how it didn't shatter into a million pieces?

He beat it down. An illusion was what it was. What it all was. And he didn't need it. He was happy with his life. Free and easy and unencumbered. And no self-respecting woman needed a man who cracked like a faulty tower every time there was a mini power failure.

He paced away, using the kitchen table as a barrier between them. 'I travel solo, Charlotte. You understood right from the start.'

'So now I'm a threat to you and your precious independence.'

'A holiday romance was all I offered and what you agreed to. I've never been anything but honest with you.'

'Honest,' she said slowly and he could hear the burn of frustration and anger. 'Is that what you're being? What about that little performance on the balcony? You'd prefer to freeze your arse off than talk to me. And tonight… Your problem's a common one and yet you deny—'

'You don't know jack.' He turned to her, his own frustration and impotence at boiling point. 'And I don't need you psychoanalysing me.'

'Is that what you call it?' Her eyes clashed with his. He could almost hear the swords cross. 'It's so much more than that, Nic, but you're not ready or willing to share, and I'm sorry for you.'

She sighed. Not an audible sigh, but one that passed from her heart to his and shadowed the world grey.

'I never meant to—'

'Leave. I don't want to hear it. I've been shut out once too often. I refuse to be shut out any more. People I love always leave—why should you be any different?'

'Charlotte…' He couldn't find the words. Why couldn't he find the right words?

'After all,' she continued, on a roll now, 'as you just stated very clearly, it was never anything more than a holiday fling.'

The way she said it, as if it were the most casual of affairs when deep down he knew it wasn't, made him want to yell something. But what? *I love you too and it might have started as a fling and now it's more but it can never work.*

'Go.'

'Okay. Calm down. Tomorrow we'll—'

She threw up a hand. 'Don't come back, Nic. I don't want you here. It's over.'

It took him a skipped heartbeat to process her meaning, then the hot taste of panic skewered up his throat. He grasped for a reason to make her change her mind. 'The benefit; you'll need some support.'

'Support?' Her laugh was harsh, scraping at his soul. 'Oh, you're a fine one to talk of support.' She curled her hands into fists at her sides. 'I planned it because I wanted to give something back to Kas and the kids. I never intended you to be involved—you invited yourself. Well, I'm uninviting you.' She rapped a fist once on the table. 'I don't *need* your support, the way you don't *need* mine, so we're square.'

He acknowledged that with a tilt of his head. 'If that's how you want it.'

'It is.'

She glared at him, eyes dry now but he knew there'd be tears soon enough. It was kinder to finish it quickly and cleanly and be done. Over. *Don't give her a reason to think there's more.*

He rubbed at the raw throbbing place over his heart, forced a smile and played his last card. 'Goodbye, Charlotte. It's been fun. Look me up if you ever get to Fiji again.' He waved a disparaging hand in the air. 'That is if you can bring yourself to leave this mausoleum.'

# CHAPTER FOURTEEN

'THAT'S the last of it.'

Charlotte dipped her thumbs into the back pockets of her jeans and watched the final box of memories being loaded into the truck. It had taken two weeks of tears and sleeplessness to sort through her family's stuff, decide what to keep and what to toss.

'You okay?' Suzette asked beside her as they watched the truck's doors close.

'I will be.' Between clearing out the house and organising the fashion show she'd had no time for dilly-dallying and broken hearts. She'd made decisions on the spot; she'd live with her choices.

At least the busyness helped keep her mind off Nic, if only for short bursts. The nights were the worst; dreams and heartache and memories. How many times had she picked up the phone to call him and say she'd changed her mind, then reminded herself he'd been the one insisting it was temporary? It had just ended sooner than she'd thought. The big surprise was that she'd done the ending.

Suzette slung an arm around her shoulders as the vehicle trundled away. 'Let's take a coffee break before that antique dealer arrives with his quotes.'

'Good idea.' Charlotte leaned into her as they walked inside to the noise of hammering and drills. In the formal lounge a guy was installing a monitoring system to keep a watchful eye when she opened the room to the public. She still had to decide which of the antiques to sell and which to keep, and that process would require more consideration. Because what stayed would be a key component of her new plans for this place.

On their way through the kitchen they passed a couple of tradesmen installing her big new oven. 'This is the right decision.'

'Yes, it *so* is. I guess I have to be grateful to that Nic guy for something,' Suzette murmured the moment they were past and out of earshot. 'If nothing else, he forced you to see what I've been trying to get you to see for two years.'

The mention of his name was like a fist at her breastbone. 'We may be over, but he's still the best thing that ever happened to me.'

Suzette stopped and looked at her deep and direct, eyes full of understanding and sympathy. 'You still love him.'

'Yes.' And that reality was a raw and open wound. 'It'll take time but I'll get through it.'

'He hurt you.'

'Because I let him, Suz. It wasn't his fault—he never made a secret of what he wanted—and I knew he had that power but I jumped right in regardless. Now I'm living with the consequences.'

She stopped at the entrance to the atrium her father had had erected the year before he'd died. The pungent smell of rich damp earth greeted them. Sunshine poured in, throwing shards of rose and emerald onto the luxurious greenery through two intricately stained-glass panels. The rest of the atrium was clear glass and allowed plenty of natural light. Sliding floor-to-ceiling windows could be opened on a fine day to bring the fragrance of the herb garden inside.

The worst had happened. It could only get better from

hereon in. But something good had come out of the bad
too. Nic had given her affirmation as a woman. She'd
bloomed like the flowering vine that climbed the atrium's walls because Nic had shown her how. She no longer
wanted to blend into the background; she wanted to shine
like the sun glinting on the glass.

'I love this room.' Smiling for what felt like the first
time in weeks, she nodded to where a stack of new café
chairs towered beside half a dozen small tables. There were
glass display shelves and clothing racks against the wall.
'And I'm going to turn it into my dream.'

Nic gazed over the white-capped ocean. Sea mist blurred
the horizon today, whipped by a strong wind. *The colour
of Charlotte's eyes.* For the third time in as many minutes
his hand hovered over his phone. Tonight was Charlotte's
big night. He should ring, let her know he was thinking
of her and wish her luck.

But she'd told him it was over. The last thing he wanted
to do was reopen fresh wounds. He should have gone back
to Fiji as he'd intended, but he'd not been able to put that
stamp of finality on their relationship.

'Why not?' he asked the ceiling for the millionth time.
She'd seemed so sure that was what she wanted on that
last night when she told him it was over. And wasn't it
what he wanted too? It had just happened too damn soon.

Tossing his phone across the desk, he brought his man-
uscript up on screen. Two solid weeks of work and he'd
almost finished, but he couldn't see the end.

*Reena is imprisoned in the Sphere of Darkness. Onyx
flies to the rescue on his trusted dragon, Grodinor. Happy
ever after...*

But how?

He drummed his fingers on his thighs. If his own life

were one of his games how would he play it? Charlotte, his real-life heroine. Beautiful. Loving and fun to be with. Unique—her understated dress code, her empathy for others, her ability to pull a fundraiser together at short notice. And trapped as surely as Reena, unable and unwilling to let go of her past.

But was Nic Russo hero material? Hardly. Was he any different to her? Suddenly, like Charlotte, he realised he was trapped in a hole of his own making, unable to unlock his fears and share them with someone who cared, someone who could help him to heal. *Someone who loved him.*

He spun his chair towards the ocean view but he wasn't seeing it. The last time with Charlotte played before his eyes like an old movie. There was something very wrong with that scene...

But what?

Had he thought himself free? Was that truly what he wanted or was it a barrier he'd erected to keep people at a distance, something to hide the deep down longing to connect with another? To trust and belong. To be accepted for his faults and failings.

He not only feared confined spaces, he was afraid of not being good enough.

*He was afraid of rejection.*

Whoa... He scrubbed his hands over his four-day stubble and let the dust of this new realisation settle. He was the independent playboy, the charmer, superficial, because that kid from the back streets was still afraid of being excluded. An outsider looking in, telling himself he didn't want to belong anyway.

He'd found solace in his safe world of make-believe. But that world was no longer enough. It was a prison, a way of avoiding reality, as surely as Charlotte's family home was for her.

He needed the real world, with a real woman. Charlotte. And if he didn't lay his fears and faults on the table, whether he was accepted with them or not, he'd never experience the freedom he really craved. And faults and all, he'd never find the love he knew he could find with Charlotte. If she'd have him back. *Real* love, a *real* life, not some fantasy world to hide away in.

His chair rolled backwards across the boards as he shot up, checking his watch on his way to the bathroom. There was still time…

'Good evening, ladies and gentlemen.' Charlotte smiled at the audience and waited for the crowd to hush. To look at *her*. The press was there at her invitation. Her parents' friends. New faces and old. Was she really standing up here in front of all these people? Her hand trembled on the microphone but she took a deep steadying breath.

'Thank you for coming and for your support for this worthy cause. As some of you know, I was recently in Fiji and had the opportunity to visit a local school.' She scanned the crowd but there was no sign of the man she'd foolishly hoped might be there. 'I'd like to acknowledge a man who not only makes generous monetary donations, but gives his time and expertise every week to support those students who play and learn under less privileged circumstances than our children here in Australia. His name's Nic Russo. Nic's kind and generous and…' her voice faltered '…and his work's the inspiration for tonight's show.' Pinning her smile back in place, she said, 'I hope you'll all dig deep tonight and purchase some of Suzette's stunning pieces that you'll see this evening.'

Nic arrived at the entrance as Charlotte finished her introduction and what he saw stole his breath—and his heart—clean away. Charlotte, *his* Charlotte, in fire-engine red. A slinky shimmering low-cut gown that clung to every curve. A poised and confident woman who'd do any damn politician proud.

And she'd paid *Nic* tribute. It made him humble and proud and very, very grateful she'd come into his life and changed it for ever.

As she turned to leave the runway he sucked in a breath. The full-length gown was backless, right down to the dip in her spine. Her shoes, glittering crimson stilettos, peeked from beneath the hem as she walked away and disappeared behind the screen.

He couldn't wait to talk to her, to touch her again and tell her... He had so much to tell her, but that would have to wait. Not wanting to distract her, he spotted a vacant seat near the back.

Fashion shows weren't his thing, especially when all he could think was, when would it finish? His attention was ostensibly on the models parading some way-out bridal and formal designs, but his mind was on the woman he'd not even glimpsed since that initial speech on his arrival.

'And now for some scintillating, sexy lingerie,' he heard the announcer say with a grin in her voice, and perked up. 'Nothing too risqué; *those* are available for your personal perusal in your catalogue.'

Models started coming out wearing what he recognised as Charlotte's work, but he wasn't prepared for the finale—the long-legged brunette gliding along the runway in a white gauze number over flamingo-pink bra and panties.

Charlotte.

He could only think...*hot*.

Too soon, she disappeared behind the screen but in no time at all she was back on the runway again wearing that fabulous red gown.

He started making his way through the audience as the announcer handed Charlotte the microphone.

'Thank you, ladies and gentlemen,' she said, her face flushed, her eyes sparkling. 'That's all and goodnight. Oh, don't forget to buy a raffle ticket or ten before you leave.' She pointed to a couple of the models starting to circulate amongst the crowd. 'The prize is a weekend getaway at a mystery location.' She handed the microphone back and began descending the steps.

Not bothering with the stairs, Nic hauled himself onto the runway and took the microphone from the surprised announcer. 'Ladies and gentlemen, before you leave…'

The audience murmured and looked at him expectantly. He only had eyes for one member of that audience and she was frozen to the carpet. Her smile had vanished; the pretty flush had leached away. He smiled encouragement at her before turning to the audience once more. 'Good evening. My name's Nic Russo.'

More shuffles and murmurs. Maybe it was a mistake to muscle in on Charlotte's event, but it wasn't his biggest mistake. His biggest mistake had been letting her walk out of his life.

'I'd like a chance to say a few words about Charlotte. I met her a month ago in Fiji. No, that's not quite correct—I met her at Tullamarine airport.' He looked down into her eyes. 'How would I describe Charlotte Dumont? She's capable. She organised this event in two short weeks. She's creative. You saw her designs up here tonight. I don't know about you, but I'll be purchasing a few pieces for my special woman, if not the entire collection, so you'd better be quick if you don't want to miss out.

'But most of all, she cares. She saw a need and made it a priority and that's why we're here tonight.' *She's the most amazing woman I've ever met. She's the woman I love.* 'So please, everyone, help her out, and help give some kids in Fiji a fantastic environment to play and learn in because that's where the money raised tonight will go.'

As he handed the microphone back Nic saw the flash of red disappear through a rear door. His heart jumped into his mouth and he followed.

Light bulbs flashed and reporters rushed him at the door. 'Does Dom Silverman have something to say?' someone asked.

Nic stopped short. Nodded. 'I'll give you guys some time to ask questions later, but can you do me a favour and disappear for now?' He shot them a grin. 'I have something important to tell Ms Dumont. In private.'

Heedless of the cold air on her bare arms and back and the glitter of flashbulbs, Charlotte fled down the wide steps and onto the lawns that lined the river. Her heart was numb with shock and a lot more.

The city's lights reflected on the water, the fountain's spray speared high into the sky, captured in changing colours of green, pink, purple, yellow.

Nic was still here. He'd come and he'd paid her the highest of compliments. He'd told the entire audience he intended purchasing her collection for his 'special woman'. He'd looked at her when he'd said it.

Shivering, she rubbed her arms and wished she'd grabbed her jacket, but she'd been in too much of a rush to avoid Nic. A couple strolled hand in hand along the bank, obviously in love.

Yes, she loved Nic, she always would and once upon a time that couple might have been them, but she'd told him no. She was strong enough to tell him no again.

She'd started a new life, one that didn't include broken hearts and dreams that didn't come true and men who weren't prepared to give everything, to share everything. Halfway was *not* enough.

She clenched her fists against her sides, summoning anger and indignation to crush the pain she'd worked so hard to be rid of. How dared he appear at her special event after two weeks of silence, smiling at her in that intimate way, arrogantly speaking of Tullamarine airport *as if nothing had changed*?

She knew he was coming for her long before he reached her. It was as if she had inbuilt radar where Nic was concerned.

'Charlotte.'

She didn't turn around. 'Hi, Nic.'

'You were sensational tonight. Congratulations.'

'Thanks.' He still hadn't touched her and, despite herself, her body yearned.

'The evening was a great success by the looks of things.'

'I hope it helps.' They were talking like two acquaintances discussing an opera performance. Two strangers who'd run out of conversation. She studied the ground as if she might find the right words to say written on the grass.

'This may not be the lake I imagined,' Nic began. 'And maybe the stars are already out, or maybe those reflections on the water are fallen stars—a bit like me. Because since we parted that's how I feel. Like I'm at the bottom of that dark murky River Torrens.'

She crossed her arms, tightened her fingers above her elbows, so tight she could feel her nails bite into the flesh. 'Perhaps you need to think about how you got there and find a way out.'

One warm finger touched the back of her neck. Gently, as if she might splinter into a million pieces. And she was very afraid it might be true.

'Where are your pearls?'

'I don't need them to remember my mother any more. She's in my heart.' *Like you.* 'I've made some changes in my life, Nic.'

'I can see that,' he murmured, his voice like velvet, and she knew he was looking at her dress. 'Told you you'd look hot in red.'

She heard the shifting of fabric and then his coat was over her shoulders, smelling warm and familiar.

His arms came around her. 'I hope there's room in your changed life for me, Charlotte, because I can't stand not being with you. Because, you see, sweetheart, I love you too.'

Tears sprang to her eyes, blurring the water's reflections, and she shook her head. 'When people love each other they talk. Flynn didn't talk to me. I never knew what he was thinking, that he was interested in politics, even whether I came up to scratch as a future politician's wife. He never gave me a chance to change and then he left.'

Nic pulled her back against him so he could feel her body tucked tight into his. Breathed in her signature perfume. 'I'm glad he did. Because now you're mine.'

She stiffened and he felt her withdrawal and a knife of panic sliced through him.

'I won't be shut out, Nic.'

'Then how about this… My name's Nic Russo, I love you and I'm also a claustrophobic. Which means I dissolve into a quivering mess in confined spaces. I'd like to talk about it with you if you'll listen.' The silence was like a dark night with no end. 'Will you listen to me, Charlotte? Will you hear my story and hold me while I tell you? Because the darkness in your cellar's nothing compared to the darkness inside me right now.'

Her silence was the longest silence he'd ever known but then she nodded slowly. 'I will.'

She turned in his arms, and stroked back the hair from his temples with fingers that were strong yet tender. Her eyes were the soft mist of the ocean and filled with compassion and love and understanding. 'You know I will.'

He was barely aware of the glitter from half a dozen paparazzi cameras. 'Then how about we get out of here?'

She jutted her chin at something over his shoulder. 'I suppose we'd better give those guys something to write about first.'

'You mean like this?' He kissed her the way she deserved to be kissed; slowly and thoroughly.

When he finally let her go, she shook her head, but her eyes were dancing. 'I meant give them a story. We've already done the public kiss. *Honey Pie.*'

'Ah, so we have,' he murmured. 'So are you up for it? For them?'

Taking his hand, she began walking up the grass towards the press, his coat swinging from her shoulders. 'You better believe it.'

He laid her on his bed and in the silvery light of a half moon, with fused gazes and hearts open and willing, they silently undressed each other. Skin on skin, nothing between them. With every touch a murmur, every breath a wish, every heartbeat, joy. They made love slowly, deeply, truly and when they'd assuaged the physical needs, they turned to each other. Only then did they talk.

'I had a mother but I raised myself,' Nic began, staring at the ceiling. He told her about his waitress poker-addicted mother and how he was often left alone as it grew dark and how his runaway imagination used to get the better of him.

'Nic, I'm so sorry.'

'It gets worse,' he went on, still unable to look at her, the words tumbling out now in the relief of sharing and his trust in Charlotte that he'd not be ridiculed. 'The school was in a rough neighbourhood. The local bullies would wait for me in the park on the way home. Sometimes they'd hold me down, kick the crap out of me and laugh about it the next day in the school yard.'

Her love and her shock were obvious in her quiet voice. 'Why didn't you tell someone?'

'I was too damn scared. But one day I did—I told my teacher. A big mistake on my part because a few days later they tied me up, blindfolded me and left me in a Dumpster at the back of some shops.'

'Oh my God, Nic...'

'I was there over twenty-four hours before the kids decided to own up and the police found me.'

The lack of emotion in his voice, as if it was just another injustice in a world full of injustices, squeezed Charlotte's heart. She touched his hair, his face, his lips, wishing he'd look at her. No wonder he was so scarred. 'That's why you didn't let me blindfold you...'

'I had a lot of time to think in there.' His tone was tinged with an odd humour. 'I found I was pretty good at making up stories of how I'd escape and discovering weird and wonderful ways to get my revenge.'

'And did you get your revenge?'

At last he looked at her. Smiled at her in the darkness. 'I got that when I made my first million from those stories of vengeance and justice and fantasy I'd dreamed up. I used them in my games.'

She smiled back. 'What happened after you were found?'

'Mum changed jobs, we moved to a new flat in a better area and things improved. But I've been claustrophobic ever since.'

'And you've not had professional counselling?'

'No. But I'm ready now. I've learnt something else in

the last couple of weeks.' He took her hand, pressed it over his heart where she could feel it beating strong and steady. 'My greatest fear's putting myself and my love for you on the line and having you not want it.'

'Of course I want it.' She covered his face with butterfly kisses. 'I want it all. It was you not letting me in that I couldn't deal with. It was like you'd already left and it hurt as deeply as when my family died and I didn't want that pain in my life again.'

His eyes were dark and filled with determination and love. 'No more pain, sweetheart. When bad things happen, as they inevitably do in life, we'll deal with it together.'

Then he spent the next little while showing her how exactly it was going to be.

Finally, pushing up to a sitting position against the bed head, he gathered her against his chest. 'Now it's your turn to fill me in on your plans.'

'My plans may have just changed.'

He stroked her hair. 'Tell me anyway.'

'I decided to use part of the house to try selling my lingerie. I'm closing off some rooms for private use and opening up the rest to the public to sell off the family heirlooms. People can come and taste Three Cockatoos wine and home-made nibbles and browse clothing and antiques at the same time.'

'But you sold the winery, sweetheart…' he murmured.

'Yes, but their daughter, Ella, is interested in my idea. She's going to come on board and help on a trial basis first. If it works out, I can put her in as a manager and it'll give me time to do other things.'

'Sounds like success all round.'

'The only problem now is the long-distance relationship,' she said.

'There's not going to be any long-distance relationship.

If Ella works out, she can take over when we go to Fiji. I can work anywhere. We'll figure it out as we go along. The important thing is that we figure it out side by side. Together.'

And the future was suddenly rosy and filled with love and hope.

# EPILOGUE

*Three months later.*

THE beach at sunset was officially perfect. The sand was pungent with the fresh scent of recent rain and strewn with petals, the air moist and warm, the sky a burnished gold shot with purple. Flickering kerosene torches surrounded the intimate circle of friends who'd gathered for the ceremony.

The only thing missing from the perfect scene was a perfect bride.

The anxious groom wore white; white trousers and a loose white Island shirt—as requested. His feet were bare. Also requested.

Nic held his breath as the faint sounds of banjos and ukuleles playing something dreamy and appropriate for the moment grew closer, heralding the bride's arrival.

And then, suddenly, there she was. His heroine. His Charlotte. For a moment his eyes blurred, because his life, his love, his whole world, was approaching him, her eyes the colour of sea mist and locked on his, her smile radiant.

For once in his life, he didn't mind traditionally conservative. Wearing one of Suzette's creations, she looked like a princess in a white beaded gown that flowed to her bare feet. She'd threaded crimson flowers through her long hair; two heavy garlands of those same flowers hung around her neck.

He let out that breath on a slow sigh of relief, and smiled back. It seemed his story was to have a happy ending after all.

'Hi, there, you,' she whispered, and lifted one of the garlands she was wearing and placed it around his neck.

'Welcome, friends.' The celebrant, a friend of Suzette's, smiled at the group. 'We're here on this glorious tropical evening to make it official between these two people...'

'So here we are.' Charlotte linked her hands around Nic's neck later as they danced—or, rather, swayed—across the makeshift dance floor under the stars to the surprise and delight of Vaka Malua's guests.

'Yep. Here we are.' He bent to place a lingering kiss on her lips. 'Did you ever think otherwise?'

'There was a time...'

'Nah. It was always a foregone conclusion.' He leaned closer, nuzzling her neck. 'I was yours from the first moment you stood in front of me in the queue at Tullamarine. And my instincts are always spot on.'

'I've missed you,' she murmured. 'I never knew a week could take so long.'

'Hmm,' he agreed, smoothing his hands over her back and sending delicious tingles all through her body.

She had stayed on in Adelaide a week longer than Nic to ensure a smooth transition for Old and New, the only place she knew that offered lingerie and antiques over a choice of wine or coffee.

Never again—from now on it was always going to be the two of them. And it was official. She wiggled the fingers on her left hand to admire her newest sparkle.

'Everything under control with the new place?'

'Ella's going to make a fine manager.' She caught sight of Suzette and Tenika grinning at her and gave them a cheeky finger wave. 'She spoke to me this morning; she's already sold three sets of lingerie and a chest of drawers.'

'Hmm,' he murmured, the rough velvet rumble hot against her ear. 'Speaking of lingerie, do you reckon this party can carry on without us? I can't wait to see what surprises you've got in store for me tonight.'

'I can't wait to see what surprises you've got for me either.' She grinned up at him, loving their sexy banter and innuendo. Loving the way they brought out the best in each other. Then she took his hand and began leading him away. 'Come on, I'll show you.'

\* \* \* \* \*

# MILLS & BOON®
# By Request

**RELIVE THE ROMANCE WITH THE BEST OF THE BEST**

---

# A sneak peek at next month's titles...

### In stores from 18th December 2015:

- **One Night With Her Ex** – Kelly Hunter, Susan Stephens & Kate Hardy

- **At the Playboy's Command** – Robyn Grady, Brenda Jackson & Kathie DeNosky

### In stores from 1st January 2016:

- **Secrets in Sydney** – Fiona Lowe, Melanie Milburne & Emily Forbes

- **A Second Chance for the Millionaire** – Lucy Gordon, Nicola Marsh & Barbara Wallace

---

# MILLS & BOON®

**If you enjoyed this story,
you'll love the the full *Revenge Collection!***

**Enjoy the misdemeanours and the sinful world
of revenge with this six-book collection.
Indulge in these riveting 3-in-1 romances
from top Modern Romance authors.**

Order your complete collection today at
**www.millsandboon.co.uk/revengecollection**

# MILLS & BOON®

## Why shop at millsandboon.co.uk?

Each year, thousands of romance readers find their perfect read at millsandboon.co.uk. That's because we're passionate about bringing you the very best romantic fiction. Here are some of the advantages of shopping at www.millsandboon.co.uk:

* **Get new books first**—you'll be able to buy your favourite books one month before they hit the shops

* **Get exclusive discounts**—you'll also be able to buy our specially created monthly collections, with up to 50% off the RRP

* **Find your favourite authors**—latest news, interviews and new releases for all your favourite authors and series on our website, plus ideas for what to try next

* **Join in**—once you've bought your favourite books, don't forget to register with us to rate, review and join in the discussions

Visit **www.millsandboon.co.uk**
for all this and more today!